Secondborn

Also by Amy A. Bartol

The Kricket Series

Under Different Stars
Sea of Stars
Darken the Stars

The Premonition Series

Inescapable

Intuition

Indebted

Incendiary

Iniquity

The Divided (short story)

Secondborn

AMY A. BARTOL

47NORTH

Text copyright © 2017 by Amy A. Bartol
All rights reserved.

No part of this book may be reproduced, or stored in a retrieval system, or transmitted in any form or by any means, electronic, mechanical, photocopying, recording, or otherwise, without express written permission of the publisher.

Published by 47North, Seattle

www.apub.com

Amazon, the Amazon logo, and 47North are trademarks of Amazon.com, Inc., or its affiliates.

ISBN-13: 9781477848357
ISBN-10: 1477848355

Cover design by Shasti O'Leary Soudant

Printed in the United States of America

For Jason Kirk,
the lion-hearted poet of
"Two thousand heartless brilliant autumns   odes."

Onward.

Nine Fates of the Republic

FATE OF VIRTUES

FATE OF SWORDS

FATE OF STARS

FATE OF ATOMS

FATE OF SUNS

FATE OF DIAMONDS

FATE OF MOONS

FATE OF SEAS

FATE OF STONES

Prologue

It's agony and relief to watch my life end.

I'm not dying, though my heart aches as if it might. Blood pounds drumbeats through my veins. My temples throb while my mother takes the podium. Spotlights shine on us, burning away the gloom of predawn light. Pausing like a seasoned conductor before an orchestra, Mother waits for the applause to die down. She's the consummate politician, serene before the gathered crowd in the courtyard. She surveys the cameras before her, knowing the effect her stoicism has on the citizens assembled beneath the grand balcony of the Palace of the Sword. Their hearts break for her—for a mother's sacrifice. These are her supporters, handpicked to be here, to witness history.

The cool morning air teases a wisp of silky brown hair from the elegant knot at her nape. Navy-colored banners twist in the wind, images of golden swords flapping behind her in the breeze. She holds back a smile.

"Citizens of Swords and all of the Fates," she begins. Her melodic voice amplifies over the grounds of her estate, the sound of it falling from the balcony like a stone, crushing the crowd below into silence. "Today, our very way of life is threatened, not only from outside the Fates of the Republic, but also from within. The destiny of our once-great nation lies in the palms of our hands, and never more than today—Transition Day."

I'm unable to suppress a shudder. Transition Day. I've heard the words often over the eighteen years of my life. It's the stuff of nightmares, what people say when they want to scare you: *one day soon you'll become a stranger to the people you love*. A picture in a frame. I've always known today would come. I thought I'd be ready for it. I'm not.

Fine beads of sweat form on the back of my neck. I clutch my hands behind me so no one can see them tremble. My long brown hair blows in the wind.

"At no other time in our history has the draft been more vital," Mother says. "We are embroiled in a fight to the death—a bloody civil war, brought on by the lawlessness of Fate traitors who would violate our very right to exist. We, the firstborns, must rule. It is our birthright to sacrifice our own for the protection of the Fates. It is an honor for secondborns to serve as champions in this proud tradition—to give their lives to their Fate and to the call of service."

Her arm sweeps in my direction. Every eye in the crowd shifts to me. Enormous virtual monitors project my image. I'm larger than life on the screens. I have to fight to maintain a serene expression. The cameras see everything, and my performance will be critiqued later. *Loyalty to the Fates above all else.*

Tiny brown holographic swords project from the lapel of my new, dirt-colored uniform. Tropo. I try not to wince. The emblem denotes the lowest secondborn rank in the military, the mark of the infantry—the expendables. My throat constricts. I swallow hard, attempting to clear it. Dune's tall frame beside me is comforting. That my mentor, the Captain of the Guard, insisted on being here for the announcement means more to me than I can say. He cares about what happens to me, maybe more than my own family does.

The holographic swords on Dune's lapels flicker in my peripheral vision. It had always been my hope that when I reached my Transition Day, I'd wear silver swords like Dune, even though I'm not firstborn.

I'd guard a Clarity—a leader of one of the nine Fates of the Republic—protecting her from threats to her life. A leader like my mother, Othala St. Sismode, Clarity of the Fate of Swords. As commander of the military, she is one of the most powerful Clarities, second only to the Supreme Leader, the Clarity of the Fate of Virtues himself. If she had granted me the rank of Iono, made me an officer in her personal guard, I could have proved my worth to her. I could have stayed with my family and Dune. I could have protected them.

But she didn't.

Now I know that it was only a fantasy. I'll never be one of them. I'll always be just a secondborn, a shadow, soon to fade from their lives.

Mother's lips are a delicate pink in the frosty air. She lowers her voice. "I'm not immune to your suffering," she resumes. "I have not placed my needs as a mother above those of the citizens of this embattled nation. No. I accept the sacrifice that we all make as just and necessary to our survival. Today, I give over to our cause my only daughter, Roselle. My heart. My life. My secondborn."

Tears wet the faces of the spectators. They believe that they know me well. I've grown up in front of their eyes—in front of the cameras. They watched me take my first toddling steps, say my first words, lose my first fight, win my second one, and train rigorously with Dune in order to one day defend the Fates of the Republic from all threats to their sovereignty.

Mother's eyes remain dry. "Roselle may be young," she continues, "but you have witnessed her evolve into a soldier. She's ready to do her duty—to join the ranks of Swords who now fight to strike the Gates of Dawn rebels from our land, from our world, and from our minds forever." The roar of applause is deafening. Mother bites the inside of her cheek. "It is a sad day for me and for my family, but we will endure the Transition. We will flourish in the knowledge that another St. Sismode will be protecting us."

She turns to me and joins the crowd in its applause. I don't move. I don't acknowledge them in any way. I'm like the banners waving behind us, a symbol, blown by forces over which I have no control.

Mother leans into the microphones. "It is my wish to have a few final moments alone with my daughter. You can follow Roselle's journey to Transition as she leaves the estate today. Thank you for your support. Long live the Fates!"

"Long live the Fates!" Chanting begins in earnest as my indomitable mother steps away from the podium. She squares her small shoulders and breezes past without looking at me.

Chapter 1
Crown of Swords

I trail my mother, her personal assistant, and four public relations specialists as they retreat toward the beveled-glass doors of the St. Sismode Palace. Clara, the newest PR assistant, hands Othala a glass of water, waits for her to sip it, and takes it back from her. Fumbling, she spills some on herself. Clara's sparkling moniker, the holographic symbol that projects up from the back of her hand, shines like crystal as she dabs at the water droplets with a lacy handkerchief.

She's a Diamond, I think. *She won't last long here among the Sword aristocracy.* I feel a twinge of pity. It's not as if Clara ever had a choice. She's secondborn. She was placed in this den of lions, and if she fails, it will be a long fall. Females who don't make it in their secondborn Transition positions usually end up in the entertainment sector. I shudder. She'll probably become a plaything for some firstborn officer. Clara teeters on her elegant high heels and tries to keep up with my mother's rapid pace.

As we enter the mansion, my eyes are drawn to the stone pediment above the doors. I wonder if Clara even notices the ancient warriors carved above the frieze, or that our name, St. Sismode, is etched upon the swords of the soldiers. Does she realize that a St. Sismode has been the Clarity of the Fate of Swords since anyone can remember?

"Let them try to criticize me for the draft now!" Mother says. She paces over the midnight-blue carpet embellished with a golden fusion-blade called a St. Sismode sword, after our ancestor who designed it. Pausing on the point of the carpet's wooly blade, she hugs herself in victory. "No Clarity of any Fate has ever given more than I have!" She turns to Emmitt Stone, her personal assistant. He's glowing with pride.

"Your Fate loves you!" Emmitt gushes, adding flamboyant applause. "All of the nine Fates love you!"

"They do, don't they?" Othala smooths her hair back, losing herself in the moment. If she were a cat, she would purr.

Dune growls low. "You don't have to do this," he says bitterly. "Roselle's still too young. She's not ready for war!"

Othala sobers. She narrows her eyes at her assembled staff. "Leave us." Clara and Emmitt nearly bump into each other in their hurry to the door. I turn to follow them out.

"Stay, Roselle," Dune commands.

I hesitate, looking to Mother for confirmation. She remains silent until the others have left, closing the bronze doors behind them, then whirls to face Dune. "It's done," she says, sneering.

"You can undo it," Dune insists. "You can save Roselle." He is rigid with barely suppressed anger, except for one hand, which twitches near the sword sheathed at his waist. My eyes widen. I know his aggressive posture well. It's the stance he uses before he attacks.

"You underestimate her," my mother replies. "She's resilient and capable of surviving whatever is thrown at her. She has my blood."

"You will spill her blood!" Dune's sand-colored eyes narrow. He takes a menacing step toward Mother. My response is automatic. I move between the Clarity and my mentor, as I've been trained to do. My hand rests on my own sword's hilt. I face Dune, my warning unmistakable. "You see?" Dune flicks his hand toward me. "She wants only to protect you, Othala. You have nothing to fear from her. She would never harm you or Gabriel. She loves you both."

"And you *care* for her," Mother hisses. She walks around the golden silk settee, putting it between her and us. Dune grinds his teeth. It's an accusation I don't fully understand.

"Of course I care for her. Roselle has been my student since she could crawl!" He rubs his hand over the short, dark stubble of his new beard. "I have always treated her with the utmost respect."

"Yes, you two are quite close. She looks at you like a father."

"You and I both know how little interest her own father has taken in her."

Othala waves her hand as if to dismiss my father from the conversation, or maybe from her life. "Kennet is not one to form attachments. But you treat her as if she were your own daughter. You've taught her everything you know about being a leader, a fighter, someone who could maybe one day be the commander of this Fate?"

"I've tried to prepare her for any eventuality."

My mother grips the back of the settee, her bejeweled fingernails digging into the fabric. "You'd just need to get rid of anything that stands in her way, wouldn't you?"

Dune rubs his eyes, for a moment looking older than his thirty-eight years. "So, this *is* revenge against me! My decision to end my personal relationship with you, Othala, has nothing to do with Roselle."

"It has everything to do with her, Dune. You're her mentor. We both know that if something were to happen to Gabriel and me, she'd be The Sword." A snarl twists my mother's lips.

My hand, still on the silver handle of my sheathed sword, grows damp. Dune meets my eyes, and his soften. "Your daughter has no idea what you're talking about, Othala. She's a student of chivalry. Her only thought is how to win your love, not steal your power."

Mother's blue eyes look upward. "Even if the thought never crossed her mind, she's still too dangerous, Dune. I have to protect Gabriel. He will rule the Fate of Swords one day, not her. It's his birthright."

I cringe, turning to face my mother. "I would never hurt my brother. I only wish to serve him—to protect him."

Mother's normally supple mouth pinches. "You say that now, Roselle, but what happens in the next few years after your Transition Day? Gabriel will marry—have children. You'll come to realize that you'll never have a family, never hold a baby in your arms and call it your own. Gabriel will inherit all our wealth and property. What will you do when you realize the only option open to you for the rest of your life is government service? You are secondborn. The Fates own your life. It's better that you leave us now. The abrupt change will be easier than a slow, excruciating march to your destiny."

"It will be easier for you, you mean." My eyes widen at my own audacity.

For once, she seems not to notice my breach in protocol. "It will be easier for us all when you're gone."

Dune glares at Othala. "You could make her an Iono soldier—part of this guard or one for another Clarity. She could—"

"Even if I concede that she poses no threat to Gabriel," Othala interrupts, "which I don't, *and* I make her the rank of Iono and assign her duties for one of the other Clarities, every secondborn of any consequence will cry 'Nepotism!'" She lets go of the settee and paces.

"You expect me to believe that's why you made her a Tropo?" Dune asks. "It's equivalent to throwing her to the wolves, Othala, and you know it! And for what? So you don't have to listen to a few complaints? They've never bothered you before. Secondborns may mutter about unfairness, but you strike them down hard whenever they do."

She stops. "I show them their place!"

"And you wonder why we have a rebellion of secondborns? You never hear their suffering."

"Their suffering?" she sputters. "You would side with the Gates of Dawn over the Fates? That's treason!"

"You of all people know that my loyalty is to the Fate of Swords and to all the Fates of the Republic. I have fought for them since the day I was born."

"Since the day you were *firstborn*," she corrects. "Never forget you're one of us, Dune."

"Othala, see reason! Once Roselle is processed, she'll be chattel. They could put her on the front line."

"She's eighteen years old—and a St. Sismode! Our commanders will have better sense than to do that."

"So you haven't even specified where she will be placed? You're going to leave it to the secondborn commanders—or whatever algorithm they're using—to decide your daughter's life?"

"I have to trust that the Fates work, Dune. Otherwise, the Gates of Dawn are right. My father believed in the system. He allowed for an organic Transition for his secondborn child. He would expect me to do the same, were he alive."

"Bazzle was dead within a month of his Transition."

"He served the Fates with honor," she says weakly. She walks to her desk and faces us from behind its broad expanse of glass and touchscreens.

"Your brother paid for your father's position as The Sword, Othala. He was murdered as revenge for what some secondborns see as injustice in a system that makes them slaves."

Dune grasps my left arm. He leads me to Mother's desk, extending the back of my hand in front of her. In the shape of a fiery sword, the chip implanted under the skin between my thumb and index finger glows golden. My moniker is who I am. All my information is stored within it, from my name to my age, address, DNA profile—almost everything that makes me *me* can be accessed by scanning it. It contains all the codes that allow me to travel both within the Fate of Swords and into the eight other Fates.

"Once they process her and find out you're her mother," Dune says, "Roselle will be made to suffer for your decisions as The Sword. Do you want that?" Othala's eyes dart to my moniker. I quickly pull my hand from Dune's and hide it behind my back. My moniker has always been a source of irritation for my mother. It isn't like everyone else's. I have a small crescent-shaped birthmark on my left hand. When the holographic image from my implant shines through my skin, it is partially obscured by the birthmark, so the hologram looks as if a dark crown rings the top of the sword. Gabriel teased me about it, calling me the Crown of Swords.

"They won't need her moniker to know who she is. Her face is everywhere. They've all watched her grow up."

Dune's eyes widen in shock. "You don't care, do you?"

"Leave us, Roselle," Othala demands. "Wait for Dune to join you in the Grand Foyer." I retreat through a bronze doorway, leaving it open a crack. "I have given her all the tools she needs to survive," Mother says. "I gave her you for eighteen years. The best strategists have trained her. She has a better chance than any one of the secondborns twice her age. We both knew this day would come, but unlike you, I was smart enough not to become attached to her. Anything you feel in this moment is on *you*, Dune."

A foot taps behind me, and I turn to see Emmitt. Sighing, I close the door and try not to show any emotion. We hate each other, but it's dangerous to antagonize him. He organizes all of Mother's appointments. For my entire childhood, if I've wanted to see her, I've had to go through Emmitt, and it was rare that I was granted an audience with her. I want to believe it was him and not her who kept me away, but deep down I know it's not true. Emmitt is vindictive, though. He once ordered all of my shoes a couple of sizes too small after I'd complained about wearing a pink velvet bow in my hair for All Fates Day.

Emmitt appraises me, taking in my unflattering new uniform. He pinches the bridge of his nose with his long fingers. "Remind me to address the hideous state of the Tropo uniforms in our next session with the Clarity," he says to Clara, who stands next to him.

"What difference does it make?" she asks, giving me a cursory glance and twirling a piece of her lavender-colored hair around a sharp fingernail. Emmitt's calm is a mask. He doesn't like to be questioned by anyone.

"This color doesn't play well to the cameras." He flails his lanky arm in my direction. "It makes her eyes look haunted and her skin too pale. And the fit!" I stand still as he straightens my already-straight collar. "It hides her delicate neck."

"She's going to war, not to tea."

"It's more important than ever to show secondborn citizens the example of sacrifice. Roselle is the embodiment of the service they owe to the Fates."

"You mean she's propaganda."

Emmitt snorts. "She's essential to our great nation and to firstborn supremacy. The Clarity of Virtues himself is adamant that she make a final statement today to show her support for the cause."

Clara sniffs and touches her stylus to her blue-painted lips. "Her support? She's eighteen. She's been raised to do whatever you tell her to do."

"And she does it so well," Emmitt purrs. They discuss me as if I'm not even here. He pauses in his fussing with my collar to take in the effect, tilting his head to one side with a delicate lift of one ruddy eyebrow.

"Will I get to see my brother before I leave?" I ask.

"Of course you'll see your brother. You just have to memorize this official statement, and then you'll have a few moments with Gabriel." He extends a small tablet with the crest of St. Sismode on its underside. "How long will it take you to memorize that?"

"'It is my honor to serve Clarity Bowie and to uphold the founding principles of the Fates of the Republic,'" I read. "'Today I fulfill my birthright as defender of the firstborn bloodlines.'" I scroll down for more, but there isn't anything else. "That's it?" I stop short of adding that I have the same bloodline as the firstborn of my family.

Emmitt wrinkles his long nose. "Do you have it memorized or do you need more time?"

"But it says nothing about the Fate of Swords—*our* Fate of the Republic—or my mother—"

Emmitt snatches the tablet from my hands. He reads it aloud in a mumbled, insulting way, then looks directly at me. "It says exactly what Clarity Bowie wants it to say. Do you have a problem with that?"

"No." I lower my chin.

Emmitt thrusts the tablet back into my hands. "You have less than an hour to practice this before you're taken to your Transition point. Follow me."

He turns with a prissy swivel of his hips. We traverse the west wing. As we pass secondborn servants in the corridors, they stand aside and bow their heads. Emmitt ignores them. Like them, he is from the Fate of Stones. He's not a Sword, but he pretends to be, as if he has forgotten that he's secondborn as well.

We enter the cavernous reception area of the Grand Foyer at the entrance of the Palace. The windows afford views of the Warrior Fountain outside, and I study the mobs of photographers and spectators gathered to watch the hovercade transport me to secondborn processing at the Stone Forest Base.

The wrought iron gates and fences outside are lined with people waiting for a glimpse of me. Young children rest on their parents' shoulders, clutching little blue flags with golden swords on them. Others carry "red Roselle roses," a fad that began when Father sent Mother flowers to mark my birth. The idea had come from one of Mother's PR specialists, intended to make my parents' relationship appear loving.

I set down the tablet on a nearby table and press my face against the one-way glass, observing the citizens who have come to wish me farewell. A commotion behind me makes me straighten. Gabriel's voice rises in irritation as he enters the foyer, descending one side of the Grand Staircase. He's arguing with his advisors. "She's my little sister! I'm going to see her before she leaves, and there's not a damn thing you can do about it!" His reflection is clear in the glass. He shakes off the hand of his mentor, Susteven. "The next person who touches me loses his hand!" Gabriel warns.

His black boots click on the marble floor as he crosses directly over the inlaid St. Sismode crest, which we've both been taught to circumvent as a show of respect. His image in the glass grows larger—dark and brooding. He stops next to me, facing the glass. He's at least a foot taller than me. Our blue-eyed stares meet in the window. Gabriel's little finger brushes mine, and he whispers, "It should be me."

Chapter 2
No Sudden Moves

Gabriel has changed so much since we last spoke. Once upon a time, he would sneak into my training sessions to watch me fight. He'd ask me to teach him combat—a boy in love with war but with no one to instruct him in the art. No one dared raise a hand to him. Now he's a man—a man doing everything in his power to forget that he's firstborn.

My heart feels sore as I gaze at his reflection. He has a puffy, night-after look about him. He's probably still coming down from some drug-induced fun. He and his firstborn crowd are notorious for their fetes, which are little more than excuses to get intoxicated and destroy their palatial apartments, leaving the wreckage for the secondborns of their estates to sort out. I hear his secondborn attendants whisper about it when they think I'm not listening.

On a normal day, they say he doesn't leave his apartment before noon. I'm a little surprised he has made this exception for me. It hadn't been easy for him, as his appearance attests. He's too thin. His shoulders lack the bulk of muscle that men of the guard achieve through constant physical training. Gabriel compensates by wearing a thicker cape. The midnight-blue wool attaches to his shoulders with golden clasps in the shape of swords, flowing down his back from his impressive height. It drapes one bicep, the other uncovered. His one-of-a-kind sword is sheathed at his waist—a gift from our maternal grandfather to the heir to The Sword.

I lean against his shoulder. "It shouldn't be you, Gabriel. You're not meant for Transition. The Fate of Swords needs you here. It's you who carries the burden of everyone's tomorrow."

Shame turns to anger. "There is no burden! I get everything I want, Roselle. I don't work for anything. I'm useless."

"You're the next Clarity of Swords."

"I don't even know how to use the sword that I carry." His chin juts out. The skin over his cheekbones is gaunt. I wonder when he last had a meal.

"I taught you to fight."

He snorts. "When you were eleven. I haven't touched my sword since." His fingers move to the arch of his eyebrow, where the hair no longer grows. A small white scar runs from his brow over his eyelid to just beneath the bottom lashes of his left eye. I remember the terror of the moment when I sliced through his skin. It had been unintentional, a lapse in concentration, but it cost me almost all contact with the brother I adore.

To my immense relief, he hadn't lost his eye. It's still as blue as ever. The wound was superficial, just a graze from the tip of my fusionblade. There was no blood. The intense heat of the golden light of my sword seared his flesh as it moved through.

Gabriel sees me staring at the scar, and his face clouds with shame. "It wasn't your fault. I begged you to show me how to fight."

"You threatened to have me sent to Transition if I didn't. Listen, you look tough, Gabriel. Practice your scowl, and you'll intimidate the Heritage Council into siding with you on all of your important issues."

He lets out a small sigh and gives me a grudging smile. "I already do. They all fear me for my ferocious glare."

They fear your temper. I think of the pieces of gossip passing between Sword guards and Stone chamber workers. "Is that why you haven't had your scar removed?" I ask. Skin regeneration is commonplace, takes only a few hours, and is nearly painless.

"Mother thought I should keep it."

His scar is a reminder not to get too close to me. I blink back tears and force a smile. "Ah. Your sneer will be legendary."

"I'm sorry I never came to see you after . . ."

A sharp pain slices through my heart, a black mark on my soul that mirrors Gabriel's scar. "I know you were forbidden to see me."

"That's not an excuse."

A part of me is glad he didn't come right away. Dune had been forced to punish me—twenty lashes with a heavy cane. I couldn't walk for weeks. But days stretched into years and not a word came to me from Gabriel. I tried to see him countless times, but my requests were always denied. I was reduced to spying on him from windows and balconies—watching reports of him on-screen while he performed ribbon-cutting ceremonies and the like. "You're here now."

His eyes blaze with restrained guilt. "You shouldn't have to go away. I'll speak to Mother. She'll see reason—"

"I missed you, Gabriel."

He fumbles for my hand. His skin is smooth, his palm not calloused from training with a sword. Turning my hand over, he opens my palm, running his fingers across it.

"You're a fighter."

"It's my destiny."

"I wish it were mine." His honesty holds a note of jealousy. He turns my hand to the side, his warm fingers following the line of the implant moniker beneath my skin. When his holographic symbol is parallel to mine, our two swords glow golden. A shiver of dread quivers through me. Soon, my sword's light will turn silver. It'll no longer be golden after my Transition. Its radiance will pale and my life will change forever.

Gabriel traces my crown-shaped birthmark. "The Crown of Swords," he whispers. "What do you think it means?"

"Nothing." I try to pull my hand away, but he won't relinquish it. His grip turns painful.

"Maybe everyone has been right about you," he grumbles, finally letting go. His head tilts. "Maybe you *are* dangerous, Roselle. Do you want me dead?"

"My fate is to *protect* all firstborns," I gasp. "It's what I'm born to do."

Gabriel suddenly unsheathes his sword. It flares golden, a glowing length of condensed fusion energy, capable of cutting diamond. It's the shape and length of a broadsword of old, but without the heavy weight of iron or steel. I back away, wary of his intentions. Gabriel's advisors watch us. A few appear horrified, but most, like Susteven, have malicious grins. They're hoping for bloodshed.

"Here's your opportunity, Roselle. If you can kill me, you can be firstborn." Gabriel's gaze is a silent showdown.

I stand immobile. "My sole purpose is to serve The Sword, Gabriel—to serve you." The pop and crackle of his weapon raises the hairs on the back of my neck. I taste its energy in the air, familiar and warm.

"Do you regret not killing me when you were eleven, when it would've been seen as an accident?" He swings his fusionblade at me in a wide, flailing arc of dizzying light. I step back from its fiery edge, but my posture doesn't change.

Gabriel's eyes turn predatory. He swings again and again—the same clumsiness. I sidestep him, and he loses his balance and staggers. His midnight-blue cape sweeps forward and drifts against his sword. A swatch falls to the floor, resting on the inlaid marble map of the nine fatedoms that surround our family crest, covering the northern district, the Fate of Stars. It's one of the regions plagued by open rebellion. Secondborn Stars have aligned with secondborns from other Fates to form the Gates of Dawn—a rebel army.

I smell burning fabric. Gabriel straightens. He swings around and grasps at his ruined hem. His advisors snicker from the gleaming stairs, and Gabriel's hand tightens on the hilt of his weapon. "Do me the courtesy of drawing your sword!" he bellows.

"No." My lips press together.

"No?" The sweet boy has given way to the bitter man. "I'm to be The Sword!"

"I know who you are, Gabriel."

"Everyone here thinks you intend to kill me! Here's your chance, Roselle! I'm attacking you. Defend yourself." He hurls himself at me again. I step back, without drawing my sword, and realize that I'm standing on the Fate of Swords crest. A small voice inside me whispers, *I could be firstborn. I could kill Gabriel, and then no one would raise a hand to me ever again.* But the penance would be too much—I'd never sleep again if I murdered my brother.

Gabriel lunges. I avoid his sword and grasp his thumb, wrenching it back against his wrist. His grip on his weapon loosens and he drops it. Catching it before it hits, I angle it away from us, and I drive Gabriel to his knees with another twist of his thumb. His head bows and he winces.

Holding his thumb, I lean down and whisper. "One day, Gabriel, you'll be a powerful Clarity. When that day comes, follow your heart. Be the leader we need, not the ruler we don't. I love you, Brother. I'll miss you every day for the rest of my life." I let go and he looks up, anguish in his eyes. I nod my head in the direction of the Grand Staircase. "And get rid of your advisors. They like seeing you on your knees."

"I know who you are, too, Roselle." Gabriel tries to control his breathing. He wears a desolate smile. "I knew you wouldn't kill me. It's never been who you are—the girl who finds wounded animals and hides them away, tending them until they're healed and she can set them free."

My eyes widen. *He has been watching me these past years.* I offer him my hand, but before he has a chance to move, my mother's shrill voice screams from the balcony above us. "Shoot her! Stop her before she murders the firstborn!"

My breath catches, and I turn to the mezzanine. Othala's torso leans over the gilded railing, pointing at me in wild thrusts. Dune is just behind her, his expression grim and drawn. Along the railing, guards raise their fusion-powered rifles. I lose my grip on Gabriel's fusionblade. It slips from my hand to clatter on the cold tile, extinguishing from loss of pressure on the hilt.

Gabriel springs up from the floor, spreads his arms wide, and moves to stand between me and the soldiers. "Wait, wait, wait!" His arms flail. "I was just demonstrating for everyone here that this is all a mistake. Roselle has never been a threat to me. I proved it! *I* attacked *her*, and she never even drew her weapon."

"Move out of the way, Gabriel!" My mother leans farther over the balcony and waves her arm at him.

"She didn't do anything!" Gabriel insists. "Roselle's innocent!" His eyes dart from Mother to Dune, and then to his advisors. "Tell her!" he shouts at Susteven.

Light from a glistening chandelier shines off Susteven's balding head. "Roselle drove him to his knees," he says with a cunning look in our direction. Bile rises in my throat.

Gabriel scoffs. "It's not what you think! She was trying to stop me."

My mother seethes. "Gabriel, move!"

I dare not breathe. Unless Gabriel convinces them otherwise, the moment he fails to shield me, I'm dead. I open my mouth to speak, but I can't manage even one word in my own defense. I should never have touched him. They can end my life for that infraction alone.

Dune moves from behind Othala and hurries to the Grand Staircase. He descends the stairs two at a time. As he approaches us, Gabriel's voice cracks—a plea. "It wasn't her fault, Dune! It was *me*—I did this!"

"I'll see to her, Gabriel." Dune moves between Gabriel and me, turning me toward the immense doors that lead to the waiting crowd outside. I take a shaky step, and then another. Dune is right behind me.

No one can get off a shot without hitting him, too. Maybe Mother still holds some affection for him, because she doesn't give the kill order.

"I'm sorry, Roselle!" Gabriel's tortured voice strains behind us.

We make it to the doors. I push one open. Squinting in the sunlight, I stop just over the threshold. The roar of the crowd is a punch to my stomach. Dune grasps my upper arm and raises his other hand in a wave. "You can't go back in. They'll kill you," he says through a false smile. "From this moment on, we go forward. We never look back."

Chapter 3
Fate Traitors

Dune ushers me to the waiting hovercar. Fine mist from the Warrior Fountain settles on my skin. Bronze statues tower fifty feet or more above our heads. I lift my eyes to their vicious-looking swords. Their snarls are ferocious even on the best of days, but this is the worst day of my life. In a daze, I duck my head and climb into the back of the driverless vehicle, a Vicolt. This model hasn't been manufactured for hundreds of years. The rear of the hovercar is made of chrome and glass. It reminds me of an overturned fishbowl, and me, the beta fish on display.

Dune gets in beside me, his shoulder brushing mine. The doors seal shut, trapping us inside. I wring my hands and attempt to explain. "I wasn't trying to kill him—I swear! Gabriel drew his sword and—"

"The Fate of Swords would be better off if you *had* killed him, Roselle."

"What?" I was expecting reprisals, not disappointment.

"Smile, Roselle," Dune orders. His tone snaps with anger. "Let them all know they can't break you." My lips move into a grin that's mere muscle memory. I grip the rounded edge of the seat. It's hard to breathe. *Mother ordered them to kill me. I'm never coming home again.* It takes every ounce of will to refrain from retching.

"Mother thinks I was going to murder Gabriel."

"She doesn't know you at all."

"Will you tell her that I'm not a monster—that I'd never—"

The windscreen illuminates. It's a heads-up display, literally; the image of a Palace guard's head fills the screen. The female face merges with the landscape outside. She has gray eyes that match her Iono uniform. "We're ready for departure, Patrøn," she says, addressing Dune as a superior officer. "The route is programmed through the city of Forge and has not deviated from the plan we discussed."

"Thank you, Seville," Dune replies. He settles back in his seat.

"Is there anything you need before we begin?"

"No." Dune glances at me. "Er, yes. Water." Two pear-shaped glasses of ice water emerge from the console between us. "Thank you. We're ready now."

"Very well, Patrøn." Seville's image fades. The Vicolt glides forward, driven remotely by a team that has been practicing for this day for weeks. The stone façade of the Fate of Swords Palace fades as we move away. I lift my water to my mouth, drain it, and set the empty glass back in the console, where it descends out of sight.

The hovercar creeps along the fence and passes through the gate. Smiling well-wishers swarm us, anxious to get a good look at me. The long tails of their brightly colored woolen coats sway in the cold breeze. Stylish high collars protect them against the autumn chill. They touch the chrome veneer of the Vicolt and wave blood-red roses in adulation. The metal pavers of the road move the magnetized hovercar forward. Because this vintage vehicle is only used in ceremonial processions, we slink along so that everyone gets a good view. I try to hide my turmoil.

An enthusiastic man about my age presses forward from the crowd and runs alongside the hovercar. The head of a red flower bounces in his clutched fist. "Wave, Roselle." I lift my hand, complying with Dune's order. The man presses his hand on the window, crushing the rose against it and leaving a smear of petals and fog from his sweaty palm.

I study the buildings, which I've only seen before from the rooftop of the Palace or in on-screen images. I've missed a lot by being tethered to the estate. The structures rise to the sky, their details coming alive. I spot the iconic Heritage Building where the annual firstborn selections are held—an event in which the elite firstborns are sworn into service as leaders of our fatedom. One day, Gabriel will go there and vow to protect the Fate of Swords, and all the Fates.

Massive streams of golden energy flow down the walls of the Heritage Building's sword-shaped tower. The source of the energy is hidden high above our heads, tucked away in the clouds, at the hilt. The base of the building resembles a mountainous rock. A channel of energy runs along the blade into the base. It's a sword lodged in stone—a metaphor depicting the Fate of Swords' supremacy over the Fate of Stones.

The Heritage Building fades behind us. My real-time image is splashed upon the next group of towers, every move I make reflected back at me. I'm tiny next to Dune, though that's not at all how I see myself. A vast world exists inside of me. I have a hard time comprehending how it all fits. Being secondborn in a world ruled by firstborns has often forced me to retreat into my imagination, to avoid the constant shame and innuendos flung at me for my inferior birth. I've filled my mind with dreams. In them, I'm not beneath notice. I'm not so low that it's impossible for my family to love me. A small tear rolls down my cheek. *I should be throwing kisses and saying good-bye to all of it.*

A round drone camera outside the hovercar shimmies closer to me, obstructing my view. Its eyes never blink as it attempts to catch my mood, my movement, any reaction that can be shared, pulled apart, and overanalyzed by a violently bored society of firstborns. I stare back blankly, giving the Diamond-Fated media nothing to gossip about.

"When we arrive at the secondborn Stone Forest Base, at the Golden Transition Circle," Dune says, "there will be more cameras. You're to make your speech there before processing." I've come to recognize Dune's brooding tone. The first time I recall hearing it, I was no more than six or seven. We were training with fusionblades on the pristine lawn behind the estate. It was dawn, and the fresh dew had turned the blades of grass silver. A pack of wolfhounds, giant beasts with vicious jaws and claws that patrol the grounds at night, was being called back to its pens for feeding. Fleet and ferocious, they raced across the wet lawn—black canines streaking like phantom shadows.

As I sparred with Dune, matching his strikes with sizzling strokes from my own much smaller sword, I stepped back, down the slope of a small hill, and stumbled over a lump in my path. Falling, I rolled away and sprang up, but what I saw brought bile to my mouth. Nightfall had resulted in the slaughter of one wolfhound, left in pieces but still breathing shallowly. Its mandible was broken. Its pink tongue hung out of its mouth. Sparking circuitry bristled beneath its organic exterior.

"Someone has slaughtered a maginot!"

I knelt by its side and reached to stroke its ebony fur, but Dune stayed my hand. He crouched next to me. "It wasn't a *someone* that did this, Roselle. Its own pack tore it to pieces." Carrion circled above our heads, waiting to move in on the carcass.

"Why would they do that?" I watched the shallow rise and fall of the wounded cyborg's torso.

"It must have displayed a weakness—a limp, a tic, an uncharacteristic frequency—something that they perceived as threatening to the pack."

I placed a childish hand on its flank, feeling its thready breathing. "But if it was broken, it could've been repaired."

"It outlived its usefulness, so it was killed. There's something to be learned in that."

"Never outlive my usefulness?"

"Never, ever trust the pack." With that, he raised his sword and sliced open the whirling brain of the canine, extinguishing its operating system. The smell of burning dog flesh rose from its corpse.

The memory fades as the drone camera veers upward from my window to get an aerial shot. I return to watching the buildings lining the thoroughfare, trying to lose my thoughts in their beauty. A golden face flashes in the crowd, distracts me from the architecture. Its featureless mask shines from beneath a shrouded hood, dazzling with rays of simulated sunlight. In a blink, he's behind us. I look back, but he has melted into the crowd. "Did you see that?" I ask Dune.

He gazes out my window. "See what?" We turn another corner. The street grows narrower.

"I thought I saw something bright." The crowd closes in, the whack of red roses growing louder with their nearness.

Dune clears his throat, touching a switch on the console that turns off the monitors and microphones. "After your speech, there won't be time for us to say good-bye, Roselle. We should do that here. Now."

A thousand things that I want to say—need to say—come to mind, but I can't seem to get them past the growing lump in my throat. My vision blurs with unshed tears.

"You don't have to say anything, Roselle, just listen. I'm going away. I've left my position with your mother."

It takes me a moment to process this. "Where will you go?" I ask, knowing that it really doesn't matter. I won't be allowed to see him again.

"I've been accepted as personal security for Clarity Bowie. I leave for the capital city today. I'll be in their fatedom by this evening."

"You're going to Purity? But what about my mother—Gabriel? They need you."

"They don't need me," he snaps, his bitterness filling the air around us. "I raised you. I trained you. You're all that matters now."

I'm stunned by his words. "I . . . matter?"

"More than you know."

My eyes brim with fresh tears. I can't imagine Dune as far away as the Fate of Virtues. He'll live in the lavish capital city of Purity, and I'll be here. I've never even been outside my Fate.

"There's a man—secondborn—Walther Petes. Say his name."

"Walther Petes." It comes out in a croak.

"Find him after they place you. He's stationed somewhere in this fatedom. He'll get word to me and tell me where you are."

"Who is he?" I ask.

"My brother."

"But . . . your last name is Kodaline."

"Is it?" Dune's eyebrow lifts.

"Isn't it?" I whisper.

He shakes his head. "You'll always be my firstborn, Roselle, even if you're not of my blood. I'll find you when it's time."

The lump in my throat bobs. "Time for what?"

"Time for our paths to cross again."

"But—" My questions are interrupted by the Vicolt's windscreen coming back online. Dune shoots me a look that orders discretion.

Seville frowns at us from her hologram. "Is everything all right?" she asks, her voice piping through our headrests. "We lost audio and our visual was obscured."

Dune leans forward and flicks the microphones back on. "We're fine. I must have tripped this by mistake."

Seville lets out a sigh of relief. "I'm so glad to hear you're doing well. Is there anything you need?"

"No," he replies.

I stare out the window once more, half listening as Dune makes small talk with our navigator, but my mind is reeling. *Who is Dune? Do I even know him?* But of course I do. He taught me everything I know. I owe him my very existence. Without him, I'd have had no love at all.

I want to ask him more questions, but Seville refuses to shut up so we can mute the microphone. I feign interest in the scenery, hoping she'll get the hint. The gorgeous buildings begin to fade from sight, replaced by less grand structures. Everything is foreign-looking now. I've not been this far from the Sword Palace estate in my entire life.

The crowds are just as ardent here, though—their roses just as bright, though their clothing is less posh, more practical.

A glimmer of light catches my eye, a golden mask in the crowd. It's really a visor attached to a combat helmet. I've never seen one like it. The visor has illuminated striations of sunlight, as if a small sun is caught beneath the shrouded hood of the man's dark cloak. Another visor passes by in the crowd—and then another. Dark galaxies obscure the faces of other masked men, their visors a swirl of stars and violet nebulae. Copper-colored atoms orbit the surface of other masks. Rippling blue water forms concentric circles on others.

Our hovercar slows, detecting an obstruction. Ahead of us, through Seville's talking head, a man stands in the middle of the road. He's wearing a mask of the night sky. His visor obscures his features. A black cape blows around his powerful shoulders. Black leather polymer covers his chest and torso. Scrolling iron gates are etched into the plates of his armor. His legs, planted in a wide stance, are clad in black combat boots.

I've never seen armor like his, only Swords armor worn by Fate of Swords soldiers. To have other Fates represented in combat is unprecedented. It violates the purpose of our Fate.

"Gates of Dawn," Dune murmurs. "Accelerate to maximum speed. Do not avoid the obstruction."

Seville's image disappears. The hovercar lurches forward with murderous velocity. Dune's smile falls when the night-faced man sidesteps the chrome hood and avoids being struck. His swirling black cape blots out the sunlight through my window. In his hand, the petals of a white flower skim past my window like lightning.

Shifting in my seat, I stare out the back, watching the renegade turn back to face us. Suddenly hundreds of white flowers pelt us from all angles. They're calla lilies—death flowers. The last time I saw them was when my grandfather died and his body was displayed in a funeral precession to his tomb at Killian Abbey.

I flinch as a stone crashes into my window, cracking the glass near my face. A mountain range shifts across the visor of the man who threw it. Other Stone-masked men begin to throw rocks, leaving dimples in the Vicolt's veneer.

Dune leans forward. He touches the navigation screens, pulling up maps and charts. A manual control panel activates, exposing the Vicolt's operating system. "Seville."

"Patrøn?" Seville's voice sounds confused.

"I'm deviating from the planned route." He engages the wings, which slip out on either side, transforming the vehicle into an aircraft.

"But, Patrøn, protocol dictates—"

"I don't care about protocol!"

The vehicle's wings begin to retract. "You're to remain in glide mode," Seville says with a phony smile. "Wingers have been dispatched to clear the area of enemy forces. You'll proceed on the designated route as planned. Everything is under control—"

Dune leans forward and disconnects the circuitry beneath the console. The heads-up display disappears. "Message received," he mumbles. He tries to engage the wings, but they're still controlled by Seville and her team. Outside, people are panicking, running from the masked men. The Vicolt slows to a stop. We idle as the Gates of Dawn soldiers form a wide circle around us. "We've become bait, Roselle. Protocol dictates we wait for troops to arrive to annihilate the threat."

"How close are our troops?" My hand grips my sword on my hip.

"I don't know. The Gates aren't attacking us, Roselle. They're waiting." He opens the Vicolt's door and climbs out. "Stay here." He closes the door. Drawing his fusionblade, he cuts through stones thrown at him, pulverizing most into dust and taking hits from others as he makes his way back to where the night-masked soldier walks slowly toward us. I wonder why our enemies are throwing stones. Surely they have more sophisticated weapons at their disposal—unless they were unable to smuggle them into our fatedom. I try to see the monikers on their hands, but gloves cover them, shrouding their true origins.

The gruesome night-faced man has already traded his flower for a fusionblade. The sword swishes in his black-gloved hand. Dune moves to meet him. My heart hammers. I can't leave my mentor out there alone, unprotected. Disobeying Dune's direct order, I fumble with my door. It swings open and I jump from the hovercar, drawing my sword. Drone cameras circle us.

The sky begins to rumble with troopships and death drones. The traitor in black tilts his masked face up. He extinguishes his sword, sheathing it. From the lining of his cape, he pulls out a silver orb that fits in the palm of his hand. He rests his thumb on top of it. Dune skids to a halt and looks up. Enormous airships soar above us. He glances over his shoulder at me, then starts waving his arms, fear carving lines in his face.

Our enemy depresses the button on the device in his palm. I squeeze my eyes shut, anticipating a catastrophic explosion. But nothing happens. I open my eyes. My sword has gone out. I shake it, hoping to reignite it. It's as useless as a brick. Confused, I search for Dune. He reaches me, grasping my shoulders, turning me back toward the hovercar. Beside us, something falls from the sky and crashes onto the metal pavers. It's a drone camera. Another one crashes and shatters, and then another. Our enemies begin retreating, melting into the fleeing crowd.

Dune shoves me in the direction of the Vicolt. I lift my face to the sky. A troopship above us pitches to the side, its thunderous sound replaced by the soughs it creates as it falls.

Chapter 4
Pulse Pummeled

The troopship plummets, clipping the side of a building and crashing through several floors. It topples over into another building in a shattering of glass that looks like sparkling, jagged rain. Black smoke turns the blue sky to night. Dune and I reach the Vicolt amid screaming and chaos. People trample each other in their attempt to run from the pelting debris.

Dune pushes me into the Vicolt. Climbing into the driver's seat, he reconnects the circuitry, and the hovercar trundles forward as he seals the doors shut. Smoke and thick clouds of rock dust overcome the vehicle, shrouding it in a haze. Thunderous rumbling drowns out the sounds of my coughs. Dune closes the vents.

The navigation system comes back online, and the hovercar resumes its course. Still panting, Dune says, "That orb was an FSP, a Fusion Snuff Pulse. It's new technology. Our spies infiltrated an enemy lab in the Fate of Stars last month and found evidence of such a device. It disrupts the atomic fusion we use to power *everything*."

"It brought down the death drones and the Wingers—the drone cameras—my sword," I reply, lifting the beautifully crafted silver hilt. It doesn't ignite.

"It probably knocked out anything fusion-driven for several miles."

But the Vicolt's power runs on old-fashioned electromagnetic cells, backed up by hydrogen cells. It slows to a stop. A soft breeze blows the dust away, exposing our path. A large portion of one of the troopships lies in a smoldering heap before us. Pieces of people litter the avenue.

A part of me is stunned, but I've been trained for this. "We have to help them."

Dune tears off a strip of his uniform cape and hands it to me. "Wrap this around your nose and mouth to keep the dust from your lungs."

We emerge, and for the next hour we work as a team, searching the wreckage for wounded, pulling debris away from bodies, checking for signs of life. Most victims are so badly crushed that there's no chance of survival. I almost lose hope until I discover a young female soldier still breathing among the carnage. Dune pulls pieces of the ship off her as I kneel and begin dressing her wounds with swatches of fabric I tear from her uniform. Her ebony hair is nearly white from dust.

The steel arm of a medical drone nudges me aside, its cylindrical silver body hovering over the soldier. A blue light scans her from head to toe, assessing her injuries. Other medical drones arrive, scouring for survivors. I step back and right into someone standing behind me. Masculine arms encircle me. Turning around in his embrace, I stare up into the visor of a Fate of Swords soldier, noting the shiny black broadsword embossed on its matte-black surface. The visor retracts in sections, revealing a wicked smile and gorgeous, steel-colored eyes.

The soldier jerks the wool away from my nose and mouth. Lifting his hand to reposition his headset microphone, his deep voice resonates into it. "I've located her." He pauses, listening. "I'm sure it's her." He grasps my wrist, takes an identification processor from his belt, and positions it over the side of my hand where my sword moniker usually glows. He pulls the trigger on the scanner. Blue light illuminates my skin. His scanner works—he must have come from outside the snuff pulse's range. My identity doesn't register on his device. Usually, a holographic screen with all my vital information would display. Frowning, he triggers the scanner again. Blue light dances over my hand, and then . . . nothing.

"Her moniker is fried, but it's her," he scowls, glancing skyward. "How do I know for sure? I've been forced to watch her every day for as long as I can remember. I think I can recognize Roselle St. Sismode. Commander Kodaline is with her."

I turn toward the wounded soldier behind me. Dune has taken my place beside her, holding her hand as the medical drone administers combat dressings and medication. The soldier's hand moves to encircle my upper arm. He turns me back to him. I wince at the pressure of his grip. "Stay where you are," he orders. His other hand examines my torso. The blood of dead soldiers smears my uniform.

"That's not my blood." I try to brush his hand from me. Chaos swirls around us. Newly arrived rescue ships and drones circle overhead. The breeze has begun to blow the dust and smoke away, allowing us to see and breathe much easier.

"Hold still," the soldier orders.

"I'm not hurt. Please let go of me." I try again to shrug away.

"Are you in shock?" he asks in a rush. "Who is the Clarity of Virtues? Do you know what fatedom we're in?" He runs his hand over my stomach, worry creasing his brow when his gloved hand comes away with more blood.

I stare at his handsome face, my heartbeat racing uncomfortably. "I'm not in shock, Fabian Bowie is Clarity, and we're in Swords. Let *go*."

He won't let go, and I'm not used to being touched, least of all by a domineering soldier whose face makes me feel like my heart is too big for my chest. I drive my elbow into his nose, not hard enough to break it, but enough to let him know he needs to let me go.

He does. He wipes his bloody nose with the back of his gloved hand. "You just struck a superior—"

I move back. "Technically, I'm still an unregistered secondborn until I'm processed. You're not my superior anything. I'm not in shock, I'm not injured, and you don't get to touch me unless I say you can."

I feel a rifle muzzle tap the back of my skull. I still. "You need some help, Hawthorne?"

The soldier's scowl deepens. He reaches out and pulls me behind him, knocking the gun away. "Gilad, don't point your weapon at her!"

Before the second soldier can comply, he's disarmed by Dune, who detaches the fusion charge from beneath the grip of the rifle, rendering it useless. Dune pockets the charge before handing the weapon back to the young combatant. "Have any of the Gates of Dawn soldiers been apprehended yet?"

The overconfident one with the incredible eyes stands at attention, giving Dune the respect owed to him by his firstborn rank. "I'm unaware of any prisoners being taken, Patrøn."

"What's your name?" Dune asks.

"Hawthorne Sword, Patrøn, 11-171971." He gives only his first name, his Fate, and his number. His last name was taken from him when he was processed. He's now required to identify with his Fate, to which he's sworn his loyalty, rather than with his family.

"And you?" Dune's gaze rests on the one who put the muzzle to my head.

The soldier's visor ticks back. He doesn't look much older than me, but he has white scars on his brow, nose, and both cheeks. "Gilad Sword, 25-135472."

"How old are you?" Dune studies them.

"Nineteen, Patrøn," they answer in unison.

More soldiers climb over the embankment of smoldering rubble surrounding us. "And how long have you been wards of the Fate?"

"I was Transitioned when I was ten, Patrøn," Hawthorne answers.

"I was ten, also, Patrøn," Gilad replies.

Dune's lips twist in a sneer. "Secondborn soldiers keep getting younger and younger. Are all of your families afraid of you?"

The question was rhetorical, but Gilad answers anyway. "Well, yeah." He smirks, showing imperfect teeth. "We're scary monsters, Patrøn."

Hawthorne glances away, listening to his headset. His eyes shift back to Dune's. "A transport is en route to intercept you here and take you directly to the Fate of Virtues at the order of Clarity Bowie."

"I will accompany Roselle to processing. She is to make her speech—"

Hawthorne raises his palm. "Negative, Patrøn. You're to leave immediately for Virtues. Those are orders. A secondborn transport is en route to intercept Roselle St. Sismode."

Two ships emerge above us and rapidly descend. Doors open from the top and form ramps leading into the bellies of the aircraft. Gilad tucks his rifle to his chest and walks toward one of the vessels. Hawthorne touches my elbow but pulls his hand away when my eyes shift to it. "We need to go, Roselle."

"Wait!" My bleak eyes fly to Dune.

"Can you give us a moment?" Dune asks. Hawthorne nods and walks away, just out of earshot.

Dune gathers me into a hug. I smell sandalwood, even through the dust covering us. I cannot remember ever being hugged by him before. I close my eyes, trying not to cry. In a hushed voice, he asks, "Do you remember the name I told you?"

"Yes."

He squeezes me tighter. "Roselle, there's something you need to know," he says, so low that only I can hear him. "Walther is not just my secondborn brother—he's my *older* brother." My eyes widen, and I loosen my grip on him. "Now you know my secret. Find me, should you need me. I will be there for you." Too shocked to speak, I hardly react when he kisses my forehead. Dune straightens and looks past my shoulder. The handsome soldier approaches us. "Hawthorne, should anything happen to her, I'll hold you responsible."

"I understand, Patrøn. I'll make sure she gets to where she's supposed to be."

I cling to Dune for a moment longer, my head on his shoulder, and then I let him go, taking a shaky step back, and then another. My vision blurs. Hawthorne walks beside me, his rifle in hand, scanning for any sign of the enemy as we move to the waiting troopship.

Near the ramp, Gilad is surrounded by a squad of soldiers, all about my age, with the glowering stares of thousand-year-old souls. Hawthorne raises his voice over the hum of the aircraft. "You're in charge of the unit until I get back, Gilad."

Gilad smiles imperiously at his assembled unit. "All right, children," he roars, "this is only a rescue mission if you find someone alive! Let's uncover Swords who need our help, and beacon them for the med drones to mend 'em and send 'em!"

Hawthorne gestures toward the ramp. "After you, Roselle." Walking to the ship, I glance back over my shoulder at the only man who ever truly loved me.

Chapter 5
Mine Now

I enter the drab interior of the aircraft. Rows of black seats line its walls and belly. The airship is empty, except for the pilots in the front and Hawthorne beside me. I select a seat by the ramp. Hawthorne reaches up and pulls down the harness. He locks it in place around me and takes a seat across from me.

Through the open doorway, I see Dune amid a unit of firstborn officers who have come to escort him to the capital in Virtues, their snow-white uniform capes turning gray with dust. They don't know that Commander Kodaline is really Dune Petes, thirdborn Sword—an imposter. *He has to be thirdborn if his older brother, Walther, is a secondborn Sword soldier.* Panic careens through my veins. If any one of those officers discovers Dune's secret—that the golden sword-shaped moniker that usually shines on his left hand is somehow a fake—they'd be tempted to execute him where he stands. By every law of the Fates of the Republic, he shouldn't exist.

Thirdborn laws allow few exceptions. It's considered greedy to deplete resources on a third child. Clarities, who are required to have two children, are usually the only ones who can produce more than the allotted offspring, but there have to be special circumstances. Gabriel or I would have to die before my mother could give birth to another child. She would need special permission acquired through a petition and legal channels. It has happened, but it's not common. A whole division of the government called Census is devoted to the detection and elimination of violators of the thirdborn rules, and its authority is almost absolute. I shiver, knowing that I can never tell anyone what Dune just told me. If I do, he will be hunted down and slaughtered.

If Walther is secondborn, then who is their firstborn brother?

"Are you okay?" Hawthorne asks. I stare at him blankly. "You look as if you might faint."

"How long until we get to the Golden Circle?" My voice doesn't sound like me. It's gravelly and raw—dry from the dust coating everything and the emotions choking my throat.

He shrugs, settling back in his seat and pulling down on the harness above his head to lock it in place. "Less than twenty."

I nod and look away from him. The ramp rises and obscures my view of Dune. It thumps hard against the side, sealing us in. The sound of it reverberates. Dim lights illuminate the interior as the aircraft lifts straight up. I get an aerial view of the destruction through the transparent aisle beneath my feet. Several buildings have toppled over. Fires rage over entire city blocks. Broken airships lie like skeletons across the scorched ground.

This is the first strike my fatedom has suffered in this war. Usually, we're pounding cities in the Fate of Stars, the Fate of Atoms, and the Fate of Suns, cities suspected of harboring Gates of Dawn soldiers or sympathizers. Mother is probably beside herself, the first Sword in several centuries to fail to protect her people—her firstborns. She doesn't care about anyone else.

I glance up through my tears. Hawthorne studies me, and I realize I'm trembling, my body reacting to trauma. Unlocking his harness, Hawthorne shifts to the seat next to mine. From a compartment on the side of his thigh armor, he extracts a square packet. He cracks it with both hands and shakes it. "Here." He places it in my hand. Heat radiates from it. He nudges my hands together, letting the packet warm them both. Unwrapping a gauze bandage from his medical supplies, he uses a water spritzer to wet the material. Setting the water aside, Hawthorne extends the cloth to my face.

I lean away from him, avoiding his hand. "What are you doing?"

"Cleaning you up. You're a mess."

"Who cares what I look like?" I ask, bumping his arm away.

Reaching for a chrome lid to a power source generator, he pulls it off the unit and holds it up so that I'm confronted by my reflection. I resemble a weeping ghost. Gray dust covers my skin. Streaks of tears create desolate lines through it.

"I'm not crying. I have dust in my eyes," I lie.

"I know," he lies, too. He replaces the chrome lid. The wet cloth nears my face once more. This time I don't pull away as Hawthorne gently presses it to my cheek and wipes off the soot.

"I'm sorry," I murmur. "About your nose."

He shrugs. "I've had worse. It's been broken a few times."

"You can't tell." I bite my bottom lip anxiously. He winks at me. My heart flutters, and my face flushes hotly.

"I get it fixed whenever it's broken. Gilad teases me about it. He says it's a waste of merits because it'll just end up broken again. Probably by him."

"What are merits?"

"Special privilege units. You earn them by doing things better or faster than everyone else. Or by doing things others can't do."

"Are there any other ways to earn them?"

"Sometimes you can earn them for being a turner—reporting other secondborns for infractions of the rules. I wouldn't advise it, though. Turners have a way of not lasting very long in most units."

"You mean they're killed?"

"I mean they have an accident that they never recover from."

"What else can you use merits for?"

He stops cleaning my face and sits back. "All kinds of things—extra rations, novel files, magazine files, soap, hair products, sweets, entertainment—"

"What kind of entertainment?"

He wads up the dirty cloth and throws it at a bin. "Well, there's films and music . . . date night." He gives me an appraising look and smiles. My heart thumps harder in my chest. "You get to go on a date—each person pays merits to meet each other. They match you with someone you'd be compatible with, and then they allow you to meet and . . ." He waves his hand in a gesture that indicates a next step. "And whatever." He raises both of his eyebrows.

I just stare at him.

He frowns. "Please tell me you know what I'm talking about."

I shake my head.

"Sex, Roselle. I'm talking about sex." I straighten in my seat and look away from him, embarrassed by the turn our conversation has taken. "You know what sex is, then?" He laughs.

"I know what it is. I don't know why anyone would waste merits on it. It's not like you're allowed to have a child. We're secondborns. We're forbidden to procreate. What would be the point of date night?"

He looks up at the ceiling. "What would be the point?" He turns to me with an incredulous look. "Pleasure, Roselle. Pleasure is the point. We both take a pill before the date starts so there's no chance of offspring."

"So you pay for the privilege of having a . . ."

"The word you're looking for is *girlfriend*, and no, no one gets a girlfriend. We aren't allowed to have an ongoing relationship. The next time I have a date, it will be with someone new."

I want desperately to change the subject. "Have they located any of the Gates of Dawn soldiers? There was one soldier with a night-sky visor. It had a swirling black hole on it"—I drag my hand in front of my face from my forehead to my chin—"here. He confronted my hover." My cheeks are on fire, and I want to slap the arrogant grin off Hawthorne's face.

"I don't know. No one is speaking to me at the moment." He taps the ear of his headset.

"How do we find out?" I try to wipe dust off my sleeve, anything not to have to meet his eyes.

"I'll probably be briefed on the status of the investigation later. You, more than likely, will be questioned for what you know about the attack. What do you know?"

"I saw the first soldier not too far from the Heritage Building."

"But the attack happened farther from there. Why didn't you alert someone to their presence sooner?" His cocky smile has evaporated.

"I wasn't sure what I saw."

His eyes dart around to see if we're being observed. He covers the microphone of his headset. "Don't tell anyone what you just told me," he whispers.

"Why? He had a golden sun mask—"

He hushes me, looking over his shoulder before turning back to me. "You didn't report the soldier immediately. It could be seen as aiding the enemy."

My voice drops several octaves. "I was confused. I'd just left my home—it was traumatic—I wasn't thinking."

He reaches out and touches my wrist. "I know what that moment is like—when you realize you'll never see home again." He stares into my eyes, and I see my pain reflected back at me. "But you can't tell them anything about that soldier. Just start at the point you were attacked. Trust me. I'm trying to protect you. Do you understand?" I nod. "Good." He drops his hand from the microphone.

Hawthorne continues to watch me with worry in his eyes. Our troopship descends in a rush of speed that makes my stomach flip. It touches down in the middle of an airship pad on the outskirts of a military Base. The door of our aircraft opens, exposing us to an overcast sky. Tall, gray pillars rise up from the ground in front of us like tree trunks in a stone forest, tapering the higher they go into the clouds. Each must be a few city blocks in diameter. Docked to each structure's tree branches are kidney-shaped airships, each large enough to harbor a few thousand troops. They're mobile barracks designed with sleeping quarters, mess hall, and training facilities that can also airlift troops to war zones and other military Bases. Assessing the stone forest of ships, I see there must be hundreds of thousands of soldiers at this Base alone.

Hawthorne rises from his seat. He takes the warming pack from my hands and disposes of it in a bin. "C'mon." He waits for me to stand. "I'll get you where you need to be." Holding his rifle close to his body with the muzzle pointed at the ground, he gazes around at the Base outside before exiting the aircraft. I follow him.

"Why didn't we just dock in there?" I ask. "It looks as if the grounds surrounding the Base have been cleared."

"You're not allowed in there until you're processed. They try to make it appear as if you're being indoctrinated into a secret society of knights."

"And you don't believe that?" I study his profile as I walk beside him.

Hawthorne scowls. "I know what's on the other side of the wall now, Roselle." When he was brought here and processed at the age of ten, he probably believed he was here for a noble cause.

"Do you think I'll still have to give my speech?"

Hawthorne looks up and frowns. The air is filled with troopships launching from their docks on the stone Trees. They resemble falling half-moon leaves being torn by the wind into the sky. "I think your press conference is canceled. There are no drone cameras here, and I've never seen so many air-barracks mobilize at once. They must be mounting a retaliatory strike. I've never seen the grounds empty like this before either—especially not on Transition Day. It's as if we're the only ones out here."

"What's it normally like?" I ask.

"Usually there are thousands of children lined up waiting to be processed. Some are crying, too young to be separated from the only home they've ever known. But some are ready—maybe they hope to fit in here like they never did with their families."

"Were you the former or the latter?" I ask softly.

"The latter." We cross the landing pad to a wide paved path that leads to an ebony wall that surrounds the gigantic forest. I have to crane my neck back to see the top. Set in the center of the wall is a gate comprised of three golden metal broadswords at least as large as five-story buildings. The center sword is ancient in design, from an era before fusion was reality. It's taller than the two that flank it by a story. *Mystical gates to an enchanted forest,* I think.

Hawthorne pauses by one of the armed soldiers stationed along the walkway. "Chet?" He offers the soldier a small white stamp wrapped in cellophane from his pocket.

The soldier looks around as if to check whether anyone is watching. "Thanks." He casually takes the offered stamp and shoves it inside a compartment on his gun belt. Scanning the grounds, Hawthorne asks him, "Where are all the Transition candidates?"

"Gone. We turned them away. No one gets inside the walls today except the secondborn Sword—orders from The Sword."

"Why just her?" Hawthorne frowns at me.

"They're worried about vetting. Monikers were coming up mysteriously inoperable. It's making everyone nervous. We can't vet candidates, so we can't take them. Anyone could show up at our gate saying he was a Sword. No one can verify it if the identifier isn't working. It's a Census problem now."

Hawthorne nods his head, looking on edge himself. "Thanks." He resumes walking.

"What's a chet?" I ask, following him.

"It's for when you need to relax and you can't. You put it in your mouth, let it melt on your tongue, and everything is okay."

"You mean it's a drug?" I frown at him.

"No, it's a chet—it's not addictive like a drug, and don't look so condescending. There may come a day when you need one. If you don't, then you can count yourself lucky and just use them for getting other things you want."

"Like information?"

"Yeah, like that."

The closer we get to the wall, the more defensive features I recognize. An iridescent shield ripples over the surface of the dark wall that surrounds the Base. The shield is more than likely fusion-powered. I cringe. This defense is useless against an FSP. "Are all our fortifications fusion-powered?" I ask.

Hawthorne pauses, turning to look at me. "Why do you ask?"

"Are they?"

"Most."

"Can they be converted to another energy source? Say—hydrogen cells?"

"Why would we do that? Hydrogen has less than a tenth of the capacity and life that fusion has."

Suddenly a drawbridge opens ahead of us. It drops from the center of the tallest sword before the Golden Circle inlaid on the ground. Sword soldiers on the other side of the threshold draw their fusion-powered rifles on us.

We enter the beautiful Golden Circle in front of the doors. In the center, an ancient broadsword rises from the ground. Hawthorne removes his black glove, exposing his moniker. He holds it to the golden light of the sword's hilt. It scans his silver sword-shaped moniker. A holographic image of Hawthorne projects from atop the hilt of the golden sword, detailing his unit, rank, and other information in flashing readouts. "Handsome devil, isn't he?" Hawthorne whispers.

"I wouldn't waste merits on him," I whisper back.

His eyebrow arches, and he's about to whisper something else when one of the soldiers at the gate focuses his attention on me. His voice surrounds us. "Scan your moniker for processing."

I hold up the back of my hand. There's no obvious glow, just the rose-colored crown-shaped birthmark upon my skin. "It was damaged in the attack this morning. It seems to have shorted out."

"Scan your moniker for processing or you will be tranquilized."

I follow his orders. No image of me projects from the podium when my hand is scanned. The soldier who spoke points to another who holds a tranquilizer gun at the ready. My heart accelerates. Hawthorne's brow furrows. "This is Roselle St. Sismode," he calls out. "You only need to look at her to know that."

"She could be—or she could be a surgically enhanced spy made to look like Secondborn St. Sismode." The soldier spits on the ground.

Hawthorne gestures toward me. "You've probably seen her at least a thousand times! Just process her and give her a new moniker!"

"I've seen her more times than I've taken a shit, but so have our enemies. She can't be processed without scanning her moniker. If she needs a new moniker, she can't get it from us. She's Census's problem now."

The very mention of Census sends raging fear through my blood. Hawthorne moves from the podium to block me from the soldier's view. I'm not one to hide, so I move around him to stand next to him. He frowns and faces the gate. "Can't we just handle this internally without Census? This is a secondborn."

An impeccably dressed man emerges from behind the soldiers. His attire would make him the envy of even the best-dressed firstborn in Gabriel's circle. A long black leather coat—tailored to show off his impressive physique—touches the calves of his high-polished black leather boots. His white dress shirt has the sheen of silk, and his black trousers have the same well-tailored lines as his coat.

But it's the tattoos near his eyes that give me pause. Thin, black lines are permanently etched from the outside edges of his eyes, curving to his temples. They make him look catlike and lethal. I know what the razor-thin lines mean. Each line denotes a hunt and kill. This Census agent has successfully tracked and executed at least fifty people—probably third-borns and their abettors.

"Whom do we have at our gates?" the agent asks, his hands behind his back. He strolls through the golden archway, chuckling. "Can it be *the* legendary Roselle St. Sismode? Why, my dear girl, what brings you to our lair? Why have they banished you to this hellish existence? Surely they could've given you a much more suitable position, considering your bloodline." He stops in front of me and grins like a deranged harlequin.

He's genuinely handsome, like some ancient king. In his midtwenties, he's as tall and graceful as a Diamond ad model. His high brows and sharp jaw are appealing, but it's his smile where things start to go wrong. His four top front teeth have been replaced with steel. So have most of his bottom teeth. I'm having a hard time not reacting to the utterly creepy look he's giving me.

I knew Census had field agents among the Swords—among all the fatedoms. I just never thought I'd meet one. It hadn't occurred to me that my moniker would ever fail—that my identity would ever be in question.

The agent's mood shifts from baiting to thoughtful. "Unless"—he keeps one hand behind his back, the other smoothing back his slick blond hair—"you're not Roselle St. Sismode. *Are* you *the* secondborn Sword—the biggest loser in all of the Fate of Swords?"

I just stare at him, absorbing his insult. He wants me to rush into some explanation—fall over myself in desperation to identify myself. I smile, even though panic is just beneath the surface, but I say nothing.

Hawthorne clears his throat. "This is Rose—"

"Quiet, you!" The agent doesn't look away from me as he growls, "You have no idea who or what this is. You picked her up on the battlefield, did you not?"

"Well, yes, but—"

"Let's not assume anything, shall we?" the agent barks. "Now, let's take this slow." The agent bends forward at his waist so that I can feel his breath on my cheek as he stares into my eyes. "Who. Are. You?"

"Roselle—"

The Census agent shoots me. I choke on pain as the steel dart cracks through my breastplate and spews venom into me. The cartridge sticks out from my chest just above my heart. He fired point-blank. I didn't even see the gun he drew from behind his back until it was too late.

The agent grins at the sounds I make as I writhe in agony. I can see my reflection in his steel teeth. His hand goes to my shoulder to steady me. He touches my hair. "Don't talk. Just panic." He breathes the words near my ear as he embraces me.

My hands reach out for his waist. He thinks I'm holding myself up, but I unfasten his leather belt and slip it from his pants. In one swift motion, I have the strap wrapped around his neck and ratcheted in a noose. The leather cuts into his throat. I use all my strength to pull on it. His eyes bulge and widen. The strength of my grip slackens and I falter. Dizziness upturns me. I drop to my knees, still holding the strap. The agent drops to his knees as well, coughing and wheezing as he loosens the noose.

Soldiers yell and run toward us. The next thing I know I'm on the ground, staring up at the overcast sky. The agent waves away Hawthorne and the other soldiers. They retreat, restraining Hawthorne. On his knees beside me, the agent smiles again. A tear slips over the inky lines near one sapphire-colored eye. "You're mine now," he whispers in my ear, scooping me up. The steel dart is still embedded over my heart. My head bobs, and I view the world from upside down as he carries me across the golden threshold into the forest of nightmares.

Chapter 6
In Census

The room is small, rectangular, and unfamiliar—dank—a cell, not a room. The only appointments in it are a small toilet in the corner and a steel sink. A steel door is across from me. I have a strange, tinny taste in my mouth. My back aches. I shift and groan from the cold and lack of movement that have made my muscles stiff. I feel buried. I reach for my sword, but it's gone—so is my uniform. I'm wearing a snug, midnight-blue long-sleeved shirt and loose, elastic-waisted trousers of the same color and coarse material. My feet are bare. I stretch my legs out from the fetal position. The ground is cold beneath me.

A long tube runs down my leg and out the loose pant leg at the bottom. It's attached to a urine collection canister, nearly full. *How long have I been here?* I pull out the catheter tube and shove it aside. Beneath the sleeve of my right arm is an intravenous device that could be feeding me drugs or hydrating me. I don't know which, but I want it out. I tug, and it stings as I extract it. My stomach growls and feels as if it's gnawing away at itself. I've never felt this kind of hunger before.

I shove myself up to my feet. Stretching my arms, I wince. My fingers brush the area where I was shot by the dart. It's sore. Lifting my shirt, I investigate a massive bruise above my heart, black and ugly but turning yellow—it's not fresh. *How long was I unconscious?*

I move to a moniker identification scanner on a panel beside the door. I glance at my hand. My moniker is still dead. I try to scan it anyway, feeling claustrophobic and desperate to get out. The blue laser runs over it. The door doesn't budge. I bang on it and yell for help until I'm hoarse, but no one comes.

The cold floor is brutal against my bare feet. I'm shivering. Crossing my arms, I tuck my hands in the crook of my armpits while jumping up and down. For a while, I pace the dingy cell, lunging with an imaginary sword. When I'm tired, I curl into a ball. Waiting. Occasionally, the sounds of feet outside the door make me brace myself, but each time, they keep going. I fall back to sleep at some point, and when I wake again, I'm not alone. My skin prickles.

"I was just wondering what it is you dream about," says the raspy voice of the Census agent. "Puppies?" He sits in a metal chair, uncrosses his long legs, and leans forward, resting his forearms on his thighs. The collar of his exquisite white shirt is unbuttoned. Red, angry abrasions stand out on his throat. His steely smile is meant to intimidate, and it works.

I sit up and lean against the wall. Rubbing the sleep from my eyes, I nod. "I sometimes dream of rainbows, too—puppies and rainbows— just like you, I'd imagine. Where am I?"

He grins. "You sleep soundly. I thought for sure that you were faking it when I first came in."

I shrug. "Tranquilizers do that to me. It feels as if we're underground."

He cocks his head to the side. "As a matter of fact, we are. You are my guest in Census." He takes off his gloves, pulling each of the black leather fingers until the wrinkles straighten. His moniker shines in a golden circlet from his left hand. Its halo denotes the Fate of Virtues— gold for firstborn or unprocessed. Because he's around twenty-five, I know he's firstborn. If he had a golden halo moniker, and he was eighteen or younger, he'd either be firstborn or he may not have been Transitioned to a silver halo of a Virtue-Fated secondborn. That happens on a secondborn's Transition Day.

My eyes widen. By any stretch of the imagination he should be in the capital right now, catered to by an estate filled with secondborn servants. Most of the firstborns who possess a Virtues moniker are from the aristocracy—or else they're the judges, legislators, ruling clergy, dignitaries, or supply-chain holders. Plenty of firstborns and secondborns reside in the Fate of Virtues, born to serve the ruling class, but they don't possess monikers from that Fate. They have stone- or sword-shaped monikers—monikers from other Fates.

My family is Sword aristocracy, on par with firstborns from the Fate of Virtues because my mother is the Clarity, but other firstborn Swords are of lower rank than those with Virtues monikers. I can't imagine why he'd be a Census agent. Most of them are firstborn, but they're from lesser Fates—like the Fate of Atoms, the technology caste, or the Fate of Seas, the fishing villages—that notoriously don't produce the kind of wealth and status as firstborn Virtues.

"What do I call you?" I ask, trying to adopt a serene mien.

"Pardon me for not introducing myself earlier. My name is Agent Kipson Crow, firstborn of the Fate of Virtues. I'm from Lenity."

Purity is the capital city of Virtues. Lenity is its sister city where most of the largest estates exist. "What are you doing here, Agent Crow? Shouldn't you be in the capital, passing laws for secondborns to follow and hoarding your wealth?"

The kohl-black lines around his eyes crinkle as he smiles. "I find that I have less interest in passing laws than I do in enforcing them."

"What do you want from me, Agent Crow?"

"Please, call me Kipson. And what should I call you?"

"You can call me by my name."

"Which is?"

"You know my name is Roselle St. Sismode."

"Do I? I'm still trying to establish who you are."

"No you're not."

"Are you calling me a liar?" He's more incredulous and amused than indignant.

"You believe that I'm Roselle St. Sismode, so what is it that you want from me so badly that you'd keep me locked away at the bottom of the Base?"

"Maybe I want to get to know you better."

"Why? I'm secondborn. You're firstborn. There's no purpose."

"You intrigue me."

"How so?" I ask.

"The Roselle I always watched seemed like such a little robot on virtual access," he replies, speaking of the drone cameras that have followed me for most of my life, streaming video for anyone to view through access channels. I was given some privacy for a few hours a day, but for the most part, my life was an open book that sadistic voyeurs like Agent Kipson Crow frequently studied. "I thought I knew her, but you cannot be her. She'd never attack me. She'd yield to her superior."

"You shot me in the heart, point-blank. Some instincts cannot be suppressed, like survival."

"What a dangerous thing to say—even treasonous," he replies with chilling amusement.

"Why are you here at a Swords Base, Agent Crow? You didn't just choose to be here, did you? That doesn't seem to fit you. Your position in Census suits you very well, but not here. It seems beneath you somehow." I watch his face for subtle cues, as Dune taught me to do when interrogating an adversary. Agent Crow doesn't give me much, a flicker of something in the squint of his eye. "You're not here by choice. You enjoy your role as hunter, but you . . . you had to come here . . . because . . ." He looks down at his moniker. "Because your moniker was not always golden. It used to be silver. You were secondborn." My heart is beating like a frightened rabbit's.

"I had an older sister once. She died." He sounds remorseless.

"What happened to her?"

"She had an accident. Unlike me, Sabah couldn't swim, you see. No one ever taught her—the firstborn—poor lamb. My parents were so cautious with her, worrying that every little thing would hurt her. They found her one morning floating facedown in the duck pond."

He killed her—it's in his eyes. I didn't think I could actually fear him more, but I do. "How unfortunate. So your parents—"

"Thought it would be better if I pursued my interests outside of Virtues for the time being." They can't condemn the murderer in their midst because he has been elevated to their only heir. The bloodline has to continue with him or it dies, too. His parents' property and holdings would be reapportioned. A small stipend would be set aside for them. Maybe they'd reside somewhere in the Fate of Stones or the Fate of Suns, but they'd never get to stay in the Fate of Virtues without an heir or the permission and ability to have another.

"What interests did they think you should pursue elsewhere?"

"Oh, I have many passions. Hunting thirdborns is one. Torture is another, but you suspected that. I can see it in your eyes—so blue, your eyes, so vast. You see everything, don't you? You recognized me immediately as your overlord, and it frightened you, so you reacted."

"I see you," I murmur. But it's more that I feel him. He has a presence that screams cruelty. It reaches out with icy fingers and chills me to my marrow.

"My parents want me to get it all out of my system, particularly before I wed and become leader of the family. But I have a little secret." Agent Crow leans nearer to me, whispering. "I don't think I'll ever lose my taste for pain."

He gets to his feet and slowly takes off his coat, draping it over the back of the chair. He undoes the golden halo cufflinks from the eyelets of his shirt, one by one, pocketing them in his black trousers before rolling up his sleeves. His fingers go to the buckle of his belt, unfastening it with agonizing deliberateness, pulling it dramatically from his belt loops. It's the same belt I used to strangle him.

I stand, planting my feet shoulder-width apart. My arms settle into a defensive position. The fear is harder to control. "I'm not going to let you torture me, Agent Crow. We both know you don't have cause. My identity is no longer in question. This isn't an interrogation."

"You attacked me, Roselle. Your aggression is suspicious. Soldiers witnessed your reaction to being tranquilized, which is standard procedure in the event that identity cannot be verified. It gives me grounds to pursue this line of questioning."

"You could simply verify my identity through a hair sample," I reply and shift away from his attempt to get closer.

"I prefer a blood sample."

I wait for his move. He winds one end of the belt around his fist, throws his arm back, and snaps it forward. The first thrash connects with my forearm, raised in a block. My coarse blue sleeve absorbs some of the sting, but it'll leave a mark. I hardly feel it, though. I allow the lash to wind around my arm, and then I grab the strap with my other hand before he can draw it back, yanking him toward me.

Bringing my bare foot up, I kick him as hard as I can in the stomach, releasing the belt. He reels back, his face a mask of surprise and pain. I don't wait for him to recover. As he bends at the waist, I drive my foot up, kicking him in the chin. He stumbles back. I roundhouse kick him in the head. He staggers sideways.

The door of my cell opens. Glancing to my side, I see a woman dressed in civilian clothing, accompanied by a Census agent in a black leather coat similar to Agent Crow's. A handful of secondborn soldiers, some of whom I recognize from the wreckage of the enemy attack, are with them. The one who stands out most is Hawthorne, almost a head taller than everyone else and scowling.

Wiping his bloody mouth on his shirt, Agent Crow shouts at the intruders near the door. "I'm interrogating a detainee!" He snaps the belt in his hand with a loud crack.

"Looks like you didn't bring enough agents for that," Hawthorne replies, gesturing at the growing red welt on Agent Crow's cheek.

"Sorry to interrupt, old man," the agent by the door interjects, "but it seems the identity of the detainee is no longer in question. Her hair sample, taken when she was brought in, has been verified. She's Roselle St. Sismode, secondborn to The Sword." He holds up a holographic chip. It shines in the dim light. "I have her new moniker here."

Agent Crow seethes. His blond hair is a mess, falling over his brow. "I didn't submit her hair sample, Agent Losif. How was it verified?"

Agent Losif shifts back and forth on his feet. "This is Agnes Moon." He gestures to the attractive woman standing beside him. "She's a secondborn advocate stationed in Swords. She has petitioned for the release of the Secondborn St. Sismode."

Agent Crow narrows his eyes at the curvaceous redhead. "Her authority isn't recognized here." The agent's cool demeanor returns. I stay rooted in the same defensive position. He's unpredictable because he believes his power to be absolute.

Agnes straightens, holding up a wristband with a shiny blue face. She waves it in Agent Crow's direction. "I really don't want to interrupt either, but I have orders to redirect Secondborn St. Sismode to a debriefing and a press conference in front of the Fates."

"On whose authority?" Agent Crow barks.

"The Clarity Bowie. He has given direct orders that Secondborn St. Sismode is to deliver a broadcast regarding the attack against her Fate. I'm sending you the authorization now." She touches the face of her wristband. A blue light shines up from Agent Crow's. He sets his belt down on the metal chair. Touching the surface of his communicator, he scrolls through whatever message Agnes sent him.

"This detainee has given me cause to believe that she has consorted with Fate traitors. I'm conducting an interrogation to ascertain her level of involvement with the attack against the Fate of Swords."

"Do you really want to upset the Clarity of Virtues?" Agnes asks, her eyebrow darting into her red bangs.

"I will take my chances," Agent Crow glowers.

"We're under orders to remove the detainee from your custody," Hawthorne says, raising his rifle and aiming it at Agent Crow. "Step away from the girl." Gilad raises his rifle as well, and two other soldiers from their unit follow their lead.

The agent directs a cold stare at Hawthorne. "You're the soldier who brought her in. Shouldn't you be out rescuing your brethren from the city that fell on them? Or better yet, finding the ones responsible? I have plans to interrogate this one for what she knows of the attack. It could be useful information to your secondborn commanders. I will share the information. It could mean merits for you."

I hold my breath. If they take Agent Crow's bribe, I'm on my own.

Hawthorne doesn't lower his weapon. He looks at me. "Roselle St. Sismode, I order you to come with us."

Warily, I start toward Hawthorne at the door. I don't take more than a step before Agent Crow barks, "Stop!" I halt. "She can't leave here without her moniker. Only we can give her that." He moves to the agent at the door and opens his palm. Agent Losif drops the shiny holographic identifier into it. Closing his fingers around it, Agent Crow lifts his other hand for the moncalate used to implant a moniker beneath flesh.

Goose bumps rise on my arms. Agent Crow opens a slot on the surgical tool and loads my moniker into it. The click of it being chambered makes me flinch. Agent Crow's eyes meet mine. A mixture of emotions hides there—rage, lust, aggression. I suppress another shiver.

He lifts my hand, rubbing his thumb over the skin between my thumb and finger. "You have a birthmark," he says. He places the tool beside my birthmark and depresses a button. A puff of white air emits from the nozzle aimed at my skin. It instantly numbs the area. A thin laser cuts a line on the back of my hand. I bite my lip as it burns, but the pain isn't unmanageable. Small curls of smoke rise to my nose. Agent Crow inhales deeply, watching me.

The laser extinguishes and a little clamp appears from the cylindrical body of the tool. It latches into the flaps of skin, pulling them apart while a tiny claw on a steel arm reaches inside to extract my fried moniker. The claw drops the broken, bloody chip onto the floor. It retreats back inside the metallic body and retrieves the new identifier, shooting it into place.

My eyelids close a fraction at the intense stinging of the new chip settling onto my sinew. Agent Crow watches, savoring my pain. The claw and the clamps retract into the body of the tool. Red laser light seals my skin closed, leaving a pink incision scar that throbs.

Agent Crow lifts my hand to his lips, kissing my incision. I try to pull my hand from his, but he holds it fast, smiling. "I will dream of you, Roselle," he promises. The flow of my blood feels thready.

My new sword-shaped hologram shines for the first time. It's no longer golden. It's silver, denoting the Transition to a processed secondborn. Agent Crow flashes me a grin. I wrench my hand from his and move to the doorway. Hawthorne, Gilad, and the other two soldiers surround me. Agent Crow's attention shifts to Hawthorne. "I never forget a face," he says, "nor an insult."

"Neither do I," Hawthorne replies, his rifle still pointed at Agent Crow. Agent Losif and the woman with the moon moniker are the first to leave. The soldiers from Hawthorne's unit direct me out. Hawthorne doesn't lower his weapon until he's clear of the cell. When he turns and looks at me, his expression is grim. "Move," he orders.

Chapter 7
Moment of Clarity

Agnes and Agent Losif assume the lead, directing us to a barren hallway in what feels like the bottom of the world. My bare feet are numb against the cool floor, but I hardly notice. I lose my sense of direction as we turn corners and cross through checkpoints where all our monikers are scanned and we're questioned. When we move again, Hawthorne's hand touches the small of my back and directs me toward an elevator.

All of us enter the lift except for Agent Losif. He holds the door and addresses Agnes. "You can make it unaccompanied to the surface from here. I'd suggest that you don't come back for a while if you can help it. Agent Crow is not one to forgive this type of transgression."

"I hope I never see any of you again," she responds tersely.

The doors close and Agnes slumps against the wall of the lift. Her green eyes pierce Hawthorne's. "You need any more favors, you can forget it. Had I known we were going to confront Kipson Crow, there would've been no way you could've convinced me to help."

"I owe you, Agnes."

"You don't have enough merits to pay me back for this, Hawthorne. And we can't meet anymore. We can't be seen together."

"I know. Thank you."

She looks at me with derision. "Roselle St. Sismode. I never would've thought you'd be a fan, Hawthorne."

"She taught me the St. Sismode maneuver. I owed her." He's talking about a series of choreographed sword attacks designed to give maximum thrust and power in fusionblade combat. I was required to do virtual-access demonstrations of the maneuver.

"I knew it had to have something to do with your sword," Agnes says sourly.

I'm trembling. Hawthorne removes a copper-colored metallic swatch from a pocket on his thigh, unfolding it into a blanket that he wraps around my shoulders. I clutch it to me. The fabric crinkles and makes noise as I shake, but it warms me, for which I'm grateful. We reach the surface and the elevator doors open into a metal bunker. The guards check our monikers once more before they open a wide steel door. The moon casts pale light high above us. The airships shine on the docks in the branches of the stone Trees, swaying in the wind.

I walk beside Hawthorne on a path that leads away from the Census bunker. "How long was I in there?"

"Three days and a dozen hours," he replies. "It took me longer than I expected to get you out, but at least we kept him occupied fighting the petitions and the onslaught of inquiries on your behalf. Agnes threw every legal obstacle she could think of at him."

"Why would either of you do that?" I ask, stunned by his intervention.

"You're one of us now. We take care of our own. Isn't that right, Gilad?"

Gilad looks me over with a sneer. "That's right. We can mess you up, but no one else gets to. It's a secondborn Sword code: mess with one of us, and we'll mess with you."

"Unfortunately, secondborn Moon-Fates don't subscribe to the same code," Agnes says, her hand worrying the band of her wrist communicator. The silver shine of her moniker radiates a small rendition of the moon above our heads. "I'm on my own, so don't think I won't call in favors with you if I need them—especially you, Roselle, although I doubt you'll be in a position even to help yourself when that freak back there comes for you again. The only thing saving you from him is the Diamond-Fated press. They're rabid for this interview with you."

"You mean there really is a press conference?" I ask. I don't know how I'm going to pull myself together to get through dinner, let alone an interrogation and a news conference.

"You think I'd have gone in there if there wasn't?" Agnes's green eyes narrow. "Of course there's a press conference. It was arranged by approaching the right people. We spun it so that they felt the propaganda was necessary. People saw the attack. They want you to reassure them."

"Why would you help me?" I wonder aloud.

"Your friend asked me to do him a favor," she murmurs. "Just say thank you."

"Thank you," I reply.

We cross a paved courtyard, passing the first of many stone and metal Trees the size and height of skyscrapers. Secondborn Sword soldiers in full combat gear patrol the lighted walkway. A fast-moving military-style hovercar approaches us. As it pulls near, I recognize Emmitt Stone as its sole occupant.

He opens the door and clucks his tongue, his eyes roving over me. "Processing doesn't agree with you, Roselle," he says by way of a greeting. "What are you wearing—and your hair—and your fingernails!" He grasps my hand. His disapproval would be comical if I had any sense of humor at the moment. He takes the metallic blanket from my shoulders and hands it to the dark-eyed girl in Hawthorne's unit. The tag on her uniform reads "Hammon."

"You couldn't have given her shoes?" Emmitt scolds Gilad, who growls at him in turn. Emmitt retreats a step, his hand going to the base of his throat in a self-soothing way. "We need to get you camera-ready." He turns to me and urges me toward the hovercar.

"Mother gave orders on my behalf?" I ask. My heart beats quicker with the thought that she cares enough to rescue me.

"No one wants you to disgrace your family any more than you already have. You'll be prepped and primped."

I pause and look at Emmitt's face. "I disgraced my family?" It's a crushing blow, more powerful than if he'd struck me.

He puts his hands on his hips and taps his foot. "You broke your moniker. Seville ordered you to remain en route, but you and your mentor exited the Vicolt. You know the drone cameras follow you. Every fatedom witnessed our shame because of you!" It's on the tip of my tongue to argue with him. Our fatedom was attacked—I was threatened—my moniker would've been ruined whether I stayed in the Vicolt or not. Did Mother think she could hide the attack?

"We're going with you." Hawthorne shoves Emmitt aside and directs me into the hovercar. He gets in beside me. Gilad slides in as well. Agnes, Hammon, and the other soldier climb into the row of seats behind us.

Emmitt sits in front. As the hovercar moves forward, he looks over his shoulder at us. "This is really unnecessary. I can take it from here. She doesn't need your help."

Hawthorne shakes his head. "She's our responsibility. We're under orders to secure her until she's delivered to her unit." I stare at Hawthorne. His exquisite gray eyes meet my stare.

"She's my responsibility now," Emmitt says. "You can come back when she's done. I have so much to do to get her ready."

"We won't interfere," Hawthorne retorts. "We'll just observe."

Emmitt pinches the bridge of his nose. "Secondborn Swords are so tedious. You don't understand the pressure I'm under to make her perform to The Sword's exacting standards."

"Do you want me to rip out his tongue?" Gilad asks Hawthorne.

"Maybe," Hawthorne replies. Emmitt pouts and turns around, slumping in his seat.

We hover near a large body of water. A sign by it reads: Aspen Lake. Silver moonlight shines off the rippling water. The Trees begin to deviate from stone-pillar trunks to beautiful glass ones the closer we get to the other side of the lake. The glass trunks shimmer in the night, regal and stately rather than utilitarian. Our vehicle pulls up in front of one of the tallest. As I look up through the transparent roof from this angle, the building with its intricate branches seems to have no end. Emmitt emerges from the hovercar and waits for me to exit.

"This way," he indicates with a gesture. He crosses to the door. I follow him, my escorts behind me. Guards confront us. We're each made to scan our monikers. A red light flashes when Agnes puts her hand under the beam. The Sword guards draw their fusionblades and move closer, barring her way. "You're not a Sword or on the approved visitor list. You don't have authorization to enter. You have to move back."

Agnes's eyes lift in frustration to Hawthorne's. An intimate look passes between them. "This is where I leave you," Agnes murmurs.

Hawthorne draws her aside. I watch them from the corner of my eye. Though they don't touch, their eyes caress. I can't hear what they're saying, but their body language reminds me of a last dance. The exchange doesn't last for more than a minute. No kiss good-bye. Agnes simply turns, climbs back into the hovercar, and departs.

Emmitt leads us into the reception area of the glass Tree. Hawthorne catches up and walks beside me. His mouth curves down and his eyes are alert with fresh hurt. He holds his rifle close, clutching it to his chest. I want to say something that will ease his sadness, but I don't have the words.

Gilad gives a low whistle. "I never thought I'd see the inside of an officer's oak."

Hammon flashes him a soft, dimpled smile. "That's because your family tree is a shrub."

Gilad details what he'd like to do to her shrub. I feel my cheeks redden. Hammon takes his comments in stride, laughing flirtatiously.

The building absorbs the noise of our boots and voices. The tapered atrium rises above our heads for hundreds of floors. Concrete pillars hold up a labyrinth of glass walkways, concrete ramps, and spiral staircases.

I straighten my neck and gaze at the walls. Enormous portraits of firstborn admirals surround the ground floor. I recognize most of them. I've even met a few. They're leaders from the best families in Swords.

In the center of the gallery is Mother's likeness. Beside her is a portrait of Gabriel, her heir apparent, and on the other side is one of Father. A golden plaque beneath his frame reads "Kennet Abjorn – *The Fated Sword.*" He hates the figurehead name for the spouse of The Sword.

Father kept his last name rather than taking Mother's because his is slightly more prestigious than hers. She didn't take his name because she's The Sword—there have always been St. Sismodes—and she would not let the name end with her. Her father stipulated in my parents' marriage contract that her children would inherit her name. It was a contentious point, one of many they still hurl at each other when they're forced to interact.

Father is in line to inherit the title of Clarity of Virtues, which he enjoys telling people. He leaves out the fact that there are four heirs in front of him who would all have to die before he could assume the title. However, he loves to rub it in Mother's face that he'd be the Clarity of Virtues before her. Her family is fifth in line. That had been the idea behind their match. Together, they're even more powerful.

I study his portrait. His hands are crossed on his lap and his Virtue-Fated hologram shines a golden halo for all to see. His dark good looks and sultry, roguish smile used to make many of the secondborn Stone-Fated servants at the Sword Palace swoon. I haven't seen him in a few years. I wonder how he's doing—if he's heard of my trouble at Transition—if he cares.

A sharp rattle of laughter from a small seating area nearby serrates the air. Firstborn officers of the highest military rank—Exos who more than likely live in this building—watch me with amused curiosity. All around us they drink golden alcohol, chatting in low voices. Their dress uniforms, adorned with immaculate black capes, starkly contrast with my detainee garb and the secondborn soldiers' black combat gear, silver Tree emblems etched on breastplates, and lethal rifles. Each Exo has a fusionblade with an intricate family crest embossed on the hilt. My own fusionblade is probably somewhere in the bowels of Census. Broken as it is, I still long to have it back.

Emmitt sidles up to me. "Feeling left out?" he asks, nodding at the portraits.

I adopt Father's smile as a defense mechanism. "I'd rather not be in a club that doesn't want me, Emmitt."

The quiet soldier who has been with us since the Census cell has his neck craned all the way back, gazing up at the levels above us. His armor tag reads "Edgerton." "It's different from our woods," he says, speaking for the first time.

"How is it different?" I ask.

He scratches his blond scruff of a beard, and I notice that he's missing a front tooth. "We ain't got windows in ours—all this here's concrete." He waves his arm at the glass shell of the building. His solemn brown eyes meet mine.

"Which one do you like more?" I ask.

He stares at me for a moment, surprised by my question—or maybe it's more than that. Maybe he's surprised that I spoke to him? He looks up again and points to a window way above my head where the light of the moon shines through. "It'd be nice to see the night sky once in a while when we ain't on point."

"It would," I agree. He smiles. A fountain in the center dances with water that's in sync with a lovely concerto playing all around us from some hidden source. I'm familiar with the song and hum along softly.

"Do you know this music?" Edgerton asks.

"I do. Do you?"

He shakes his head and shrugs. "Naw, what'd I know about music? I've been Transitioned since I were ten, same as Hawthorne. We come up together." He shuffles his feet on the marble floor's inlaid mosaic leaves of orange, crimson, and gold. It's as if the Tree itself had shed them.

"It's by Sovenagh—her ninetieth symphony. It's called *The Rape of Reason*."

We enter an elevator car. None of us speak as we rise to somewhere in the center of the trunk. When the doors open, Clara Diamond, Mother's personal public relations assistant, greets us. "You found her!" Clara bleats to Emmitt with visible relief. "The Sword is threatening to have me killed if I don't report back to her soon." She's not joking. The terror shows on her white-lipped face. Mother's temper is legendary.

As we exit the lift, Clara reaches for my arm. I allow her to take it because I need her support as much as she needs to assure herself that she won't be dying today. "We have to get you to the debriefing. We can clean you up later."

I fall in step with her and Emmitt. The Sword soldiers trail us, rubbernecking in awe. The décor lacks the sophistication that I'm accustomed to, but the carpet is soft beneath my bare feet. Clara leads me down a long hallway that skirts the atrium.

We pass a few gangways that lead to round platforms that hang in the air above the ground many stories below. Clara pauses at the largest. Emmitt shoos me ahead, urging me over a lighted-glass gangplank with glass railings. I stop midway.

Emmitt holds the others back. "She has to go alone. You will wait here." Hawthorne brushes him aside, but Emmitt manages to get back in front of him. "I'm only trying to save your life. This is a private conversation. You don't have the security clearance level to attend. *I* don't have the security clearance to attend." He holds his hand on his chest to illustrate his point. "You can protect her from here. She can't go any-where, and Clara made sure that we're the only ones on this entire level."

Hawthorne gives me a reluctant nod. I turn and follow the gang-way, holding its glass handrail until I make it to the rosette-shaped platform. Dangling over the atrium gives me the feeling of floating on air. About a hundred feet away, surrounding me on all sides, are tiers of balconies. As I peek over the railing, it's as if I'm trapped inside the rib cage of a giant leviathan.

A dome of darkness forms around the suspended platform. I can no longer see the soldiers or the staff from Mother's Palace. The floor illuminates. I'm now being viewed as a holographic image by whoever's vetted into our meeting.

A holographic image of an elderly admiral projects before me. His white handlebar mustache is extremely outdated but well groomed. He's attired in a highly decorated dress uniform. I straighten. He's a firstborn Sword that I've met many times before. His name is Admiral Yarls Dresden. He's a lecher and an alcoholic. The secondborn Stones of the Palace fear him.

Admiral Dresden doesn't acknowledge me. I have to hold back a sigh of relief. Another holographic image of a slender woman in a beautiful silver ball gown made of light walks off the adjacent balcony and into the air, approaching my island platform. She wears a half-moon-shaped tiara atop her ebony hair. She stops just feet away from me. I recognize her as Clarity Toussaint Jowell, the leader of the Fate of Moons. She greets Admiral Dresden, and they engage in quiet conversa-tion about the weather, ignoring me entirely.

Someone else winks into view—an attractive older man, maybe in his early forties, with a golden shooting-star-shaped moniker that indi-cates he's firstborn Fate of Stars. His long dark hair is held back from his face with a leather tie. No gray taints the ebony of his full beard. He's not dressed in formal attire, like the other two; rather, he wears a black woolen cloak that would be perfect for a midnight stroll in the crisp air. The Star-Fated man acknowledges the other holograms. "Admiral Dresden." His accompanying nod is perfunctory.

"Daltrey." Admiral Dresden spits his name like he has tasted something spoiled.

Daltrey greets the Clarity. "Clarity Jowell."

"It's been a trying day for you, I'm sure, Daltrey. Our thoughts are with you," she says in a sympathetic, yet flirty, way.

"It has. I thank you for your thoughts."

"Your house still standing?" Admiral Dresden smirks at Daltrey and twists his mustache.

"It is. Thank you for your concern," Daltrey replies with a cutting glare.

"Pity," Admiral Dresden drones, "that our assault against your Fate was necessary, but we must rid ourselves of these Fate traitors. The Gates of Dawn seem to like your Fate too well. Or maybe your Fate fosters their particular brand of secondborn rebel."

"My Fate is comprised of freethinkers. One needs a special sort of mind to harness and engineer power and energy."

"Too bad it also breeds traitors."

"Yes. Too bad," Daltrey agrees, but it rings insincere. I stare at him.

Mother winks in, interrupting any further conversation. She's elegant in a ball gown of midnight blue with pinpoints of silver that mimic stars in the night sky. A delicate silver tiara is woven in her chestnut-colored hair. She doesn't acknowledge me but greets each of the other participants with brief exchanges about their health. Her mouth pinches in agitation as she falls silent, scowling at her timekeeper.

Clarity Fabian Bowie's firstborn son, Grisholm Wenn-Bowie, joins the circle after Mother. I recognize him without an introduction. He's been to the Sword estate many times in his youth to beat up on Gabriel. He's only a few years older than me. At twenty-one, he's passingly handsome but could use a more rigorous training regimen.

Clearly this meeting interrupted some kind of celebration because I don't think Grisholm wears his golden, halo-shaped crown over his dark, shaggy mane just to tame it. *His hair must take him hours of styling, though.* Not only is Grisholm's grooming glorious, so, too, is his evening attire. The firstborn heir to the fatedoms is a contrast in black and white. Skin-hugging black trousers that don't leave much to the imagination meet the shiniest black boots I've ever seen. A golden belt with a halo-shaped buckle gleams at his waist. His silken white dress shirt and an intricately tied cravat are as immaculate as his snowy-white cape.

Grisholm appears bored. He ignores everyone else and studies me with a condescending curl of his lip, taking in my attire and my hair, which probably has knots in it. I smooth a hand down the side of my Census-issued rags, adjusting the hem so that it lies flat on my hip.

"Can it be the Secondborn St. Sismode?" Grisholm smiles like he smells something delicious. "Why is it that you still resemble a little lost waif, Roselle, even when you're all grown up?"

"Clean living, Firstborn Commander," I reply. It elicits a chuckle. I'm thinking, *I can still kick your ass, Grisholm, like I did when I was ten and you smashed Gabriel in the head with the clock from the hall table.*

His eyes skim over my criminal attire and long, messy hair. "Had a brush with the authorities, have you?"

"Census was gracious enough to put me up for a few days while we sorted out my disabled moniker. I'll have to send them a spa basket. What would you recommend, First Commander? Assorted soaps?"

"With bubble bath," he plays along, smiling evilly. He's just as I remember; he loves a good snubbing. "Shall I send it for you on your behalf?"

"That is a generous offer, First Commander."

"To whom shall I address it?"

"Agent Kipson Crow."

"Ooh." He mock-winces.

"Ah, you know him."

"I do. The Fate of Virtues is smaller than you may think. You never have had much luck, have you, Roselle?"

"The only thing I've had in abundance is loyalty, First Commander."

"I recall your loyalty," he replies, rubbing the side of his head where I'd clocked him as retribution for what he'd done to Gabriel. He was too embarrassed then to have been beaten by a little secondborn girl to tell on me, so I never had to pay for what I did. "Too bad your loyalty is not reciprocated." His words sting. "I'll make sure Agent Crow receives your gift."

I worry for a moment about baiting Agent Crow, but the agent will do whatever he plans to do, regardless. A basket sent on my behalf by the First Commander, heir to the Clarity of Virtues, might be the one thing that makes him hesitate to act.

Everyone quiets when the next participant joins the circle. A halo-shaped circlet crowns the Clarity's salt-and-pepper hair, thinner than his son's. Thinner, too, is Fabian's physique, attired for the evening in a similar vein as Grisholm. In his late forties, he's a man of action who, I'm told, rarely sits down, and that comes across even in holographic form.

I've seen Fabian Bowie every day of my life in one capacity or another, be it on the virtual screen addressing the fatedoms or inside Mother's office when I was much younger. On the occasions when we've met, he's always been cordial, if somewhat dismissive. I've never minded being dismissed, though. Being less than perfect in his presence is never a good idea. I've witnessed some of his more ruthless decisions, like assassinations of firstborns who displeased him. Mother arranges these killings, usually by finding an assassin from the pool that Admiral Dresden cultivates. I learned early that Fabian Bowie demands absolute submission from all his subjects. The only exception is his firstborn son.

Clarity Bowie's attention is focused on me when he asks, "Are you having any trouble stepping in for the Clarity in his absence, Firstborn Leon?"

The handsome Star-Fated Daltrey clears his throat. "No trouble, Clarity Bowie. It's an honor to serve my Fate in his absence."

"He's never one to stomach bloodshed," our leader says, disdain written on his features. "I have not seen Clarity Aksel sober since his arrival here in Purity. He has more of a taste for women than he does for ruling his fatedom."

"It's a difficult time," Daltrey says in a noncommittal way. "It's my duty as second Star family to see to all the needs of our Fate while he's away." Clarity Bowie glares at Othala.

"Are we secure?" Mother addresses her wrist communicator. She's not looking at any of us.

"Everything is locked down here," Emmitt replies, his voice piping through the circle of glass on her wrist. She turns off her communicator so that he can no longer hear the conversation.

"Roselle Sword." Mother calls me by my processed name for the first time. I lift my chin in her direction. My stomach churns as I realize that she's distancing herself from me by using it. "Describe for us your version of the attack perpetrated against the Fate of Swords three days ago."

My mouth feels dry, but I manage to sound passably normal as I recount the events of the attack upon Dune and me. I leave out seeing the first golden-masked man, as Hawthorne suggested. No use muddying the water. I finish by saying, "The enemy combatants brought down our airships, my moniker, and my sword by using a Fusion Snuff Pulse."

"How did you know what it was—a Fusion Snuff Pulse?" Daltrey is the first to question me. His intense stare holds a note of fear. I take a step in his direction, studying his features closer. "Perhaps you overheard something at the Sword Palace regarding such a device?" His sand-colored eyes give me a look that I know well—it demands discretion. I've seen that look from Dune a thousand times. This man is somehow related to him, but how, I don't know. He's a Star-Fated firstborn, but I'm sure nonetheless. Their manner is the same. Their features are similar. He's an older version of my mentor.

I look around at the faces of the others. They have no idea that Daltrey is anything other than what he says he is. They're not even looking at him. My attention goes back to Daltrey. "I heard about the device at the Palace of Swords from my mother's advisors. They were discussing it when I was called to see her regarding details for my Transition Day."

I wait for Mother to call me a liar. A second ticks by and then another. I glance at her. She appears to believe me—and why not? I'd lived among them at the Palace. Everyone was lax around me because I was a phantom to them. My eyes lift to Daltrey's. His relief is clear, but I seem to be the only one who sees it. He nods ever so slightly, and Clarity Bowie starts demanding answers from Othala. "What are you doing to keep us all safe from this fusion pulse, Clarity St. Sismode?"

Fear eats at me with ferocious bites. *I just lied to The Virtue and The Sword—the two most powerful people in the world. Why?* My hands are shaking so much I have to press them against my thighs.

Clarity Bowie is unimpressed by Othala's lack of decisive action to shield the fatedoms from this new weapon. "Our enemies have become bolder, Othala. They assault us at the heart of our military, and yet, you do nothing!"

"We strike their Bases when we locate them," Othala reasons, "but we cannot continue to assail Fates like Stars and Suns the way we have. We're disrupting their workers. We need to keep Stars producing energy and Suns yielding food supplies. Their firstborn citizens are with us. It's pockets of rogue secondborns whom we have to stamp out."

"What are you doing about the threat to our power sources, Daltrey?" Clarity Bowie points at the Star-Fated firstborn.

"Cages can be built around the power sources to protect them from a pulse. But you need to do it on a massive scale, which requires around-the-clock work from Star engineers—Atom engineers can help as well.

They'll need access to every fatedom of the Republic to accomplish this task, especially the capital. We should start with your Palaces."

"Clarity Jowell, see that Daltrey and his engineers get the access they need from Census."

"It will be difficult, Clarity Bowie," the diplomat from the Fate of Moons replies. "Census doesn't like granting special access to anyone. They feel it impedes their tracking of thirdborns."

"Would you rather sit in your palace in the dark, Clarity Jowell?"

"No," Jowell replies. "I'll see that it gets done. Firstborn Leon, I'll need a list of workers as soon as you can get them to me."

Daltrey Leon nods. "You will have them within the week."

Grisholm makes a rude sound as he rubs his face with both hands. "This is all very interesting, Father, but we've heard all of this from your personal guard, what's his name—Sand?"

"Dune," Clarity Bowie corrects him. My heart beats faster at his name. He's safe for the moment.

"Yes—him." Grisholm points his finger at his father like they're in the room together. Maybe they are. "Take care of whatever you have to take care of, Daltrey, and let me get back to the Opening Ceremonies of the Secondborn Trials. I have a very healthy bet on a secondborn from the Fate of Stars—Linus Star—and I want to have a chance to speak to him before the first match tomorrow."

Othala's indulgent smile is faked. "You should never bet against the Fate of Swords. We win The Trials almost every year."

"The odds have plummeted on the Sword champions—the attack, you know. Your Fate suddenly doesn't seem infallible."

Mother looks as though he's slapped her in the face. She tries to hide it, though, forcing a grin. "It will be interesting to see who comes out the victor."

"The victor of The Trials never returns to his Fate, does he?" Grisholm asks, baiting her.

Gritting her teeth, Othala forces another smile. "I believe you're correct. Balthazar chose to leave Swords and live in Virtues after winning last year's Trials."

"You can't resign them to their Fates after they've seen Virtues," Grisholm quips. "Plus our women are"—he evaluates me from the floor up—"more discerning in their fashion sense than those of other Fates." I consider jumping over the railing of the island module and falling to my death—anything to get away from Grisholm's smirk.

"Forgive my son, Roselle," Clarity Bowie says with resignation. "He has avoided the responsibilities of his birthright ever since he could crawl."

"There's nothing to forgive. I am, as ever, at your service," I respond, forcing a smile of my own.

"Your mentor speaks highly of you—or should I say your ex-mentor?"

"I will always consider Commander Kodaline to be my mentor, even if I never see him again."

"He says that you'd make a fine leader." Mother's face loses color.

"I hope one day to lead a secondborn regiment of my own. I will train rigorously that I may achieve my goal."

"There are other ways to differentiate yourself as a secondborn. You're quite skilled with a sword, or so Dune tells me."

"I have trained with one most of my life."

"You could be useful. We have many enemies in our Fates." Clarity Bowie casts a glance at Admiral Dresden. "Wouldn't you agree, Dresden?"

The admiral scrutinizes me. "She has potential for special operations."

"Father," Grisholm sputters, "are you trying to make us late for the fete? Mother will be beside herself if she's left alone among the second-born pod-dwellers of The Trials."

71

"She'll be fine. She has quite a taste for secondborn pod-dwellers. Go if you must." The Clarity waves his son away.

Grisholm doesn't need to be told twice. His holographic image blinks out. For the next hour, the remaining council grills me as I rehearse a crafted set of answers to all the questions the press will be allowed to ask. When the gathered holograms are satisfied that I'm ready, they wink out, all but Fabian and Othala.

The Clarity of Virtues gives me an approving nod. "I will leave you to it, then. Make us proud, Roselle."

"Excuse me, Clarity Bowie?"

He looks surprised that I would address him, but he indulges me. "Yes?"

"We never spoke about what I'm to say about the Fusion Snuff Pulse. What do I tell people about the weapon that brought down the airships and destroyed power in part of the city?"

"It was an explosion, like we said before."

"But it wasn't an explosion. It was a total loss of power."

"If that were to become known, we'd have widespread panic."

"If we don't tell people, they'll think it's something that can be avoided with bomb-detection units. They won't know that they could be flying in an airship and suddenly lose all power. We need to build everyone pulse-protection cages around their energy sources and tell them to stay grounded until the threat has passed. Or at least have them convert to hydrogen power in the meantime."

"You will say nothing. Everyone has to keep working and living as if nothing can touch them. Do you understand?"

"But if we teach them how to build their own anti-pulse cages—"

"Then they'll be doing the work of Star-Fated secondborns. That cannot happen. Your Fate is your fate and you must adhere to it or bad things happen."

"Bad things *are* happening," I insist.

"You will not say a word about the FSP! Do you understand?" he shouts.

"I understand." I've never felt more intimidated in my life, not even by Agent Crow. I'm trembling for real now, and there's no hiding it.

"Don't make me regret trusting you."

In an instant, only Mother and I remain. She looks me over. "You're a disgrace. Couldn't you have cleaned up before tapping in?"

"I was told this meeting was to be conducted with all due haste—"

"Do *not* disappoint me again, Roselle. You're on a very short tether now. I will personally see to it that your life is filled with misery if you mess this up."

"I won't let you down."

"You already have. Clean yourself up! I want this finished first thing in the morning before The Trials begin." Her hologram extinguishes without a good-bye.

Chapter 8
Exo and Ohs

I stand on the island platform in shocked exhaustion for several moments, until I realize that I'm no longer in a bubble of secrecy. Turning toward the gangway, I'm confronted by six curious faces. "The press conference is in the morning, before the first test of the Secondborn Trials," I say numbly.

"You have to get some sleep. I can only do so much with your puffy eyes—I'm not a miracle worker!" Emmitt replies in a panic.

Hawthorne joins me in the center of the island. "We'll take Roselle to our air-barracks and return her to you in the morning."

Emmitt wags his finger at Hawthorne. "No, no, no. You're not taking her from this building. I'm going to be up all night planning her hair and wardrobe as it is. She stays here. You can come back when we're done."

Emmitt bickers with Hawthorne. The Stone's voice has a hollow sound. The hanging trees surrounding us wait like gallows as they fight over me. Hawthorne stops abruptly. "When was the last time you ate?" he asks.

"I don't know," I reply. I don't feel hunger, just terror.

"Right." He turns to Emmitt. "Roselle needs to eat. Take us to our quarters and send for rations so that she doesn't collapse, or you can explain why she's not at the press conference in the morning."

Emmitt takes a hard look at me, his gaze with the weight of a thousand eyes. He must agree with Hawthorne, because he lifts his hands for Clara to come forward. "Have you secured quarters?" Emmitt asks. "We need to accommodate"—he waves his hand in the Sword soldiers' direction with a disdaining look—"them as well."

"I have access to an apartment several levels up in the Treetop. A firstborn officer agreed to let us use his suite." She glances at her wrist communicator. "Clifton Salloway. Apparently, he's a fan of our Roselle." She nods in my direction. "This way." Clara leads us to the elevators.

The lift takes us up to the top floor. The doors open on another that leads to a suite. The drawing room has a multilayer air-billiards table in the center of it. A wet bar and lounge area intermingle, while five or more private rooms hide down side hallways. Gilad activates the wall-sized virtual screen with a voice command. Almost every channel is broadcasting commentary on the hunt for the Gates of Dawn rebels who perpetrated the act of violence against our fatedom, or live-streaming feeds of the Secondborn Trials Opening Ceremonies, or presenting reports about the participants in this year's Trials.

Gilad settles on the champion profiles, as the Diamond-Fated commentators discuss our fifty or so Sword representatives, among them Tilo Sword, 61-924501. They rattle off his statistics, strengths, and attributes. Tilo, a veritable giant of a man on the screen, has an insolent smile, as if he fears nothing. I study his sword work, knowing that a fusionblade is the great equalizer between us. I wouldn't need the kind of power he possesses to defeat him. He's slow and my fusionblade is quick, but now, my weapon of choice can be rendered obsolete with a push of a button—the right kind of pulse—an FSP. If I had to fight someone like Tilo with a steel blade, mine would have to be small and light, giving him the advantage because he could wield a broadsword with ease.

I walk away as Gilad and Hammon debate the weaknesses of the next set of champions from the Fate of Seas. Edgerton uses an airstick to blast billiard balls around the obstacle-laden, air-powered table. Emmitt and Clara converge in front of a conference wall unit, haggling with the glass Tree staff about the rations we need to see us through until morning. Emmitt, as always, is winning the argument.

Slipping out onto the balcony, I find we're not in one of the docked ships on the branches; rather we're in the trunk, with balconies that jet out over the lake beneath us. This Treetop view of the stone-and-glass forest must only seem commonplace to avian and Firstborn Exo officers. The moon illuminates flat landing pads that cover some of the tops of the Trees along the canopy, but not ours. We're so high up, nestling between the clouds.

The unfamiliarity of it all is almost as frightening as being in Census. Goose bumps rise on my skin, and I try not to think about the scorn on Mother's face. *What happens if the Gates of Dawn use the FSP again, and I fail to warn everyone? Will those deaths be on me?* Tears prick my eyes and slide down my cheeks. My hair, long and loose, tangles in the breeze.

"I've never been in a Treetop apartment before," Hawthorne says as he joins me at the railing. I quickly wipe the tears from my face with my sleeve. He pretends not to notice. "I've only ever seen this kind of luxury on the virtual screens." I don't comment because to me, this isn't luxury. "I bet you're used to this."

I clear my throat, but my voice is still thick. "This is all new to me as well."

"Yeah?"

"Yeah. I'm used to a more lavish cage than this one." I cross my arms and rub my hands over them. The breeze is cold, but I don't want to go inside and watch the other soldiers debate the merits of champions who will almost certainly die in agonizing ways in the next couple of days. I glance at Hawthorne and see him frown. He has taken off his helmet. His hair is sandy blond, a little longer in the front than I'd expect from a soldier. It suits his roguish nature. "Forget I said anything," I mumble.

"You always looked so focused."

"When?" I ask. I've felt off-kilter since I've known him.

"When I watched you on-screen. You always seemed so grateful to be a secondborn and to serve our Fate."

Another voyeur. "What makes you think I'm ungrateful?"

"I wouldn't have expected you, of all people, to call your home a 'lavish cage.'"

"It's not my home any longer, and please, forget I said anything."

Hawthorne moves away from my side. He descends a few stairs into a sunken seating area and lights a fire table in the center. Simulated flames rise up from its core, illuminating his face with a golden glow. I move to the fusion-made heat, stretching my hands out to it.

Hawthorne faces me across the table. "Did Agent Crow hurt you?" The simulated firelight reflects in his eyes. "You were there for days."

"I only remember the last dozen hours. I don't know. He tried to, but I wouldn't let him. It would've been worse if you hadn't—thank you."

Hawthorne's jaw tightens as he grits his teeth. "I wouldn't leave a drone down there with him." My heart sinks. A part of me was hoping he'd come to help me because it was *me* down there. "You seemed to be holding your own when we got there."

"Agent Crow underestimated me. He won't make that mistake again."

"No, he won't," Hawthorne agrees with a frown. "Men like that don't stop, Roselle."

"Maybe, if I'm lucky, a city will fall on him." I'm so tired that I'm forgetting to be cautious about what I'm saying—or maybe I trust Hawthorne, even though I hardly know him.

"We can hope," Hawthorne replies. My eyes widen at his treasonous agreement.

Attempting to change the subject, I ask, "Are you okay?" His stare shifts away from the flames to me. "About Agnes. You said good-bye to her. It looked . . . permanent."

He shrugs. "We had a date night once."

"That was much more than a date night," I reply. "That looked like a relationship."

He scowls at me and gazes around to see if we're being overheard. "You don't know what you're talking about!" he growls. "You know it's forbidden for us to have relationships—casual encounters only."

"I would never tell," I murmur. "Did you two meet in secret?"

"It's over, Roselle! Whatever we had is finished now. We can't be seen together, not with Agent Crow's threats. I won't risk her further."

"I'm sorry," I offer, and I mean it. He acknowledges me with a curt nod.

Clara opens the balcony doors and beckons us inside. "The rations are here. You'd better come in before everything is gone. Honestly, do they not feed you soldiers?"

I cross the balcony and enter the suite. The soldiers have shed their weapons and body armor, resting them against walls and sofas. Hawthorne follows suit and takes off his rifle and chest armor, depositing them in a neat pile in a corner. I thought his armor was the reason for the breadth of his chest, but I was wrong. The armor is thin and lightweight. All of the bulk is Hawthorne's muscles. My face flushes, and I look away.

A servant has set us a table in the dining area, and a buffet has been laid out on the lavish side table. Large trays display selections of meats and cheeses, bread and pastries, vegetables and fruit. The soldiers load food onto their plates. Hawthorne hands me a porcelain dish and insists that I serve myself before he takes anything. He sits next to me at the long table. Emmitt sits on my other side.

Gilad, Hammon, Hawthorne, and Edgerton attack their food as if they've never tasted anything quite as good. I eat at a sedate pace, trying not to gag. It's not that it's entirely bad, but the meat is salty, the cheese isn't very creamy, and the fruit isn't as fresh as I'm used to. Emmitt pronounces his meal inedible and pushes it away. Gilad looks up from his plate and stabs Emmitt's steak with his knife, confiscating it.

Emmitt scowls at him. "Must you?" he asks.

Gilad doesn't answer, just keeps chewing while staring at Emmitt like he's next to be stabbed. By the end of the meal, I can barely keep my eyes open. After stifling several yawns, I give up trying to be polite. "I wish everyone a good evening," I say, pushing away from the table and standing. Hawthorne stands, too, but the other soldiers choke on laughter.

Gilad catches his breath for a second. "Good evening to you, too." I can tell when someone is mocking me, I just don't know why. Apparently, neither Clara nor Emmitt knows either, because they're as baffled as I am.

"Don't be savages," Hawthorne says with a scowl at his team. "You could all use some manners."

"What good are manners in a battle?" Gilad asks.

Not waiting to hear the answer, I walk away to the farthest door at the back of the suite, and Hawthorne follows. "Who is Walther Petes?" Hawthorne asks, his voice low enough not to be overheard.

Hesitating, I turn back from the doorway and stare at him blankly. *How does he know that name?* "I'm sorry, who?"

"Walther Sword—his last name was Petes until his secondborn processing—I don't know his number." He has an intense look, as if he sees right through me.

"I don't know. Why?" I reach for the doorframe. My knees feel weak. Walther is a secret that I need to keep, no matter what.

Hawthorne seems not to notice my weakness. "He commands a unit at the secondborn Base near the border of the Fate of Stars—the Twilight Forest."

I shrug and lean against the doorframe. "So?"

"So he's a combat commander for Vector Company. What does a combat commander want with you?"

"I don't know," I lie. Dune must have gotten word to his older brother to find me—maybe Dune's not leaving my placement to chance like everyone else has. "Why do you ask?"

Hawthorne leans against the other side of the doorframe. "I was under orders from my commanding officer to extract you from Census, but it was to be a covert mission. I had to work it out on my own—assemble my own team. They sent me because you're familiar with me. I assured them that you'd trust me if I found you."

"How did you know I'd trust you?" I ask.

"I just knew." I turn away to retreat into the private room and evade any more of his questions, but Hawthorne holds my arm. "I caught the tail end of a briefing between Commander Aslanbek—he's my CO—and Commander Walther."

"What did they say?"

"They were arguing about you—about who ultimately keeps you."

"I don't know anything about it. I thought you were acting alone." I don't know why I'm crushed by disappointment, but I am. I thought Hawthorne came to help me because he's my friend—my only friend. I should've known better. I've never had a real friend apart from Dune. I don't even know how to be a friend, let alone make one.

Hawthorne squints at me, as if he notices my disappointment but not the reason for it. I straighten. "I'll see you at first light," he says. He lets go of my arm.

I can only nod. Entering the bedroom, I slump against the door to close it. I don't even bother to wash my face before falling headfirst onto a pillow.

∽

My neck is sore when I rouse from a nightmarish sleep. It's still dark as I lie in bed, looking around at unfamiliar shadows as dark as the folds of Agent Crow's leather coat. My heart slows, and I wish that I had thought to pour myself some water before bed.

In my dream, I'd been searching the wreckage of the airships for bodies. Coughing on rock dust, I couldn't find anyone alive, only pieces of people—hands with red roses still clutched in their fists. Some of the mangled corpses had stumbled from beneath the rubble, their limbs crushed so that they lurched and jounced, dragging broken legs and feet. Some of the dead soldiers had twisted jaws hanging sideways and heads held at strange angles. They crowded around me, pawing my uniform, until I realized I had a silver-sphered Fusion Snuff Pulse in my hand. Pressing the button, it stole their power, rendering them dead once more.

Rising from the bed, I stumble to the bathroom. Undressing and kicking away the ugly blue clothing, I turn on the shower and step in. The heat of it soothes the kink in my neck. When I'm done, I wrap myself in a robe that I find in the cabinet. I leave the bathroom and venture into the drawing room. At the bar, I find a glass and pour myself some cold water from the tap. Sipping from it, I see Edgerton, alone and staring at me. He's made a bed of the enormous sofa.

"Hello," I whisper, not wanting to wake anyone else.

"Sun ain't up yet. You shouldn't be neither," Edgerton whispers. He's shirtless, his gun propped next to his hand. He's skinnier than Hawthorne and Gilad, but he has the wiry muscles of someone who knows how to fight.

"I had a bad dream." It's such an awkward thing to say. I immediately regret it.

He doesn't know what to make of me standing in front of him with wet hair, in a robe that's four sizes too big, its hem dragging on the ground, sleeves hiding my hands. "Oh," he replies. "I despise bad dreams."

"I do, too."

"You gotta close the door on 'em."

"How do I do that?" I set the glass down. He has my full attention.

"You gotta tell your friends about 'em—talk it out—no matter how many times it takes, and then poof"—his closed hand opens and his fingers spread apart—"the monsters go away."

"I don't have any friends."

"I'm your friend."

"You are?"

He nods.

"Why?"

"Because when you look at me, you're seein' me, not some good-for-nothin' cold-water hick from the mountains of Swords. You can tell me about your demons—I've experience with 'em."

Sitting beside him on a fluffy chair, I tell him about the dismembered corpses, the hands that don't match their arms, the heads on sideways. I leave out the part about the Fusion Snuff Pulse. I'm forbidden to tell him, and he'd be in danger from the authorities by knowing it. He listens, not making a sound until I finish.

"Erebody dies, Roselle. It were their time. This is war. Nobody gets to pick when they go or how. It just happens when it happens. Ain't no sense worrying about it."

"They were murdered, Edgerton."

"Most of 'em Swords done some murderin' of they own—it's been going on longer than the few days you've been in it. We're soldiers. We kill things. We get killed by things. That's the job. You want a different job, you picked the wrong birth order and the wrong Fate to be born into."

"What if I don't want to kill things—what if I want to save things?"

"You mean, not be a secondborn Sword?"

"Yes."

"If there were a choice, what Fate would you pick?" he asks.

I chew on my bottom lip, thinking. "I don't know. They all have drawbacks because I'm secondborn. I have no voice in any Fate."

"That's never gonna change. You have to make peace with it or it'll destroy you." He reaches for the strap of his gun. Fishing through a compartment on it, he extracts a white stamp wrapped in cellophane. "I have a chet. I was savin' it for something really bad. Here," he says as he extends it out to me. "You can have it. It'll relax you."

"No, you keep it." I rise to my feet, not taking his offer. "I have to be sharp for the press conference." Edgerton nods and puts it back.

"She's too strong for that, Edge," Hawthorne says from the archway. He has his arms crossed, his back against the wall.

"How long have you been there?" I ask. My face burns with embarrassment.

"We all have night terrors," Hawthorne replies sympathetically.

"Hammon has bad ones." Edgerton sits up and reaches for his shirt, dragging it on. "Sometimes I have to hold her all night, which ain't as easy as it sounds cuz neither of us is allowed in the other's capsule."

"You and Hammon are . . ."

"She's my girl."

"But that's . . ."

"I know. That's why we hide it. I'm telling you cuz you'll find out anyway. You see erething. Are you gonna keep my secret?"

I nod. "You wouldn't have told me if you thought I wouldn't."

"You're right. You strike me as someone who has secrets of her own that are a lot bigger than mine. You're no turner."

"I thought Hammon and Gilad—"

"They're best friends," Edgerton interrupts, "but she and me has always been together."

"Ham and Edge," Hawthorne acknowledges.

A door opens down the hall, and a blurry-eyed Clara Diamond shuffles into the drawing room, almost running into Hawthorne. "Ugh, why are you people *up* when you don't have to be?" she asks, combing a hand through her hair. She trudges to the bar and inputs a selection for coffee. It arrives piping hot in the instant-carousel unit. She takes a sip from the mug and looks at me as if seeing me for the first time. "Ah, good, you're awake. We have to get started on your look. Follow me." She walks toward my bedroom.

"You have to get started on your look," Edgerton teases me softly. I reach for the pillow on the chair and toss it at him. He catches it, his laughter following me as I trail Clara.

I admire Clara's lavender-colored hair as she spends the next couple of hours styling mine by hand, not leaving it to the bathroom unit's automated groomer. She arranges it in long, loose curls, then applies cosmetics to my face, sighing over every scrape that she finds.

Emmitt breezes into the bathroom in a whirlwind with clothing draped over his arm. "I had seamstresses up all night creating this masterpiece for you, Roselle, even though I know *you* won't appreciate it."

He carefully unwraps a Tropo uniform unlike any I've ever seen. The top is made of two different fabrics, suede and silk. The suede corset squeezes me at the waist and fits so tightly, it makes it hard to breathe. I shrug into it, and Clara fastens the line of golden hooks and eyes along my spine. The beautiful beige suede creates an hourglass effect.

A beige silk panel, sewn into the bodice of the suede just above my breasts, creates the neckline and the sleeves. It's so fine as to be transparent, showing off my collarbone and shoulders. The neckline at midthroat has a thicker panel of silk like a choker. Trousers of the same supple suede fit me like a second skin. Knee-high, matte-black leather boots finish the outfit.

The black bruise over my heart is a dark shadow. I touch it, and my fingers press into the beige silk. It still hurts, but not as badly as when I'd first awakened in Census. "What about this?" I ask. "You can see this bruise."

"I have a solution for that." Emmitt holds up a long leather jacket. "This should hide it." I attempt to put my arms in the sleeves, but he stops me. "*Uhht, uhht,*" he says, pulling the black leather jacket back, "let me just drape it on your shoulders and see the effect." We both gaze into the full-length mirror in front of us as he sets it on me. It marries the look of a cape and a coat. The jacket resembles Agent Crow's coat, clearly a knockoff of Census uniforms, except that this one has a row of golden sword-shaped buttons on either side of its lapels.

Emmitt smiles. "The way you're wearing this denotes a certain negligence, as if you're unconcerned with the attack. Rebels don't scare you."

"It looks like a Census coat."

"It does, but it's different enough that people will automatically feel you have authority, though they won't know why."

I now see how brilliant he is. He lifts a kohl stick from among the cosmetics and pulls a thick line across my bottom lashes at a catlike angle. If Agent Crow were here, he'd probably accuse me of stealing his look. Emmitt reads my mind as he stares at my reflection. "You'll be responsible for more kills than any agent can ever hope for. Here." He reaches into his jacket pocket, and then slips a sharp-pointed ring onto three fingers of my left hand, like brass knuckles in the shape of jutting talons, but in gold.

"What's this?" I ask.

"If you run into a question you didn't anticipate, look down at this ring while you think, as if you're too bored by the question to answer it."

"Won't people find that offensive?" I lift my hand, trying not to poke my eye out as I study it.

"No. They're looking for someone to believe in. You, showing no fear, is what they need. Be infallible. Be fearless. We'll hold the press conference on the balcony of this Treetop penthouse. Eat something now before your crude entourage consumes it all."

I hope for rain as I follow Emmitt. I peek outside as we approach the windows to the terrace. Drone cameras are already arriving for the press conference. Floating platforms levitate like flat tarmacs, carrying high-profile celebrity commentators. I'd expect this caliber of on-air talent to focus on the Secondborn Trials rather than me. They embrace frivolity. Dune always said it's because any serious journalism is subject to severe censorship. I've mostly avoided them until now because my virtual access had its own dedicated channel, mostly drone and stationary cameras that I rarely interacted with.

I follow the scent of breakfast into the dining area. Gilad and Hawthorne are already working through huge plates of food. They haven't bothered to put all their armor back on yet. Edgerton and Hammon are at the sideboard, dishes in hand. Hammon leans closer to Edgerton, selecting a roll from a basket. Her torso brushes against his wrist. His hand rests lightly on her side, caressing the curve of her hip. His mouth lingers close to her ear. Her face flushes. She closes her eyes and turns so that her neck brushes his lips. The intimacy makes my face flush as well.

They notice me beside them and move apart from one another. I follow them to the table with my full plate and sit across from Gilad. I start eating, my fork and knife making soft sounds against the plate. As I chew, every eye is on me. "What?" I ask after swallowing.

"What are you wearing?" Gilad asks.

I look down at myself. My cleavage presses provocatively against the beige suede and silken fabric. "A uniform."

"Whose uniform?" Gilad asks, his eyebrows arching up. "That's not a Sword uniform."

I smile and resume eating. "Don't worry, Gilad. You'll get one in the next requisition."

"I'm not wearing anything that looks like that," he growls.

"You wouldn't fill it out half as well," Hawthorne teases. His gorgeous storm-colored eyes linger on me. We eat in silence until I set my fork down. Hawthorne lifts his chin. "You ready for this?" He indicates the assembling crowd of reporters outside. I can just see them through the archway of the dining room.

"We'll know in a few minutes," I reply. "Please excuse me." He stands as I do. I take my dish to the clearing tray near the sideboard. After depositing it, I join Clara at the glass doors that lead to the balcony. She doesn't speak as we both gaze outside at the mass of reporters on mobile platforms, vying for airspace near the railing. As soon as I come into sight, the drone cameras perk up, flying nearer.

The screen in the main room is tuned to a channel covering this news conference. Desdemona Diamond, secondborn, narrates my appearance inside the Treetop apartment. "Roselle Sword, formerly St. Sismode, has just made her entrance to the lavish apartment of Clifton Salloway, firstborn Sword and heir to the Salloway Munitions

Conglomerate. We have yet to see Clifton himself, but we know this inter-Fate pleasure seeker by his reputation for the lovelies."

Desdemona details my lavish ensemble with fascination and a touch of envy. My eyelids narrow at the screen. She is making this all sound nefarious, treating me as if I'm an adulterous Diamond-Fated firstborn actress found in the hideaway of a clandestine lover.

Desdemona turns to her co-anchor, Secondborn Suki Diamond. "Where has Roselle been for the past four days since her ill-fated procession through the streets of Forge?"

"I don't know for sure where she's been," Suki replies giddily, "but it's all too curious that we find her here, in the Treetop love nest of Clifton Salloway." She clasps her hands in her lap and leans closer to Desdemona, her long black hair hanging to her ankles in a shimmering cascade. "Maybe we should reach out to his ex-flame, Firstborn Celestial Bastille?" I don't know who that is, but I hope with a rising panic that they don't.

Hammon joins me at the glass doors, but her focus, like mine, is on the wall screen. "You've made it onto the *Daily Diamond!*" she breathes in awe.

Desdemona flips her long hair as she discusses Clifton Salloway and his string of broken hearts. Her hair is gorgeous, seven shades of blue, sewn to her head with the darkest of thread so that the seams form diamond patterns. Diamond sparkles glisten from her long eyelashes and over her dark cheekbones. Her blue lips are painted with a white diamond in the center, and so are her long blue fingernails.

"This is a delicious turn of events, Roselle," Emmitt whispers in my ear, almost preening when Suki and Desdemona begin discussing my outfit again. They note its exquisite fit and speculate that designers might favor a military cut and style in their spring collections. "Use this to your advantage. Clifton Salloway is a dream come true, *and* he wants to meet you."

"He's here?" I ask. I couldn't feel more awkward if I'd walked into the glass doors in front of me.

"He's right over there." Emmitt puts his hands on my shoulders, turning me in the direction of the bar. In the corner of it, a firstborn officer stands with a three-finger glass of light blue liquid. He's leaning against the back counter, watching me. I'm startled that I didn't notice him before. While Hawthorne is the rugged kind of handsome, Clifton is the film-star kind of gorgeous. Attired in a black Exo uniform similar to Gabriel's, Clifton is the highest-ranking Sword outside of an admiral. Exo is the rank given to both exceptionally well-trained firstborn soldiers and a few aristocratic firstborns with very little military prowess. I don't know where he falls.

As if my eyes on him are an invitation, he pushes away from the counter and prowls nearer. Stopping a foot away, he takes my left hand, bringing it to his lips. He kisses the crown of my birthmark, causing my silver sword moniker to shine on the bridge of his nose. My heartbeat hammers in my ears.

"Roselle," he murmurs, "Clifton Salloway. It's an honor to make your acquaintance." Behind him, on the screen, the co-anchors of the *Daily Diamond* are in a frenzy, commentating on the "primal chemistry" between Clifton and me. Clifton gives a soft chuckle. "We've been found out, Roselle," he teases.

My laugh is more nervous. "I hate when that happens, Patrøn. It ruins the fun."

"Someone as lovely as you should never have her fun ruined. And I insist that you call me Clifton." Clifton looks to be in his midtwenties, although his clean-shaven cheeks might be making him look younger than he is. Sultry green eyes, with flecks of gold that resemble the tails of shooting stars, stare back at me from beneath a whiplash of blond hair swept to the side. His eyes grow brighter as he releases my hand with some reluctance.

"So, this is your apartment, Clifton?" I ask as he straightens.

"One of them. It's where I stay when I'm required to fulfill my active duty tours."

"I see. Thank you for the use of your apartment. It was generous of you."

"It was no trouble, I assure you. I am a fan of yours."

My eyebrow lifts. "A fan of mine?"

"You have taught me a fair number of sword maneuvers. Tell me, would you consider giving me private lessons?"

"I—" I look away from his handsome face in utter bewilderment. Surely he must know that I'm not in charge of my own destiny. I'm told when I must rise and when I'm to sleep, when to eat and when to train, when to study and when to bathe. It's all out of my control—everything about my life is out of my control.

Hawthorne joins me. "I believe they're ready for you outside, Roselle." His hand gently angles me toward the glass doors.

"Excuse me, Patrøn," I murmur to Clifton.

"Of course," Clifton replies with a wink.

As I turn away, Hawthorne growls low to Clifton. "She doesn't give private lessons. Go find someone your own age to train with."

I glance over my shoulder at them. Clifton stares at my backside. "I'm bored with my trainers. They lack the kind of ferociousness that I see in Roselle. She would give me quite a workout."

"She's only eighteen." Hawthorne stands rigidly between us.

"So it's okay to send her to war, but not to allow her to—"

"If it were up to me, she'd never see a battlefield."

"Then tell her to consider training with me, and I'll make sure she never sees combat."

Hawthorne turns. "Gilad, this Exo wants private lessons. He's looking for ferociousness. You up for a training session?"

Gilad looks like a malignant hobgoblin with his scarred face and his dead man's stare. "Anytime," Gilad replies.

"Are you her unit commander?" Clifton asks Hawthorne with a speculative look.

"No. I'm just someone who looks out for secondborns."

Emmitt is positively gleeful beside me. He claps his hands and whirls me toward the drone cameras outside, whispering in my ear. "You are fast becoming my favorite person in the entire fatedom! *Gah!* Clifton Salloway and that gorgeous Sword are fighting over my little Roselle. What's next?" He stops at the threshold, drunk on the testosterone in the room. "Now," he says as he puts his hands on my shoulders and squeezes, "keep your wits about you, and you'll survive this to live another day."

Another day may be the best that I can hope for. The doors open, and he gives me a little shove out onto the balcony. The doors close behind me, and I'm alone with a wall of reporters. The sun rises slowly beside us. I squint a little as my eyes adjust. I pull the leather coat tighter around me. Squaring my shoulders, I walk a few more steps to meet the strobe flashes and jockeying reporters beyond the railing.

Questions are shouted from many angles. "Roselle, are you and Clifton Salloway lovers? Where have you been for the past four days? How did you and Clifton meet? Did Clifton rescue you from the Gates of Dawn soldiers? Does Clifton Salloway know that you're secondborn? How long have you been keeping this affair a secret? What does your brother think of your affair with Firstborn Salloway? Does Gabriel feel threatened by this relationship?"

"Hello," I greet them. I look at everyone, allowing the photographers and drones to get their pictures, pausing a few seconds in as many directions as I can.

"Roselle, Roselle." Desdemona Diamond vies for my attention. I shift in her direction, and she asks, "Is Firstborn Clifton Salloway your lover?"

Instead of frowning or scowling as I'd like to do, I laugh softly. "I only just met Firstborn Salloway a few moments ago. He very charmingly introduced himself near the door there." I point over my shoulder at the silhouette of Clifton in the glass. He waves to the reporters. "And I could no more have a relationship with him or any other man of my acquaintance without violating a hundred different laws. The last time I checked, that was forbidden."

Suki Diamond shouts the loudest. "How do you explain your appearance in his apartment, then?" The reporters crowd toward her.

"Firstborn Salloway was gracious enough to offer his apartment to us last night to prepare for this press conference."

"Who is the *us* you're referring to?"

"The team of secondborn soldiers who have accompanied me to the press conference."

"How come you need a team of soldiers to accompany you while in the Stone Forest Base? Do they fear for your safety? Are you a target for the Gates of Dawn?"

"I don't have an answer for that question. You'll have to address it to the company commander or the admiral of the Stone Forest Base."

"Do you believe that the Gates of Dawn were specifically targeting you in the attack on the Sword capital of Forge?" asks a dark-haired secondborn man with a small scar through the center of his top lip. He doesn't look at me but holds an audio dictator out, reading its screen as it takes notes for him.

"The enemy soldiers were along my route to the Stone Forest Base, so to a certain extent, I believe they targeted me for the media appeal of the event."

"How did you know they were enemy soldiers?" he asks.

"They had visors and helmets that were different from Sword soldiers."

"Why would they attack you, do you think?"

"I don't see this as a personal attack. I believe they wanted to do as much damage as possible and scare as many people as they could. My Transition fit that profile."

The man looks impressed by my interpretation. "Do you have any insight as to how they entered the Fate of Swords?"

"No."

"But if you had to guess?" he presses.

"I'm sorry. I don't know."

"Did you like the white flowers they brought you?"

I don't answer right away. His question brings unbidden tears to my eyes. I swallow hard and look down at my ring, trying to look bored rather than shocked by his callousness. The platforms have grown quiet. The clicks of drone cameras are loud and rapid. When I'm certain my voice won't betray me, I look up and give my best impersonation of my father's fatal smirk. "I find calla lilies more appealing than roses. I'll be sure to bring them some in return the next time we meet."

The reporters swarm, understanding my meaning. Voices shout questions. "Will you deploy with the next wave of Swords to the battlefield?"

"I haven't yet gotten my orders."

"Did you witness the explosion that brought down the airships?"

I pause. "No. I didn't witness an explosion. I saw one airship crash." It's a lie of omission, and it bothers me.

Most of the questions that follow I rehearsed with the panel of leaders last night. My answers are short on details and heavy on things I didn't see. I drill through them quickly. Eventually Emmitt emerges from the apartment behind me, stops at my side, and says, "Roselle only has time for a few more questions." Most of them are about my current uniform and whether I plan to set new style trends for secondborns and firstborns alike. I allow Emmitt to answer those, though he pretends that a secret Diamond-Fated designer had done the work.

The final question interrupts my thanking everyone for coming. "Do you have plans to see Clifton again?"

I groan inwardly. *What is the fascination with my so-called love life? Do they really not get that if I were to have an affair with Clifton, I could be jailed or killed?* I look over my shoulder at Clifton standing inside his apartment. He steeples his hands, as if he's praying for me to say yes. This gets a chuckle from the men and sighs from the women. My eyes drift to Hawthorne's. He looks worried. I face the reporters once more. "I don't make plans. I follow orders."

"Okay," Emmitt says, waving to the reporters. "Thank you for coming today. You can pick up press packets from the Base Commander at the Warrior Gate. Have a pleasant journey back to your Fates." Emmitt links arms with me, as if we've always been the best of friends, and we stroll to the glass doors. "Well done, Roselle! You were flawless!"

Hawthorne meets me just over the threshold. Re-dressed in his combat uniform, he has his rifle slung on his back and his helmet on his head, without his visor deployed. The downward slash of his eyebrows feels ominous. Angry-faced, he grasps my upper arms and growls, "We're leaving. Now." I let go of Emmitt's arm as I hurry to keep up with Hawthorne. He marches me to the door.

I try to stop him. "I should say good-bye to our host and thank Emmitt and Clara for their help. It's rude just to leave like this."

"Move," he barks. "That's an order." I stop resisting. My leather coat slips from one shoulder. We are at the door of the apartment in a couple of heartbeats. Emmitt blusters behind us, shocked by our lack of decorum. Gilad holds the door open for Hawthorne and me while Hammon holds the elevator doors and Edgerton points his rifle menacingly at some target over my shoulder.

From behind me, Clifton Salloway calls out, "Consider my offer, Roselle. I'd love to work with you."

Hawthorne swears under his breath. He stomps right past Gilad, who slams the door behind us. We enter the elevator and face the glass that overlooks the immense drop to the ground. Gilad and Edgerton step into the lift as well. Hammon closes the door and selects the ground floor. As we descend, I try to ease my arm away from Hawthorne's grip. He tightens it, and then realizes that he's hurting me and lets go. I take off my coat, folding it over my arm to hide the bruises that Agent Crow left.

"Do you mind explaining what just happened back there?" I ask.

"Whoo!" Edgerton yells. I flinch from the surprise and sheer volume of it. It takes all my willpower not to throat-punch him. He slaps his thigh, and then doubles over, hands on top of his knees, laughing.

"Damn, that was fun!" He wipes a tear from his eye. "Did you see the look on his face when we evac'ed to the elevator without giving him a chance to worship at the altar of Roselle?" Hammon snorts with laughter beside Edgerton, and even Gilad cracks a smile. "That ol' boy can hunt!" he continues. "He wants Roselle somethin' fierce!" He points at me. "And you! You got to be the coolest customer that I've ever set eyes on when it comes to handlin' those Diamond-Fated douchebags!"

I rub my forehead, at a complete loss. "Who is *ol' boy*?" I ask.

Hammon takes pity on me and explains. "We sometimes call a first-born *ol' boy* or *ol' man*. He was talking about your boyfriend, Clifton, back there."

"Don't call him *her boyfriend*," Hawthorne scolds. He's really angry. "Talk like that could get her killed! That kind of relationship isn't just flirting with danger, it *is* danger." Hawthorne points at me. "You, stay away from him. He's no good for you. He asks you again for private lessons, you tell him no, and then you tell your commanding officer that you're not interested in training anyone. Do you understand me?"

"I take it *private lessons* have nothing to do with weapons training." I lean my forehead against the glass of the elevator and watch the rapidly approaching ground. A part of me hopes to be splattered by it so that I don't have to face the soldiers in this lift.

"Aw, he wants his weapon trained, all right," Edgerton hoots, doubling over again.

"Thanks for the warning," I reply. "I'll stay away from him."

We reach the ground floor and Gilad is first off the lift, followed by Hammon and Edgerton. Hawthorne holds the door open for me. I'm glad he doesn't touch me. I've reached my limit for being manhandled today. The next person who tries will wind up hurting.

Chapter 9
That's Mine

We file through the ground floor of the firstborn officer Tree. Hawthorne still radiates rage. Gilad marches beside him. Hammon and Edgerton are ahead of them. I trail behind, my heeled boots and shorter legs making it hard to keep up.

My entourage walks right by the cluster of chairs closest to the outer doors without seeing the devil seated in one of them. I slow my pace, staring at Agent Crow. He smiles. Steel teeth shine. Pointing to the life-size virtual monitor encompassing the nearest pillar, he directs my gaze. My image is on it, a replay of the news conference. I blink. I seem so much older than I am—it's the air of confidence I'm feigning, a trait I've learned from watching my mother. It exudes from behind my carefully applied war paint.

I come to a stop when I notice the hilt of my fusionblade on Agent Crow's hip. It's unmistakable, bearing my family crest. My heart squeezes tight. My grandfather gave me that sword when I was born. It's the only thing I ever received from him.

Agent Crow says, "You didn't even mention me once in your news conference."

"You're not important, Agent Crow."

"You wound me, Roselle."

"I'd like nothing better."

"Don't tease me," he replies.

"That's my sword," I state. The fact that he's wearing it on his person is so offensive that I'm laser-focused.

"*Was*, Roselle. This *was* your sword." His eyes almost sparkle.

"No. It *is* my sword. You stole it from me."

"Careful." His smile evaporates. "You don't want to go around making accusations you cannot possibly prove."

"I can prove it's my sword. It has a rose embossed on the center of the hilt."

"I like roses." He shrugs with an amused smirk.

"The rose is interwoven into the St. Sismode crest."

"Coincidence."

"I think not. I want my sword."

"Well, you cannot have it."

"Why not?"

"Your commanding officer is only going to take it from you anyway. You're no longer a St. Sismode. You're Roselle Sword. Roselle St. Sismode no longer exists. This is just a representation of who you used to be. What do you say I keep it for you . . . for later?"

"I say no."

Hawthorne is so close behind me that he accidentally brushes up against me as he whispers, "Stand down."

"No."

"Agent Crow's right," Hawthorne explains. "They'll only take it from you, Roselle. Let it go."

"No. It's my sword." It's the only tie I have left to my identity—my family. I'd rather fight and pay the consequences than back down. I lunge at Agent Crow.

Hawthorne is ready for my attack. My feet lift off the ground as he pins my arms behind me before I can touch Kipson Crow's smug face. I struggle against him, and he wrestles me down onto the marble floor. My cheek hits hard and bounces. On bended knee beside me,

Hawthorne grits his teeth. "Calm down, Roselle! You die if you hit him unprovoked in public. Be smart!"

I kick Hawthorne in the knee with the heel of my boot. It doesn't hurt him through his combat armor, but his knee slips out from under him. He crashes to the floor beside me and loosens his grip on my arms. I shake free, but Gilad's knee digs into the middle of my back, keeping me down. I throw my head back, connecting with Gilad's nose. He moans and swears. Hawthorne tries to get up, but I pull him by the ear until his head hits the floor like mine did. The golden ring on my hand leaves claw marks across his cheek.

As I struggle, I almost have Hawthorne and Gilad off me, despite their size and weight. I crash back down, though, as Edgerton tackles me, too. The wiry soldier from the mountains of Swords gets my arms behind me once more. Everyone hangs on. Wrist restraints clamp onto me while Gilad and Hawthorne hold my legs.

Hammon gets down at eye level with me. Her brown ponytail sticks out from her helmet and sweeps the floor. "Look at me!" she orders. "You'll survive this! We won't let you die for a family that no longer wants you. You're a secondborn Sword. You're our family now!"

All I can do is pant, unable to take a full breath with their weight on top of me. Gilad and Edgerton slide off. Hawthorne hauls me to my feet by my wrist restraints. I refuse to cry out, even though it's excruciating.

Agent Crow starts clapping. "This is so touching. What a little family unit you've become in such a short time." He's less than pleased, though. He wanted me to hit him.

Hawthorne shoves me into Gilad and Edgerton with a murderous look. They each take me by an arm and lift me off the ground, though I'm no longer struggling. They walk me out of the building while Hawthorne stays behind with Agent Crow, who calls out after me. "I'll keep your sword safe, Roselle! Not to worry!"

Outside, the sunlight makes me squint. "Secure a hover," Gilad growls to Hammon. She complies, asking the Tree valet to call a lightweight commuter hover for us. She motions for Gilad and Edgerton to bring me, and I'm half dragged, half lifted off my feet and pushed into the vehicle. Gilad and Edgerton place me between them, their broad shoulders squashing me. Hammon gets in and sits in the row behind us.

I taste blood on my tongue. I lick my lips. They're bleeding. Hawthorne appears a few moments later. He gets into the front of the vehicle, throwing my leather jacket at me from over the seat. It hits my chest and falls to my lap. The sleeve of my blouse has torn at the shoulder, exposing my skin. I squeeze my eyes shut, willing tears to recede. I open them when I have my emotions restrained. My throat aches with the effort.

"Sector 4-15. Tree 177," Hawthorne hisses, touching the scratches I left on his cheek. His fingers go to the shell of his ear, presumably to feel if it's still attached. The hovercar moves forward, navigating the traffic on its own.

Gilad wipes blood from his nose onto the sleeve of his combat armor. It doesn't do much to stem the flow of it. He says nothing.

Edgerton chuckles. "You're a spitfire, Rose—"

"Shut it!" Hawthorne orders, glaring at him from the front seat.

"Well, she is," Edgerton mutters under his breath. He tosses the golden claw ring that I was wearing to Hawthorne. "Here, I got you a souvenir." Hawthorne catches it and files it away in one of his armor compartments.

Not another word is spoken in the fifteen minutes it takes to travel to the concrete Tree. Gilad gets out of the commuter vehicle first, followed by Hammon. Edgerton makes a spinning motion with his fingers while he whistles. I turn and present him my back. He takes off the wrist restraints. I straighten in my seat and rub my wrists while he clips the cuffs back onto his combat belt, and then exits the vehicle.

I slide over to get out, but Hawthorne stops me. "A word, Roselle." I pause, staring out the windscreen. He sighs in frustration. "Do you know the average life expectancy for a secondborn Sword from the aristocracy after his or her Transition Day?"

I don't answer.

"It's four weeks. That's around thirty days. Do you know why they don't last very long?"

I don't answer.

"It's because no one likes them. They're unlikable. They usually don't know how to do things, and they're arrogant and lazy and expect things to be done for them. They believe their hardships are worse than everyone else's. I can tell already that that is not you. You're strong, capable, and you don't complain. But you're arrogant, and arrogance will get you killed faster than the other traits combined. Listen, I know what it's like—"

"You don't know what it's like. You don't have any idea what *my life* is like!" My throat constricts. "I know things you couldn't possibly know. No one expects anything from you, Hawthorne, except for you to follow orders. Go where they tell you. Sit where they tell you. Sleep where they tell you. And you do everything they tell you, and when you do it well, you get merits."

"How are you different than that?"

I don't say anything.

"Aw, I get it," he says disgustedly. "You think you had so much more to lose than I did. You're from a better family than mine, is that it?" That's partly it, but not all of it. What I don't tell him is that no matter what I do, I'm always at a disadvantage. Everyone has a preconceived notion of who I am *because* of the family I was born into. Everyone has had virtual access into my life. The idealized role I have had to play as a symbol of a secondborn Sword follows me, makes me different. The worst thing that I can be in a situation like the one I'm in is different.

Hawthorne sees none of this. "Well, like it or not, Roselle, we've wound up in the same place. You're no better than me now and, unlike you, I know how to survive here. You still have to figure it out." I hug my leather coat, pulling it closer to my chest. Hawthorne rubs his temples with his fingers, like he's trying to think. He drops his hands, and his eyes meet mine. "Just so you know"—his hand gestures in my direction—"there are already bets on how long you'll last."

I lower my chin, feeling ill. "I'll make it."

"Will you?" he asks softly. "Then I'll double down on you."

"Just stay away from me. I don't need your help."

"Yeah, like you didn't need me in Census?" Derision is written all over his face.

"That's done now. You don't have to watch out for me anymore."

He sighs. "You're gonna need a friend."

I stare him directly in the eyes. "A friend wouldn't have stopped me from getting my sword back." I slide out of the car and wait for him to join us. He does, looking grim-faced. Holding my coat over my arm, I smooth the fabric so that my hands don't shake.

Turning to the other soldiers, Hawthorne says, "Rejoin the unit and resume your duties. Dismissed." Gilad walks away without saying anything.

"See ya around, Roselle," Edgerton says.

We are stopped before we enter the concrete-and-metal military trunk. Our monikers are scanned. A brawny soldier at least ten years older than us reads the monitor of the scanner. "Roselle Sword, you're to report to Intake—sector 23, level 5, subsection 7Q." His deep voice is sharp. He motions to a soldier near him.

Hawthorne holds up his hand. "I'll take Roselle there." Hawthorne taps the face of his wrist communicator. A map readout projects up from it.

The older soldier gives him a sharp nod. "Patrøn." Hawthorne gestures for me to come with him. We enter through a hangar door fortified with artillery shields. As soon as we cross the threshold, there's an antechamber with metal benches. On the other side of the room is a huge oblong-shaped archway that opens into the trunk of the Tree.

Hawthorne takes off his helmet. His hair is matted down. He swipes his hand through it and moves toward the automated conveyor system.

Wall ports of various sizes and shapes cover one side of the small room. One of the conveyor ports activates the moment Hawthorne tosses his helmet onto it. Air catches it and lifts it up through a clear tube, into the ceiling, and out of sight. Hawthorne strips away his rifle, depositing it onto another port conveyor. The air catches it, and it's gone in seconds.

"When we return from active duty," Hawthorne explains, "there are drop-off points for your gear. Everything is coded for you, so it'll be returned to your pod cleaned and conditioned. You want to do this every time you use your armor because it'll get rank quickly if you don't."

"Who cleans it?" I ask.

"Stone workers assigned to our Base." The stream of air takes his combat boots the moment he throws them through a hole to the conveyor. He removes his remaining weapons—his fusionblade, fusionmag—a handheld fusion-powered gun that fires bullet-like bursts of energy and knife—and they whisk away through the hole. He strips off his chest mail and armor, placing them in the conveyor. Barefoot and attired in combat leggings and a clingy combat shirt, he shifts to an adjacent wall unit. Tropo-ranked soldiers wait in line for automated stations that line the wall. Hawthorne goes to an empty one marked "Strato." He scans his moniker. Holograms of clothing flash in front of him, all higher in rank than Tropo. He selects a midnight-blue Strato uniform, socks, and training boots. A parcel wrapped in clear plastic descends into a bin next to the wall unit. He unwraps the package and quickly dons the shirt and trousers. I wait, trying not to admire the way his muscles bunch and stretch beneath his shirt. He sits on a bench and bends to fasten the buckles of his boots.

He finishes, straightens, and stands. "C'mon," he says.

We enter a cargo area. It takes a few moments to adjust to the dim interior. Without windows, this Tree is dark and oppressive compared to the glass one. Natural light is replaced by ghostly bluish tracks of incandescent bulbs. It's bustling, though. Soldiers are everywhere. No one is sitting around. Whereas the ground floor of the officers' glass Tree is made for gathering and social interaction, this one is purely utilitarian, with massive storage units and pallets of everything soldiers need for survival.

Hawthorne grabs my sleeve. "Careful," he says, yanking me back from a shiny, sharp-nosed drone. It flies by at eye level above an outlined track on the floor painted in a wide yellow band. "You'll want to make sure the stingers aren't coming through. They travel the perimeter of stone Trees."

"What do they do?"

"Security patrols, automated drones that catalogue and ping monikers. If you're not where you're supposed to be, they'll deviate from their route and confront you. Never cross a gold road without looking."

I nod, resuming my rubbernecking. A stinger makes its way around the circumference of the trunk, passing a familiar type of bunker. More stingers are stationed outside the thick metal doors. "What's that there?"

"That's a Census access station."

My heart beats faster. "You mean they live beneath this Tree, too?" Goose bumps form on my arms as I remember Census's cold cells— the feeling of being buried alive. I imagine the guards stationed on the other side of those heavy doors protecting the elevators that lead underground.

"They live and work beneath most Trees in this area. They have a network beneath this whole Base. We share some of the tunnels. If we're attacked, all noncombatant personnel will go below ground. Some triage units and medical facilities are also below us."

Around me, automated heavy machinery moves supplies onto airpowered conveyors that lift into tubes. These tubes form arteries into the Tree, carrying everything from munitions to rations and cartons of new boots and blankets. Hawthorne points. "Those tubes are called phloem. Everything gets unloaded and coded, then transported along the thousands of phloem to different departments and distribution centers within the trunk. Those pipes there," he says as he points to liquid-filled pipes of different colors, "are called sapwoods. They carry water, fuel, waste, et cetera, up and down the trunk, to and from the branches above."

A unit of soldiers runs by us in formation, using a green track that spans the perimeter. Soldiers hang from the sheer cliff faces of the trunk by harnesses and rock-climbing gear. Zip lines connect levels. Soldiers use handheld trolleys on the zip lines to descend floors and automated ones to ascend. Looking up, dark hallways are visible everywhere in the trunk, leading in every different direction, presumably, to the branches and then the exterior hanging airships that make up the leaves of the Trees. Unlike the officers' Tree, the open air of the trunk does not extend all the way to the canopy. Solid levels begin far above us.

I follow Hawthorne, circumnavigating the cargo areas, and we arrive at the center of the trunk. "This is called the heartwood," he explains. A series of poles with steps on either side moves continuously up or down. Fifty or more are clustered in this one area. Soldiers grab the poles and step onto stairs that either lift or descend, like a ladder, but with the rungs on the outside at alternating heights.

"Have you ever used one before?" Hawthorne asks. "They're easy. Just get on a step, secure yourself by holding the pole, and then step off when you reach your level. In your case, it's level five." He walks toward one and pauses, blocking the flow of traffic onto one of the heartwood lifts. Tropo soldiers move to different lines to avoid the delay. "Whenever you're ready, Roselle."

I climb onto a step and clutch the pole with both hands. It lifts me, and my leather coat slides to the crook of my arm. Hawthorne steps onto the same lift at the same time, taking the adjacent step slightly lower than mine. I gaze into his gray eyes, feeling my face redden and my heartbeat rush in my ears. We enter a glass pipeline, and now it's reasonably hard to fall off the lift and very intimate.

"Approaching level one," a feminine robotic voice announces. As we reach the floor, there's an opening to step through, but we continue upward, encircled once again by the frosted glass tube.

Hawthorne reaches out and touches my cheek. His fingertips are warm and rough. He caresses the sore spot where I hit the marble floor when he stopped me from retrieving my fusionblade. "I'm sorry I hurt you." He frowns. "You're so light. I used too much force. I was afraid you were going to hit Agent Crow, and then you'd be taken from us. I didn't think I could get you out of Census twice."

"I *was* going to hit him." I can hardly blame Hawthorne. He probably saved me from much greater torture, maybe even death. What he doesn't understand is what my fusionblade means to me. Everything here is considered disposable—including people. "Don't worry," I murmur. "It's not my first bruise."

"Approaching level two." We pass the floor.

His thumb traces my bottom lip as we slip hidden behind frosted glass again. Longing like I've never felt before shatters the anger that I felt earlier. "It may not be your first bruise, but it's the first one from me, and I'm sorry for it." My insides tighten, and my whole body floods with heat. The violence of the ache leaves me breathless.

"Should I punch you in the face and call it even?" I ask, leaning my hip against the pole between us for support.

"Approaching level three." I don't even glance at the platform as it goes by.

He grins. "Would you? It'd make me feel so much better."

"Some other time, perhaps."

"Approaching level four." The floor glides by us.

Hawthorne drops his hand. "The next level is five. We'll step off there." The heady rush of being near him is knee-weakening. I've been surrounded by powerful men all my life, but not one has affected me like this. It's a vicious craving for something that I don't entirely understand. I want to touch his hair, to slide my fingers over the angular planes of his face.

It suddenly occurs to me that we may not see each other again after today. This Tree alone is the size of a city, and either of us could be reassigned to another Tree or a new Base at any time. Maybe it's smarter not to grow too attached. I crave connection, but the thought of missing Hawthorne the way I miss Dune is heart-wrenching.

"This is us," Hawthorne says, threading his fingers through mine. We jump from the heartwood, landing gracefully on the glossy metal deck. I gaze at our clasped hands. His is sun-kissed and strong, capable. Mine is so much smaller in comparison. I can't remember the last time someone held my hand. Hawthorne's voice is tender. "It's this way."

We merge into a stream of brown and blue uniforms and move with the flow. Hawthorne doesn't let go of my hand. The ceiling has the same exposed girders and dull lighting as the cargo area. Light panels line the sides of the hallway like long windows.

Every few steps, someone's arm bumps into my shoulder. I'd drown among them if Hawthorne weren't here to keep me afloat. We turn so many corners that I lose count. Finally, we come to a gateway that reads "Intake." Hawthorne lets go of my hand, but I still feel the echo of his. Soldiers surge around us. No one turns down the short hallway to the Intake facility. "Are you ready?" Hawthorne asks.

It doesn't matter if I'm ready. This is my life now. This Tree is my home for as long as they say it is. From this moment on, most of the decisions that affect my life will be made for me by Sword commanders who don't know me at all.

"I'm ready," I lie.

"I'm around, you know, if things go wrong and you need me. You can find me."

His earnestness makes my heart contract, and my entire being longs to reach out and hug him. "I'm around, too," I say softly. "You know, if things go wrong and you need me."

Hawthorne gives me a sad smile. He lifts his hand and rubs his ear where I'd wrenched it. "I just might need someone like you in a fight."

"Good," I reply. I turn and square my shoulders to the empty hallway. "I'll see you around, Hawthorne." I pass through the sliding doors into the Intake facility, then glance back over my shoulder. He's still there, watching me as the doors close.

Chapter 10
Intake

I walk past empty turnstiles and corrals that must be used to funnel new recruits along on Transition Day. It feels weird being the only one here. I reach two glass doors that slide open as I approach, leading me into a waiting room filled with rows of metal benches bolted to the floor. Soft chamber music plays through speakers in the ceiling. A beautiful blond woman about ten years older than me sprawls on one of the benches, gazing up at the ceiling, listening to music through wireless earpieces. It must be different music than the song playing overhead because the beat she taps with her black-booted feet is so much faster. Her hair is swept up in a tight twist above the collar of her red uniform. A loose overcoat of the same bright red hangs open and drapes from either side of the bench. She holds a stylus between her top lip and the bottom of her nose. Beside her on the bench rests a medical tablet, adorned with the Atom-Fated symbol of a carbon atom.

"Excuse me." I try to get her attention by waving my hand.

No response. I walk nearer and stand over her. She squeaks in fright, almost tumbling from the bench, and scrambles to her feet. The stylus hits the ground. "I didn't hear you come in!" She pulls the earpieces from her ears and shoves them into the pocket of her overcoat. "Intake has been suspended since the attack. No one is being processed until new monikers are issued. I wasn't expecting you." I hand her back the stylus, and her eyes widen. "You're Roselle St. Sismode!"

Her awe might be funny if I wasn't so nervous. "I'm . . . well, I'm just Roselle Sword now."

She realizes her breach of etiquette and nods, composing herself. "Of course. So, you've been assigned to Tree 177?"

"Yes." I thought that was obvious.

"Me, too!" She grins at me and holds her hand to her chest. I'm not sure what she wants from me, or what I'm supposed to do. She's grinning at me like we know each other, but I've never met her before. I fidget, feeling awkward. "Oh! You're here for intake!" she says, like the thought just occurred to her.

"Yes."

"I never dreamt I'd be the one to intake Roselle St. Sismode." She doesn't try to mask the giddiness in her voice. She retrieves her tablet, assuming a much more professional mien. "If you'll follow me." She leads the way through metal doors and down a hallway of doors to private rooms. We pass by other professionals in red coats, looking bored as they sit at desks and stare at walls, their chins resting in their Atom-monikered hands.

"My name is Emmy, by the way, and I'm here to make your intake go as smoothly as possible. If you have any questions, just ask." She guides me to a private room with an examination table and medical machinery. I cringe. The machinery seems archaic compared to the infirmary at the Sword Palace.

"Please take a seat on the table, and we'll get started."

The metal slab table in the middle of the room is less than inviting, but I take a seat. Like everything else here, the room has dark metal girders with exposed bolts. "Let me pull up your files, Roselle." Emmy sits beside me on the table with a friendly smile, then she gasps with a loud intake of breath. "You've been given a new moniker! You're a beta tester, like me. I thought only Atoms were testing it!"

I glance at my moniker. The sword-shaped hologram on my hand shines brighter than my old one, the crown more pronounced. "I was given a new one yesterday."

"Can I look at it?" She takes my hand, gently touching the small scar that the moncalate device left when Agent Crow implanted the new processor. "Your sword has a rose-colored ring around it. Why was it never removed?"

"The stain of the birthmark is deep, so the only solution would be to cut out the area of skin and regenerate tissue over it. My mentor was against it because he didn't want my training delayed for something he thought was frivolous. Since I'm secondborn, no one argued with him."

"Well, *I* think it's interesting," Emmy replies with a conspiratorial wink. "Have you used your new moniker yet?" She goes to the side table and retrieves a shiny silver, laser-like tool.

"What do you mean?"

"You're equipped with the latest technology. This is top-secret Atom device-ware. Your moniker is state of the art, impossible to clone. The Gates of Dawn will have a difficult time sneaking into our Fates when these beauties get implanted. They're going to start phasing them in soon to the general population."

"What's new about it?" I ask.

"Didn't anyone tell you how to use your moniker?"

"No."

She lifts my hand in her own again. "First of all, let's take care of this scar."

"I don't have any money to pay you."

"Oh, this one is free. They should've done this for you when you had it installed." She passes the laser over the incision mark. I feel heat, but nothing more. She sets the laser aside. Reaching into a drawer under the table, she extracts a handful of test-tube-shaped vials. She holds the shades of them to my hand until she finds a match for my skin tone.

She removes the cap to reveal a roller-ball applicator and rolls the vial over my incision mark. A cool, fleshy gel covers the scar. She caps the vial and drops it back into the drawer. Lifting the laser once more, she passes it over the gel. The gel melts and blends with my skin. The scar disappears.

"Thank you," I murmur. I've had this procedure done often. Training with fusionblades is dangerous.

Emmy lets go of my hand and sets the laser aside. "Here, let me show you what your new moniker can do. I just had mine installed last week." Holding up her hand, she shows me her silver moniker in the shape of a carbon atom—six electrons circle a cluster of six protons. "Mine will only respond to my own touch. It's a series of taps along the length of the moniker. Think of it as a keyboard." She taps the skin. A holographic screen alights. "Once you activate the screen, you can use this simple menu to interact with it."

"What does it do?" I ask.

"Well, that depends on your clearance level. I only have some of the most basic functions for my personal use. This will eventually replace our wrist communicators and my tablet. I'll be able to access files directly from my moniker. It's supposed to make my work more efficient. Here, let me show you." She looks at her menu bar, choosing options by glance alone. My profile alights on her holographic display. "This is the best function I've found so far! I'm going to contact you." She stares at my profile on her display. Menu items blink as she chooses them. The moniker in my hand vibrates. My eyes widen. "Aren't you going to answer it?" She laughs.

"How?"

"Tap the tip of the sword—long–short–long."

I do as she directs. A holographic display alights from my hand. "What now?" I ask.

"Okay, stare at the menu display that reads 'Incoming contact.' Now choose 'Accept.'"

I do, and the holograph above my hand changes to display the side of her face. She peers into her own screen. Her full-faced grin broadcasts in a tiny hologram. "Hi!"

"Hi!" I can't help but smile. We play around with the contact feature until I get the basics of it down. Emmy insists that I add her to my contact list. She shows me other features, like the guidance system that will help me navigate Tree 177 and other areas of the Stone Forest Base.

Finally, Emmy sighs. "You should explore your moniker more in your downtime. Just remember that whatever files you access are logged."

"What do you mean?"

"They can track your location, what you've been looking at, and who has contacted you. It's all logged."

"Oh," I murmur. "Is there a way to turn that off?"

"I don't know. I think you'll have to ask one of the programmers. I'm medical." She lifts her tablet once more. "What would you like to do next, the med exam or placement?"

"Placement."

She nods. Her blond eyebrows lower in concentration, a tiny crease forming between them. "You're Tritium 101—T-101 for short. You've been assigned to the ambulatory brigade for active field operations. For now, you'll be tagging casualties in the field during active duty." She must know how grim her news is because she forges on with a fake optimism. "They have you slated for aviation training when you cycle out of active duty—whoa . . ." she says. "You must be seriously smart to have tested into pilot training."

"When does Tritium 101 go active?" I ask.

"You'll ship out to the front line in a few days."

"For how long?"

Her eyes are apologetic. "A rotation usually lasts a few months." My odds of making thirty days just dropped significantly. "You can contact me anytime you want while you're in the field. I'll always be available to you for counsel. I'll check in on you. I promise."

"Thank you."

"Ready for the medical exam?"

I nod numbly. She has me lie on the table and does a quick body scan with a handheld device. She asks about my bruises, but I tell her I fell and they don't bother me. She gives me a skeptical look but doesn't press. Instead, she has me sit up once more. "Everything looks normal—it all matches up with your records from a few months ago. Do you have any questions?"

"No."

"Let's get you outfitted then, shall we?" she asks with feigned brightness.

She guides me from this room to another down the hall. It's a shower facility of sorts. She directs me to take a shower. I've had one today, but I don't argue. When I'm done, I wrap myself in the coarse robe. My long hair is sodden and heavy. I towel off and exit the stall.

Emmy already has a uniform for me. The holograms on the lapels shine with brown swords, T-101 emblazoned on the glowing blades. Quickly, I change into it. It's the coarsest dull brown and beige I've ever worn. The boots are hardly better, stiff and unyielding.

Emmy bites her lip. "Normally, we'd cut your hair, but there's a note in your file that it's not to be cut. I have these." She holds up hair ties. "I'll show you how to style it a few different ways that will be acceptable to your CO. Don't deviate from them or you'll earn demerits, which will result in the loss of privileges."

"Why can't we just cut it?"

"I can't." She looks almost embarrassed. "I see this sometimes, when an intake subject is exceptionally lovely. There's sometimes a proviso that stipulates details about appearance."

"Who wrote the stipulation placed on me?" I ask.

She looks at her tablet. "Who *didn't*? There's a list."

My eyebrows slash together. "Who?"

"Sword Admiral Dresden, Sword Exo Clifton Salloway"—her voice goes up an octave—"Virtue Census Agent Crow!"

A parade of horribles. "Let's cut it," I reply.

"No!" She throws out both her hands, looking panicked. "I'm dead if you do." Although I think she's overreacting, I don't fight her. Instead, I sit in a chair in front of a mirror and study the way she styles my hair. "You're going to be a distraction in the ranks."

"Then let's cut it," I reply. I was never allowed to cut it before because Emmitt was in charge of my appearance. Maybe it's time to do what I want. I cast a defiant look in Emmy's direction. "What are they going to do, send me into battle?"

"Don't think for one second that your situation cannot change, Roselle. There is *much* worse than this. Do me a favor—try not to anger the powerful people who take an interest in you. It's bad for your survival."

I know she's right, but ever since I left my home, I've wanted nothing more than to rebel. A hollow darkness grows in my chest. I feel betrayed by everyone. Maybe this is how every secondborn feels when she finds herself here.

Emmy gathers a package filled with clothing that looks similar to what Hawthorne wore under his combat gear. She places it in a hoverbin to send to my quarters.

"Can I keep those?" I ask, indicating my discarded uniform and leather jacket. I don't know how things work here, but if chets are traded for information, then I wonder what one can get for leather, suede, and silk.

She bites her bottom lip. "I'm supposed to discard them. It's contraband." She looks around, and then picks them up and quickly stuffs the items underneath the other clothing in the hoverbin. "I know nothing about this if you get caught."

"Understood. Thank you."

She programs the drone, and it disappears into a wall tube unit. "Are you ready to see your capsule?" Emmy asks, referring to my sleeping quarters in the dormitory of one of the airships docked on the branches above us.

"I'm ready."

She leads me to the door. "I'm supposed to call one of your shipmates from Tritium 101 to come and retrieve you, but"—she looks around at the empty hallways—"because no one is here, I could take you there and show you around—if you don't object."

I smile. "I don't object."

"Yay! I can get out of here for a few hours!" She raises her arms over her head and scrunches up her face with exaggerated excitement. Dropping her arms, she calls down the hall. "Stanton, I'm taking a new recruit to her air-barracks!"

A bald man pokes his head out of a doorway. "Oi, bring me back a crella from the Base Exchange."

She shoots a finger gun at him with a wink. "You got it, even though those things are toxic for your blood. All that dough and sugar's gonna give you a heart condition."

"Only if I'm lucky," he calls back.

Emmy helps me program my guidance system to locate Tritium 101. We leave the Intake facility together, following the glowing map on my hand. We take a heartwood up to level 772, where she shows me which training facilities and dining hall are assigned to Tritium 101. "Don't make the mistake of failing to report for your ration rotation. If you miss mealtime, you're not allowed to make it up."

"Okay." We continue to an area that resembles a storefront.

"This is the Base Exchange where you can find edibles, entertainment items, personal items—you pay with merits. You can track your merits here, on your moniker." She shows me my profile menu on a different screen.

"I don't have any merits. I'm broke," I muse.

"You'll earn some. I have faith in you," she says. "But be careful how you earn them." Her warning hangs in the air. She purchases a few crellas for the staff back at her post, and we make our way through Deck 772. Branches split off, dark hallways that lead to ports where hanging dormitory airships attach to the exterior of the Tree. The trunk in the center has several sectors: hangars for fighter planes, training facilities, dining facilities, and communications and debriefing areas.

Following one of the branches off the deck, we enter a dark, winding hallway. An airlock to our right has a wide octagonal archway. Above it, the illuminated sign reads "Tritium 101."

We enter the dormitory airship. The inside is kidney-shaped and tiered like an amphitheater. Each tier has an iron-mesh walkway and columns of capsules stacked five high with round hatch doors. Ladder-like rungs and handrails alternate between columns. The doors are color-coded and numbered. Heartwoods move up and down the catwalks at intervals. The place is almost empty, just a few soldiers here and there.

"I'm Section Black, row 102, capsule 1001D."

She looks around. "There." She points to the section with black doors. "We can take that heartwood." Catching a step up, I hold on to the pole, taking it with Emmy up to row 102. We step off onto the iron catwalk and follow it until we locate capsule 1001D, the fourth in the pillar. I climb the rungs on one side. Emmy climbs the other. The round door has a scanner. It opens upward when I press my moniker beneath the laser. The capsule has a three-foot radius and about a nine-foot depth.

I climb inside. A thick white pallet, a thin white blanket, and a plump white pillow are the only items inside. I lie on the pallet.

"There's storage for some personal items beneath the pallet," Emmy says, pulling aside the mattress to uncover a shallow cubby beneath the metal slat. I fold the pallet back down. I can sit up without hitting my head. The ceiling is made of the same material as a virtual screen.

Emmy pushes a few buttons on the console by the door. The virtual screen turns on, dialed to live coverage of the Secondborn Trials. "Aw, that Petree Atom is divine, don't you think?" Emmy asks, sighing over the secondborn Atom champion as he enters a labyrinthine obstacle course that looks like it was designed by a complete sadist.

"He looks scared," I observe. And who wouldn't? All The Trials are designed to kill him.

Emmy climbs in next to me and we watch the screen, shoulder to shoulder. "He doesn't look scared," she disputes. "He looks determined."

I shake my head. "He looks like he's having second thoughts."

"He looks dreamy."

"Where are my clothes?"

"In your locker, in the shower facility in this sector. Do you want to see it?"

We leave the capsule. The door closes and locks automatically. We take the catwalk over to the lavatory. The room is used by both sexes. Rows of sinks and mirrors are everywhere. Individual shower rooms resemble small closets, timed for a five-minute shower in the morning and another after training. I have a designated locker with the same number as my capsule. Inside is a beige-and-brown active-duty uniform, one set of beige pajamas that resemble the clothing I got from Census, a pair of boots, shower slippers, socks, underwear, bra, combat armor, helmet, generic fusionblade, fusion rifle with cartridge, and personal items, all perfectly situated. "Everything a Sword needs to survive," Emmy says with a hint of sarcasm. "You have a schedule, Roselle. As soon as I release you into the system, you'll need to follow your schedule and join your unit. Failure to report for duty on time will result in demerits. Get enough demerits and there will be consequences."

"What kind of consequences?" I ask.

"Depends. Could be loss of meals, loss of privileges, detention—or more painful consequences. Read your Intake manual in your files. Here, this icon on your moniker has your schedule. You see these little icons?" A sword, a rifle, a uniform, armor, and more. "They will appear on your schedule so you'll know what you'll have to wear and bring with you for training. Your Stone-Fated locker room attendants will know what you need, and they'll have it ready for you. Just place your dirty gear back in here and it will be cleaned and returned."

I nod.

"You'll need to take your fusionblade with you everywhere you go from now on. You can leave your rifle here unless otherwise directed for training or combat purposes."

I take the fusionblade from my locker. It's not nearly as nice as my other one, the one from my grandfather, but it feels better to have it all the same. The smooth hilt is generic, except that it has been coded with my number: 00-000016. I buckle the thigh harness to my right leg and sheathe the weapon.

Emmy shows me the rest of the dormitory airship. There's a deck below our quarters where fighter planes are stowed. Mechanics and pilots work on the sleek vehicles and the troop movers, readying them for combat missions. The rest of the air-barracks is restricted to higher clearance levels and off-limits to Tropo soldiers like me.

"Most of what you'll do will take place in the trunk of a forest Tree or on the battlefield. This is really just your quarters. So now, I'll release you into the system and you'll get your first activity." She takes her tablet and stylus from her pocket. "Okay, open your schedule and tell me where you're supposed to be."

I open my schedule on my moniker. "Lunch," I say, "and then fusionblade training in facility Q."

"I'll walk with you as far as the dining hall. I'd eat with you, but I'm not coded for your facility," she explains. "And you wouldn't want me tagging along with you anyway. I may scare all of your potential Sword-Fated friends away—Atom-Fated, you know—we've sort of got a bad reputation lately because of the Gates of Dawn and all."

"I could never see you as the enemy, Emmy," I reply. "It would be nice to have a friend like you."

She grins at that. "You're special, Roselle. Try not to change."

A loud siren sounds, startling us both. I look around in panic. A red light blinks above one of the branching hallways. "It's okay," Emmy says. "That siren is a call to all the soldiers on this level to gather. A new airship has docked—returning soldiers from the front line. More airships will return over the next few days because a cycle is ending. This is a way of welcoming them back. Whenever you hear that siren, you have to drop whatever you're doing and go to the designated area."

We follow the flood of soldiers gathering in the trunk. Thousands of us crowd the main deck in front of a branch hall airlock. The airlock opens, and everyone around me applauds. The first grim-faced soldiers emerge from the dark tunnel and file by. Their uniforms look new, like mine, but the soldiers in them are as different from me as they can be. New fusionblade scars have turned faces to railway lines. Eyes are missing. Ears are missing. Fingers and hands are gone. These are just the ones who can walk.

The applause fades. Harrowed looks and a growing sense of horror ripple through the crowd. No one among the thronging crowd expected this kind of parade. They expected a victory celebration, not a procession of haunted stares. Red-coated medical professionals move through the crowd. Doctors rush soldiers past us on hovering gurneys to hospital facilities beneath the trunk.

As the last of the wounded are cleared, we move to leave, but the siren sounds again, and we both still. The red light turns on above the adjacent hallway. The hangar door lifts. Tropo, Strato, and Meso Sword soldiers file out of the tunnel, none of them injured. The crowd erupts. Hats fly into the air as war heroes file by, their expressions grim. The crowd quiets. The returning soldiers don't disperse. Instead, they wait in a wide circle with their backs to us.

Amy A. Bartol

The last two soldiers drag a severely beaten Tropo soldier across the floor. His head hangs listlessly as they carry him to the center of their ring. Then the unit commander appears from the shadows of the corridor. Battle scars etch his face. He surveys the gathered crowd. When he speaks, his voice booms throughout the deck.

"Soldiers!"

"Oosay!" Everyone answers as one.

"We have a coward in our midst!" He walks to the bleeding young man in the middle of the circle. If he's even conscious, he cannot hold his head up. Two soldiers hold him up by his arms.

"This man is a traitor!" the commander shouts. "Why, you may ask? What has he done, you may wonder? Nothing! He has done absolutely nothing!"

Confused chatter breaks out among the soldiers.

"His job," the commander continues, "is to beacon wounded soldiers in the field for evac. Did he do his job?" His hand shakes back and forth. "Passably. He tagged some wounded soldiers. Medical drones came to help the fallen. He did the minimum required of him."

He fishes into a pouch and holds up a black circular disc the size of a thumbnail. He holds it aloft, turning it. "This is a death-drone beacon. It is used when ambulatory medic soldiers come across a wounded *enemy* combatant! Simply place this beacon on the body of a wounded enemy soldier and alert a death drone. The death drone will arrive and interrogate your enemy for you! The *death drone* will determine whether that *enemy* should be transported to a Base for further interrogation. If there is no need for your *enemy* to continue breathing the air that belongs to *you*, the death drone will deliver swift and righteous justice to your *enemy*!"

Manic applause ripples through the onlookers. The commander nods. "Do you know how many death drones were summoned by this soldier?" the commander asks. "Zero." He makes a 0 with his hand and

118

turns so that everyone can see it. "He did not tag a single one of your *enemies* for termination."

Soft hisses build among the crowd and the soldiers.

"That *means* that those of you who are about to ship out on your next active tour will have to face the same Gates of Dawn soldiers that could've been killed if he'd done his *job*!"

The commander points to the unconscious soldier, circling. After a full rotation, he approaches the wounded man. Holding the pouch of beacons above the Tropo's head, the commander empties the satchel. The discs cascade down, sticking like black rain to the soldier's skin and uniform. A deafening surge of cheers erupts again.

The other soldiers drop the wounded man and back away. Death drones pause at the threshold of the hallway where the soldiers emerged. The entire deck grows silent. Everyone backs away from the tagged man.

Except me. I step toward him.

Emmy grasps my sleeve. "Roselle," she hisses. "There's no saving him now." I yank my arm from her and push through the crowd.

Black-bodied death drones emerge silently from the adjacent tunnel, like giant bats from the maw of a cave, following the call of the beacons—the sound too high-pitched for us to register.

Hovering over the wounded soldier's body, one death drone flashes blue laser lights upon its bloody target. The other drones join it, and the soldier is covered in blue triangles. A moment passes, then two. My throat tightens. I try to get closer, but broad shoulders block my advance, and before I can find a way through, the death drones begin to fire steel slugs into the brain of the Tropo soldier.

I turn from the carnage, feeling ill. Emmy, who had been following, takes me by the arm and wrenches me away from the cheers and jeers of the overworked mob. She drags me into a lavatory and pushes me into a private stall near the back. "Breathe slower," she says softly. I bend and try to catch my breath. She places her cool hand on the back of my neck.

"They never even gave him a trial!" I whisper.

"There are no trials here, Roselle. There's only survival. You go against them and you forfeit the right to breathe their air."

"You can't believe that," I mutter.

"It's true." She takes a few deep breaths with me. "I can't save everyone, but this is my shot at saving you. Keep your head down. Do your job and you'll get through this. The harder you work, the faster you'll rise, and you could make it out of here. It won't always be like this. This war will be over one day and things will go back to normal."

"What's normal?"

She shakes her head. "I don't know—less violence, more boredom. Listen, let me show you to your dining hall, get you some water. You can schedule time to come and talk to me during my office hour rotations when your unit is stationed here. You'll be okay."

Straightening, I nod. A smile of relief crosses her lips. We leave the bathroom together, and my hand shakes as I raise it to look at the map above my moniker. Emmy pretends she doesn't see my overactive nerves. We follow the map to the nearest cafeteria.

"This is where I leave you, Roselle," Emmy says at the entrance. "You can contact me on your moniker if you have questions."

"Okay." I nod. But it's not okay. I'm numb.

"Here." She shoves the bag of crellas into my hand. "You need these more than Stanton. Remember what I said. Contact me if you need me." With that, she turns and walks to a heartwood, steps onto it, and disappears from sight.

Chapter 11
That Newcomer Smell

There's almost nowhere to be alone here. The mob sweeps me into the dining hall. Overheated boys slap each other on the backs and shout boisterously to companions. Those who seem disturbed by what they just saw are harder to find.

I scroll through the carousel of cuisine options, the bag of crellas under my arm. The selection of palatable food is limited. The meat options look suspect. I opt for porridge with fruit, toast, and cheese. Ample portions are jettisoned onto a hovering tray that trails me, tracking my moniker as I walk through the seating area. Most of the tables are completely occupied. Every time I think I locate an empty seat, someone looks up, sees me coming, and slides a tray into the empty space at the table. After the fourth time, I begin to take it personally.

Farther back in the dining hall, the uniforms change from beige and blue to other hues. Golden-colored uniforms—Fate of Stars power and technology engineers—are also assigned to this facility. But there is no intermingling between Swords and Stars. I see the red-colored uniforms of the Fate of Atoms medical and science engineers, but not the orange-colored uniforms of the Stone-Fated workers.

I attempt to join a table occupied by four Star-monikered engineers. They seem alarmed as I take a seat and my hovering tray settles in front of me. Three of them rise and depart, leaving half-eaten entrees behind. The trays quickly clear themselves from the table. I turn to the Star-Fated man beside me. The tag on his uniform reads *Jakes*.

"You must be new here," he mutters. He shovels food into his mouth as if he's never eaten before, or else he's trying to eat fast so he can leave.

"I was processed this morning." I rest the package of crellas on the table beside me. I unfold a cloth napkin in my lap, pick up my spoon, and stir my steaming porridge. I have no appetite for it, but I know I need to eat it. I have training after this. "Why did they leave?"

"They don't want any trouble."

"Am I trouble?"

"Not only are you a Sword, you're *The* Sword."

"My mother is *The* Sword. I'm just the secondborn Sword. I should be treated like everyone else here."

He snorts. "Good luck with that. If you're looking for fairness and equality, you've come to the wrong place. Let me clue you in. We're not supposed to sit together, even if you weren't St. Sismode. Fates don't intermingle."

"Where's it written that I'm not allowed to sit with you?"

"It's not written—everyone just knows it."

"It's a ridiculous rule, and I don't see you leaving."

He doesn't look at me. "I'm hungry. I missed breakfast and I don't have a lot of success earning merits." His thick glasses are proof. He could correct his vision if he had the merits to do it. "Why did you sit with us anyway? Don't you want to fit in with your own kind?"

"I couldn't find a seat with them."

"They're giving you the hot end of the sword, are they?" he asks with a sarcastic smile. "I'm not surprised. Most of them have under-developed brains coupled with mommy and daddy issues. They were turned over to the government before they got their first pimple because their families began to fear them." His scorn is sharper because it's true.

"You act like you fear them."

He waves his hand, gesturing to the sea of brown and blue uniforms around us. "I am somewhat outnumbered here."

"True." I try a bite of my porridge and wince. It's awful.

"Not what you were expecting?" he asks, gesturing toward my bowl.

"That would be an understatement."

He sets aside his fork and wipes his mouth. "If you live long enough, you'll still never get used to it." He begins to stand.

"I didn't sit at your table looking for a friend, Jakes." Our eyes meet.

"What do you want?" he asks, sitting back down on the edge of his seat.

I take my fusionblade from my thigh-strapped scabbard and slide it onto the table between us. "Can this be converted to hydrogen power?"

He looks at the weapon, then at me. "Why would you want to do something like that? Fusion is so much more powerful than hydrogen."

"I'm asking if it can be done. Can it?"

His hand reaches out and touches the cool silver hilt. "I think so. I'd have to play around with one to be sure, but I think you can swap out a fusion-powered cell for a hydrogen-powered one and still keep it in the same housing."

"I don't want to swap it out. I want a way to switch it over. A fusionblade and a hydroblade in one unit. Is there a way to toggle between them? I'll make it worth your while. I never forget a kindness."

He leans back in his chair. "What do I get in return?"

"These, to start." I push the paper bag toward him.

He looks at it warily, then pulls it nearer and opens it. His face brightens. "How did you get these?" he asks. "There are four of them here! I've only ever had a small piece of a crella."

"Consider this a payment for hearing me out. If you can't help me, all I ask is that you don't say anything to anyone else. If you can help me, I'll be in this dining hall for every meal until I ship out for active duty in a couple of days. We can discuss payment when you have something for me."

Jakes closes the bag and tucks it inside a small satchel. "I'll think about it." He rises as if to leave.

I grasp his wrist and squeeze it lightly. "Think about it fast. I don't have much time."

Jakes begins to nod when a rough hand falls on his shoulder and forces him back down into his seat. "Aw, this is a pretty picture." A snub-nosed Sword cadet with a shaved head crouches between us. "Are yous having a date night or something? Is this an automated pay-to-play meetin'?" Behind us, four Tropos laugh. "I says it has to be random because no one would ever sleep with *this* guy on purpose." The beefy hand of the Sword comes down hard again on Jakes's shoulder.

The malicious man turns to me and sneers. "Look here! We have a celebrity in our midst! Tell me, Roselle"—his eyebrows come down in a thoughtful look—"do you plan to sleep with every male you meet? I hear that you and Clifton Salloway are quite the thing. What would your mother say?"

I reach up, grip the back of his bald head, and slam his forehead on the table. His head bounces and leaves a bloody indentation in the veneer. He slides to the floor and groans. I lift my fusionblade, ignite it, and swing its golden glow between me and the man on the ground's entourage. They back away warily. I look at Jakes's pale, strained face. "You can go now."

He lurches to his feet, a bead of sweat dropping from his brow. Gathering his possessions, he slips away from the table and out of the dining hall. I extinguish my sword, tuck it back into my scabbard, sit, and resume eating as if nothing had happened. The groaning soldier's friends drag him away as he holds his head. I pretend not to notice the thousand pairs of eyes fixated on me. I finish my meal and leave the hall in time to make the next appointment on my schedule.

Jump training is my first class. I suit up in lightweight combat armor and am pushed out of a simulator module that mimics the velocity of being tossed out of a troopship. The free fall to the simulated terrain is the easy part. I learn to stretch out as the air pushes against me, and the terrain detector on my suit activates, creating a force that fights gravity and slows my descent. Then I feel as if I'm being torn apart; my limbs want to keep falling while my torso is held back. The instructor screams, "Back straight and chest out!" I use every muscle available as he hollers at me to lift my head before it smashes into the ground when the gravity regulator turns off. I hit the simulated dirt hard enough to knock the wind out of me.

I'm not unhappy to strip off the armor at the end of the training session. I rub my sore neck and hurry to my next class: weapons training. I'm instructed on the parts of a rifle. I listen to the instructor with only half an ear because I already know everything he explains. He notices my inattention and calls on me. "You there. Come 'ere. You think you're too clever for this class?"

"No, Patrøn."

"I want you to reassemble this rifle and shoot that target there." He pulls a timepiece from his pocket. "Go."

I reassemble the rifle in under ten seconds and shoot the target. The shot is dead-on. An unbidden smile crosses his lips, and his eyes narrow in mirth. He turns his timepiece to show the other instructor, whose mouth shapes an *O*. For the rest of the session, they make me shoot at everything that moves on their simulated battlefield. A crowd forms to watch me take down simulated enemies with one-shot-one-kill accuracy, eliciting wary and envious stares from my fellow classmates.

My next class is fusionblade training. I'd like to skip this one. I'm already a pariah, my advanced training alienating me from my fellow Tropo cadets, but there's no way of avoiding it, so I enter the training room and stretch while we await the instructor.

The instructor's name is Chaplan. He's Meso, two ranks above me. Tall and strong with a full beard and green eyes, he instructs us to call him "Master of Swords" or "Master" for short. He gives us an initial demonstration of his skills, and although he has a decent understanding of how to wield a fusionblade, he doesn't strike me as someone who has mastered it.

We pair off and use modified training swords capable of leaving burns and bruises but not removing limbs. The first cadet I pair with has had next to no training. He's not happy that I know more than he does and asks to switch partners during our first break.

I beat several cadets in mock battles, and then I'm asked to spar with Master Chaplan's assistant, Brody. Master Chaplan stops the fight when it's plain that I could take Brody's head off. The Master taps in, relieving his assistant. He indicates that I should switch from my training fusionblade to my combat sword.

I bow to him as is customary, straighten, and stand before him, watching as he executes a series of moves. I'd be impressed if they weren't my moves from a virtual access instructional training session recorded a few years ago. *Is he trying to let me know he has trained with me, or is he trying to pass that off as his own work?*

Whatever the case, he gets cheers from the cadets. They're waiting for someone to take me down a notch. Apparently, no one likes a know-it-all. I consider deference for a few seconds, and then my pride kicks in, and I change my mind. "Are you ready, cadet?" Master Chaplan asks with palpable condescension.

My chin dips, a small assent. I hold my sword with both hands, the hilt near my right shoulder. He circles me, his back stooped as if he's more inclined to wrestle than to battle with swords. I stand perfectly still. Waiting. He charges at me from behind. I easily catch the angle of his sword with my own, blocking him. He lunges. I sidestep, planting my left foot on his thigh, twisting my body, and wrapping my right ankle around his throat. Then it's only a matter of arching my back and throwing my weight backward, which chokes him and causes him to fall flat on his back lest I snap his head from his neck. With a small backflip, I land on my feet.

He struggles to rise from the mat, startled and winded. He gazes around at the silent crowd, rattled by the takedown, but instead of acknowledging my skill, his pride gets the better of him. He begins to stalk me again.

I wish he wouldn't take this personally, but he has. He lowers his eyelids and puckers his mouth. I kick him in the side and block his sword as it descends from above my head. My kick moves him into position in front of me, and I swing my fusionblade across my body from right to left. At the last possible second before striking, I loosen my grip. The blade extinguishes as I sweep it across his body. Everyone cries out, certain that they'll see him fall in pieces. My grip tightens again once the blade has cleared his body, the move so quick it creates the illusion that my sword passed right through him.

It's a parlor trick, and if Dune were here, he'd scold me for it, but I don't feel the least bit guilty. Master Chaplan drops his sword and touches his chest with rising panic. He stares at me as understanding dawns. His mouth is no longer pinched in anger. It contracts in fear as he realizes he's punching above his weight.

From behind me, someone claps slow and loud. "Bravo! Brav-o!" It's Agent Crow. A group of black-coated Census agents wind their way around the room, taking up positions by the doors. I extinguish my sword and sheathe it.

"You do have a knack," Agent Crow says, "for making people look ridiculous." He turns to my instructor, whose face is mottled and flushed. "Don't worry. I once underestimated her, too. It's a failing that we cannot be too hard on ourselves for committing. We must both promise each other never, ever to do it again."

Agent Crow strolls toward me, his black leather coat flaring in his wake. The training facility has grown quiet. "Agent, to what do we owe the honor of your presence?" Chaplan asks.

"Census has been given a new assignment. It just came down to us today." Agent Crow indicates the other Census agents lining the room. Soft murmurings of unease ripple through the crowd. "I've been tasked with transitioning this Base to new monikers." The Census agents begin lining up the soldiers against the wall and scanning their existing monikers with handheld devices. "If you would please, step that way, Master of Swords. All of your questions will be answered by my associates." He raises his hand and gestures in the direction of another Census agent. I try to leave as well, but Agent Crow blocks my path.

"I already have a new moniker, Agent Crow. There's no need to detain me. I'll leave you to your duty."

He lifts my left hand, admiring the glow of the silver sword hologram. He frowns, his thumb running over my skin. "You had your scar removed." His look is accusatory, as if I'd removed his brand of ownership.

I pull my fingers from his grasp, my back rigid. "This must be a boring job for you, Agent Crow, being the hunter that you are."

He smiles, showing the gleam of steel teeth. "I thought that at first. This kind of work dulls the senses, but it's proving to be interesting."

"I'm sure you'll enjoy tearing into people's flesh." I try to walk away again, but he grasps me by my upper arm, staying me. I shake him off and back away a step.

"Don't you want to know what I've discovered?" he asks. "Or should I say, who I've discovered?" *Does he know about Dune?* I raise my eyebrows because I don't trust my voice enough to speak. He comes closer, touching his halo-shaped moniker. The hologram changes to an image of Agnes Moon. "It would seem that your friend had a few secrets of her own."

Agent Crow stares at the menu on his moniker, selecting another option. It changes from Agnes's profile to an image of her beaten almost beyond recognition. "The woman who came to take you from my custody was an imposter. She had a cloned moniker." Bile rises in the back of my throat as I view the gruesome postmortem image. Agent Crow leans in close. "Thank you for the soaps, by the way. Did you know that if you wrap them in a towel, they become quite an effective bludgeoning weapon?"

I shudder. The thought that I may have provoked him is not something I can just shove away. "You murdered her. She was no more thirdborn than you or I."

He grabs my elbow. "Careful, Roselle. Questioning the integrity of a Census agent has consequences." I clench my teeth, knowing that there's nothing I can do to prevent him from hurting whomever he wants, and calling it justice.

He strokes my hair. "What I find most intriguing is that this Moon-Fated Agnes would be an advocate for you. Why would a thirdborn enter Census knowing that she could be discovered?"

I shy away from his touch. "I'd imagine that she was instructed to do it. Grisholm Wenn-Bowie was particularly interested in you, Agent Crow, in my debriefing. He found the idea of sending you that basket amusing." *Disinformation. Steer him away from Hawthorne.*

"The First Commander is interested in very little that happens outside the Fate of Virtues, that I can promise you. You must have made an impression on him."

"I've known him for a long time. One could say I've left a dent in him," I reply. "Did Agnes say someone sent her?" How much does he know? I cannot allow this to lead back to Hawthorne, Walther, or Dune. The thought of Dune at the mercy of Agent Crow pains me.

"I never got around to asking Agnes about her connections—I know it was bad form. Anger does not usually overwhelm me, but she was solely to blame for it. She provoked me at every turn. Her relentless pursuit of your release was something I found . . . personal."

"It wasn't personal. It was her job as a Sword advocate."

He ignores me. "In light of this new information regarding Agnes Moon, her being thirdborn, I have some questions for you, Roselle.

It'd be more appropriate to ask them in the secure surroundings of an interrogation cell in Census." He raises his hand to my mouth. His thumb brushes my cheek, skimming over the scab there. It's still sore from Hawthorne wrestling me to the floor. "I'd like the chance to taste your blood." I pull away.

Four military policemen approach us. A dark blue armband, bearing an emblem of a golden sword over a black shield, encircles each soldier's left arm. "Roselle Sword," the lead MP addresses me, "you've been found in violation of code 47257. You're ordered to come with us."

I know the code he's referring to. I violated it just a few hours ago. It's called brandishing. I'm not allowed to ignite my fusionblade in noncombat or non-training situations. I don't resist when cuffs restrain my wrists.

Agent Crow scowls at the MP. "I have reason to suspect this soldier has information regarding an investigation into thirdborns."

"She violated code. She gets a couple nights in the cooler. You can visit her there, at the detention center, and ask your questions. Contact her commanding officer if you want to make arrangements to see her."

Agent Crow's eyebrows slash together. "I cannot possibly ask the kind of questions that I need to ask in your facility. This is classified information." They ignore him. I'm relieved of my weapon by the youngest of the soldiers.

The one in charge is a middle-aged man with the lined face of someone who has seen a lot. The creases around his mouth deepen. "Then I guess you're gonna have to wait until she gets out," he says. "Oh, but her regiment is scheduled to go active in less than forty-eight hours." He snaps his fingers, like the thought only just occurred to him. "You'll have to follow her to the battlefield to get your answers." He leans closer to Agent Crow. "But then, men like you don't fight when your enemy has a weapon and can fight back, do you?"

Agent Crow gives him an icy stare. "You'll live to regret this." The dark lines by his eyes bunch together.

Secondborn

"I've lived to regret a lot of decisions, Census. This ain't one of 'em."

"Who's your commanding officer?" Agent Crow demands.

"Commander Aslanbek," he replies in a bored tone. I bet a lot of people ask him that, hoping to intimidate him. "Say your good-byes. You can see her in a few months when she gets back from active duty."

My smile for Agent Crow is forced, intended to make him believe that I don't fear him. Right now, it's the best I can do. I'd been waiting for the MPs to arrive and arrest me since lunchtime, but I hadn't known I'd be grateful to see them.

"Don't get comfortable, Roselle," Agent Crow murmurs.

I don't respond as the soldiers march me out and onto a heartwood.

Chapter 12
Detention

We travel almost all the way down the Tree's trunk to the detention center on the second level. The lead MP scans his moniker at the steel doors. One thick door opens. Inside is a small antechamber with a glass divider to a larger area. We walk to the glass. Behind it, a lone guard waits.

"One for detention. Detainee was quiet," the lead MP says to the female guard on duty behind the glass. "No additional charges to assess, Tula." The guard, in possession of my generic fusionblade, deposits the weapon into a phloem. The air-powered pipeline sweeps it away.

"Scan her over to us," Tula replies without inflection.

The lead MP takes me to the panel on the wall. My cuffs are taken off and my moniker is scanned. A piece of the glass that separates this room from the rest of the facility descends into the floor. "Step through," the lead MP orders. I obey, passing through a laser that scans my entire body. On the other side, I look at the glass, which projects my complete body-image scan. I can see all my vital organs and the moniker chip inside my hand. The missing piece in the glass ascends from the floor and seals shut.

"Present your hands," Tula orders. I do as she says, and she cuffs my wrists in front of me. We walk a few steps to another guard. "One for cell 685." She lets me go and returns to her post.

I'm remanded into the custody of an older guard with thinning hair. He leads me away and scans me through several corridors to a hallway of individual cells. He opens one and indicates that I should enter. I do. He formally reads me my sentence of forty-five hours' confinement. The officer takes off my cuffs and leaves, closing the cell door behind him. Sinking wearily onto the bottom bunk of a stack five high, I cover my eyes with my hands, thanking whatever providence allowed me to escape Agent Crow for a third time.

"Brandishing is sort of an asinine thing to get arrested for," a lilting feminine voice informs me from a bunk above mine. I thought I was alone. She sticks her head over the side of her berth, two pallets up, and looks down at me. "Are you thickheaded or something? Why would you threaten some heathens with a sword in front of everyone? I can think of better ways to get your point across."

"I find that being direct works for me," I reply.

She snorts. "Being direct here isn't the best strategy." Her black hair falls around her face. She has a line of star tattoos over each of her eyebrows. "It gets you thrown in the cooler faster than you can say 'St. Sismode Sword.' Would you look at that? I just said your name, and I didn't even mean to. It's just a saying we have here."

"It's a stupid saying," I mutter.

"Aye, maybe 'tis at that, but I'm not wrong about what I said. Brandishing is a threat for the slow-witted. Never threaten. Promise—in private—and back it up with something more than words."

"I'm sorry, I didn't catch your name."

"Flannigan, but my friends call me Flan."

"What are you here for, Flannigan?" I ask.

"Ah, this and that, if you know what I mean."

"No, I'm fairly slow-witted, so you'll have to explain it to me."

"I get things. Things people need. Useful things."

"You're a thief?"

"I'm a privateer," she retorts. Her hand hangs over the bunk, showing her Stone-Fated moniker.

"Those stars above your eyebrows, what do they mean?" I ask.

"I fell in love with the night." They look as if they're ascending over the peaks of her eyebrows, like rising stars over mountains. "I have a business proposition for you."

"A what?"

"I need your assistance. In return, I'll be indebted to you until such time as I can return the favor."

"Why would I need the services of a failed privateer?"

"I'm very good at what I do." She narrows her eyes at my insult.

I can't believe I'm having this conversation with her. "If you're such an exemplary privateer, why is it that you're locked up in a cell?"

"I wanted to get caught." She sniffs and looks at her black-painted fingernails.

I think she must be joking, but her expression doesn't change. "Why would you want to get caught?"

She climbs down from her perch and stands by my bunk, waiting for me to move over. I grudgingly scoot to the wall and she lies beside me, her black hair covering mine. "I wanted to get locked up because it'll give me time to figure out a strategy to escape," she whispers.

The thought of escaping this existence is a tempting one. I have no idea where I'd go, but anywhere seems better than here, within reach of Agent Crow. "Why would detention be any easier to escape than your air-barracks?"

"It isn't, but I needed a place to hide."

"From whom?"

"Monsters in black coats."

"You're hiding from Census? In here?" I gesture to our cell.

"That's right," she whispers. "They're changing out monikers. Mine is cloned—they'll be able to tell when they extract it. I must find a way off this Base without getting caught. They're working on the Tritium

101 monikers right now because we're scheduled to ship out soon to the Twilight Forest, and from there, the front line. I just have to avoid them until we do."

I'm shocked. "You're in my air-barracks?"

"Aye. It was me who put your leather jacket in your locker for you. I never felt leather that nice before. It's contraband, mind you, and if they catch you with it, you'll do time in here again. You're in Section Black, same as me, except I'm in the underdeck, where they put all Stones who assist Swords."

My eyebrows lower in confusion. "I didn't see my leather jacket in my locker."

"Oh, I hid it for you. It's there, in the false bottom that I created for you. You're welcome, by the way."

"Thank you."

"I can find a buyer for you, if you're interested. You can get quite a few merits for it, if you go through me."

"Are you thirdborn?" I ask, on a hunch.

She wrings her hands, the first sign of fear I've seen from her. "No. I'm secondborn. I just don't come from the Fate of Stones."

"You're from Stars."

"Aye." She points to her tattoos. "I got these beauties before I became a privateer."

"Why would you change your moniker?"

"Stone-Fates don't have many advantages. It's probably the worst Fate to be born into if you have ambition, but it's the best Fate if you want to become invisible. No one sees us, even in our orange uniforms. We're beneath notice. Being invisible is an advantage for someone in my profession."

"What will happen if you're caught?"

Her face pales, and she looks away from me. "They may think I'm a good-for-nothin' thirdborn, but even if they do believe that I'm secondborn, they'll want to know how I came by my cloned moniker, and that I can't tell 'em. If I do, people will die. So they'll torture me until I talk, or until they kill me. Either way, it's not worth livin' for. I have this." She holds up a small white capsule. "Cyanide. It's a better death."

I rub my forehead. The stress of the day has brought on a headache. "Listen, I'll help you avoid Census. Please get rid of that."

"I promise you that I will pay you back."

"You don't have to."

"Why would you help me and not expect payment in return?" She's studying me.

I lower my chin, unable to meet her hazel eyes. "I'm responsible for Census's getting someone who tried to help me—a Moon-Fated advocate. An agent named Crow killed her. In a way, I owe a debt."

"Then, you'll help me . . . for real." She expels a pent-up sigh.

"I'll help you. What's your plan?"

&

A little more than thirty-two hours later, at around midnight, I'm writhing on my bed, pretending to be ill, watching as Flannigan tries to get the attention of the MP on duty. It takes a lot of door-banging, jumping up and down, and hand-waving, but she finally gets a detention guard to come into the cell.

"Oi, are you sick?" the guard asks, twisting his mustache like he doesn't believe a word.

I groan. "I'll be okay," I reply, holding my hand to my stomach, lying on my bunk in the fetal position. "Stomach problems. I ate the porridge."

He's not unsympathetic and calls an Atom-Fated medic for me. The medic dispenses a couple of antacids and tells me to drink water. Before the guard leaves, Flannigan rests her hand on his arm and thanks him. The guard sees the doctor out and closes the cell door behind them.

When he's gone, I sit up, drinking water to wash away the taste of the chalky antacids. "Did you get it?" I ask.

"Aye." She sits beside me on the bunk, showing me her moniker, which has changed from a brown mountain-range symbol to a silver sword-shaped symbol.

"How did you do that?" I ask.

"'Tis my processor. They call it a copycat. It cost me a fortune, and by tomorrow, it'll be absolutely worthless. The new monikers repel its ability to infiltrate the technology. Until someone comes up with a way to beat the new moniker processors, I'm in serious trouble."

"Do you still have your old moniker?"

"I do, but it's not here. It's back in Stars. I couldn't let it be found on me when I crossed fatedoms."

I lift her hand and admire the sword hologram. "Have you been many places?" I ask.

"I've been everywhere. I've had thousands of lives that were not my own." She doesn't look much older than twenty as she stands and crooks her finger at me. "And now, whenever you're ready, I'll have one more to share with you. Follow me, and we'll be Holcomb Sword for a while." She giggles, like this is a game, but it's a deadly game, and I'm just waking up to the fact that I'm ready to play it.

When the hallway is clear, Flannigan scans her cloned moniker at the gateway. Circumventing the guarded hallways, we reach the heavily guarded outer gate of the detention center, and Flannigan pulls me into a room filled with cleaning equipment. She opens a grated vent at the back wall. "Follow me," she whispers and disappears into the vent. I climb in next to her, and she pulls the grate back into place. We crawl through a metal shaft that leads to another grate. This one empties out into a dim concrete tunnel.

This tunnel is empty and dank, lined with sapwood pipes that transport water, fuel, and waste along the trunk of the Tree. It also has clear tubes filled with data lines. Flannigan looks directly at one of these and follows it down the tunnel until she comes to a small access panel with a holographic scanner. "There it is," she says, rubbing her hands together.

"What is it?" I ask. My heart is pounding. I'm afraid we'll be caught at any moment. Flannigan doesn't seem to share my concern and places Holcomb's moniker under another scanner. "What are you doing?"

"I'm accessing the detention center's inmate roster, making it look as if you were in our cell all night. I'm scheduling you for release at five a.m. I, on the other hand, was never even there. No connection will exist between us. You won't have to go back to the cell. I'll make the action log close out seamlessly."

"You can do that? You can take yourself right out of the detention center logs?"

"I can do anything," she says. Her grin is full of bravado. "Watch—I just erased myself from this Base."

"What happens if we get caught?"

"We won't." She winks at me. "This is like a golden halo stroll down the streets of Purity," she whispers.

"How do you know how to do this?" I ask.

She quirks her eyebrow. "I'm a Star, remember? I was born to create this kind of technology for the ease and comfort of the aristocracy. I got bored and decided to see the world instead." She plucks at holographic screens with her index finger.

"Of all the places to go, I'm surprised that you ended up here." Something isn't quite right about Flannigan. She may try to appear as if she's just a free spirit, but there are an underlying intensity and drive that don't quite fit what she's telling me.

"I took a wrong turn." She shrugs. "Believe me, I want out of here as fast as I can manage it." That I can believe. She closes down the holographic screen. "There," she says triumphantly. "We are officially free women." She links arms with me. "C'mon, let me show you my world. But first!" She holds my hand and lifts her boot up. Sliding the heel to the side, she reveals a small compartment. From it, she extracts two pieces of thin metal, two inches by four inches. She slides the heel closed and extracts a couple of fingerless gloves from the heel of her other boot. Both are left-handed.

"This," she says, holding up one of the pieces of metal, "is lead." She opens a small slot between the finger and the thumb of one of the gloves and slides the metal into it. She hands me the glove. "Put this on."

I slide the black glove on my hand. The lead covers my moniker.

"Your moniker can be tracked. Right now, your signal is coming from the detention center. When you move away from it, you leave a trail, unless your moniker becomes invisible by blocking that signal. With that glove, you can walk right by a stinger and it will never know you're there. It won't challenge you. It won't report you to the MPs. It will be blind. Stinger drones send out high-frequency pings that interact with your moniker. With the source covered, they get no feedback." She puts her own glove on. "Now, let's see what mischief we can find."

We set off. She locates internal heartwoods used solely by the Stars, Atoms, and a few Swords who maintain the Tree Base's infrastructure. I head toward the one that leads up, but she grabs my arm. "We can't go up," she says. "Most of the Census agents are up, replacing monikers. We go down."

One level down, we come to a laundry. Even at this hour of the night, Stone workers are busy washing bedding and uniforms. We bypass them by sneaking behind the large industrial machines. The tumble and hum drown out our sound. Coming to a separate aisle, we're hidden behind large racks of black leather coats.

"Here." Flannigan takes a long black coat from the rack and holds it up to me. She hands it to me, along with the white uniform shirt and black trousers of a Census agent.

"What is this for?" I ask, as she chooses a tailored coat for her small frame.

"Don't you want to get your fusionblade back?" she asks, slipping on the white Census shirt. She stares at me, a challenge.

"How do you know about my fusionblade?"

"I make it a priority to know all there is to know about the soldiers I serve."

"No," I murmur, shaking my head. "Something's wrong. You know entirely too much about me. Did you know I was going to be put into detention?"

"It was over three hours from the time you brandished to the time they picked you up. In that time, Census made a move on you. You can connect the dots."

"You had me picked up?"

"Of course I did. No one reported you—it's the Sword secondborn code never to rat on each other or you're labeled a turner, and turners die badly. I had to do something or Agent Crow was going to kill you." She slips into the black trousers.

"Who are you?" I ask, not moving.

"I'm a friend. Now do you want to get your sword back or not? This is the only chance you'll get. The Census agents are busy changing out the Tritium 101 monikers, which means there are only a few left behind to guard the lair." She completes her ensemble with a black-leather flat cap that hides her hair and shadows her face. It's not the uniform of a Census agent, but it may go unnoticed.

"How would we ever find it? There's a network of tunnels below this entire Base."

"I have the schematics," she replies. She locates a bag stashed among the coats, and reaching in, she extracts a wrist communicator. "I can't turn on the communicator until we're underground or it will be noticed." She puts on the powered-down wristband.

"This is insane."

"No more insane than them taking away everything you cherish in one day. In light of that, I think this is a very sane decision."

She walks toward the heartwoods, taking the bag with her, slinging the strap of it over her shoulder. I follow, and we descend together toward ground level. Flannigan tries hard to hold back a smile. "I'm glad you could make it," she says. I stuff my hair up into the flat cap and pull the short leather bill down low to shadow my face.

When we reach the ground floor, we cross out of the utility corridors and exit into a warehouse area. Crossing it is simple. We just move as if we own the place. Stingers patrol the perimeter, but they're blind to us.

We approach Census's steel bunker doors. Two more stingers, like enormous hovering wasps, vibrate in the air on either side of them. Icy fear prickles my spine. I swallow down bile. We stop by the door's scanner. The hum of the automated sentinels grows louder. Every impulse tells me to turn and run. Instead, I stand absolutely still between a stinger and the privateer.

Flannigan eases a small box from the bag. It contains a row of moniker chips individually encased in lead sleeves. She chooses one and slips it from its cover before returning the lead sleeve and box to the bag. The moniker's hologram shines with aqua light, resembling a cresting wave of water in Flannigan's palm.

It's a firstborn's Sea-Fated moniker.

I have a moment of sheer panic, thinking the stingers will turn on us when they read the pings from the roiling moniker on her palm. Neither one moves. The identity must have authorization to be in this area. The scanner illuminates when Flannigan flashes the shiny, tumbling wave beneath it.

The bunker doors roll open.

Flannigan steps inside the bunker. I follow behind. The doors slide closed. Two armed soldiers stand across a narrow hallway ahead of us, guarding elevators. The men are protected by armor, but their visors are open. A crooked smile forms on the smaller soldier's face as we move toward him. His flirty voice is directed at Flannigan in front of me. "And who might you b—"

In a blink, Flannigan pulls a Census tranquilizer gun from the bag. Aiming it at the one speaking, she shoots him in the cheek. Surprised, the soldier is slow to react. He doesn't raise his weapon. Instead, his hand lifts to the silver dart embedded in his flesh. Flannigan pivots. The second guard reaches for a rifle propped against the wall. The dart from Flannigan's gun strikes this soldier below his temple. Neither Sword drops right away, but both of them stagger, stunned. Flannigan fires two more darts, striking each man just above his jaw. Eyes roll upward. The smaller one falls first, followed close behind by his partner.

"Help me," Flannigan whispers, thrusting the tranquilizer gun back into the bag. I grab one of the guard's feet while she gets his arms. We struggle to pull him into a dark room, out of sight. The next one is harder to move, but we manage it.

Flannigan hurries to the elevators. I follow her. Using the stolen identity, she calls a lift. The doors of one slide open. We step inside.

"Is that a copycat moniker?" I ask as the elevator begins to descend.

"Yes, the firstborn profile belongs to a Census agent stationed in the Twilight Forest Base, but he has access to Census in this Base as well." She slips the copycat into the slot in the side of her glove *on top* of the lead that covers the moniker implanted in her skin. The Census agent's crashing wave shines dimly through the glove. "I keep a few of these handy for the doors that are hardest to open. It won't matter in a few days. They'll all be useless." Switching on the wrist communicator, she pulls up the schematics for Census's underground lair. "The key to getting around is to project confidence. Try not to look anyone in the eyes, but don't avoid them either."

"How am I supposed to do that?"

"Privileged boredom works with the aristocracy, especially in Virtues. Census agents are different. You have to behave like a predator. You fear nothing. You're the hunter. Hunt."

Flannigan stops the elevator at a floor near the lowest point in the Base. When the doors open, cold air wafts over us. The black leather coats make sense now.

What the privateer said earlier is true. Unlike the last time I was here, there are very few Census agents guarding the corridors. The ones that should be stationed by the elevator on this level are absent from the post. We just pass by the checkpoint unchallenged. The few agents we encounter in the corridors move with purpose, barely giving us a look. Their arrogant conviction that they can never be infiltrated is almost funny. If I weren't so terrified, I'd laugh.

We hurry through a mile of corridors, following the wrist communicator. "We're beneath Aspen Lake," Flannigan informs me. She stops abruptly at a couple of nondescript metal doors. "They're in here."

She removes another cloned moniker from her case and opens the doors. I recognize the holographic image of Grisholm Wenn-Bowie displayed upon the access panel of the scanner. "How do you have Grisholm's cloned moniker?"

"He was easy to get to. He enjoys the touch of lovely women."

We enter. Flannigan closes the doors behind us and sets her bag down on the granite table in the center of the room. Shiny steel mesh covers the doors of the elegant cabinets lining the walls. Priceless items—jewels, art, prototype weapons—sparkle behind the mesh. On the far wall sits a vault.

"You said we were coming here to get my fusionblade," I mumble numbly.

Flannigan rummages in her bag and takes out a small device, which she pockets. She reaches in again and extracts a fusionmag. When the bullets from the weapon hit a target, they break apart and extinguish, killing the target without exiting and doing further damage. She arms the fusionmag with a cartridge and hands me the gun. "I lied. This is much more important than a fusionblade. Cover the door."

She goes to the vault and uses the copycat of Grisholm's moniker to open it. Inside are rows and rows of new moniker chips, moncalate tools used to implant the chips, and processor boxes used to program them with identities. "I needed someone to help me break into Census so that I could get new monikers. You were my best option."

She deftly chooses one processor box and one moncalate tool from the vault and puts them in her bag. Removing another device, she shoves it in her pocket, then steals row after row of new moniker chips from the vault until the bag is full. With a rueful sigh for the monikers still left in the safe, she sets the device from her pocket beside them.

"This is an incendiary, Roselle. It'll explode in five minutes and make it look as if we blew up the new monikers rather than stealing them. That way, they won't come looking for them. Are you ready?" she asks as she arms the device.

"How could you do this to me?" I whisper.

"I'm not doing it *to* you. I'm doing it *for* you." She secures the bag, moves to the door, and opens it a crack. Seeing no one in the corridor, she steps out. The moment she does, I hear shots. Blood spatters my torso, chest, and face. Flannigan falls against the door and slides to the floor.

Instinctively, I step over her with the fusionmag raised. Four agents are approaching from down the corridor. I fire four shots, striking each agent in the head. The bullets explode, spreading bone fragments and brain matter on the walls. I pivot. The other side of the corridor is empty.

Flannigan breathes raggedly, a shaky hand covering the hole in her abdomen. "Take these to your locker," she says in a raspy voice. "This bag will fit in the false bottom. On the shelf, you'll find a handheld welding tool. Seal the bottom of the locker." Blood drools from her mouth. "Tell him it was nearly flawless. Tell him to miss me. Every day."

"Tell who?" I demand, my heart pumping wildly.

She smiles. "The man who'll ask you about me." She reaches into her pocket and extracts the cyanide capsule, places it in her mouth, and convulses until all that looks back at me is her lifeless stare.

In a daze, I take a few steps, but then I turn back and gather the bag she dropped. Securing the long strap over my shoulder, I reach inside her glove and find the copycat moniker for the Census agent. I slip the crashing aqua wave into the slot above the lead covering my own implanted moniker. Flannigan's wrist communicator still works. I slip it from her and strap it to my wrist. Then I run.

When I reach the next corridor, I slow and peek around the corner. Three agents run toward me. I step from around the corner and take one down with a fusionmag shot to the head. My next two shots find their marks before the agents can raise their drawn weapons. Running past their bodies, I turn another corner, the labyrinth of passages seemingly endless. I keep running, watching the map on my wrist so that I don't get lost.

Suddenly the ground shakes. The loud noise of the incendiary device careens off the tunnel walls. As it subsides, a new sound—the sound of rushing water—replaces it. The floor continues to shake. I don't wait to see what's coming.

Someone behind me yells, "Stop!" I pause, glancing over my shoulder. A tall male agent stands at the junction of the corridors. He raises his gun, but before he can fire, a wall of Aspen Lake water strikes him and he's gone, swept down the other corridor. I run again. The sound behind me is deafening. Ahead of me, the elevator looms. Only one Census agent guards it. He looks up and sees me coming. Behind me, a thundering river of water crashes and churns.

The agent backs away and scans his moniker on the elevator's call-box. The doors open. He backs into the car. I lift my fusionmag, pointing it at him as I run, and shoot him in the neck. The bullet explodes and sparks fly out of him. Arterial blood sprays the wall of the elevator. He holds his throat and slides to the floor.

Leaping across the threshold of the elevator, I'm just in time as its doors roll closed behind me. Water slams against them, pushing them apart again. I'm drenched by the tidal wave as it fills the car. Coughing and panting, I tilt my face toward the ceiling, trying to tread water, but before the wave can drown me, the car lifts up and out of its path. The lake water rapidly drains through the open doors and falls down the shaft. The doors slide closed, finally.

I clutch the railing, gasping out choking sobs. My trembling knees threaten to fold beneath me. The dead stare of the Census guard on the floor is more than I can take. Before I know what's happening, though, the elevator stops. The doors open. I force back tears and turn, raising my fusionmag and pointing it at an empty hallway ahead of me. Nothing moves.

Is this the same bunker?

I pause, listening. My foot slides forward and I take a tentative step from the lift. Water in my boots makes squishing noises. I sweep the fusionmag, its aim following the path my eyes take as I scan the area. The sound of heavy breathing to my left rattles my nerves. I swing my weapon in that direction. The door to the dark room beside the elevator is ajar. I creep to it, peeking inside. The two unconscious soldiers stunned by Flannigan are still sprawled out on the floor. I back away quietly.

Shoving the fusionmag into my jacket pocket, I strip off the wrist communicator and toss it back into the elevator. The car descends into a watery grave. The fake moniker frees me from the bunker's prison. I stand between the open doors and covertly stow the copycat back into its lead sleeve and drop it in the bag.

The buzz from the stingers makes my heart thrum wildly in my chest, but my own moniker remains covered in the leaded glove, undetectable. Crossing the warehouse floor, I leave a trail of dripping water in my wake. I take a heartwood up to the laundry. The welcome hum of washing machines drowns out my footsteps.

My trembling hands strip off the wet uniform. Slipping on Flannigan's orange jumpsuit, I find that we're virtually the same size. I keep the flat cap, pulling it down once more over my hair to shadow my face. Retrieving the fusionmag from the Census coat, I shove it in the bag.

The heartwood line looms ahead. I stumble from the laundry and jump on one. About midway to my floor, a blaring siren rings, accompanied by a robotic, feminine voice: *"All personnel, please report to your air-barracks and to your capsules until further notice. We are on lockdown. Please report to your capsules immediately."*

By the time the heartwood reaches my floor, I'm a trembling mess. I take the corridor used by Stone-Fated workers. The orange-uniformed personnel don't give me a second glance. Posted signs lead me to my air-barracks. Soldiers guard the door to Tritium 101.

A worker ahead of me tries to scan his moniker, but a soldier stops him. "You're getting new monikers in your designated areas. Report to your capsules, and you'll be summoned throughout the evening." I pull my gloved hand inside my sleeve so only my fingers show. When I reach the soldier, he waves me through.

Before I reach the underdeck capsules, I branch off and take the staircase up to Section Black, open the door at the top of the stairs, and find myself in the back corner of the locker room. An eerie silence greets me. No one is about. They've all returned to their capsules. My wet boots echo on the tile floor.

Finding my locker, I'm about to strip off my leaded glove when I stop. The clock on the wall indicates that it's half past two. I can't open my locker yet. I can't take the risk of my moniker showing up here while I'm supposed to be in detention. My scheduled release is five thirty. I have to wait.

Seeking a hiding place, I go to one of the individual toilet rooms and close the door. The moment I enter it, I begin to retch. Leaning over the steel commode, I vomit until there's nothing left in me. When I'm finally able, I rise and lock the door. Then, I sit and wait.

Jolting awake, I look around. Bathroom. Bag. Orange uniform. *Panic.* I jump to my feet. My head spins and I see spots. With my forearms against the wall, I wait until the world rights itself, then I open the door. No one is in the locker room. I listen, but the thundering of my heartbeat is all I hear. Gathering the courage to leave the bathroom, I step out with the bag. The clock on the wall reads five twenty. *Close enough!* I strip off the leaded glove and shove it in the bag.

I hurry to my locker and scan my moniker. The door pops open. Dropping to my knees, I pull apart the false bottom and cram the bag inside it, on top of the outfit that I wore to the news conference. I strip off Flannigan's orange uniform and the flat cap and thrust them into the hollowed-out bottom. Covering the hole with the piece of metal, I rise to my feet. I tug on my beige pajamas, warm against my cold skin.

Rising up on my tiptoes, I reach and search the top shelf, knocking things over in my haste to find the welding tool that I'm too short to see. It's there in the back. I drop to my knees again. A golden flame ignites when I pull its trigger. I put it to the floor of my locker and weld the seams. The melting metal blows curls of smoke up. I try not to look directly at it, but I'm partly blind when I finish.

Easing my locker door closed with a soft *click*, I hurry back to the toilet closet, shutting the door and locking it. With trembling hands, I begin to take the welding tool apart. Footsteps sound outside the bathroom door. The first part of the tool unhinges. I drop it in the steel bowl. My fingers work furiously on the next part.

Someone beats on the door. "Come out of there!" a deep voice shouts.

I take a deep breath. "Just a minute!" My voice is raw and raspy.

"You're not supposed to be out of your capsule!" The door rattles on its hinges. Gut-wrenching fear squeezes my heart. A fist hammers again. Another piece of the welding tool slides free. I drop it in the toilet. Sweat slips down my face.

"It was an emergency!" I call back. My fingers bleed, cut by the sharp edges of the tool.

"I don't care if you shit all over the inside of your bunk, Soldier! I want you out here now!" The door rattles on its hinges.

"Okay!" I answer as the final two pieces come apart. I drop them in and flush. When I'm sure that all the pieces have been swept away, I unlock the door. The door is thrown open by a Strato soldier, red-faced, towering over me, looking as if he's about to breathe fire.

"Tropo! What are you doing?" he demands. Anger gives way to annoyance when he sees my face. I must look petrified.

"I had to go to the bathroom, Patrøn."

"We're on lockdown!" he bellows. "You're not allowed to leave your capsule!"

"I just got here, Patrøn. I spent all night in detention."

He rubs the stubble on his chin. "Get down and give me fifty push-ups!" I exit the bathroom closet and drop to the ground. The act of doing something so commonplace makes me feel better. When I'm done, I stand and face him. "Now get to your capsule," he orders.

"Can I wash my hands first?"

"No, you cannot!" he yells. He calls to someone over his shoulder. "Can you take this Tropo to her capsule?"

I look over his shoulder to the soldier standing by the lockers. Hawthorne stares back at me. "Yeah, Barkley," he says, "I'll take her."

Chapter 13
Ugly Moles

I don't realize that my feet are bare until Hawthorne asks, "Do you want your slippers?" I shake my head no because I don't trust my voice not to be thick with emotion, and I don't know exactly what he'll see if I open my locker. I try to walk to the door that leads to the tiers of capsules. Hawthorne stops me with a gentle tug on my arm. "Sorry about Barkley. He's a head case. Stay away from him if you can. He has a crazy fascination for the rules, and I know you don't."

Hawthorne's strong hand on my arm loosens. He's about to let go of it when I turn and rest my forehead against his chest. I inhale Hawthorne's scent that I now associate with safety. My shaking shoulders hunch toward him. A sob that I can't force down breaks through and chokes me. He moves his rifle so that it rests against his back on the gun strap. I hide my face against his chest once more. His hands come up to rest on my shoulders as he holds me to him. "Shh," he hushes softly, brushing my hair back from my hot face, tucking it back behind my ear. "Whatever it is that's making you cry, look away from it. It doesn't have you. I do."

I can't get close enough to him. He lifts me up in his arms, and then sits down on a bench, settling me in his lap. He leans his back against the wall. I don't know how long it takes me to stop crying, but I get the hiccups toward the end. Hawthorne doesn't tease me about them. He reaches into the pocket of his gun strap and extracts a cloth used to remove condensation from the barrel. "It's clean," he says when he uses it to wipe my face.

"I'm sorry," I murmur.

"About what?" He stuffs the cloth back into the compartment. "I've never cleaned my rifle with Roselle's tears before. I'll let you know how well it works." He waits to see if I smile. I don't. "Are you okay?"

"No," I reply with a watery look and a set of sniffles.

"You look exhausted. I know you were picked up for brandishing."

"Who told you?"

"Agent Crow, when he gave me this." Hawthorne shows me his new moniker and scar. "He also told me he wasn't done with either of us."

"Is that all he said?" I ask.

"Yes. Why?" he replies. I cringe. Hawthorne doesn't know about Agnes Moon. Agent Crow didn't tell him. How do I tell him that his girlfriend was murdered because he wanted to help me? He'll never forgive himself . . . or me.

"He killed her, Hawthorne. Agnes is dead. Agent Crow beat her to death. He showed me the photos." Exhale—that's how I tell him.

Hawthorne shakes his head. I'll never forget the look of horror on his face for as long as I live.

"Agent Crow accused Agnes of being thirdborn. Was she?"

His eyes smolder. His nostrils flare. "No! She was secondborn, like us! She was just a Moon. She's never even been trained to defend herself!"

"He was going to kill her either way, for helping me. He's insane, Hawthorne. I'm sorry." I don't know what else to say. I feel powerless to take away his pain.

"She didn't want to help. I convinced her to do it." His lips thin in despair. "I'm going to kill him."

"One day. I'll help you." Rubbing my eyes in exhaustion, I rise from his lap and sway on my feet. Hawthorne stands and catches my shoulders.

"I'm taking you to your capsule." I don't argue. He places a comforting hand on the small of my back, and we walk.

"How do you know which one is mine?"

"I asked around once I found out we were in the same air-barracks."

I pause. "That's more than coincidence, Hawthorne. There are literally a million capsules on this Base and thousands of air-barracks."

"I know," he says grimly.

"Who put me here with you?" I stare at him accusingly, searching his eyes.

He cups my cheek. "I swear to you that I don't know, Roselle."

"I don't either."

We continue walking until we reach my capsule.

"Get some sleep," Hawthorne insists. "I'll check on you later."

I climb the ladder up four levels, open my capsule, and crawl inside. The door shuts. Resting my head against my pillow, I pull my blanket over me, but for hours, I lie awake in total darkness.

My thoughts turn to last night. Flannigan planted herself in my detention cell. The privateer manipulated me into helping her steal monikers, but for whom? She died to get them. What am I supposed to do with them? Turn them over? Say that I accidentally shot eight Census agents and helped blow up and flood the tunnel-dwelling hunters and their scary interrogation rooms?

A part of me wants to rationalize the eight deaths as mercy killings. They would have died anyway—drowned by the wall of water—except for the one in the elevator. He probably would have made it. But how many thirdborns had he murdered? He had at least twenty kill tallies by his eyes. Maybe I brought justice.

All I know is that I'm in possession of contraband that will get me tortured and killed. Now that I have time to think, I can see every mistake with glaring clarity. I was released a few hours before my sentence was officially over. Strike one. If anyone asks Holcomb Sword, he'll be able to say he hadn't released me. Strike two. They won't find a moniker trail of my leaving the detention center at five a.m., or arriving at the air-barracks at five twenty, except for the login at my locker. And there won't be a record of my entering the air-barracks at all. Strikes three and four.

I feel more and more confident that at any second, Agent Crow is going to bang on the door of my capsule and arrest me. But one hour slips by, and then another, and another, and nothing happens. I switch on the virtual-access screen on the ceiling. No one is reporting on the bombing of the Census Base. The news is all about the semifinal rounds of the Secondborn Trials. Half of the competitors scale the side of a mountain. From a bluff, the other half picks them off, one by one, with fusion arrows. Something inside of me feels like it's dying.

∽

I'm startled awake. The visual screen above my head is still on. Commentators discuss the deaths of several of the champions from the Fate of Seas, burned up in a fiery crash when an incendiary device ignited their ultra-light aircraft in the aviator challenge. A fist bangs on my door, and Hawthorne's voice calls, "Roselle?" I scoot down to the panel and open the door outward. He gazes at me from the ladder.

"Hi." He fakes a smile. "How are you feeling?"

"Like I just had a coronary. I thought you were Agent Crow." I rub sleep from my eyes.

"He's back at the Stone Forest Base," Hawthorne says, a look of hatred in his eyes. "We're in the air, en route to the Twilight Forest."

"How long have I been asleep?"

"You missed breakfast and lunch. It's fourteen hundred." He hands me a silver foil ration pack. "It's turkey pasta—one of the better ones.

You know you can come out now? We're no longer on lockdown. Whatever was worrying them while we were docked at the Base has passed now that we've left. We were cleared for active duty."

"You're serious?"

He's worried, but I'm relieved. It'll be harder for Agent Crow to get to him. After Agnes, I don't know how to protect him, beyond not telling him anything about the thousands of monikers hidden in my locker. He can't be involved in that.

"Would you like to go for a run with me?" Hawthorne asks.

I nod, set aside the ration pack, and climb out of my capsule, meeting him on the catwalk. We head to the locker room, where I pick up a workout T-shirt and sweats from stacks of them. No one here is shy, I'm learning. Naked bodies, male and female, walk around for all the air-barracks to ogle. I take my clothes to a bathroom unit and change there.

When I come out, Hawthorne is leaning against my locker with his arms crossed. "Do you intend to do that every time you change your clothes?" he asks with an amused grin.

"Yeah. I do," I reply. I kneel on one knee and secure the straps of my running boot.

"Why would you want to hide your body? Do you have an ugly mole or something?"

"Uh, no. No mole."

"I can lend you some merits to get that thing removed, you know."

"Hawthorne," I say, my face reddening by the second. "You've been getting naked with these people since you were ten. I've never changed my clothes in front of anyone since I could change them by myself."

"Your access feeds showed you training, your diet, your lessons, almost every aspect of your life, but they never showed us your room or anything like that."

"That whole place—everything you saw—those were all my rooms. I had an entire wing of the Sword Palace to myself." We exit the locker room and walk along a row of capsules to a heartwood. We step on facing each other. It takes us down to the lower floors.

He leans toward me. "What was that like?"

"It was lonely, Hawthorne. There were days when I thought that if someone didn't speak to me, I'd go mad. And then there were times when I thought I was a ghost, and only drone cameras could see me. Now it's as if *everyone* sees me, and they can't look away."

We step off the heartwood onto a training deck. A track spans its circumference. Soldiers stop talking as we pass, their eyes on me.

"I see what you mean," Hawthorne says. "It won't last forever. The regiment will get used to you, and then they'll stop paying attention."

Hawthorne and I keep pace for the first fourteen miles. It feels right to run after days of not training. I haven't had a decent workout since I left the Sword Palace—since I lost Dune. We pass other runners, but no one passes us. In the final mile, Hawthorne pulls away from me. I try matching his stride, but it's impossible, and he beats me by a hundred yards. He has the decency to breathe hard afterward. I have to pinch my side.

"You don't lose often . . . do you?" he asks.

"I believe . . . you went easy . . . on me." I give up trying to play it cool and hobble around outside the track, staring up at the black ceiling and panting like I might die. "That last mile . . . was painful."

Sweat dripping from his face, Hawthorne offers me a towel. "I have something I want to show you." He guides me to the other side of the deck. "We're close to the Vahallin Sea. We'll fly low, near the water. Do you feel us descending?"

He motions for me to wait, goes to a small compartment door, and unlatches it. He slides the door open, securing it from closing with a hook. Wind whips around us. He holds out his hand to me. I inch toward him, my hair pulling free in wisps from its stays. The wind is so loud that I'd have to scream to be heard, so I don't even try. I grasp Hawthorne's arm and cling to it. I long to explore the world drifting by beneath us, knowing I've squandered my existence by never having trudged through these green fields dotted with sheep.

We fly over a cliff, the land falls away abruptly, and the Vahallin Sea moves as if it's breathing. Its scent is a primal thing, bringing tears to my eyes, as if some ancient part of me remembers it—knows what it feels like to swim in its depths, its vastness.

Hawthorne taps my shoulder. I look up at him, tears on my cheeks. He brushes them away with his thumb, then takes my hand and helps me up, sliding the door closed.

"That was—" I have no words to describe it. "Thank you."

"It's nice to share it with someone." I nod, my throat tight. "C'mon," Hawthorne says, "I could use a shower." My eyes widen. "I don't mean together."

"Oh."

We make our way back up to Section Black. At my locker, Hawthorne asks, "Have you put on your combat armor yet?" I shake my head no. "Okay, when you're finished with your shower, put these on." He indicates the tight black shirt and leggings that go beneath the armor. "I'll show you how to armor up."

Hawthorne walks away. I gather the special shampoo and detangler that Emmy had requisitioned for me, a razor and shaving cream from the shelf of supplies available to everyone, and a towel from the stack. Then, following Hawthorne, I find that his locker is two rows over from mine.

I peek around the corner. Hawthorne strips off his sweaty T-shirt. His broad shoulders and back muscles bear witness to his intensive training. His skin is perfection. His training trousers hang low on his narrow hips—so low I get a glimpse of the two dimples just above his rounded backside. I back away, my cheeks burning. *He's right, I am weird, and right now, I wish he had an ugly mole.*

An empty shower closet isn't hard to find at this time of day. I step inside one, close the door, and lock it. I strip off my clothes and turn the water on by scanning my moniker. I only get five minutes.

But five minutes isn't long enough. I finish shaving one leg, sans water. After towel drying my hair, I wrap the damp cloth around my body, exit the shower closet, toss my dirty clothes in the clothes chute, and run my fingers through the tangles in my wet hair. Rows of sinks are located near the lockers. Putting toothpaste on my toothbrush, I begin brushing my teeth in front of one. Two buttons are on a panel near the side of the mirror. Above them, a label reads "dryer." I push the top one. Warm air blows down on me, drying my hair. Soft waves form as I run my fingers through it. On a shelf behind me are grooming supplies—razors and shaving cream. I take a new razor and some shaving cream to finish shaving my leg properly.

I set the items on the edge of the sink. With my toothbrush still in my mouth, I bend over at my waist, flipping my hair over so that the underside can dry. Running my hands through it, I feel the curls loosening. Reaching for the shaving cream, I rub some on my ankle before pulling the razor across it. I rinse the blade in the sink without looking up, and then drag it across my skin again. Large feet stop right next to me. I flip my long hair out of my face and look up. Hawthorne is there, with just a towel wrapped low on his hips. He is knee-weakeningly handsome.

"What are you doing?" he asks.

"Bruwshing my teef," I reply, my mouth full of foam. Beyond him, a group of male soldiers watches in fascination. I turn and spit. "What?" I ask Hawthorne's reflection in the mirror.

"I meant what were you doing with that razor?"

"Shaving my legs. I don't have wax to remove the hair, so—"

"I thought only Diamond-Fated women shaved their legs—models, and you know, *feminine* women, not soldiers."

"No one here shaves their legs?"

He shakes his head. "I don't. Hammon doesn't." Putting toothpaste on his toothbrush, he turns around and scowls at the males still watching me behind us. "Show's over. Go on now." The men laugh, telling him to lighten up. They push each other around before dispersing.

"I didn't know," I mutter, embarrassed. "We do things differently at home. Every woman shaves or waxes her legs and her armpits—all the aristocracy does it. Do you find it disgusting?"

"No."

"They think it's disgusting though, right?" I wish someone would tell me these things *before* I make an ass of myself.

"Roselle, you just made their top-five lists," he says, pointing in the direction of the other soldiers. "Honestly, you were probably on that list anyway, but now it's a safe bet you're number one."

My nose wrinkles. "What's a top-five list?"

"You don't want to know. Rest assured, they find you the opposite of disgusting."

I gesture with my thumb over my shoulder. "All right. I'll just go—"

"Change in the bathroom—yeah, that's actually a good idea."

◇

Hawthorne is in his uniform when we meet later at my locker. Tossing my long hair into a ponytail, I tuck it into the neckline of my undershirt. My clingy under-armor attire doesn't leave much to the imagination, and Hawthorne's eyes rove over me. My cheeks flush with color. He looks away, reaching past me to retrieve the armor from inside my locker. His arm brushes up against my breast. I bite my lip and move back, giving him more room.

"Excuse me," he says.

"It's fine," I assure him. "Thank you for doing this." My fingers tangle together nervously. "I've never used this kind of combat gear before."

"It's no problem." He inhales deeply, then leans close and sniffs my hair. "You don't smell like a soldier," he jokes. His nose brushes my neck.

"Oh." My blush turns to one of embarrassment. "They gave me this special detangler because they wouldn't let me cut my hair."

"Why wouldn't they let you cut your hair?"

"Oh, you know—I need permission from Admiral Dresden, Clifton Salloway, or Agent Crow in order to change how I look." Admitting my total lack of freedom regarding my own body is humiliating.

Hawthorne's jaw ticks.

"So, how does this work?" I ask, gesturing to the combat suit, changing the subject.

He shows me, and it's ingenious. A catheter lines the interior of the armor for long missions. He describes how to position the collector so that I don't wet myself and how to change it when it becomes necessary. I step into the suit, sans catheter. Armor plates run over my calves, thighs, torso, and arms. Hawthorne tightens my elbow buckles, tugging on my armor like he's trying to protect me. I want to lean into him, gently brush my lips against his. He has no idea.

Hawthorne pulls the armor breastplate from my locker. "You can put this on a couple of different ways," he explains. "I usually unclip the right buckle of the waistband, shrug into it, putting my head through this hole, and secure the waistband clip. Some soldiers lift the breastplate over the head, and then tighten both the waistband clips. Whatever works for you."

I do it the way he does it. The wide armor-plated straps hang on my shoulders, holding the armor in place. I secure the right clip of the waistband. He tugs on the belt to cinch the waist, hands me a headset, and passes me a helmet. It fits me like it was made for me. The visor clicks out in sections to cover my face.

Hawthorne hands me elbow-length gloves and a fusion-powered rifle. He steps back from me and admires his handiwork. "Goodness, Roselle. You look like a soldier!"

"I *am* a soldier."

He pulls a tin of wax from his pocket. "Rub this on all the shiny parts of your armor. Some of the clips need to be dulled down so that they don't reflect light and give away your position. Don't go using it on your legs. I only have this little bit."

I nudge him with my shoulder. "Very funny."

"Ration rotation happens in ten. I'll wait here for you while you change." He leans against the lockers and crosses his arms.

Dining in the air-barracks is as informal as you can get, just bins of premade food in foil packages. We line up for the bins. There isn't much to choose from. I pick up a red foil package and begin to read the label, but Hawthorne snatches it out of my hand and tosses it back in the bin. "Don't eat that. Remember: 'Red for a reason.' Here." He thrusts a green foil package into my hand.

Hawthorne takes two of everything except the red package.

Tables and chairs occupy most of the room. We spot Gilad, Hammon, and Edgerton at one. I follow Hawthorne to the table and sit down next to Edgerton. Hawthorne sits beside me. I strip off the long plastic spoon from the foil pouch, tear away the top of the foil, and stir the contents—creamy chicken salad.

Hawthorne hands me a package of rolls. "It's better with these."

I take one. "Thank you."

"Why's she here, Hawthorne?" Gilad growls.

"She's hungry," he replies.

"All you'll get from her is trouble," Gilad grumbles. He's not wrong.

"So I should run panic-stricken from her?" Hawthorne asks. "Like most of these soldiers around us? Isolate her because she's different?"

"It's called caution," Gilad says, looking straight at me. "She may not last long here. No sense in getting attached. No hard feelings, Roselle. I'm just a realist."

"Sure, Gilad," I reply. "Let's just get all our awkward moments out of the way now."

"So, Roselle." Edgerton addresses me from his seat next to Hammon. "Tell me why you shave your stems—and what else do you shave?" Hawthorne begins to choke. Hammon elbows Edgerton.

"What?" he queries Hammon. "You're the one what wanted to know. I was just going direct to the source. Roselle and me has that kind of relationship. Don't we, Roselle?"

I pat Hawthorne on the back as he tries to catch his breath. Red-faced, he wipes his eyes. "Where I come from," I answer Edgerton, "females shave their legs, armpits, and . . ."

"You don't has to do that. We'll like you just fine with hair," Edgerton replies, as if he's sorry that I've been raised by savages. Hammon elbows him again. "What?" he asks her, dismayed. "We will. She's our friend, even if she does strange things."

"Thank you, Edgerton," I reply. "That means a lot to me."

Hammon gives me a friendly smile. "Sorry. Edge still has mountain sensibilities. Things that appear impractical are lost on him. He forgets what it was like to be newly processed."

"I know that a lot of things from my world don't make sense here," I reply. "How long has it been since you were processed?"

"I was eleven," Hammon says. She looks over at Edgerton, her adoration obvious. "We were all processed on the same Transition Day. That's how we all met. You make most of your core friends on your first day."

"We was just sayin'," Edgerton chimes in, "how hard it must've been for you not to Transition with anyone else."

"I didn't say that," Gilad interrupts, not looking up from his food. "I said you'd be puking up sunshine to be the only one."

"Gilad and I were best friends from the start," Hammon says. "Then Gilad brought Hawthorne in, and I brought Edge in."

"So you've all been together for years?"

"We've been lucky," Hawthorne replies. "None of us has been trans-ferred. We were assigned to Tritium 101, and it's been home ever since."

"We all made the rank of Strato together. Well, Hawthorne made it first. He's up for Meso now," Hammon says proudly. "I bet he gets it by the time we're done with active duty. We'll have an officer in our midst soon."

"I might not get it," Hawthorne says.

Edgerton rolls his eyes. Gilad says, "You'll get it. You earned it."

There's genuine love here, even between Gilad and Hawthorne, maybe especially between them. A cold sort of anger bubbles up in me. It's hard to name what it is at first, but then I realize that it's jealousy—of their relationships with one another, the camaraderie, trust, respect, and love. I've never had that.

I glance away from them. A familiar face catches my attention over at a different table. Jakes sits with a few other engineers. I haven't thought much about him since I was thrown in detention. He nods and points his chin toward the door. He gets up from his table and leaves. Crumbling the foil meal package in my hand, I stand. "Please excuse me, I have something I have to do. I hope you have a lovely evening."

I hurry for the exit, following him. Jakes is at the end of the corridor by a heartwood. I move in his direction. He takes the heartwood, and I follow him down. We pass a few decks. He steps off into a hangar that houses combat troop movers and Winger aircraft. Most everyone is still at dinner. He pauses by some metal crates, and I join him.

"I looked for you before we deployed," he says by way of a greeting. He pushes his thick glasses up on the bridge of his nose.

"I was in detention. I was picked up for brandishing."

"I heard. No one has ever stood up for me before."

"It was my fault you got harassed in the first place. I'm sorry there was trouble, but I'll always take the consequences."

"Maybe I'm tired of being cautious," he mutters. "Maybe it's time for a little danger."

"Do you have something for me?" I ask.

"I do. I was looking through schematics for some older weapon designs in the archives." He touches the scanner on the metal crate, opening it. "What you wanted isn't so far-fetched. Most of the old designs were scrapped when fusion came along, but I was able to use existing diagrams and parts to create this." Inside the crate is a fusionblade housing, but it's unlike any I've seen before. The silver hilt is longer than a normal fusionblade's. Not only that, a regular sword of this caliber has only one strike port where the energy flows from the weapon. It's the source from which a fusionblade glows with golden power. This weapon has two strike ports: one at the top of the hilt, and the other at the base of the hilt.

I lift it from its case. When I squeeze the hilt at its center, two light-infused blades ignite from it. At one end, a golden fusionblade; at the opposite end, a silver hydroblade. It's truly a dual-bladed sword.

Jakes comes nearer to me. "If you choke up by moving your grip toward the fusionblade's strike port, Roselle, the hydroblade will extinguish. The opposite will occur if you place your hand closer to the hydroblade. Or you can have both if you keep your grip centered on the hilt."

Most of the time, I'll only use one side of the sword or the other because to have them both lit at once is dangerous, unless I use it like a staff. Jakes shows me how to switch off each side so that it won't pop on accidentally.

"This is remarkable. You've done it, Jakes!"

"It wasn't that hard. The hydrogen cells are abundant," he explains. I wave the dual-blade around, trying out complex maneuvers. "We use hydrogen cells for powering some of our burners in the lab—it's heavy hydrogen—condensed. I can show you how."

"I'd like to learn that." I want to learn everything he knows about everything. I'm tired of being ignorant. I want to be able to break into consoles, like Flannigan could. I want to write the story of my life to suit me. I want to see the world without restrictions. I want to use my mind to obtain freedom, like she had.

"We get these hydrogen cells in bulk," Jakes continues. "They last about a thousand hours before you have to change them out and recharge them." He holds it up. It resembles a silver bullet with a clip on the back of it. "You can put them in one of your armor compartments, or maybe even in your hair. They have clips on the backs." He slips a hydrogen cell into my hair like a decorative pin. "Just open the housing on the hilt here to reload."

"Am I interrupting something?" Hawthorne asks from behind us.

Jakes looks startled. "It's okay. Hawthorne is a friend," I tell him.

"What's this?" Hawthorne asks, indicating my new weapon.

"Something we need. Hawthorne, how many merits do you have?"

"A lot. Why?"

"Because I need some to get an ugly mole removed, and so do you."

"I don't have an ugly mole."

I blush, remembering catching a glimpse of him in the locker room with just a towel on. "You have a mole, Hawthorne, and it will kill you if you don't have it removed. This is the tool that's going to remove it. Everyone will need to get a mole removed, and Jakes here is the one who's going to do it."

I extend the dual-bladed sword to Hawthorne. He takes it, examining it closely. "This is . . . handy," he says, in awe.

I turn to my Star friend. "Jakes, anyone who comes to you wanting a mole removed, you give him the means to remove it. If he needs to do it on credit, you extend him credit. Do you understand?"

"How many moles are you expecting to remove?"

"An entire regiment's."

Hawthorne and I haggle with Jakes over the price of the new sword. He has already made two of them, and I intend to take them both. "When can you have more ready?" I ask.

He shakes his head. "I'm going to need more help—parts—time."

"Do what you can. Also, look into converting existing fusion-powered rifles to hydrogen. We'll need hydrogen magazines. If you can think of a way to make it work, I might be able to get a message to Clifton Salloway."

Hawthorne grasps my arm. "Excuse us for a moment," he growls to Jakes. He drags me a few paces away around the side of a shipping crate. He positions me with my back to the metal box, his face close to mine, his eyes as dark as storm clouds. "What's going on?"

"I can't tell you—you just have to trust me. We have to spread the word about this new weapon, but it has to be a subtle infiltration. Soldiers have to want them because they're new and in demand, and for no other reason. I don't know how we're going to do that, but we have to try."

Hawthorne's expression softens. "You just need to be seen using one, Roselle. That's all it will take. You're Roselle St. Sismode. They may pretend to despise you, but they've watched you for years and copied your fighting moves, your mannerisms, your style—everything about you."

"You're an influencer, too, Hawthorne. Soldiers follow you because you're trustworthy." I grip his biceps. "Use your sword with me tonight. Practice with me, somewhere that we'll be seen."

"You're acting as if this is a matter of life and death."

"I'm not acting."

His eyebrows slash together. "I don't want you to contact Clifton Salloway—for any reason. Is that understood?"

I drop my hands. "Why not? I'm not going to get personally involved with him. I'm just going to, you know, ask him to mass-produce dual-bladed swords. And maybe a new hydrogen version of a fusionmag. And a fusion rifle with a hydrogen-powered option. And maybe see if he has connections to major airship manufacturers."

Hawthorne stares at me like I'm insane. "Roselle, Clifton Salloway is not someone you want to owe a favor."

"Hawthorne, I understand firstborns like him. He's violently bored. He craves purpose. I can give him that purpose."

"His purpose will be to get you in bed."

"I'll worry about that later. Right now, we have to make this weapon seem like the only one worth having."

Frustration plays upon Hawthorne's face, but he nods in agreement. "We're merely tabling this conversation about Salloway for now."

"Thank you," I murmur. He backs away, just a step. I squeeze by him and walk back to Jakes, who is drumming his fingers on the dual-blade's case.

He straightens. "I have some ideas about who can help me. It'll be less expensive to convert existing fusionblades."

I agree with a nod. "We focus on conversion, then. Soldiers will have to bring their fusionblades to you."

"I'll get started right away," Jakes replies.

"Good. I'll find you later and check on your progress." Hawthorne and I turn and move toward a heartwood.

"You're a regular arms dealer, Roselle," Hawthorne says. I want to tell him everything. I want him to know that I'm doing this to protect secondborn Swords because my mother won't.

"No, Hawthorne. I'm not an arms dealer," I say instead. "I'm a privateer."

Chapter 14
Little Fish

Hawthorne and I face off on the training mats. I want to correct the slope of his sword arm, but I refrain. I'm not here to teach. I'm here to make our new weapons look sexy. The killer-come-to-call stare in his eyes is completely attractive, though. I'm glad we don't have to fight on a regular basis. I don't know how he'd take me dominating him, wrestling him to the ground, having my way with him.

He moves first, stalking me. He has a natural instinct for the dual-blade, holding it in balance, twirling it. That's a relief. I was worried because he isn't considered a "Master of Swords," and I've already wrecked one of them. His first strike is a wide-arcing thrust, his golden blade whining through the air. I counter it with a similar move. Because the blades are alike, their golden energy repels. A few soldiers stop their training to watch. I try to make whatever Hawthorne does look valiant and virile. It pains me. I have to clamp down on my ego.

When he counters with the hydroblade, I do the same, and they repel each other once more. Our silver blades of energy smash with a fantastic hissing. He pivots the fusionblade toward me in a counter-strike. This time, I meet the golden energy of his sword with my weapon's silver energy, and Hawthorne's golden fusionblade cuts through my silver hydrogen blade like it's air. I'm ready for it, and I compensate by dropping to my knees and rolling away. My hydroblade assumes its full length again. I demonstrate a move that could shear off Hawthorne's ankles, powering the hydroblade down at the last second. A dither of conversation ripples through the crowd.

We mock-battle for almost an hour. Turning backward tumbles to make his aggressive, lopsided maneuvers look spot-on and deadly, I get a decent workout. The crowd around us chatters excitedly. A few male soldiers approach Hawthorne to congratulate him on a rousing match. One claps him on the shoulder, asking about his weapon. Hawthorne hands it to him, showing him its features.

By evening, the demonstration is already yielding results. We haven't even docked yet at the Twilight Forest Base, and Hawthorne has fielded a score of questions about his new weapon. No one has approached me. But the men have begun complaining about the sudden shortage of razors in the locker rooms.

⌒∽⌒

We dock on a Tree in the Twilight Forest Base around midnight. The jarring *bump* shakes me awake inside my capsule. My eyes open to darkness. The sinister demons in my dreams were just gathering momentum. Sweat beads on my upper lip. The slaughterhouse scent of the newly dead is still with me. The Gates of Dawn's strike was over a week ago, but I'm unable to close the door on it.

I lie awake, shivering. I'm still getting used to my little capsule. It affords me solitude, which is something I crave now, but when I'm inside its hollow shell, the world disappears. I'm lost, a collection of atoms scattered in black space. The darkness wraps around me, and just when I think I'll go mad from it, the pendulum of fate swings. Bright white light illuminates my capsule. I flinch and blink. Blinded.

The door of my capsule opens automatically. From the speakers near my head, a feminine voice says, *"Attention Tropo soldier, you*

168

have been selected for an active duty campaign departing Twilight Base in twenty-nine minutes. Report to Deck 134, Hangar 12 for further instructions." The message repeats on a continuous loop, counting down the minutes. I shove aside my blanket and rub my eyes. If they want to keep me mean, this is the way to do it.

I jump from my capsule to the catwalk below. Very few doors are open. I'm alone, save for a few other females in this section. Hawthorne's capsule remains closed. My moniker vibrates, and I touch the glowing sword. A countdown clock shines upon the holographic sword. I head to the locker room to collect my armor.

The moment I cross the threshold, my skin prickles with unease. Twilight Forest soldiers are inside. They're the type of dangerous animals who only come out in darkness. "Well, well, the conscripts have arrived," says a thuggish one with a scar across his chin, his fusion rifle in his hand. Other soldiers are with him, leaning against lockers, their arms crossed, the Twilight Base emblem etched into the breastplates of their black combat armor. The emblem's violet Tree branches spread out with a soft glow, as if lit from inside.

More female soldiers trickle in, all attractive. Hammon is among them. A soldier trails her.

"I've fallen into the deep end," a soldier murmurs near me, close enough to cast his shadow upon me. "Little fish, little fish," he whispers, "you're a rare one. What's your name?"

I ignore him, gather up my armor, and try to squeeze by him. He closes the gap, his mouth looming near my neck. "Don't swim away, little fish."

"I have twenty minutes to report for duty."

"I could get you tossed back into your pond, but you'll have to do something for me first."

"I could gut you," I reply, the unlit hilt of my fusionblade pressed to his groin. "Back. Up."

He does. Another soldier near us laughs. "She's no little fish, Carrick. You hooked yourself a whale there. She's Roselle St. Sismode."

The soldiers trade looks. "So it is," Carrick says. "You won't last the day with what they have planned for you. You should take my offer. Someone else could go in your place, if you're nice to me."

"I'm never nice." I leave to change in the bathroom.

When I return, Hammon is beside me in her combat uniform. The emblem on her breastplate glows with a silver-etched Tree, like mine. She has her helmet on, but her visor is up. "We're being drafted by Protium 445. They went through our rosters and chose only the soldiers they deemed the most attractive conscripts."

I put my helmet on. "What are they going to make us do?"

"I don't know yet. Stay close to me, and I'll have your back."

I nod. We make our way to Deck 134. The moment we enter Hangar 12, a gruff soldier shoves me in the opposite direction from Hammon.

"Can we stay together?" Hammon asks him, indicating me.

"Aw, that's so cute. They want to stay together, Tolman."

Tolman sneers at her. "Sorry. We don't take requests from Stone Forests. Anyway, you don't want to go where St. Sismode is going. Trust me." He raises his rifle and aims it at her. She backs away, her eyes on me, as we're moved toward different airships.

The troopship I enter is almost full. Soldiers twenty or more years older than me, in blood-smeared armor with grimy faces, sit wearily on shallow seats.

"Why, if it isn't the St. Sismode secondborn," a soldier says as I approach him, looking for a seat. "Come to grace us with your presence, have you?" He spits at my feet as I walk past. Others follow his lead, and soon my armor is dotted with sputum. I find a seat near the front, by the pilots.

Another soldier walks up and hands me a pouch. I'm the only one who gets one. I strap it to my armor. One side of the pouch is filled with red medical-drone beacons, the other with black death-drone signals. Otherwise they look virtually the same.

"Where are we going?" I ask.

The soldier scowls at me. "You're bailing out between the enemy's line and our line just east of the current battlefield," he replies, "where the fighting has already taken place. We're going to the trenches west of your position. The fighting could shift back to you. Stay on your toes."

"If it does, you'll be trapped in the middle, between both of us," a soldier beside me cackles. "Dead center." He shoots me with air-gun fingers.

The soldier across from me chimes in. "If it was up to us"—he swings his head and looks down the line of soldiers in the unit—"you'd be fighting, not scouting for broken bodies, but there are rules now about young soldiers in combat."

"Swords have gone soft, is what it is," another says. He spits through the hole of his missing front tooth. "In my day, you'd be the first to die on the battlefield, you bloodsucking St. Sismode. Now you get to wipe what's left of our asses for us when we get 'em blown off."

"Yay for progress," I mutter.

The soldier next to me laughs, though it sounds more like a death rattle. "You got moxie, I'll give you that. I used to think you looked like your mother, but it's your father you take after. Him and his Virtue-Fated cronies always did have a one-liner ready."

Whether this man knows Father or has merely watched him on the visual screen is unclear. The fact that he thinks I'm anything like him is unnerving. I hardly know my father. "Kennet is the kind of person you don't sit down next to unless you're sure he hasn't moved your chair," I answer.

"You're not the kind to be hollowed by a firstborn's cuts, though, are you, girl?"

I lift my chin a notch. "The secret is to leave before their insults slice too deep. The fools on parade never notice when a secondborn escapes their carnival."

He gives me a grunt of approval. "Maybe you're not just a pretty visitor on her way through. We'll have to see how you do."

"I'm still not wiping your ass for you," I reply, which leaves them all laughing despite themselves.

The door to the airship closes and we settle in for the journey to the front line. It's the wee hours of the morning, and most of us haven't gotten more than a few hours of rest. Once we're airborne, some soldiers sleep. Snores issue from the bobbing heads around me. I'm too wired, and I don't trust any of them enough to close my eyes.

A couple of hours into the flight, the hatch opens. Wind whistles through. The cold of the first gust makes my teeth chatter. Fear rattles through me, too, as if the hammer of some long-dead god is beating my heart for his war drum. I've only had one jump simulation.

I close the visor of my helmet against the frigid air. The visual access monitor lights up. A beautiful woman's face and bare shoulders appear across it. She's from the Fate of Diamonds, her perfectly coifed hair and ruby lips as unmilitary as one can get. Her voice is low and sultry, as if she's outlining plans for an upcoming date night, rather than the mission at hand.

"Soldier," she breathes with a come-hither smile, "you have been chosen as our first responder. Your mission is to locate wounded Sword soldiers, your brothers and sisters, and tag them with the red beacons you have been given. Once a disabled soldier has been tagged, a medical drone will be summoned to assist him with his injuries. After you have dropped your beacon on him, do not wait for the medical drone to arrive. Move on to the next soldier who needs your help.

"You have also been given black beacons in your first responder kit. It is vital that you place black discs on any enemy combatants that you discover wounded or active. This beacon will dispatch a death drone to your position. Once an enemy is tagged, it is best to move on, making sure that your pouch is closed and that other black beacons on your person have not been activated. In the event of multiple black-disc activation, discard the beacons and move away from them quickly. Failure to utilize black beacons will result in severe penalties. Remember, the more black beacons you place upon your enemies, the faster we can end this terrible war and enjoy the peace and prosperity we each so desperately crave and deserve.

"In the event that you are able to secure any weapons from the fallen and wounded, it is imperative that you collect them. Automated hoverbins will circulate through the battlegrounds. Simply place all discarded weapons into the hoverbins as they pass. Good luck, soldier, and thank you for your service. Long live the Fates of the Republic." The visual screen turns off.

The soldier who gave me my pouch earlier walks up the aisle toward me and stands by the open door. A green light turns on. He walks down the line and thumps each soldier on the top of the helmet except for me. He goes back to the front of the airship. Holding out three fingers, he draws one back. Two fingers. One finger. All the soldiers on the airship rise and lurch toward the door, jumping two by two into the night.

The soldier directing the exodus waits for a few seconds, then he comes over to me and thumps me on the top of the helmet. My heart races. My knees shake. I rise from my seat and walk to the open doorway. It's total darkness below me. The only light is above, a half-moon and the pinpoints of stars. The soldier holds out three fingers. Then two. Then one.

I jump.

For a few moments, I see nothing. Green outlines form as my night vision picks up the heat signature from the ground. The ground detector initiates the gravitizer in my suit, triggering the repelling force of a magnet that pushes against the molten metallic core of the planet. The pressure punches my chest painfully, making it feel like a safe has fallen on it. I try with all my might to keep my neck up and my chest out, grunting and gasping from the effort. The force eases as I fall the last few dozen feet to the ground, but the impact still knocks the wind out of me. Wheezing, I lift my head from the soil. The impact left an impression of my helmet. I search around for other soldiers, but I can't see anyone.

It's silent, and I'm alone, pinned down by the night. Pulling my glove back, I check the time on my moniker. It's nearly dawn. Crawling in the dirt, I take refuge behind a small clump of trees. I check my rifle to make sure it's fully armed. Leaning against a trunk, I hold the rifle on my lap and wait for sunrise.

As dawn rises over the field, the ground around me is brown and cloying. White wisps of fog and mist shroud the battlefield ahead of me, and I can hear something now, the sound of weapons fire and incendiary devices. Less than a quarter of a mile away, the sky lights up through the dense fog.

Barren trees twist deep purple in this light. I rise and walk toward the fighting. Near the former frontline trenches and bunkers, the bodies begin to pile up. Blood soaks the muddy terrain. A tide of war washed through here at some point during the night, laying waste. The carnage is everywhere. I lift my face to the sky, looking for an answer to it all. Mist on my visor is the only response.

I hear a groan near me, drop to my knees, and begin digging through mud and pieces of soft flesh. Wiping grit from armor, I see the sword-shaped emblem that indicates one of us. A wave of relief washes over me. I open his visor to see his face. He's older, maybe in his thirties. Blood trickles from one of his nostrils.

"Help me," he begs, his eyes unfocused.

"You're going to be fine," I assure him, hoping that it's true. I fumble with the pouch clipped to my waist. My gloves are too thick, so I strip them off and clip them to my waistband. The air is cold. My fingertips turn pink. From the beacon pouch, I extract a red disc and place it on his armor. It sticks like a magnet. A red light flashes on and off, signaling a medical drone.

I begin to stand, but the soldier grasps my hand. "Please help me."

"A med-drone is on the way. You're going to be fine, soldier." My voice is strained and low.

"Please," he begs. I take his hand, holding it until the medical drone arrives, then I move back so it can work on him. Its blue laser light flashes over him, giving him a full-body scan. A robotic arm emerges from the drone, ratchets down, and sticks the soldier in the neck with a syringe full of white liquid. The soldier stops moaning and closes his eyes.

Two more claws emerge from the medical drone. One attaches to the armor of the soldier while the other stabilizes his neck and back. Together, the claws lift him from the ground while a third arm emerges and places a swatch of cloth beneath the soldier's body. The swatch inflates into an air-pallet. The claws lower the soldier to the pallet, securing him to it with straps. The air-pallet lifts from the ground and hovers away with the soldier in tow, in the opposite direction of the battlefield. The medical drone retracts its arms and flies into the mist. I move on, pawing through bodies, checking for pulses, opening visors to check for breathing. No one is alive—not Swords, and not the Gates of Dawn soldiers in their warrior armor and unique helmets.

At midday, the sky is just as gray as it was at dawn, and the mist is no less thick. I take a sip of water from the straw in my helmet. The supply is running low. I'm not sure when, or if, they plan to pick me up.

I'm so near the battle now that the noise is no longer muffled. An arm moves in my peripheral vision. A dark-armored soldier with heavy black gates etched into his breastplate lies on the ground amid others with violet-colored Tree emblems on their breastplates. His visor is down, a swirling night sky engulfed by black holes. I've seen it before, like the one the Gates of Dawn leader wore when my hovercade was attacked. The one I dream about almost every night. It can't be the same man. They're probably just both from the Fate of Stars.

He reaches for his fusionblade, but a body bogs him down. He struggles against the dead weight as he sees me nearing him. One of his arms is useless. His armor is sliced open from his shoulder to his abdomen.

I'm close now. He tries again to grasp his fusionblade, but it's just out of his reach. I kick it away, he stops struggling, and his head drops, his breathing coming in heavy pants from beneath his visor. My hand trembles. I have to see him.

I inch nearer, drawing my fusionblade. I hold it close to his neck. "Open your visor," I order.

"Why?" he asks in a deep voice.

"Do it."

The visor skips back to reveal his grimace. He squints in pain. I stare at him for a long moment. "What are you looking at? Just do it! Kill me already!" My hand trembles, and he sees it. I extinguish my fusionblade, attaching it to the weapon's clamp on my thigh armor. "Aw, I thought you were brave, Little Sword," he says. I unzip my pouch and fumble for a black death-drone beacon. "But you're a robot, same as the rest of them. They programmed you not to think for yourself. To follow orders. To do as you're told. I bet you don't even know why you can't think for yourself. It's the way you were raised, indoctrinated into their society—and it is *their* society. It was never yours, not since the moment you took your first breath. It was always theirs."

I set the black beacon on the side of his boot. He tries to scrape it off, but it holds firm. The ominous black light blinks on and off, calling to the nearest death drones. The ground rattles beneath us, the battle growing louder. The injured man tries again to reach his sword. He groans in anguish and tries to scrape the beacon off his boot again, but it clings with the tenacity of a parasitic insect.

He's not the one who attacked me in Forge. I know he's not. He was probably never even there. The wrongness of summoning the death drone tortures me. I move to pick up his fusionblade to give it to him so he can defend himself. As I grasp the hilt, sparks pierce my skin. Molten heat burns me. I scream in agony and drop the sword. Red welts bloom on my right palm in the perfect outline of the crest etched into his fusionblade.

"Hurts, doesn't it?" he asks. "It knows you're not me." The smirk of vengeance on his feverish face is more acrid than the smell of my burnt flesh. "You can't shrug that off."

I turn my head and hit my visor button with my chin as I retch. It ticks back enough so that my vomit only splashes on the ground. When I'm done, I walk a few steps and sit down, cradling my swollen hand in my lap. The compartment on my gun belt holds my first aid supplies. I fumble through it with one hand for some ointment and a clean bandage. The ointment cools the burn on contact, and I breathe easier. Tearing the bandage package open with my teeth, I wind it around my palm and tie it off. I lean back against a rock and stare straight ahead.

The wounded Gates of Dawn soldier reaches to his waistband. I tense and make to stand, but he doesn't pull a weapon. Instead, he extracts a little white pill. Raising it to his mouth, he's about to swallow the cyanide when I lurch forward and knock it from his hand.

He groans and closes his eyes.

"Shouldn't you at least go out fighting?" I kick his fusionblade closer and back away.

"No one fights to stay in hell." He doesn't reach for his fusionblade. "Your drone will interrogate me, Little Sword. I'd rather not stick around for it." Drool runs from his mouth. "Do you know where the phrase 'stick around' came from?" he asks. His hand searches the ground for the cyanide capsule.

"No." I pull at the dead body that has him pinned.

He seems not to notice. His breathing slows. His skin is losing color. "It's from a book. 'A friend *sticketh* closer,'" he grunts, "'than a brother.'"

The dead body slides free, and I let go of its limp arm, seeing his wounds for the first time. His collarbone is cut clean through, but it can be mended. "What does it mean?" I ask.

"It means that even when your brother goes away, a true friend will remain forever."

"Sounds like something a firstborn would say," I reply.

He laughs in delirium. "It does, but . . . I think it means something else. Why are you sticking around?" he asks.

I kneel beside him and place my good hand on his forehead. He's clammy. He's trembling—going into shock. A death drone emerges from the fog. A steel rope slithers out from its belly and wraps around my enemy's neck, pulling tight. The drone attempts to scan his moniker, but all it finds on his left hand is a scar where the processor chip has been removed.

"*State your Fate of origin,*" the eerie machine demands. I know the soldier is Star-Fated—it's obvious from his armor.

The pressure on his neck eases so he can speak. He gasps but refuses to answer. I ease my fusionblade from the scabbard with my left hand. The moment it ignites, I slash the death drone in half. It falls in two pieces.

I kneel beside the soldier and untangle the steel rope. He gasps. My cold fingers pry off the death-drone beacon. Standing, I toss the blinking black summoner into the air and swing at it with my fusionblade, disabling it.

"Why . . . did you . . . do that?"

"It isn't right," I reply. "You're helpless."

It doesn't mean he'll live. I reach into my pouch and extract a red beacon, placing it on his boot where the black one had been.

"What? Why?" His face scrunches up in agony.

"Because you'll die if I don't get you help. You don't have a moniker. The medical drone won't help you if it can't identify you."

I use my fusionblade to slice off the hand of the dead Sword soldier, pick up the hand, and hurriedly rest it on top of the Star-Fated man's. The medical drone arrives and scans the moniker. Nothing happens. It hovers idle. Then, a bright burst of laser light shines from the belly of the automated medic. It cuts the Gates of Dawn soldier's armor open. I hold my breath as the medical drone goes to work. A syringe emerges and sticks in his neck. He closes his eyes, and the pained expression on his face eases. He loses consciousness. I release the breath.

The ground shakes again. A mortar shell explodes so close that dirt rains down upon my head. I have to stay until the medical drone finishes. If I don't, he'll be shipped away on a hovering stretcher to a medical evacuation ship that will take him to the Twilight Forest Base, right into the hands of interrogators who will do far worse to him than what the death drone had planned.

Sword soldiers stumble past, retreating. I close my visor and move around the man I've chosen to *sticketh* with, pushing corpses to shelter him. Crawling to his side, I make myself as small as possible. The robotic arm sutures singed edges of his skin. It dresses the wounds when it's finished. My resolve to stay begins to wear thin.

The medical drone hoists the Gates of Dawn soldier, loading him onto an inflating stretcher. It secures him to it and flies away. The stretcher lifts to hover, but I destroy the homing mechanism on its side with my sword. It rapidly deflates. With the toe of my boot, I kick the soldier's fusionblade next to his hand, then extract my penlight and prop it against his left thigh, turning it on and facing it toward the sky, hoping it will help his people find him. Then I run.

The roaring thunder of an explosion sends burning flack streaming down on me. I'm knocked sideways. Falling, I'm stunned for a few breaths. I rise to my feet and keep running. Fear makes my stomach heave, but I swallow the bile down. I glance behind me. The flash of fusion fire singes the side of my visor, just skimming over its surface. I turn my head back and keep going.

Ahead, troopships are firing up. The closest one shuts its door and lifts off, leaving me behind. I force myself to push on. My thighs burn with exertion. More fusion fire flies past my shoulder. I get closer to the next troopship, but the door of it closes before I can make it there. It lifts off right in front of me.

I cry this time. "*Stop!*" I scream. "*Please! Stop!*" Panicking, I sob as the ship ascends and grows smaller in the sky.

All around me, broken boy soldiers lie discarded. I trip over one, almost falling, but I right myself again and keep going. The pull of changing wind sucks me forward as a small airship descends in front of me. The door is already open, lined with Sword soldiers. Fusion-rifle fire hums by, the airship soldiers shooting into the gathering storm of the enemy behind me. A few of them jump from the belly of the airship and surge out near me. One tall Sword soldier grabs my arm and drags me back toward the aircraft. No ramp extends when we reach its open door. The tall soldier picks me up and throws me inside, where I hit the floor hard and tumble. The other Sword soldiers jump inside one after another.

The tall one makes a circular gesture with his finger, and we ascend amid exploding mortar shells. The airship shakes and I'm tossed around. The tall soldier falls on top of me, holding me to the floor. The other soldiers hold on to grips on the walls.

I wheeze and try to catch my breath. We stabilize, and the bucking of the airship eases. The tall soldier slides off me. He presses the external button that retracts my visor, and the sword-shaded screen ticks back. Reaching out, I push the button on the side of his helmet. His visor falls away, and the most beautiful storm-cloud eyes gaze back at me. *Hawthorne.*

Chapter 15
A Beautiful Crime

Back at the hangar, I lean against the airship wall, feeling the warmth of Hawthorne's hand next to mine. All the other soldiers have left the aircraft. It's just Hawthorne and me who remain. Our fingers touch. He doesn't say anything. He doesn't have to.

"How did you find me?"

"Commander Aslanbek gave me clearance to track your moniker." He probably thought I was dead. My moniker didn't move for a long time out there. But Hawthorne fought to find me anyway.

"Thank you," I murmur.

His hand moves to cover mine. I wince and cradle it in my lap.

"You're hurt." Hawthorne tries to look, but I won't let him touch it.

"I'll get it looked at later," I reply. The crest etched into the hilt left its mark, and it will be like a death warrant for the Gates of Dawn soldier and his family if my regiment discovers it. It was monumentally stupid of him to use his family fusionblade in combat, or else extremely arrogant. If I ever see him again, I'll *sticketh* my boot up his ass.

Hawthorne's voice is soft. "Do you know what went through my mind when I found out that they took you in the middle of the night and dropped you off somewhere on the battlefield, Roselle?" I shake my head. His expression turns bleak. "I thought, 'Well, that's it, then.

She's gone. She won't survive that. They've figured out a way to kill her as some kind of sick revenge against her mother, and now my life will go back to normal.'" He scowls. "Then I started imagining you on the battlefield—abandoned. Alone." His teeth clench. "I had this pain—this unbelievable ache in my chest. I didn't know why at first, but I do now. I used to worry about active duty because I might be killed. Now I'm terrified that it'll be you who dies out there, and I'll have to go back to a life without you in it."

"You hardly know me, Hawthorne."

"I've been in love with you since I was ten, Roselle . . . maybe even before that."

I shake my head slowly. "I don't understand."

"I've watched you forever—for as long as I can remember."

Disappointment rises in me. "I'm not that person you grew up watching, Hawthorne. I mean, I *was* her, but ever since I left home and Transitioned, I'm not her anymore. She's not me."

"You're right. You're not her. You're better. You think for yourself, and you never back down when you believe you're right. And you're not perfect, like they made her seem. You have flaws, but your flaws are sexy. You're naïve and jaded, smart and gullible, ferocious and delicate. Men will break themselves against your fragile smile."

"And you? Will you break, too?" I ask, a little breathless.

"I'm already broken, Roselle."

His hand reaches over to cup my cheek. For a moment, his warm fingers rest on my nape, his thumb brushing my skin. I've lost the ability to breathe, as if the air is too thin. His face is half in shadow. He leans closer.

Something rattles outside the airship. Hawthorne drops his hand from me. We move apart, afraid to be seen. Another airship is landing in the hangar. We peek through the open door. Twilight soldiers are waiting outside. I recognize a few, Carrick among them. Tolman is with him.

"I know them, Hawthorne," I whisper. "They sent me to the front line this morning."

Hawthorne points with two fingers, first to his eyes, then toward the front of our airship. I nod and follow him to the cockpit. He switches on an audio feed that picks up voices from outside our airship.

"Why is that St. Sismode brat still breathing my air?" an angry voice barks.

"She got lucky. We'll take her again tonight," another voice responds. "No way she survives a second time."

"I want you to deliver a dead secondborn to me!" the first voice screams. "It has to look like the Gates of Dawn are responsible. Contact me when you have her body. I'd like to deliver it personally."

The door of the other airship closes, and the gathered Twilight soldiers move away. Hawthorne is the first to speak. "I'll take care of it, Roselle. I have friends. I'll reach out to everyone in our unit who ever owed me a favor."

"That was a commander. This goes higher up than even him. You can't help, Hawthorne. I'll think of something. They cannot suspect that we know or they'll act sooner."

"They're going to act tonight!"

"Then I've got time."

◦�〷◦

When I get back to my capsule, I decide I have no other option but to talk to Clifton Salloway. I search my moniker for his contact information. Surprisingly, he's not listed under "Inter-Fate Playboy" or "Panty-Dropping Smile." I'm forced to resort to Salloway Munitions. I expect some kind of secretary, but I'm linked directly to the man himself.

"Roselle St. Sismode. What a pleasure it is to see you." His good looks shine through even in holographic form.

"We need to meet."

"Would this be for business or pleasure?" He grins.

"Business."

"Pity," he sighs.

"I have a proposition. When can we speak?"

"How about this evening? I'm en route to Twilight now. We can discuss your *proposition* at my private quarters on the Base."

"I would love to, but some Twilight Forest officers have been having a bit of fun with me. They plan to send me out to the front line again this evening. In a few hours, I'll be knee-deep in mud and blood."

"Don't worry about armoring up tonight. I'll take care of it. I'll send a hovercar and an escort for you at twenty-two hundred." His tone brooks no refusal. I nod and sign off.

I have two hours.

Slipping from my capsule, I make my way to Hawthorne's bunk. I knock gently on the door. It opens almost immediately. I put my finger to my lips and climb down the steps. He follows me. I lead him to the locker room, into an empty shower closet. I lock the door behind us and face him. "I found a way to avoid being sent to the front."

"How?"

"You're not going to like it." His face loses its cautious smile. "I contacted Clifton Salloway. I'm going to meet him."

Hawthorne closes his eyes and turns away. "When?"

"Tonight. It's not what you think. I'm going to make him an offer— one that will be profitable to him. It'll ensure that he'll do everything in his power to keep us from the battlefield."

"Explain."

"Later. I have to get ready to meet his escort. You have to trust me."

Hawthorne leans against the shower door. "You think your plan is going to work?"

"I do. I'll be safe tonight anyway."

"You understand who he is, right?" Hawthorne asks. "He's an arms dealer. He sells weapons, legally and illegally. Men like him make their own rules. Men like that don't do favors for free."

"I'm going to make him seem more legitimate. I still have the St. Sismode name. It's synonymous with weapons. I'll use the name they tried to take from me."

Hawthorne holds me in his arms. "I wish I could protect you."

"I wouldn't be here now if you hadn't found me today." My fingertips slip beneath his shirt, inching it up, exploring his ribs. As I lift the shirt over his head, it turns inside out, like my heart. I let it drop on the floor. Hawthorne's chest is broad and strong.

His hands go to the hem of my shirt, peeling it away over my head, exposing my military-issue bra. Midnight-blue cotton covers my breasts, a light blue string cinching in a crisscross at my back. Hawthorne reaches around me and unties the lace. The string slips from my back. He keeps the ribbon, tucking it inside the pocket of his pajama bottoms.

I arch my brow.

"It has your scent," he answers in a gruff voice. He leans his face nearer.

I tilt my lips up to meet his mouth. His kiss weakens my knees. He gathers me closer to him, and the warmth of his forearm against the small of my back is seductive. His fingertips move to my shoulder, sliding off the blue strap. He kisses my skin, and I shiver. An ache builds inside me. My hand slips to his back, feeling the play of his muscles beneath his smooth skin. The tips of my breasts rub his chest. An explosion of heat drenches me.

Hawthorne lifts me in his arms and presses my back against the wall. My legs wrap around his narrow waist. I feel the hard length of him against me. My mouth finds his again. He holds my bottom, his strong fingers digging into my flesh, his tongue caressing mine.

"I don't want your first time to be in a shower closet," he says.

"What does it matter where," I whisper, "as long as it's with you?"

"When I make love to you, Roselle, it's going to take longer than a few minutes, and we'll need protection. They'll kill our baby and you, too, if you get pregnant. I'll never let that happen."

Being secondborn is a curse that never ends. "I hate them," I hiss. "I hate them all." Hawthorne sets me on my feet. I pick up my shirt and hold it to me. Angry tears threaten.

"Shh . . ." He embraces me again. "Don't cry. It's no good hating them. They can't feel it, and it will only turn you bitter."

"We need to change things."

"We need to stay alive, Roselle. We can work around the rules and still be together. Let me show you."

He takes my shirt and tosses it to the floor by the door. Blue light flashes from the scanner on the wall when he swipes his left hand beneath it. The showerhead turns on. Warm water soaks us both. A smile tugs at my lips. I look up at him. Water runs over his face and drips from his chin. He returns my smile, staring into my eyes. His hands cup my cheeks. His mouth finds mine again, kissing away everything awful about today.

I lean against him. Hawthorne's hand strokes my wet hair. His steely muscles tense under my fingertips. I discover he's a bit ticklish when my unhurt palm caresses his side. He chuckles, his lips grinning against mine. I feel his hands go lower, following my spine to the waistband of my pajama pants. His hand slips underneath the fabric—past my sturdy underwear—to my bare skin. He cups my bottom. I almost melt in his arms. My heart flutters wildly as he explores my body. Eternity wouldn't be long enough to discover the vastness of him, but the seconds tick by. My fingers tangle in his wet hair. The water turns off. Hawthorne reaches over and swipes his moniker again. It turns back on.

"How did you do that?" I ask.

"I'm a higher rank than you. I get a longer shower."

"That's not fair," I say breathlessly.

"Are you complaining?" he teases. "Because I could—"

Rising up on my tiptoes, I kiss him. His tongue strokes mine. He inches my pajamas down, and I step out of them.

I'm naked. With him.

I slide my hand inside his waistband, over the smooth skin of his backside, and his clothes pool with mine on the floor. He groans. "You're so beautiful, Roselle." Softly uttered, his words fill my head. Tender kisses fall on skin. Desire tears through me like fragments of an artillery shell. Its sharp shrapnel travels everywhere with devastating effect. The heat of it is almost too much to bear. "Terribly beautiful," Hawthorne amends.

I'm inexplicably linked to this man, as if he owns pieces of me—shards of my heart. The intimacy existing between us was forged in battle and by circumstance, sealed by a searing need for something real to cling to in a world of disposable people. And I do cling to him, consumed by the upheaval of passion that he elicits in me as I learn his body and he, mine.

The water turns off again. Hawthorne hangs his head. "I'm out of shower credits for today."

It's difficult for me to let go of him, but I must. I move away to the shelf by the door. I take a towel from the small stack of them, wrapping it around me, and then I hand him one. "I'll leave first, and then you," I whisper.

"Wait!"

I turn back around.

Hawthorne takes a step to me and kisses me again. "I didn't get to kiss you good-bye."

I want to linger here with him, but I force myself to leave the shower. On the way to my locker, I toss my wet clothes into the phloem. Selecting my uniform, I take it to the bathroom closet, towel off, and put it on. Back at my locker, I apply cooling ointment to my hand and rewrap it in a dry bandage. Closing the narrow door, I walk to a sink with a mirror above it. I twist my hair into an attractive coil and secure it with pins. I pinch my cheeks, adding some color, but they're already flushed, and my lips are full, swollen from kissing Hawthorne. Evaluating myself in the mirror, I have a glow that was never there before.

"You're stunning, Roselle," Hawthorne says behind me. He has changed back into dry pajama bottoms. His T-shirt is draped over one bare shoulder. The other shoulder leans against the wall. He's so handsome that it's hard not to melt into the floor.

"Do I look different?" I ask as I blush. "I feel different."

"To me you do, but I don't think anyone else will notice," he replies softly.

"I don't have any makeup. Firstborns are used to makeup."

"You don't need it."

"You're biased. You've loved me since I was nine," I tease him.

"I have. I still do—love you."

"How could I not feel pretty now?" I whisper.

My moniker vibrates. I have a message. I read the holographic words.

Meet me at the main gate atrium of your Tree in twenty minutes.
—Clifton

I frown.

"What is it?" Hawthorne asks.

"It's a message from Firstborn Salloway. He wants me to meet him at the main entrance of the Tree. He was supposed to send an escort, not come himself. I'll see you soon." Impulsively, I move toward him to kiss him good-bye, but then I stop and look around. At the other end of the row, soldiers are brushing their teeth. I look down. "This is going to be difficult—not touching you."

"I know. My instinct is to crush you to me and never let you go."

I look into his eyes. "I love your instinct. Try to get some sleep while I'm gone."

"Impossible. Find me when you get back."

I leave the locker room and go to the main gateway of Tritium 101. In the branch hallway to the main trunk, I have to cross through a checkpoint. I scan my moniker. From behind me, a voice says, "Little fish, little fish, we was just comin' to scoop you up in our net. So nice of you to swim downstream to us." Protium 445 soldiers shuffle over to me like a bunch of thugs, their rifles slung on gun straps that hang nearly to their knees. Instead of looking lethal, it looks stupid. I could shoot them with their own rifles.

"I don't have time for you, Carrick. I'm under orders to meet an officer."

"We're under orders to find conscriptions for our next mission, and we choose you." He pokes his finger into my chest.

"You won't like what I do to you if you touch me again," I warn him. He laughs, thrusting his finger into my chest. I snatch his rifle on its low-slung gun strap, shoving it against his heart with one hand on the barrel and one bandaged finger on the trigger. He stills. "Look, little crocodile, I've got you by the tail," I murmur.

His friends scramble to lift their weapons. I unclip the gun strap from Carrick and step back, pointing it at them. "Aw, what happened to the babbling brook?" I ask them.

One of the guards at the checkpoint calls for MPs, who arrive within seconds. I lower the rifle and stand down, offering it to them.

The lead officer speaks to the guards at the checkpoint. I don't say a word. Carrick and his friends try to talk over the guards, explaining their orders to gather conscriptions. I remain silent. No one has spoken to me yet. It's not my turn.

The lead MP faces me. "They say they're under orders to gather conscriptions." Carrick smiles smugly. I want to beat it off him.

"I believe they are, Patrøn."

"And you refuse to go with them?" he asks.

"I do, Patrøn."

"Why? You're a cadet. You follow orders."

"I'm under orders, to meet Exo Salloway at the main atrium. I'm late. I was to be there fifteen minutes ago, Patrøn."

"Why would Exo Salloway want to speak to you?"

"I'm a munitions expert, Patrøn. He's a munitions manufacturer."

"It's past twenty-two hundred," he says, with a skeptical raise of his eyebrow.

"There's a war on, Patrøn. Our enemies don't stop for us to rest. You'll have to address any further questions to my commanding officer."

"Who is your commanding officer?"

"As of twenty minutes ago," a deep voice behind me says, "her commanding officer is Exo Salloway." Clifton approaches from the shadows of the checkpoint. "I have jurisdiction over this cadet."

"She's Tritium 101. She falls under the jurisdiction of Commander Aslanbek," the MP replies, checking his tablet.

"Commander Aslanbek and I are good friends. He understands how important the welfare of this cadet is to me. You can confirm this with whomever you like. Make your contacts. We'll wait. In the meantime, I want a list of every one of these petty criminals' names." He gestures toward Carrick and his men with an easy wave of his hand. Then he reaches into the interior pocket of his long, tailored coat and draws a small silver case from it. He opens it and takes out a slender brown cigar, which he lights. It smells a little bit like burning rose oil.

In a couple of minutes, the lead MP returns. "Our apologies, Exo Salloway. You are free to leave. The Tropo as well."

"The list?" He looks in the direction of the other soldiers.

"Will be sent to you without delay."

"Thank you. Have a pleasant evening." He drops his cigar, stamps it out on the floor in front of them, and offers me his arm. It would be rude not to take it, so I do. We walk together to the nearest heartwood.

As we descend, Clifton says, "You seem to draw a crowd wherever you go."

"Apparently, I'm the most interesting woman in the world," I reply.

"You are," he agrees. "I'm sorry that I haven't intervened on your behalf before this. It was negligent of me not to have realized what was going on here. I've been preoccupied. Will you forgive me?"

"There's nothing to forgive. There's no reason for you to intervene on my behalf."

"Oh, but there is, Roselle."

"I don't understand, Firstborn Salloway."

"It's Clifton. Please, call me Clifton. And I'll explain, but not here. Has your unit been informed of the attack against the Stone Forest Base? I believe it was right after you left."

It was before I left, but I reply, "No."

"Census was destroyed—an explosive beneath the lake flooded the entire place. Took out all of their tunnels."

I feign alarm. "Was anyone hurt?"

"Some agents were killed, but most survived. They were switching out monikers at the time. They've discovered quite a few spies since. The new monikers are impossible to clone. We've been uncovering spies and thirdborns masquerading as firstborns. It's been extremely tedious. I don't want to bore you with the details."

"I'm not bored," I reply. "I didn't know you could clone a moniker."

"You can't anymore. We've stepped up the process of switching out monikers on the Base. They should be starting the process here at Twilight soon. It's only a matter of time before we detect every single traitor in our midst. And then, we'll move on to the general population."

"I thought Exos didn't really work."

He laughs. "You are adorable."

I don't feel adorable. I feel alarmed. The network of thirdborns will be cut down. I try not to think about Dune. He must have found a way to get a new moniker, or they would have just killed him when his was destroyed during the strike against Forge.

Outside, the wind is biting. Clifton puts his gray coat around my shoulders, and we walk to his impressive hovercraft. His hand moves to the small of my back as his driver opens the door for us. I climb in and move over, making room. We fly to a glass Tree very much like the one Clifton occupies at the Stone Forest Base. The driver docks the craft on the edge of the balcony. Clifton gets out and holds the door for me. After we exit, the aircraft slips away to park elsewhere.

Clifton points to mountains along the stunningly beautiful horizon. "Have you been to the Tourmaline Mountains before?" he asks. He reaches into the inner pocket of the coat I'm wearing. It's such an intimate action. If I move my lips, they would brush his cheek. I don't.

He steps back and takes a cigar from the case. Before he can reach into his other pocket, I hold out his lighter to him with my injured hand.

"You're hurt," he says, taking the cigar from his mouth without lighting it.

"It's nothing—a small battle wound. I'll have it taken care of soon."

He lights his cigar. "I'm extremely rotten at my job," he says, puffing out a curl of smoke.

"Again, I thought Exos didn't do anything."

"Not that job, my other job."

"You mean as an arms dealer?"

"No, I have another job that interests me far more than that. I'm one of the active members of the Rose Garden Society. It's a very important position. I wanted to tell you about it before, but you didn't want to give me private lessons."

"Did I hurt your feelings?" I tease.

"You hurt more than my feelings. My ego was severely tested." A genuine smile curves my lips against my better judgment. We walk the balcony, gazing at the canopy of Trees. I try to figure out where my airbarracks is docked.

"You're just over there," Clifton says, pointing over my shoulder, his warm breath on my cheek.

"How do you know that?"

"It's my job to know."

"Your job as a Rose Gardener?" I reply.

"That's right."

"Am I the Rose you're tending?"

"Let's just say that it's in the Rose Garden Society's best interests that you remain alive."

"Why would you care? I'm not the heir."

"Do you know your brother, Roselle?"

"Of course I know Gabriel!"

"Yes, but do you *know* him? He's into some things that make the odds of his surviving to assume your mother's position . . . highly unlikely."

"What things?"

"Bad things. I'm not at liberty to elaborate further at the moment."

"Shouldn't you at least be protecting *him*, then?" I'm powerless to help Gabriel, and it scares me.

"Your mother is doing everything in her power to keep him out of harm's way, but he is who he is."

"What does that mean?"

"It means if something were to happen to him, The Sword would be forced to accept you as her heir."

"So you're hedging your bets. My successor isn't appealing?"

He laughs as if he finds my question delightful. "If you should die, and then Gabriel should die, your mother would have to have another heir. She's still young enough, but getting your father back to do the deed would be asking a lot of the ol' boy. He hates her. An infant isn't what we need. We need a strong leader. Someone fit to be the Clarity of the Fate of Swords, which is not the doughboy next in line should you die."

"The doughboy?"

"Harkness Ambersol. Try saying that five times fast. He's not fit to rule a crella."

"And you think I am?"

"No one has ever been more fit to be The Sword than you—not even your mother."

"That is treason."

"That is the truth. You have a certain moral ambiguity that can get you into trouble, but with the right advisors, you can overcome that."

"So your Rose Garden Society is dedicated to me—to keeping me alive."

"We're just, as you say, hedging our bets."

"This is pretty complicated for you, seeing as we're at war and I'm on active duty."

"It was until recently. Commander Aslanbek has decided to join the Rose Garden Society. It didn't take much convincing. He just had to meet Harkness, and he took a pin from me on his way out the door."

"A pin?" I ask.

"May I?" He indicates the pocket of his coat. I lift my arm so he can reach inside. He pulls out a pin in the shape of a rose with thorny vines wrapping around an ancient sword. "You have quite a few followers, Roselle."

I take the pin and hold it up in the soft light. "Aren't you worried that your secret society will be found out?"

"Not really. We actually do have a Rose Garden Society, all very legal. We commission Sun-Fated workers to do some beautiful landscapes for less fortunate firstborns. But secretly, the society is only interested in keeping you alive. And that isn't illegal either."

"Why are you telling me all this?" I ask.

"There are people who'd like nothing better than to see the St. Sismode name die forever. We want you to know that you can come to us for help."

"There'll be no favors here. I'll pay my way."

"How do you expect to do that?" he asks.

"I told you when I contacted you that I had a proposition for you. Do you know what I did when I first shot a rifle in training at the Stone Forest Base?"

"No . . ." he replies, intrigued.

"They made me assemble the rifle and fire it at a target."

"Ten seconds?" he guesses.

"Seven."

"Bull's-eye?"

"Of course." I smile. "The parts were all Burton. So why don't we use Salloway?"

"Burton was the lowest bidder, and Edmund Burton has worked hard to win your mother's favor."

"How about I make it sexy to have a Salloway weapon?"

"I'm listening."

"I will demo every new weapon you manufacture. I will be your spokesperson. I will make Salloway the brand that everyone has to have. You will own the private sector market. We'll work together on the military, sway the right people in the Sword hierarchy."

"What do you want in return?"

"I want you to start making these." I show him my dual-sided weapon.

"Who made this?" he asks. He takes the weapon and ignites it with surprising grace.

"You'll have to pay a friend of mine for the design. Some money, but mostly you can pay him in merits. I also want you to make a rifle that uses fusion power but can be switched over to hydrogen."

"Why?"

"Because I know something you don't. There *will* be demand, and you'll be in a position not only to fulfill that demand, but to put Burton out of business in the process."

"What do you know?"

"I'm not at liberty to say. You'll have to trust me, Clifton."

I scan my moniker and enter the air-barracks. Everything is quiet; most of the soldiers are slated for medical-rescue detail in the morning. I go to the locker room, change into my pajamas, and climb to Hawthorne's capsule. I rap lightly on the door. It opens immediately.

He grabs my wrist and pulls me inside. It's impossibly tight in here. I practically have to lie on top of him in order for us both to fit. He shuts the door with a touch of his foot to the console. The Secondborn Trials play out on the screen above our heads. They're down to the final competitors—a burly male Sword, a wily female Star, and another male Sword. They look battered and bruised, almost incapable of remaining on their feet for much longer.

"What happened to Linus Star?" I ask, remembering Grisholm's favorite to win.

"He made it pretty far, but he blew himself up when he attempted to use an incendiary to take out a bridge in the 'Up You Go' challenge. He misjudged his fuse timer." Hawthorne's voice rumbles through his chest as I lie against it. It's such a lovely sound—I could lie here forever and listen to him talk. "How did it go tonight?" he asks.

"Better than expected—and worse."

"What do you mean? Will he help you keep Protium 445 off your back?" he asks anxiously.

"He'll take care of them." I kiss the fabric of his shirt over his chest. "Clifton is part of a secret club that plans to kill my brother. I don't know how to stop them short of exposing them—and I need them, so you can see my dilemma."

"He told you that?" Hawthorne asks incredulously.

"No. He said he wants to protect me should anything *accidentally* happen to Gabriel."

"How do you know they'll try to kill him?"

"I don't, but it's the logical next step. Secure me. Make me an ally. Take out the weak player. Put your ally in a position of power. It's a good strategy. They just haven't accounted for my mother. She'll eviscerate them if she hears a hint of this Rose Garden Society."

"If your brother dies without an heir, you're firstborn."

"It will never happen."

"But if it did, you'd leave."

"Theoretically, I'd have to return to Forge—to the Sword Palace."

Hawthorne rubs his hand over my arm. It's comforting. I had no idea how nice this could be, snuggling with him. His voice vibrates my ear. "I'll be twenty next year—old enough to enter the Secondborn Trials. If I win, I could elevate to firstborn status."

"That's the most asinine thing I've ever heard, Hawthorne." I rise up on my elbow and glare at him. "Don't ever say that to me again. Don't even think it!"

"Why not? If I win, we'd never have to sneak around. We'd be able to be together. I could bring you with me. I could marry—"

"You could die for the entertainment of firstborns everywhere!" I snap. "One person wins The Trials. One. That's it! One out of close to a thousand entrants—you have only the slightest chance of making it out alive!" I rest my cheek against his chest again. "I can't do anything right now about the Rose Garden Society. I need Clifton's help. I'll have to rely on Mother to keep Gabriel safe." He kisses the top of my head. "Hawthorne, I have something to tell you, but I don't know how you're going to take it."

"What is it?"

"I did something good and bad. I meddled in your life."

"What did you do?" he asks.

"Promise you won't be mad."

"I can't promise that. You're going to have to tell me what you did and hope for the best."

"I gave Clifton a list of demands. One is that you be pulled off active duty and placed in pilot training—flying medical rescue airships. It's dangerous, but it's noncombat. You won't have to kill anyone—you can save them instead."

His hand stills. "How did you know that was a goal of mine?"

"I made Clifton give me access to your file. You made Meso—they plan on telling you next week."

"You read my private files." He sounds angry.

"Not all of them—and you're not allowed to be mad about that."

"Why not?" he growls.

"Because you've been watching me since you were a child without my permission."

"True," he mutters between tight lips. "But it feels wrong to be taken out of active combat duty when my entire regiment is still in it. They count on me."

"I know—that's why I pulled your closest friends, too."

"So what's the good part?"

"That *was* the good part, Hawthorne."

He sighs. "What's the bad part, then?"

"Clifton knows how to hurt me now—he can hurt you and that will hurt me. It was a risk. I don't know if I should've taken it. I can't see his next move yet."

"You're worried about what he can do to me? Aren't you afraid they'll get to you?"

"I don't know who *they* are. Until I do, I'm vulnerable. You have to know that if you intend to be anywhere near me. I just made your life extremely complicated and incredibly dangerous."

Chapter 16
Where They Bury Me

ONE YEAR LATER

Risk-taking is becoming more and more a part of my DNA. I see it in every secondborn Sword. We're adrenaline junkies, living for the highs because the lows are so low. Too low. Most of us don't expect to make it past the next birthday. The average life expectancy of a Sword during wartime is a year and six months. If that's the case, I only have a few months left to live. My friends are all past due.

I've made it through two tours of active duty, and my third is fast approaching. Trained in combat rescue aviation, I'm now able to fly all types of airships. At first, my job was dangerous, but nothing compared to what a normal soldier faces on the ground. Clifton made sure of that. Mostly, I've been relegated to resupply runs that don't require me to be near the front line. The same can't be said for my friends. Hawthorne, Gilad, and Edgerton fly rescue missions that often require them to pass into enemy territory.

Toward the end of my last tour, though, everything changed. My missions became increasingly harrowing. It alarmed Hawthorne, but Exo Salloway might have been the most furious. He quickly amended the situation, pulling me from duty and ordering me back to inactive status a few weeks before my tour was officially over. Ever since, I've done nothing but work for him as a spokesperson for Salloway Munitions Conglomerate. But my most recent briefing in our Stone Forest Base command center indicated that when I go active again, I'll be on point for more combat missions. It has changed my outlook. I'm growing increasingly reckless—finding it difficult to hide my all-encompassing relationship with Hawthorne.

That's not all that's different. The night terrors sometimes follow me around during the day as well. I try to hide my shaking hands when I'm struck with a bout of crippling anxiety. We all do. The only thing that keeps my mind off it all is my illegal boyfriend. When I'm with him, nothing can touch me.

"Do you think he knows?" I ask Hammon again. "He was acting like he knew something was up when I contacted him this morning. Do you think Gilad told him?"

"Gilad would never tell Hawthorne about your surprise," Hammon replies. She sticks her head out from under the bottom of my Anthroscope airship and holds out her hand. "Air-wrench." The noise in the hangar is irritating. I can barely hear myself think as airships land and power down. Our Stone Forest Tree is especially busy today because several air-barracks are returning from active duty. A new rotation will deploy in a few days.

"Do you see a problem?" I shout. "I think I have to recheck the weld on the magnetizer."

She shakes her head. "It's just a flap rotor. I can adjust it." She slides back under the aircraft.

Clifton has loaned me the sleek-bodied Anthroscope for my commute between the Base and his warehouses, laboratories, and testing facilities. I try to take care of its mechanical problems myself because this isn't a Base ship. The airship is hardly military. It looks like a first-born's ultimate sports-airship fantasy. It has a cockpit control room with two seats and a little apartment in the back where I can change.

Hammon slides back out from under the airship and hands me the tool. I place it in her toolbox. "Done," she says. "When are you headed out next?"

"I'm scheduled to be in the Fate of Diamonds in two days to film an ad campaign for the new Salloway fusionmag. It's the one with the hydrogen-powered magazine option. They're calling it the Culprit-44."

"That's exciting! The glamorous life of the 'Face of Salloway Munitions' never ends," she says with a grin.

I make an ugly face. "Technically, I'm a Weapons Liaison between the Fate of Swords and the Salloway Munitions Conglomerate. Which means that, like you, I'm a secondborn Sword owned by the Fate of Swords. Only now, Clifton is my commanding officer."

"I know, but having Clifton Salloway as your CO is extremely different than having Commander Aslanbek. I don't get to leave the Tree or the Forest Base and fly around the Fates consulting on weapon designs, or have dinners with important Salloway *clients*."

"Some of those *clients* have wandering hands," I reply dryly. "I sometimes have to threaten to break a finger or two."

"Yes, but *he* takes care of you."

"My relationship with Clifton is complicated. He's my boss . . ."

"And he's hot for you."

"He's just used to having any woman he wants, and I keep saying no."

"The thrill of the hunt." She gives me a coy look and wipes some smudge off the side of the gorgeous airship.

"Something like that. He's being *way* too overprotective lately, though."

"How so?" she asks.

"Ever since we returned from our last tour of active duty, it's like he's afraid something bad will happen to me. I know he's been working angles with the powers that be. I just don't know what he's planning."

"You think he's planning something?" she asks.

"He's always planning something, Hammon. He's a master of strategy. And he wants me out of the air-barracks. It's like a thing with him. We argue about it a lot."

"Where does he want you to live?" she asks.

"Ideally, with him. That's completely out of the question, though. I'm staying here."

"You're worried that if he moves you, you won't be able to see Hawthorne?"

"Yes." Hawthorne has been gone for advanced pilot training. I miss him so much as it is. "If Clifton moves me, I'll never get to see him."

"You have Clifton wrapped around your little finger. I'm sure you'll figure out how to get your way."

"No one has Clifton wrapped around her finger," I reply.

She puts away her tools and wipes her hands on her uniform. I hand her a clean rag from the bin. "Do you ever take your gloves off anymore?"

I look down at my black leather gloves with the fingers cut off. The one on my right hand covers my scar. I researched the crest and found out the Gates of Dawn soldier's family name. It's Winterstrom. That's all I've been able to get on him, though. I don't have clearance for anything else.

"I have to handle weapons at Salloway's testing facilities. Most of the handgrips aren't exactly fit to be used yet. Metal filings and spurs sometimes cut me if I don't have gloves on. It's a habit now." Hammon doesn't know about my scar. I keep it a secret from everyone.

Hammon checks the time on her moniker. "Edge should be back soon! *Eeep!* I can't wait!"

"You're sure Gilad won't tell Hawthorne about the surprise?"

She rolls her eyes. "He'd never ruin the surprise. Edge, on the other hand, can't keep a secret to save his fool life." She smiles at me with her beautiful dimples. "You worry too much, though. Hawthorne won't care about a surprise party. He'll only care if you're there. He's been gone for ten days. He's going to need some serious Roselle time."

We enter the Anthroscope's control room. I sit in the pilot's seat and Hammon climbs into the copilot's chair. The engines of the airship fire up so Hammon can check the gauges. "We should take this for a test run," I say nonchalantly. "You know, to make sure."

"Let's!" she squeals. She reaches for a headset. I put mine on, and we strap in. I get clearance from the Tree Fort to take the aircraft to the testing airspace for a mechanical adjustment run-through. We ease out of the hangar. I follow protocol and don't exceed regulated speeds until I reach the testing area. Then I flood the engines, and the ship molds into an aerodynamic, needle-like shape. I turn spirals, listening to Hammon's peals of laughter. We make several circuits until we're ordered back to the hangar.

"I love that so much," Hammon says, during our return trip. "Just getting out of the Tree for a second and seeing the sky. I sometimes forget there's a world outside."

My heart sinks. "Do you hate being a Sword mechanic?" I ask. I got her the job so she wouldn't be forced into infantry combat.

"No, I actually love it. I'm good at it—much better than being shot at all the time. And I hate search and rescue. The mutilated bodies give me nightmares, and *that's* when I *can* sleep. If it wasn't for this job, I don't think I'd still be here. Something would've wasted me a year ago."

After each tour, new Sword faces flood into Tritium 101 capsules, replacing the dead. None of us tries to make new friends.

"What would you be," I ask, "if you could be anything?"

"I don't know. I used to dream about living by the water—like being born in the Fate of Seas. What would it be like to work on a boat and just fish all day?"

She doesn't dream of being firstborn. "That sounds like a nice life."

"Can you see Edge working as a fisherman? My mountain man," she says with a twang.

"I think he'd do anything for you."

"He would." She smiles.

"What are you going to say to him when you see him?"

"Nothing. I'm going to find a quiet nook and jump him—it's been ten days, Roselle. Ten!" She holds up both of her hands and spreads her fingers wide. "How about you? Have you and Hawthorne . . . ?"

My cheeks flood with color. "Nope."

"He's still holding out on you? I have to hand it to him, the boy has willpower."

"Way too much."

"Make Hawthorne forget about caution. Show him that sometimes you have to take risks to prove you're still alive."

"You're right." I power down the Anthroscope and take off my headset. We disembark.

The smile on my face evaporates. Agent Crow stands in front of the airship. He walks the length of it, passing me, with his hands behind his back. When he gets to the nose, he turns his eyes toward me. At least ten more inky kill tallies curve from their corners on either side of his face, and now he also has them notched on his neck. They're thin, but together they represent a seriously frightening number of dead bodies. He presses his finger to the Anthroscope and trails it along the length of the airship's body, stopping in front of me again. "Roselle Sword."

"Agent Crow."

"You never show fear, do you?"

"Why should I fear you?"

He leans near me and sniffs loudly. "I smell it on you, though. You're afraid."

"That's wintergreen. You should have one." I raise my package of breath mints.

His steel teeth grind, but he presses on. "Did you know that it's been a year since Census was attacked here at the Stone Forest Base? It took us a while to sift through the bottom level of our underground facility. It was a swampy mess of muck and water from the lake. They just recently uncovered my quarters. I've been away, living beneath the Platinum Forest Base. Are you familiar with it?"

"No."

"It's in the Fate of Stones. But I'm back now, and I wanted to let you know."

"I'm sure the Fate of Stones will miss you terribly."

"You'll also be pleased to know that I've recovered a certain item that had been lost to me." He pulls back the side of his black coat and shows me my fusionblade in the sheath at his side. The St. Sismode crest is unmistakable. He has had it restored; there's no outward damage that I can see.

A part of me still aches to take it from him, but not a large part. My identity was so wrapped up in it a year ago. Since then, I have come to accept some of the things that I cannot change. This is one of them. Or maybe it's because I have more now—I have friends who love me. I manage a genuine smile.

"I guess I'll always know where it is. You should really try the new sword we designed." I take my dual-bladed sword from its scabbard and ignite it nonthreateningly. "We're coming out with an upgrade in the next few months. It should be a top seller. And, you know, Salloways really are the best weapons now."

He makes no move to take it. Maybe he knows that I could cut him in half without even trying. "They uncovered the vault room," he says. "Some items that were in it have gone unaccounted for."

I extinguish my sword and replace it in its sheath. "You had a vault?" I ask. "I thought you just used your lair to torture unsuspecting young women. Did they steal all your belts?"

He leans back, watching my body language. "No, but we did find a severely decomposed corpse of a young woman. We can't account for her. But it's her copycat moniker that intrigued me most. Do you want to know why?"

"I love a good mystery."

"The last moniker she cloned belonged to Holcomb Sword. Remember him? Twisty mustache . . . MP . . . stationed at the detention center . . . on duty and servicing your cell the night you were there . . . the night of the explosion . . ."

"Huh. He sounds familiar, but it's been so long . . . I couldn't be sure."

"Oh, *I'm* sure, Roselle. It was Holcomb Sword who released you from your cell in the morning."

"If you say so," I reply.

"I do say so."

"I think what you have there is called a coincidence, Agent Crow."

"In my line of work, there are no coincidences. She had other cloned monikers on her, but the one still inside her had his identity."

"Who else's did she have?" I ask, like we're gossiping and I want all the juicy details. "You know who I'd want to be, if I could clone someone?" I turn to Hammon. "Strato Hammon, that firstborn singer who just ran away with that really good-looking Diamond who sings that song I like?"

"Sarday?"

I snap my fingers. "Yes! Sarday!" I turn back to Agent Crow. "Did she have a cloned Sarday?"

"You really are very clever," he replies. "It will be such a triumph when I have you all to myself."

"If you'd like me all to yourself, you'll have to clear it with my commanding officer, Clifton Salloway. Otherwise . . ."

"You think he can save you?" Agent Crow leans in near my ear. His breath is warm against the shell of it. "He can't." With his hands behind his back, he walks away.

"I hate that guy." Hammon shivers. "He makes my hair stand on end."

"He's a psychopath."

"You attract all the fun ones, Roselle," she replies. "Here comes another one now."

Hawthorne strides over from an airship that just docked. Gilad and Edgerton are with him. He looks from me to Agent Crow's retreating back. He lurches in the direction the agent went, intending to go after him. I grab his arm and hold him back.

"Hawthorne, no!"

He turns to me, and for a moment, there are pain and anguish in his eyes. It's Agnes. He still wants revenge for what Crow did to her. "When did he get back? What did he want?" Hawthorne growls.

"He wanted to let me know that he's returned," I reply. Hawthorne is visibly shaken. I've still never told him about stealing the monikers. I won't make him my accomplice.

"I won't let him hurt you. I'll kill him first." He once told me men like Crow never give up. I can tell he's thinking about that now.

A shudder travels down my spine. I focus on Hawthorne's stormy expression. My heart melts a little, and my worry loses its sharp edge. I'm not alone anymore. I have him. I stroke Hawthorne's arm. "Please don't let him spoil your homecoming," I murmur. He gazes at me, and his shoulders ease. He relaxes and loses some of his anger. "Did you have a good flight?"

Hawthorne and Edgerton reply in unison. "No."

"I have something planned for all of you that will alleviate some of your stress," I reply. "If you'll all follow me to Deck 227, I'll show you the surprise."

"I thought it was just a surprise party for Hawthorne," Edgerton interjects.

"Nope," I reply. "I missed *all* of you. Even you, Gilad. So come this way . . ." I gesture and start walking. Hawthorne catches up, his hand brushing mine. That one small touch sends an electric current through my body. My knees feel weak.

"I missed you," he says, so softly that only I can hear.

"What, no date nights while you were gone?"

"No. This really pushy soldier I know spent all my extra merits financing dual-bladed swords for my unit."

"That's unfortunate," I reply. "I'd loan you some of mine, but I used them all for the same purpose."

"I guess we'll have to figure out our own date night then."

"Way ahead of you."

"Where're we going, Roselle?" Edgerton asks.

We take a heartwood down to the lower deck and step off into a sea of soldiers. Hawthorne uses the cover of the crowd to take my hand. His strong fingers thread through mine. I want to wrap my arms around him. "We're just over here," I call behind me. I raise my moniker to the scanner. A steel door opens into a private shooting range. Hammon closes the door behind us.

It's quiet, the walls soundproofed. I hand everyone eye protection. "What about ear protection?" Gilad asks.

"You won't need it." I try to suppress a smile. He gives me a skeptical look. Each station in the gallery has a black box. "This is your surprise," I murmur. "Everyone line up in front of a black box. You, too, Hammon."

"Why me?" she asks with a crooked smile.

"Because it's a family party."

She takes a place in front of one of the black boxes. So do the men. "You can open them," I say. Hawthorne lifts the lid of his box, as do they all. "This is a Culprit-44," I announce. "It's equipped with both a fusion-powered magazine and a hydrogen-powered magazine. Note the dual sides. You will find two extra hydrogen magazines in your black boxes. You will need to swap them out more frequently than the fusion side."

I walk past the tall walls that separate each station. "Do not let that deter you," I continue. "The hydrogen-powered magazine is just as effective in most combat situations as its fusion counterpart and can fire five times faster. It has automatic action. You can trigger continuously, not just in bursts. The weapon maintains accuracy even with the increased rate of fire and frequency because the hydrogen barrel doesn't overheat. The fusion barrel requires a slower rate of fire and frequency because its projectiles are hotter, so it'll warp and lose its precision with automatic action. And, as we all know, switching out a scorched fusion barrel on the battlefield can get you killed. Thus, the need to curtail the frequency of its bursts. You won't run into that with the hydrogen-powered barrel.

"The weapons before you are prototypes. Only a few of them exist. We'll be rolling them into production next week. I wanted my friends to be the first to have them."

Hawthorne, Gilad, Edge, and Hammon slip on their eye protection.

I show Hammon the proper way to load the weapon. Edge aims at the target downfield. Gilad fires several bursts with the hydrogen barrel. "Notice how quiet it is?" I ask. Then I show him how to switch to the fusion barrel, with just a flick of my thumb.

I move on to Hawthorne. He has destroyed the Gates of Dawn silhouette at the farthest point on the range. "What do you think?" I ask him.

"Can you strip this for me and show me how to reassemble it?" he asks, setting it down on a stone slab counter.

"Of course," I reply. He takes a step back. Lifting the weapon, I take out the magazine and begin to disassemble it. Hawthorne inches closer. His nose touches my hair and he inhales. His arm slips around my waist from behind.

Strong lips find the sensitive spot beneath my ear and nuzzle it. "I've missed you," he breathes. Setting the pieces of the Culprit on the counter, I reach up and cup the side of his face, leaning into his kisses. Then I turn in his arms. His hands reacquaint themselves with my curves.

Edgerton's voice hollers from two stations down. "*Whoo!* This is better than flying upside down in a vector spinner!"

I giggle against Hawthorne's lips. "What's a vector spinner?" I whisper.

"You don't want to know. I feel like I'm still wearing his puke from it, though."

"Aw, you poor thing." My hands on the back of his neck gently guide his mouth back to mine.

"I like my present," he murmurs. "Thank you."

Edgerton peeks around the wall. "Hey," he says, chewing on something. "Are these crellas for us, too?" He holds up an already-bitten pastry.

I nod. "Yes, and drinks to go along with them on the bar next to the—"

He shows me his other hand. "This?" he asks. Both hands full, he steps toward me and hugs me with his forearms. "You're the best, Roselle." Hammon joins us with two sparkling wines. She gives one to me. Gilad passes another to Hawthorne.

"A toast," I say, holding up my glass. They look at me funny.

"It's wine, Roselle," Edgerton whispers.

"Er . . . a toast means . . . never mind. Let's drink a sip in honor of our little secondborn family."

"To family," Hawthorne murmurs, looking like he'd prefer to have his mouth on me.

"Family," I say and take a sip.

Hammon chokes on her drink and coughs. Eyes wide, she stares at Hawthorne as if he has ordered her into active infantry duty. "Hawthorne," she gasps with gut-wrenching dread in her voice. "Your moniker has gone golden."

He focuses on his left hand. The holographic sword is no longer silver. Hammon's eyes dart toward me, then to the floor. Gilad stares at Hawthorne as if he has become a walking corpse.

Edgerton is the first to speak. "Hey, congratulations, Hawthorne. Looks like you won the lottery. We're all really happy for you."

"This can't be right," Hawthorne mumbles, as if to himself. "Flint can't be dead."

I turn away, tears stinging my eyes, and pick up the pieces of his Culprit-44. Reassembling the weapon, I place it back in the velvet-lined box and close the lid.

Hawthorne grasps Hammon's upper arms. "How long has it been like that?" She stares at him, growing paler. "Do you know?" He shakes her a little.

"Hey, now," Edgerton says, touching Hawthorne's arm. "Take it easy. Erething's gonna be—"

"How long?" Hawthorne repeats, more desperately.

"I don't know," she replies. "I just noticed it."

Hawthorne turns. "Did you notice it before, Roselle?" I shake my head. I don't want to face him because I don't want him to see my tears.

Edgerton tries a softer tone. "Hawthorne, take a breath. This ain't such a bad thing."

Hawthorne growls. "I have a life here! I have someone I love—who loves me! I have nothing out there!"

"I get it. I do." Edgerton rests his hand on Hawthorne's shoulder. "But there ain't nothin' to be done about it. You're firstborn now. You has to go be firstborn."

Hawthorne backs against the counter next to me. Edgerton's hand falls from him. "I can fix this. I have to fix this," he mutters aloud, but he sounds as if his thoughts are in disarray. He grabs me to him. My tears wet the front of his flight suit. He strokes my hair and rains kisses on the top of my head.

Pounding on the metal door breaks us apart. "Military Police," a deep voice yells through the door. "We're looking for Hawthorne Trugrave."

Hawthorne and I are bred to be cautious. We've trained ourselves always to show restraint, to avoid getting caught, to stay one step ahead of anyone who would tear us apart. But as Edgerton moves to open the door, I know it really doesn't matter now. Hawthorne and I will be separated, and there isn't a thing either one of us can do about it. All of our concealed caresses, all the times I forced myself to look away so no one would notice the love written all over my face—all for naught. I'm still going to lose him.

MPs wander into the gallery. The one with the bushy eyebrows gazes at the holographic image of Hawthorne shining up from his moniker's screen. He finds Hawthorne. "You've Transitioned, Firstborn Trugrave. We have you scheduled on an airship leaving in twenty minutes for Forge. Your possessions will be sent to you. We need to go—"

"I'm not ready," Hawthorne growls, like a cornered animal.

The MP remains friendly. "Of course you're ready. Just come with us. Everything else can be taken care of. Your family needs you now."

"I said I'm not ready!" Hawthorne's hands ball into fists.

The MPs look at one another with here-we-go expressions. "Everything will be fine," one says in a placating tone. "You're going home." All three MPs grab Hawthorne, who thrashes and bucks like a wild beast. Edgerton holds my arm.

"Roselle!" Hawthorne yells. "Just wait!" He struggles against the MPs. Spittle flies from his mouth. The cords of his neck muscles strain as he wrenches. "Roselle! You don't understand. I need to protect her. They'll find a way to bury her. This is where they'll bury her! I have to fix this. I need to fix this!"

"Nobody's going to kill anybody," one of the MPs growls as they drag him toward the door.

"Don't hurt him!" I shout through tears. Edgerton holds me back. I clutch the black box.

"Let 'em take him," Edgerton growls in my ear. "He'll fight harder if you get in the middle of it, and they'll hurt him worse." I know he's right, but it takes every ounce of willpower not to pull the firearm from the box. The MPs drag Hawthorne from the room, and it's over almost as soon as it began. And then he's gone.

I don't remember returning to my capsule, but I can't imagine ever leaving it again. This is where they can bury me.

Chapter 17
Shattered

No one, not even Gilad, has heard from Hawthorne in two weeks. I'm becoming desperate. Tritium 101 is scheduled to go active soon. If I can't get in touch with him, I might not talk to him until I return from the Twilight Forest Base—if I return. I've tried to contact him, but all the overtures I've made have been declined. Whether by him or by my commanding officer is unclear.

I can hardly sleep. But finally, I get Hawthorne's address, and from an unlikely source. As it turns out, Emmy can be bought with crellas and a daily gossip visit. I hate using her, but I'm desperate.

It's been hard waiting to leave the Stone Forest Base, but first I have a private luncheon scheduled with Clifton and some buyers. I haven't asked who, and he hasn't said. It's better this way.

At least I get to pilot the Anthroscope to Copper Towne. The moderately sized city is near the border of Swords and Seas. Usually Clifton and I leave together from his apartment on Base, but he has something scheduled this morning in Forge and requested that I take his chauffeured airship, but I harassed him until he agreed to let me meet him in Copper Towne. I'll dine with Clifton, and then if all goes well, have dinner with Hawthorne.

I change into a stunning rose-red dress and black heels that I find in my locker. Clifton's assistant provides my "uniforms," coordinating them through my Stone attendant. Pulling the long, fingerless satin gloves to my elbows, I breathe easier, knowing my scar is covered. The thigh-high stockings are next. I pick up my black wrap and clutch, and make a dash for the hangar.

After receiving clearance for takeoff, I plot a course for the border of Swords and daydream about what I'll say to Hawthorne when I see him tonight. The trip takes several hours, but I arrive at the Salloway warehouse a little before our appointment.

I walk unhurried to the front offices of the Salloway Munitions satellite warehouse and testing facility. It's not the exquisite headquarters—that's in Forge. This building is "serviceable" and "secure," according to Clifton. Entering through the front doors, I pass through a full-body scanner. Inside the large lobby, sophisticated, masculine-leaning furniture sits beneath a sword the size of a blue whale. I choose the leather chair directly beneath its sharp point.

Ordering a very potent alcoholic beverage from the table unit, I watch as a short, fat glass with two perfect ice cubes pops up through a hole in the veneer. I touch my lips to the rim, marking it with red lipstick, and take the tiniest of sips, just enough to have it on my breath. Then I lean back in my seat, cross my legs, and wait. After ten minutes, Clifton approaches. I let him devour my legs with his eyes. "Abandon all hope, ye who enter here," Clifton remarks by way of greeting.

I try not to giggle. My boss reaches down and takes my hand, helping me to my feet. He kisses both of my cheeks. His lips linger a little longer than appropriate. Then he indicates a brutal-looking man with a thick red scar that runs from his temple to his cheek. "This is Valdi Kingfisher."

I'm given first names only, with last names of birds—it's a hallmark of the business. I nod. "Firstborn Kingfisher."

"This is Pedar Albatross," Clifton continues.

"Firstborn Albatross," I reply, with another nod.

We take the hallway to the main weapons-testing room. Clifton runs through the specs of the new prototype Culprit-44. He gives them each a weapon without the magazines and gestures in my direction. "Roselle, if you would." I approach the station, and they crowd around behind me as I assemble the weapon in under five seconds. I enable it and pop off twenty shots at twenty targets in twenty seconds—all head shots. Clean. They're duly impressed. I casually look at my red-painted fingernails and trigger the weapon, spraying the targets in a barrage of silver hydrogen energy, decimating them. *That* has them whooping with glee.

Pedar sidles up to me as I put the weapon into its case. He leans in close, about to say something, and then I feel his hand on my bottom. I'm debating the best way to kill him when the distinct whine of the Culprit-44 powering up sounds next to us. Pedar and I glance at Clifton. His face twists in a scowl. "Never touch her. She's not for sale, only the weapons."

Pedar drops his hand. Valdi smacks him upside the head, ordering the smaller man out of the building to wait in the airship.

"My deepest apologies," Valdi says to both Clifton and me. "He's an animal. I will deal with him later, on your behalf." I nod, but Clifton is fuming.

"Shall we have lunch?" I interject.

Clifton takes my arm and places it in the crook of his own. Wordlessly, we leave the testing room. A light repast is set up in the penthouse office suite. We sit around a table with luxurious white linen. Above the table, a chandelier with hummingbird crystals sparkles with golden light. As we eat, I sit quietly while Clifton and Valdi discuss quantities and delivery dates.

Dessert arrives, a confectionary bird's nest with two ice cream eggs. I eat some, then sit back and sip coffee. The conversation turns to the Secondborn Trials. Valdi and Clifton discuss the merits of last year's competitors, especially the winner of The Trials, a burly Sword-Fated man named Nazar who decapitated a Star-Fated woman in the "Headless-Friendless" challenge and torched a Sword-Fated man in the "Shade of the Sun" winner-takes-all finale.

"I'm sorry," Valdi says to me. "Are we boring you with our talk of brutality?"

"No," I reply.

"Were you able to follow it?"

"Quite able. You're an odds maker, Firstborn Kingfisher. You make money not only by calculating the likelihood of a winner, but also by making sure that the person who's least likely to win doesn't."

He chuckles. "That's exactly right. I'm curious, Roselle. Why is it, do you think, that a Sword wins the Secondborn Trials each year? One could argue, and many do, that a Star or an Atom, with all of their ingenuity, should have better odds of winning the title."

"You're asking me if I have a theory?"

"Yes, Roselle, what's your theory?" He raises his cup to his lips, watching me over the rim.

I set down my cup. "The average secondborn Sword soldier is Transitioned by the age of twelve. Many of us go earlier, though, as young as ten. I was taught to fight since I could walk, by one of the most skilled assassins of our lifetime. By the time you stopped sucking your thumb, I knew a thousand ways to kill you with mine." I hold my red-painted thumbnail out to him. Then I lift my spoon and pick delicately at my bird's nest. "That's not strength, that's ingenuity, problem-solving, and training. The average secondborn Transition age for the other Fates is eighteen. No one fears them like they do us, because only secondborn Swords have to struggle every day to survive, with or without a Trial."

Valdi sets his cup down on the table and holds out his palm to Clifton. "I'd like one of those rose pins, if you have one to spare."

After we say our good-byes to Valdi, I check the time. It's taken longer than I thought, and I'm anxious to leave. Clifton sits back in his chair, stirring his coffee. "I'm sorry about Pedar. That will never happen again, I promise you."

"I wasn't surprised."

"You weren't?" His golden eyebrow rises in a cunning arch.

"You named him Albatross for a reason."

He chuckles. "You are insightful."

"I can see why he was confused, Clifton. You weren't just selling arms today—you were selling me and the Rose Garden Society."

"I was garnering support for the cause."

"That cause being keeping me alive?"

"That is my main concern."

I set my napkin aside and rise. Clifton frowns. "You're leaving so soon? I thought we could spend the evening in Copper Towne. We have another luncheon scheduled tomorrow. It will save you the trip back and forth."

"That sounds lovely, but I can't. I only have day-pass access codes. I have to be back on Base by lights out, unless you've cleared it with Tritium 101?"

Clifton sighs, annoyed. "Forgive me, I forget sometimes that you're not . . ."

"One of you?" I ask.

"Precisely . . . you're not one of us, and you're not one of them. You're something else entirely." Whether he's speaking of firstborns and secondborns, I'm not exactly sure. Clifton rises from his seat. "I will walk you out."

He takes my arm, and we catch an elevator to the lobby. He kisses my cheek at the door. "I'll see you tomorrow. Plan on staying in Copper Towne tomorrow night. I want to take you to a show."

I cannot get to the Anthroscope fast enough. I plot a course to the address I have in Forge. On the way, I go over all the things I want to say to Hawthorne. My palms sweat as I enter Old Towne, the historic district in Forge. Goose bumps break out on my arms as my airship approaches the Sword Palace. I hadn't recognized the address, but it is among the residences of the Sword aristocracy.

The sun has gone down by the time I find an available hoverpad about a block from the address. Gigantic old buildings line this street. They're classic estate homes that have the feel of the Sword Palace in their stone and design. Old trees line the walk.

Pausing in front of a gray stone residence, the largest estate on the street, my stomach churns. The home takes up almost the entire block and the block behind it, with unimpeded airspace above. The flag above the frieze has an elaborate crest. *Who are you, Hawthorne?*

I move down the street and around the block. A high security wall encloses the back of the estate. If I attempt to scale it, it will likely trigger an alarm, and the last thing I need is to get caught in Forge stalking a firstborn. I walk back to my airship in the dark and retrieve my emergency bag from the storage unit in the back, where I have a training outfit, tools, and a half-dozen weapons. I quickly change into the midnight-blue outfit and boots. Disassembling the rifle's scope, I bring the eyepiece with me, leaving everything else behind.

Returning to the estate, I climb a tree until I'm above the security wall. I lift my scope and place it to my eye. A part of me knows just how wrong this is, stalking my love at his home, but I'm way past talking myself out of it. What I see through the windows makes my heart squeeze painfully. Hawthorne is having a dinner party.

I lean forward on a branch. Soft lights shine through the windows of an elegant dining suite. Hawthorne is dressed in an exquisitely tailored black coat, laughing, a beautiful blond female seated next to him. He lifts a glass of wine from the table and takes a sip. She touches his other hand. My face floods with heat. I feel the burn of tears rising and force them down.

He's not hurt! No one is preventing him from contacting me. He can visit me anytime he wants. He can accept my transmissions. He can do anything he pleases. He's firstborn!

He flirts with the young women at his table. Jealousy devours my heart. Some of his friends look familiar, but I can't place them. It doesn't matter anyway. What matters is that they're all firstborn, and Hawthorne is one of them now. A part of me knows I should be happy for him. A part of me will try to be. The other part of me has to leave now if I plan on surviving this.

I jump out of the tree and storm all the way back to my Anthroscope. Wheeling the airship around, I break several safety laws as I blast out of the city. Somewhere between Forge and Iron, I wipe my wet cheeks with the back of my sleeve, vowing never to cry for another firstborn again.

Chapter 18
Flannigan's Man

The next morning, I apply more concealer under my eyes at the locker room mirror.

"Do you think I could use some of that?" Hammon asks.

I pass the makeup stick to her. She brushes it on beneath her eyes, covering her own dark circles. "Are you okay?" I ask.

"I'm fine. I think I just ate something awful last night."

"Maybe you should call a medical drone."

"I feel okay now," she replies. "I'm afraid to ask you how it went last night."

"Do you want to help me prepare my ship? I'll requisition for maintenance, and then we can talk about it."

She brightens. "Put in the requisition, and I'll meet you in the hangar after I get my tools."

I head to the hangar, and I'm almost to my airship when I see Agent Crow lurking near it. I turn to leave, but he catches me. "Roselle Sword, I need a word with you."

"Good morning, Agent."

"Good morning. You look tired. Did you have a trying evening? Losing sleep over something, perhaps?"

"I've had a few nightmares lately, but none while I've been asleep."

"The hazards of being you, I presume. I've actually heard that you recently lost your friend. The MPs tell me Hawthorne Trugrave put up quite a struggle."

"I'm sure he's over it now," I reply.

"Quite. You wouldn't know how it is, but the Transition from secondborn to firstborn is illuminating. It's like being reborn."

"You would know that better than I." *Because you murdered your own sister.*

"Yes. I also know that he has all but forgotten you by now. You probably never even enter his mind." I try not to wince. Agent Crow smiles. "I had a chance to interview the MPs who took you from me that day a year ago. They said Tula did your detention intake."

"And?"

"And she remembers you."

"That's not surprising. A lot of people remember meeting me. Unfortunately, it doesn't work both ways."

"I believe that. You're something of a celebrity, aren't you?" he says with faux sympathy.

"I'm just secondborn."

"The thing I find surprising," he goes on, "is that Tula seems to recall another young woman who was processed into detention before you came in."

I know he's talking about Flannigan. "They made a lot of cells for a reason. Bad girls are everywhere."

"I have an interview with Holcomb Sword in about"—he glances at his moniker's timekeeper—"thirty minutes. I can't wait to find out what he remembers about that night."

"Good luck with that," I reply, with all the confidence I can muster.

Agent Crow turns to leave just as Hammon arrives with her toolbox in hand. A look of pure joy crosses his features, and he begins to circle back to us with a wicked silver-toothed grin. Hammon becomes alarmed.

"You're right, Roselle. Bad girls *are* everywhere." He scans Hammon from head to toe. "You're pregnant, secondborn." All of the color drains from Hammon's face. It's like an aphrodisiac to Agent Crow, and he moves closer, touching her cheek with the back of his fingers. "The thing is, we, in Census, don't lock up bad girls. We kill them." He casts a glance at me. "I'll be back for you both shortly."

He strolls away, leaving the hangar. The moment he's gone, Hammon falls into panicked gasping. Her hand reaches out, bracing her against the side of my airship. I touch the back of her neck. "Take deep breaths, Hammon. Slow and easy. You're all right." I feel my own panic rising.

"He's going to kill me, Roselle," Hammon wheezes.

He is. He's going to kill her for getting pregnant. He's going to murder her in the most desperately painful way, and there isn't a thing I can say or do to stop him. Unless—

"Hammon, we have to act now. Can you pull yourself together?"

"He's going to kill me, Roselle."

"I won't let him. We're getting you out of here. It's going to be fine. Ask Edge to meet you in our locker room. Don't say anything else, just get him there."

"Right now?" she asks.

"Yes, right now."

With trembling hands, Hammon sends the message to Edgerton as we walk—fast but without being obvious—back to my locker. Opening it, I grab for the black glove that I wear to cover my moniker. "Put this on." I look around to see if anyone is watching us, but no one is in our aisle. I unhook a latch and slide the heel of my boot aside. Inside are two lead squares. I take them both out and hand one to Hammon. "Put this inside the glove, over your moniker."

I stand up and put both hands on her shoulders. "Go to your locker and take out anything you think you'll need to survive. Put it in a small bag. Bring it back here in two minutes."

Hammon nods and leaves. People walk by, but no one is paying attention. I take out my fusionblade and thrust the hot edge against the welds in the floor of the locker. The soldered fragments bend. I pry open the bottom. Inside is the bag full of stolen Census monikers. I pull out the bag and set it aside. With shaking hands, I weld the bottom back in place with my fusionblade.

Sweat slides down the sides of my face, and I nearly scream when I notice someone beside me. "It's just me," Hammon whines, sounding terrified. "I don't know where Edge is! He's not responding!"

I close my locker and settle the strap of the bag on my shoulder. "If he doesn't make it here in the next few minutes, Hammon, we're going to have to go without him."

"Go where?" Her bottom lip trembles.

"I'll explain when we're in the hangar."

My heart is in my throat as we go to the door of the locker room and wait one minute . . . and then two . . . and then three. Edgerton strolls in with a ration packet in one hand and a canister of water in the other. "I told you you'd be hungry after breakfast when you didn't eat anything," he says casually. "I just have a second to drop this off to you, then I have to be—"

I grab the water canister from his hand and thrust a glove into his palm before tossing the water in a bin. "Put this on. Don't ask questions. I'll tell you everything you need to know when we get to the hangar. Move!" Edgerton is a soldier. He follows orders. When he has the glove on, I shove the lead square over the top of his moniker. It goes dark. "Follow me."

We make it to the hangar. No one is watching us. Entering my airship, I wave Hammon and Edgerton in and close the door.

"What is going *on*?" Edgerton demands.

"I'm pregnant," Hammon whispers. "Agent Crow knows, and he's going to kill me."

Edgerton is struck dumb.

Amy A. Bartol

"We're leaving," I tell him, "and where we're going could get us all killed, but it's the only shot Hammon has now, so we have to try. Agent Crow doesn't know you're the father, Edge. You don't have to come with us. It's up to you, but we have to leave now, and when we do, you'll never see Hammon again. So decide what you want to do while I go get clearance to leave the Base."

"I'm coming," Edge says before I can move.

"Good. There's a compartment under the floor. You can hide in it. Stay here until we clear all the checkpoints. I'll come get you when it's safe." He nods. Hammon moves to the seat beside the door to the cockpit and straps in.

I turn and run to my seat in the front of the airship, skip the pre-checks, and contact the Tree Fort to get clearance for the flight. Clifton has arranged for overnight access codes. I just have to hope that Agent Crow doesn't detect that I'm leaving. As I wait for the Tree Fort to respond, every movement in the hangar gives me panic attacks.

"I think I'm going to be sick," Hammon moans behind me.

"You can be sick," I reply in the calmest voice I can manage. "I've got you, Hammon. I'm going to take care of you."

She groans. "They're going to kill us all, Roselle. I'm murdering you and Edge." I hear her vomit.

"No one is murdering me," I reply. "We're at our best in our darkest hours. This is pretty dark, so we're going to be okay."

"He knew, Roselle! He just looked at me, and he knew!" Hammon sobs.

"His super power is observation," I reply. "That's why he's so good at his job. He's only around because of me—it's my fault this is happening. I have a plan, but I don't know how it will play out. Luckily, I have a bargaining chip."

"It better be a big chip."

"It's the biggest."

My headset turns on with a soft hum. *"You're go for mission, 00-000016."*

I hardly wait for the hangar door to open before lifting off and setting a course for a Salloway Munitions facility that borders the Fate of Stars.

"You can go get Edge out now," I tell Hammon when I cross the final checkpoint.

I hear her unbuckle her harness. She stands, comes to me, and rests her hand on my shoulder. I reach up and cover her hand with mine. She lets go and walks back to the hold.

Edgerton joins me a while later, settling into the copilot's seat. "Hammon is lying down in the back. She's a wreck, Roselle."

"How are you, Edge?"

"How am I?" He curls his bottom lip out. "I'm pretty bad. I really messed up erething. I've killed my best friend. She's dead if they find her—all because I couldn't leave her be. And I just allowed another friend to smuggle me out of the place that has been my home for most of my life—from the only world I know how to operate in. I'd say I'm pretty messed up right about now."

"Yeah, but other than that, how are you?" I ask.

He laughs grimly. "You're what my granny called an ol' soul, Roselle. I knew it the first time I seen you atop a pile of rubble, siftin' through it like the people underneath it meant somethin'."

"They did mean something."

"To you, maybe, but not to this world. This world just don't care."

"Someone once saved my life, Edge, and when he did, you know what he said?"

"Wha'd he say?"

"He said, 'You can't go back in. They'll kill you. From this moment on, we go forward. We never look back.'" A tear rolls down my cheek.

"Was that when you left home?" he asks.

"Yeah," I answer in a raw voice.

"But Hawthorne's back there." He gestures with his thumb.

"I haven't heard from him since he left, Edge. It's like you said, he's firstborn now. He's gone."

"Nothin' is too late if you're still breathin'."

I wipe my tears on my sleeve. "Then we'll have to keep breathing."

"What's your plan?"

"We're never going to make it to the Salloway Munitions testing facility."

"We ain't?"

I shake my head. "I'm going to make it look like this airship malfunctioned, and then I'm going to land it in enemy territory. We're going to the Fate of Stars."

His face falls. "That's your plan? We're going over to the other side?"

"It's our only shot to keep Hammon alive."

"Then what—the Gates of Dawn kill us, right?"

"I hope not. Your job is going to be to protect Hammon—you tell them whatever you have to tell them. You make sure they know she's pregnant, and you're seeking asylum. Just keep saying it."

"What about you?" he asks.

"They're going to hurt me, Edge." My voice cracks. "There's no getting around that. They're going to hurt me until I can get someone to listen to me—then everything will be all right. I have something they want."

It's dodgy near the border. Alerts ping my headset, one after the other, warning of the dangers this close to the border of Stars. Airships do enter the Fate of Stars, but they have authorization and take secured routes patrolled by fighter pilots. Edgerton takes the controls and shows me how to fly at a low altitude to avoid detection. He guides us into the area where the most recent fighting took place. The ground below is covered with bloated bodies and blown apart by war machines.

He lands us in an open field. "What do we do now?" he asks.

"We wait."

Soon a crowd of Gates of Dawn soldiers circles us. My knees knock as I rise from my seat. "This is it, Edge. I'll go out first. You stay with Hammon and protect her for as long as you can."

"I should go first," he retorts.

"No. You should stay and protect your baby. I know what I'm doing." It's a lie.

He grits his teeth and nods. With Flannigan's bag over my shoulder, I walk out with my hands raised. Armed soldiers shout conflicting orders at me. I walk a few feet, and then stop. "I need to talk to a man, to Flannigan Star's man. I have an important message for him."

"Never heard of him," a brutish soldier replies.

The crowd of warriors begins shouting: "Kill that bloody bitch!" "It's Roselle—The Sword's daughter!" "Take her head off!" Mud is flung at me, striking me in the face and chest. I don't try to wipe it off.

"I need to speak to Flannigan's man," I insist. "I have something for him."

The man in front of me snarls and spits in the dirt. "I have something for you!" He swings his meaty fist at me—a left hook.

I sidestep it and try again. "Flannigan Star is female—a privateer. I need to talk to the man who will ask about her. I have a message from her. An *important* message!"

An ugly soldier throws an uppercut. I jump back, colliding with someone else's fist. It knocks me sideways. My ear rings. The crowd around me cheers and laughs. My instinct is to reach for my fusion-blade, but I can't. Someone will kill me before I can get away, and then they'll kill Hammon and Edgerton. I have to take my beating.

Fists rain down on me from every angle. I stagger and vomit, wheezing and doubling over. The blows to my kidneys are excruciating. I don't remember hitting the ground, but the sharp edge of a boot in my sternum leaves me seeing spots, and then nothing.

࿇

My head feels solid. I can't see anything except a red light. I try to open my eyes but my eyelids won't move. "Hey, you. Wake up!" Someone slaps my cheek.

"For your sake, don't hit her again!" a man roars. "The next person who hits her is dead! Do you understand? If she dies, I'll slaughter every last one of you stupid, filthy animals!"

"You weren't delirious, Reykin," another voice says. "Roselle St. Sismode really did save your miserable life. Look at her hand!"

"I can see it!" the first man barks.

I retch again, my body wracking with dry heaves. An arm behind my shoulder and another behind my knees pick me up. I moan. My head slumps against a solid chest. "I know it hurts," a low voice says. "I'm not going to let them near you again. Get her bag, Danny, and take it to him. Tell him she's with me in triage."

❧

I smell like blood, pee, and vomit, but mostly pee. I try to open my eyes, but something slimy covers them. I try to pull it off, but someone grasps my hand and holds it gently in his own. "Don't touch them. The leeches will fall off on their own." A man's voice.

"Medieval . . . torture . . ." My voice doesn't sound like mine.

"The leeches will take the swelling down so that you can open your eyes. Do you know where you are?"

"Stars . . ." I rasp. "Dawn."

"That's right—a Gates of Dawn base. Do you know who I am?"

"Flannigan's . . . man . . ."

"No. I'm not Flannigan's man."

I growl in despair. "Need him."

I feel his thumb trace the scar on my palm. "I'm a friend . . . and a friend *sticketh* closer than a brother, even to a black-hearted angel."

I lick my lips. "You."

"Me."

"Hurts . . ."

"I know. You can sleep now." Something sharp jabs into my arm.

⌒⌒

I jerk awake, groaning with a half sob. I'm in a bed in a beautiful room, but I feel as if I'm lying on embers. I've been in pain before, but never like this. Everything aches. My eyelids feel thick and heavy. My head throbs. *Focus,* I tell myself.

Mahogany wainscoting lines the walls. Snowy-white curtains drape over the large windows. I see a high ceiling with decorative molding and bright chandeliers above me. *Maybe this is what death is like.*

My hand moves over the blankets. The bedding is masculine, but no less gorgeous for that, soft sheets like those at the Sword Palace. As I turn my head on the plump pillow, my neck muscles revolt. I wince and moan.

The man has aquamarine eyes and dark hair shaved close on the sides, but the top is longer, like Gabriel's fashionable style. He looks to be around twenty-four or twenty-five, a year older than when I last saw him on the battlefield. "Winterstrom."

"You know my name," he replies in the deep voice that I sometimes hear in my dreams. I lift my right palm out to him so that he can see his crest burned into it. "Why didn't you get it removed?" he asks.

I drop my hand, mostly because holding it up hurts so much. "I would've had to tell the physician how I got it. They make a point of reporting wounds like this. They would've researched the crest, like I did, and then Census agents would've been dispatched here to find you." I look down at myself. I'm clean. Someone bathed me. I hope it wasn't him.

"So you protected me yet again. Why?"

"I wanted to find you myself and tell you what a stupid move it was to bring your family fusionblade to a war."

"Really?" He leans forward, forearms on his knees. His shoulder doesn't seem to be troubling him. His right collarbone is straight under his fashionable dress shirt.

"No," I reply. "Not really. I never thought I'd see you again." I touch my head. It's wrapped in a bandage, which I begin unwinding.

Winterstrom sits down on the mattress next to me. He tries to stay my hand. "What are you doing? You have a concussion." The bandage is bloody by my temple. I probe the wound. It's deep.

"I need you to stop fixing me! I need every single bruise and contusion your soldiers gave me. My Fate needs to see my wounds so that they don't accuse me of being a traitor."

"You plan to go back? You're going to have to explain yourself."

"My friends—the ones I came with—are they here, too?"

"Yes."

"Are they hurt?"

"The male is. The female was untouched."

"How bad is he?" I ask.

"Better than you," he says grimly. "They're safe."

I exhale in relief. "Flannigan's man?"

"He's here as well. He's waiting to speak to you."

"I need to meet with him now. I don't have a lot of time." I inch toward the far side of the big bed. Every move is a struggle. The metal apparatus attached to my right arm slides a little as I straighten my elbow with a small stab of pain. I yank its needle out and scoot to the edge of the mattress.

Winterstrom rises to his feet. "You're in no condition to move. You're weak. You've been sedated for two days."

"Two days!" I breathe hard with fear. I stand and immediately regret it. A disorienting rush of blood to my head almost knocks me to the floor. I catch myself with both my hands, and Winterstrom helps me back into the bed. I realize that the only thing I have on is an oversize shirt, and by the smell of it—a soft scent of lemongrass—it belongs to him. "How is it that they haven't found me yet?"

"We've been jamming your signals since you entered our airspace—that includes your moniker. No one knows you're here. Why did you come?" he asks. "Are you seeking asylum, like your friends?"

"I have to make a deal—with Flannigan's man. Do you have my bag?"

"I gave it to him."

"Did you see what was in it?"

"State-of-the-art moniker chips, thousands of them. Moncalate. Profile programmer. Worth a fortune."

"Flannigan died for it. Was it worth her life?"

"I don't know. You'll have to ask him."

"What's his name?"

A deep voice behind Winterstrom answers me. "We've been introduced. My name is Daltrey Leon." He enters the room and closes the door. I remember him as a hologram in the middle of the night at the debriefing with the Clarities. In person, he's not ghostly. He's tall, with long dark hair tied back at his crown. His full beard is meticulously well groomed, and his sandy eyes bear an uncanny resemblance to Dune's.

"Is that your real name?" I ask. "Your brothers have different ones. It's so hard to keep up."

"So you did recognize me that night we met. I often wondered. I took a chance by not wearing the colored eyewear that I normally use. Your mother is usually so observant, but I think she only had you on her mind that night."

"Are there more of you about?" I ask wearily. "I know of three—you, Walther, and Dune."

"I'd rather not answer that question."

"Why? You know everything there is to know about me. I'm at a disadvantage."

Daltrey's eyes don't leave mine. "Thank you for arranging this meeting, Reykin. I'd like to speak with Roselle alone."

"I'll stay," Reykin Winterstrom replies.

"This is family business, Reykin."

"I wasn't aware she was a member of your family, Daltrey."

"She's my brother's daughter."

"By blood?" Reykin asks.

"No, but there are stronger ties than blood. Ask her who her real father is. I doubt she will tell you Kennet Abjorn."

"She has my protection," Reykin says.

"Are you both serious right now?" I ask. "I have a list of demands, and then you're going to let me return to the Fate of Swords. You can argue about who has more right to hear what I'm about to say after I'm gone."

"I think she's delirious, Daltrey," Reykin says, reaching out to touch my forehead. I would swat his hand away, but it's cool and soothing against my skin. "You should come back after she's had more time to recover."

"No, this is who she is," Daltrey responds. He picks up another chair and brings it to the side of the bed. "She's been taught to think— to reason—to strategize. She's performing to the high standards of her training, and I'm very interested in what she has to say." Reykin's hand slips away, but he doesn't leave my side. He's sticking around. It's somewhat endearing.

"You have Flannigan's bag?" I ask Daltrey.

"I do. Thank you for delivering it to me."

"She had a message for you."

"I'd like to hear it."

"She said, 'Tell him it was nearly flawless.' And then she said to tell you to miss her every day."

A sad smile touches his lips. "Tell me how she died."

I explain in detail our meeting and subsequent foray into Census. "I've had the monikers for a year. I haven't known what to do with them—who to contact."

"You didn't need anything until now," Daltrey replies. It's a harsh assessment that paints me in a self-serving light.

"Oh, I've needed plenty, Daltrey," I counter angrily. "I just had to survive on my own."

Daltrey studies me. "Until now, but you have very little to bargain with, Roselle—I'm in possession of everything you and Flannigan stole from Census. You held nothing back from me. You've lost your position of power."

"Have I?" I ask calmly. "That's interesting, because I feel like I have all the power in this room. You may have the bag, but it's useless without a way to upload your fake profiles. If they never make it into the Republic's networks, then what do you really have? A bunch of holograms that won't scan."

"We're Stars—infiltrating networks is what we do."

"It's what you *used* to do. Your network of spies has been decimated. Admit it. Your operatives in the field couldn't get out with their copycat monikers and were all cut down. Those still alive have had to go to ground. You're losing everything."

He's unruffled. "You have set us back as well, Roselle—you and your hydrogen-powered alternatives. You've made the antiquated method of weaponry sexy. Our best hope for winning this conflict is being thwarted by you."

"I'm interested in saving the lives of secondborn Swords. All your Gates of Dawn soldiers are doing is killing secondborns. It's completely senseless, your war. You're changing nothing. If you want to rebel, rebel against firstborns. Instead, you've let them go on with their lives while you murder us in droves. You can choose to walk away anytime you want. Secondborn Sword soldiers have no choice but to fight you or die. Either you kill us or they kill us. There are zero options for Swords."

"Secondborn Swords have options," Daltrey replies. "You could lay down your weapons and revolt against firstborns. You can join us whenever you wish."

"We can cross your line and get our heads beaten in, you mean." I touch the wound on my temple.

"The secondborns of your Fate need a leader to show them the way," he replies.

"I can help you with your moniker problem, and then you can leave me alone. I'll never tell who is really a thirdborn or a spy."

"You have no power to make demands, Roselle."

"I fail to see your point of view."

"I have your friends. You'll do as I say or I'll kill them, and then I'll kill you."

"I think this is called mutually assured destruction, Daltrey. Without me, there *is* no more you. I'm your best chance to operate in the Fate of Swords—or any of the Fates of the Republic. If you don't return me, a certain arms dealer will come looking for me. He makes weapons that are not currently accounted for in any ledger. A lot of those weapons find their way here. He'd hate it if his spokesperson didn't come back. It could make him very angry."

Daltrey gives me a genuine smile. "Dune will be so proud. What are your demands?"

"My friends each get a new moniker and new lives as firstborns—someplace near the sea where they can live without the constant threat of war. You protect them with everything you have. I'll provide currency for them to live on. We will make arrangements for the transfer when I'm back in my Fate."

"You have money?" he asks. He doesn't seem at all surprised.

"I'm a spokesperson for a weapons dealer during a civil war. Money is not hard to come by."

"How will you convince your Fate that you were the victim of circumstance here? You look guilty—flying in here with your friends and landing in enemy territory."

"It's not going to be easy. I might not be able to convince a certain Census agent, who wants me as his personal punching bag, that I'm innocent. He might have to die."

"That can be a problem for you. Maybe you should rethink your options and remain with us."

"That would be bad for you. You need me to go back. You just let me win our argument—you want me to think I'm not being controlled, but I'm really doing exactly what you want me to do. All this, this war, it's an exercise in futility."

His stare sharpens, and he sits up straighter, waiting for me to explain.

"This has all been a lesson so that when you make me The Sword, I do things differently—so that when I have true power, power you've given me, I change things."

He tries to suppress a smile, but it's there, in his eyes. He's impressed that I've figured it out. "You know what it's like to be a Transitioned secondborn, Roselle. The one person you've loved your entire life is a thirdborn. Your moniker was disabled before you were processed. You were exposed to the lawlessness of Census, hunted by an agent who subjected you to his unwavering cruelty. You've been embroiled in a war where no one wins—where you're expected to slaughter wounded soldiers." He gazes at Reykin before looking back at me. "Many people have died to show you just how bad things are in our world, and you alone will be in a position to change things."

I was only guessing, but it really is true. "If I become The Sword, I'll have Fabian Bowie and his son Grisholm as my constant adversaries. One word from either of them and my position of power would vanish in the wind."

"Your charisma and your mind far exceed theirs. They are pure entitlement, but you will win the hearts of your people. I have faith in you, Roselle. You have not disappointed me once since you were born. You are the Crown of Swords."

"There's just one thing—I love my brother."

"I'm sorry about that."

"It changes nothing in your eyes, does it?"

"No. It doesn't."

"I need to go back to my airship. I'd like to leave by tonight."

"I don't think that's the best option. You'll leave the airship here. They won't be able to check the logs and your ruse of a malfunction won't be discovered. We'll get you passage back to Swords on a watercraft. Reykin can make the arrangements. He'll also provide the self-replicating malware that will allow us to penetrate their industrial control systems. You'll simply have to find a way to deliver it. And since you and Reykin have an affinity for each other that goes deeper than with anyone else I could assign, he'll be your contact. It's best to have a natural connection, and he's smarter than he seems. With the exception of your scar, he rarely makes a mistake. And he's a bit more ruthless than most, which has its uses. I trained him myself to fight—I also trained Dune, so you're well matched." Daltrey rises from his seat. "If you need me, get a message to me through Reykin." He glances at the younger man. "Make sure her scar is removed before she returns to Swords."

"It'll be done," Reykin agrees, then he stands and walks Daltrey to the door.

"Hawthorne . . . Hawthorne Trugrave," I call after them. "Was he ever a part of this?"

Daltrey looks back. "No," he replies. "He was never one of us."

"Did you kill his brother Flint to separate us?"

"No, we liked the secondborn Sword. He made you happy. I believe it was your other ally who killed his brother—your arms dealer."

And there it is. The thing I feared since asking Clifton to take Hawthorne out of the infantry. I showed Clifton how to hurt me.

"The Gates of Dawn are interested in change, Roselle," Daltrey continues. "Your other allies—the Rose Garden Society—they're committed to the status quo, the preservation of the firstborn hierarchy. Don't confuse us. We only overlap when it comes to your welfare."

The door closes behind Daltrey. I stare at the ceiling. My head pounds. I can't find a comfortable position. Everything hurts. "What would you do if someone killed your brother, Reykin?"

Reykin is quiet. He walks to the window. Standing in the sunlight, he resembles a sculpted god. "I'd take my fusionblade to the battlefield and kill as many of my enemy as I could find until I was cut down, and then saved by a little Sword soldier." He pulls something from his pocket. It's my penlight. He studies it. "I'd return this, but I've grown rather attached to it."

"What happened to your brother?"

"A Census agent killed Radix. He was only ten years old."

"Was he thirdborn?"

Reykin gives a humorless laugh. "He was fifthborn, but they don't know that. They thought he was thirdborn. They killed my mother as well, and dragged her body through the streets of our town."

"I'm sorry." I glance at his left hand. He has a new golden shooting star moniker. "You're firstborn."

"Yes. I still have three younger brothers. The two youngest are in hiding. I'll make sure they both get one of the new monikers you brought."

"Where is your secondborn brother?"

"I haven't been able to locate him in the two years since he Transitioned."

"What's his name?"

"Ransom Winterstrom. My father had an offbeat sense of humor. I'd introduce you to him, but he died last year, defending my mother."

It's no mystery now why Reykin was on the battlefield that gray day last year when I found him. "I'm sorry. I don't know Ransom, but I'll make inquiries for you."

"Maybe he's better off not knowing anything that happened here. I wasn't always the best brother to him. Maybe he wouldn't want to see me."

"Do you love him?"

"Yes."

"Then he'll want to see you. Trust me, I know what I'm talking about."

He turns to face me. Something about him tugs at me. Maybe it's the sameness I see in him. He was trained like I was—his mentor trained mine. I recognize the intensity and control with which he holds himself. He looks at me as if he sees me, not just the girl that grew up in front of cameras. "You're going back to protect your brother," Reykin says softly. "It's what I'd do, if I were you. Know this, Roselle, so that there are never any lies between us. I'll kill Gabriel if or when I'm ordered to. I won't hesitate to cut his throat, and there will be nothing that you can say or do to stop me."

Chapter 19
A Serious Hat

The girl who comes to bring me clothes gives me a once-over and sets a pile of fabric on the bed. "I'm Mags," she says with a conspiratorial wink. "I work for Firstborn Winterstrom. He said you need something to wear." I sift through the stack of extremely feminine clothing and groan in irritation. "What? You don't like them?" Mags asks, eyeing me like I'm a spoiled firstborn.

"It's all very lovely, but . . ." I study her outfit, a serviceable ensemble of black trousers and a simple white blouse. It will blend in with everyone around me. She's about my size, just a little taller. I can work with this. "Could I trade you?" I ask. "I promise you won't get in any trouble for it."

"Oh, I never worry about getting into trouble here. Firstborn Winterstrom is like family. He lets me see my own family whenever I want to, and they come here to stay sometimes."

It irritates me that Reykin is beloved by his staff. He's a ruthless killer who I let live and who is now a credible threat to my family. The irony is almost more than I can take. "He sounds like the best firstborn ever," I reply, trying to keep my total lack of sincerity from eking out. "I'm happy for you."

She begins to unbutton her blouse. "I know what you did for him." My own hands pause on the buttons of Reykin's oversize shirt. "He was in a bad way when he left to join the war. At first we thought he was no better when he came back. He used to scream for you in the night—he'd call you 'Little Sword' or 'black-hearted angel.' We were all scared that he was losing his mind after all he'd been through with his parents and Radix."

"He told you about me—about how we met?"

"He did, but that was one of the reasons we thought he was losing his mind. He said Roselle St. Sismode saved his life."

"I don't know if I saved him. I just didn't kill him, which is not the same thing."

The Stone-Fated girl takes off her blouse and hands it to me. She puts the new one on. "You saved him. You called a medical drone and it patched up what was torn apart in him—and I'm not just talking about his sword wounds."

"What do you mean?"

"I think you mended his faith in humanity. He'd lost it the day they killed Radix." She locates my boots and helps me put them on. I walk slowly with her through the enormous house, more modern than the palace I grew up in. Its beauty is tempered by its size. She takes me to the back door of a kitchen the size of our locker room in the air-barracks. In the closet, she finds a cloak and hands it to me. Once outside, we follow a stone path to a small cottage behind the main house.

"Knock, knock," she says, pushing open the front door.

"We're in here," Hammon calls from the next room. I follow Mags and find Hammon sitting on a sofa with Edgerton's head in her lap. He looks kind of like me—like he got beaten by a mob of soldiers.

"Roselle!" Hammon gasps. I must look really bad.

"It probably looks worse than it is," I insist.

Edgerton sits up. "No, it don't."

I limp toward them. "You're right, it doesn't," I agree. They make room for me on the couch, and I settle between them. Hammon moves to hug me, but I stop her with a raised hand. "Please don't touch me. I don't think I can bear it."

"I took the beating of my life, Roselle," Edgerton says. "You look like you took a fall off a cliff."

"I don't remember much about it once I hit the ground."

"I don't either, to tell you the truth," Edgerton replies. He must have gotten the leeches, too, because his eyes are less swollen than the rest of him.

"You don't want to know what happened to you," Hammon says quietly. "It was your hand that saved us, Roselle—your scar. Without that, they'd have killed you and Edge for sure. That man— Winterstrom—he saved us all. How come you never told us about him? You hid that scar under a glove for an entire year."

"He told you?" I ask.

"Mags told us," Edgerton replies.

"I didn't want to involve you. Only Hawthorne knew about it. The less you knew, the better."

"Apparently, we're still five steps behind you," Edgerton says. "Reykin was just here. He told Hammon and me about the deal you made for us."

"There's no way we can ever repay you, Roselle," Hammon adds.

"You can name the baby Roselle if it's a girl," I tease.

"That goes without saying," Edgerton replies. "So you're going back?"

"I have to. It's like you said, Edge. I'm still breathing, so there is still a chance, right? I'll get word to you as soon as I can. Hopefully, one day, when it's safe, we can all be together."

We say our good-byes. Mags leads me back toward the main house, and I pause by the garden gate to keep from passing out. "You shouldn't be out of bed," Mags scolds me.

"I've run out of time, Mags. I have to leave now or I might have to stay forever."

"Would it be so bad?" she asks.

Here among the beautiful grounds of the Star-Fated estate, war seems distant. A glass gazebo borders a small, serene lake. Well-groomed horses run along the paddock fences. I can see why Reykin's parents were lulled into a false sense of security. One could feel untouchable here.

"Forget what I said, Mags. There's no forever. There's only now."

I lose my balance. Someone behind me breaks my fall. "You're going back to bed," Reykin orders. He lifts me into his arms. I wince at the pressure on my ribs. He takes me back to the room I was in before and lays me on top of the blanket. Mags comes in with a cold compress. Reykin takes it from her and lays it on my forehead. With my eyes closed, I murmur, "This changes nothing. I'm still leaving by tonight unless you have another one of those cyanide tablets. I feel bad enough to take one of those. Either way, I'm not staying here."

Mags snorts in derision. "We don't have cyanide here. The mind of this one." I peek at her. She gestures with her thumb in my direction. Shaking her head as if she never heard of such a thing, she leaves the room.

"You wouldn't let me take the easy way out," Reykin says. "I'll return the favor."

"You're just being cruel now."

"I've booked passage for you on a very low-budget cargo watercraft leaving for Bronze City late this afternoon," Reykin says. I can't hold back my sigh of relief. Reykin notices. "Did you think I was going to hold you hostage here, Roselle?" From the pocket of his coat, he extracts a laser tool and a small vial that matches my skin tone.

"It's hard to know what you'll do, Reykin," I reply. "You're somewhat unpredictable. It's the austerity of your stare. I thought before that you'd protect me, but then you promised me that my brother is as good as dead—so you can see my dilemma. I believe people like you should come with a warning label."

"My intention isn't to harm you. My intention is to make sure no one ever harms you again." He reaches for my right hand, taking it gently in his. His fingers run over the crest that his fusionblade left there.

"Why can't you protect me without killing my brother?"

"You know what I thought about when I was lying in this very same bed," he asks, "recovering from the wounds I received the day I met you?" He seems almost reluctant to apply the skin tone to my palm, as if he'd like me to keep my scar. "I kept thinking, 'Why was she there—that girl with the perfect lips? Roselle St. Sismode is the secondborn to The Sword. Why wouldn't they protect her?'" The skin gel is cool as he brushes it on my palm. "'Who wants her dead?'"

"Why would someone want me dead?"

"I can think of at least two reasons, Roselle. The first is the fear of what you'll do with the power you'd have if you ever became The Sword."

"What's the other reason?"

"With you dead, there would be very little reason to kill Gabriel. The alternate to your brother, if he dies without an heir and you're already dead, is a man named Harkness, and trust me when I tell you that he'd be disastrous as The Sword. Now that I know that the Rose Garden Society exists, I'm leaning toward the second reason. It'd be easier to kill you than to take out a whole society of firstborns, with their rose-shaped pins and secret handshakes. If you die, the point of their club is moot. If you die, they lose their power."

"Who do you suspect?" I whisper. My throat feels tight. I have my own ideas, but I want to hear his.

"It's a long list, but the ones at the top are Gabriel, Admiral Dresden, Grisholm Wenn-Bowie, Fabian Bowie, and Othala St. Sismode." "Admiral Dresden does nothing without my mother's approval."

"I know. The order to send you to the front line had to come from Othala. Whether or not it originated with her is the only question. She'd have to know about it either way."

"So my mother wants me dead for sure."

"Does that surprise you?" He sets the laser on the bedside table. "Your death would serve two purposes: protecting Gabriel and making you a martyr in the fight against the Gates of Dawn."

The sting of betrayal burns. "You must be so disappointed," I mutter, a hitch in my voice.

Reykin moves closer. "I'm not disappointed." He touches my hair, stroking it. "Othala might be having trouble getting to you, but like you said, your arms dealer is a very powerful man. He has more connections within the ranks of secondborn Sword soldiers than even your mother, because she doesn't bother to pay for information. She expects loyalty. He's more practical and has the resources to back it up. Your arms dealer is an excellent ally, but he's also a very serious enemy should you cross him in the future."

"You mean that if I decide to change things for secondborns, he would resist those changes?"

"That's precisely what I mean, Roselle."

"Answer a question for me, Reykin. What's the difference between the Gates of Dawn and the Rose Garden Society? It's my understanding that you both want me to be The Sword."

"Ah, there's a world of difference there. The Gates of Dawn want change. We want the destruction of the Fates. We want to live, work, and love as we see fit. Have you ever asked yourself why you have to be a soldier? Would you have chosen it for yourself or would you have become something else if given the freedom to do so? And why are you made to support firstborns? It's not your destiny, it's their greed."

"But *you're* firstborn."

"I am, but I was raised not to let that go to my head," he replies.

"So you see me as someone who can one day bring about the destruction of the Fates?"

"Yes, with you as a leader, we'd have a chance to topple the Fates Republic and form a new system of government."

"And the Rose Garden Society?" I ask.

"They want things to remain the same—a Fate-based system with a formidable ruler—only I suspect they have aspirations for power that go beyond what they lead others to believe."

"What other aspirations?"

His stare is piercing. "On the surface, they speak of maintaining a dominant military hold over the Fates. They see Gabriel as weak—and he is. You'd make a more competent commander."

He bows his head over my hand and continues to work on my palm, filling in the scar with regenerative cells. "What do you want most, Reykin?" I whisper.

A vengeful glint enters his eyes. "That's very simple, Roselle. I want the complete and utter decimation of Census."

Finally, something upon which we can both agree.

He finishes his work on my palm, and then checks his timepiece. "If you insist on leaving Stars tonight, we'll have to go now." I wipe my face with the compress and wearily set it aside. Reykin rises from the bed and helps me to stand. "You have to meet a ship at the docks in Brixon."

"Will I be recognized?"

"You don't exactly look like yourself, Roselle." I haven't seen myself in a mirror yet and don't intend to look now. He goes to the closet and comes out with two flat caps. He hands me the black one, and he puts on the charcoal gray one. He holds up a radiant golden star made from metal and only a couple of millimeters thick. "This is a device loaded with a malware program I created. It will infiltrate their technology and allow us to gain access." He slips the star into a small compartment in the brim of my hat. "You need to upload the program into one of the secured networks. We only know of three locations. One is in the Stone Forest Base of Census, guarded by hundreds of agents, and they've been extremely vigilant since you helped blow them up."

I shake my head and pay for it with stabbing pain. "I don't think I can get back into Census. We're not on friendly terms. Where are the other two access points?"

"One is at Fabian Bowie's Palace in Purity."

I cringe. "And the other?"

"The Sword Palace."

Why I thought I could do this is beyond me.

Reykin reads my mind. "One thing at a time. You get access to one of these places, and we figure out our next step together."

"How? You'll be here, and I'll be in Swords."

"You let me worry about that." I put the cap on and stuff my hair into it, pulling the brim down low over my face. "You look like a proper Star from Brixon," Reykin says.

The hat reminds me of Flannigan. "It's a serious hat."

Clearly, he approves. He hands me a pair of gloves. Slipping the left one on, I notice that it has lead inside. "So that you don't ping on any of the drones that might be looking for you," Reykin offers.

As I put on the other one, I realize that there's a faint little star still visible on my palm. "Did this one *sticketh*?"

"Sometimes Stars are like that."

We take his well-designed hovercar down a lane lined with oak trees. Their leaves scatter like sparrows as we pass. I rest my head against the soft seat and giggle when he switches to flight mode and scares the crows, who fly from the black-railed fences as the engines radiate. The horses run in protest, too, their manes waving good-bye. I glance at Reykin. He's staring at me.

"What?" I ask.

"I've never heard you laugh."

I look away and sit up straighter. "How long until we get there?"

"Not long."

"Explain to me how your program will work."

Chapter 20
Sword-Shaped Heart

I'm at sea for about an hour when I take off my leaded left glove. A half hour after that, a very expensive airship pulls up to our port side. It's a Verringer. The only person I know who owns one, besides The Virtue, is Clifton Salloway, who owns five. This one is entirely black, with black fairings and camouflage capabilities. It sets down on the water like some enormous long-legged insect. An impressive array of munitions level at the lumbering cargo vessel I've taken passage on.

A wide black gangway protrudes from the Verringer, latching on to the railing of our hull. Heavily armed bodyguards emerge from the luxury airship. The captain of my watercraft scratches his beard, unsure what to make of all these goings-on. Clifton's personal bodyguard, Crucius, approaches him, and a flash of currency quickly subdues any protest.

I stand on the deck with Mags's shabby cloak wrapped around me. It doesn't keep out the cold wind, but it looks like something I could've acquired on my own. I've taken off my hat, tucking it inside the pocket of my cloak, and my hair falls loosely around me, wisps of it blowing in my face. Clifton disembarks from the Verringer and boards the rusted deck. Pulling the collar of his long coat closer to his neck, he has a look of relief on his face, but it turns to an angry scowl the closer he gets.

Stopping in front of me, he reaches his hand and gently grasps my chin, turning my face to get a better look at my black eyes.

"Who did this?" he demands.

"I ran into some trouble in Stars, not far over the border. I had to abandon your Anthroscope. Sorry. I really loved that airship. I can pay you back."

"I don't care about the airship. Are you hurt worse than this?"

"There's a probable concussion and a couple of broken ribs."

"It was against my better judgment to let you pilot that aircraft alone. It's way past time that you had bodyguards. I'm not listening to any more of your excuses about being your own protection. You're vulnerable. You could've easily been killed." Despite his scary manipulations, I believe Clifton has genuine feelings for me. Maybe he sees me as more than a possession—maybe I'm his friend as well.

"Come, let's get you out of the cold," he says, putting his arm around my shoulders. We cross the gangway and enter his mobile apartment. Leading me to a comfortable seat, he takes my cloak and urges me to sit, grabbing a soft blanket from another seat and laying it in my lap. I snuggle into it.

"I'm glad you're not very mad at me," I say. "I think I'm going to need your help explaining myself to my unit."

"I am mad at you."

"But not *very* mad," I cajole.

"The problem has always been *staying* mad at you, Roselle, and you don't have to worry about your Sword unit. They know nothing about this. I told Commander Aslanbek that you've been with me since your airship went missing. They think you've been collaborating on weapons and product strategy at our facility. I've had a difficult time fending off a certain Census agent, though. He's convinced that I'm harboring you and two other Sword soldiers from your regiment—a Hammon Sword and an Edgerton Sword. Do you know them?"

"They're my closest friends. You helped them about a year ago, remember?"

"Vaguely. I don't remember the specifics."

I pluck at the blanket in my lap. "I won't involve you in it. It's really not something you'd be interested in."

He leans back in his seat, his eyes roving over me. "Worth getting your face beaten in for?"

"Only just slightly," I reply with a rueful smile. "Had I known how awful I'd feel now, I may have reconsidered helping them." Everything with Clifton has to be minimalized. He understands loyalty, but only to an extent. He expects me to cut any ties that he does not consider advantageous. If they infringe upon my time or my person, or take me from him, they have to go. He'd consider this ordeal a grievous crossing of that line. "I will never see them again, so the point is moot," I add.

"Then we won't speak of it again."

"The Census agent will be a problem, though." Agent Crow will never leave this be. He'll hunt Hammon and Edgerton to extinction if he's able.

"He'll be dealt with. Your airship veered off course and went down today behind enemy lines. Gates of Dawn soldiers attacked you, but you managed to escape with some injuries. You contacted me because I'm your commanding officer. I came to your aid. I will have my team issue a statement, and I'll field any and all inquiries on your behalf."

"Thank you."

"We'll have to wait to fix your face until after the press sees you. It is, after all, part of the alibi. Then I'll have my private physician personally see to you."

"You're very good to me."

"I'm exactly what you need, Roselle." He lifts my hand and kisses the back of it before holding it upon the armrest between us. "I was worried about you. I'm glad you're in one piece."

"I'm grateful that you came to find me. Are you taking me back to the Stone Forest Base?"

"No. Your air-barracks has gone active. They're stationed in Twilight now."

"So, you're taking me to Twilight?" I didn't think I could feel worse, but my fear of combat raises the bile in my throat.

"There's no reason to return you to Tritium 101. In the last few days, I've permanently phased out your duties there. You'll have a place closer to me now. You'll move in tonight."

"You already have a place for me?"

"I've had it for a while." I wonder if he's had it since he decided to kill Hawthorne's brother, and then I wonder if he's been making sure that no messages come to me from Hawthorne. "We'll return to my office, and then I'll take you home."

True to his word, Clifton masterminds my alibi. He contacts only the Diamond reporters that he has in his pocket. When we arrive on the rooftop landing pad of Salloway Munitions Conglomerate's headquarters, the press already have their drone cameras strategically positioned. They capture me disembarking with Clifton's assistance, huddled in Mags's shabby cloak.

The amassing correspondents ambush me with hundreds of questions all at once. Clifton shields my face, walking me to the private entrance of his empire in the sky. "Roselle has had a trying day," he calls to them. "All of your questions will be answered in due course."

The entire top floor of the headquarters is Clifton's personal domain. I haven't been to his secluded suite before. When I consult on weapons, it's usually in a manufacturing facility, in a laboratory, or in the field. I wander around, studying the prototype weapons behind thick security glass. Clifton contacts his personal Atom-Fated physician, demanding to know his estimated arrival time. When he's done, he asks me, "Can I get you a drink, Roselle?"

"Water, please."

He turns on the visual screen. Commentators are already narrating the thirty seconds of "Roselle" footage they received only a few minutes ago. My fusionmag ad campaign and the campaign I did for the newest version of our dual-bladed sword are spliced into the footage, along with old news items. The strike against the Fate of Swords on my failed Transition Day is among them.

I don't want to relive that, so I walk to the window overlooking the balcony. It faces the sword-shaped Heritage Building. The windows of Clifton's office are mirrored on the outside, so no one can see me. I take in the view. What I find is telling. Every day, Clifton looks down on the hilt of the Heritage Building from these windows. The Heritage Council is the sole occupant of the spherical penthouse just a few floors beneath me.

I'm about to turn from the window when one of the sword-shaped doors of the Heritage Building opens below. A tall man with sandy-blond hair in an Exo uniform emerges. He takes a few steps onto the penthouse's grassy balcony, scanning the buildings around him until he finds ours. His face tilts upward. *Hawthorne.*

My hand presses against the glass. Then Gabriel joins Hawthorne at the railing. The shock of seeing them together brings a rush of blood to my head. My hand slides down the window as I crumble onto the floor.

Chapter 21
White Rose

I awake in a sterile bed. Medical monitoring machines blink and beep. The walls of a hospital room take shape. Across from me, a life-size visual screen plays newsreel taken outside the Salloway Munitions Conglomerate's headquarters, drone footage of me being transported on a hoverstretcher. I have no memory of it. I gaze around for a way to turn down the volume, and my eyes fall on a black-coated man sitting in the chair near my bed, his blond hair slicked back. He's riveted by what he's watching.

"Agent Crow," I growl. I find a switch on the bedside railing and press it. My bed slowly tilts up.

"Roselle." He says my name as if it's his favorite word. "Did I wake you?" He turns down the volume so that it's barely discernible over the pounding of my heart. "They're calling you a heroine"—he indicates the visual wall with a flick of his wrist—"for repelling the Gates of Dawn soldiers when your airship drifted off course and crashed in rebel territory. It's amazing that you made it out with your life."

"It's not that amazing," I reply. "I got my head beaten in."

"Yes, a severe concussion. Someone wasn't fooling around." He flashes me a steel-toothed grin.

"It was more of a mob than a someone."

"How ever did you escape?" he asks, leaning closer.

"That's kind of fuzzy. I can't remember—head injuries are tricky."

"Did you leave Edgerton and Hammon behind to fend for themselves?"

"I don't know what you mean," I reply.

"The friends you took with you. Did you leave them in the Fate of Stars?" He twirls his fingers as if unraveling a plot.

"I was alone."

"Think harder, Roselle," he growls. "You weren't alone. You hid your pregnant friend and her lover in your airship and smuggled them out of the Fate of Swords."

"If she's gone, then someone took her, like a Census agent. Your lawlessness is legendary. You think you can disappear anyone for any reason. As a matter of fact, I saw her talking to you before I left. It would be interesting to find out just how many secondborns go missing after they speak to you, Agent Crow."

His face darkens. "You think you're powerful now that you're with Clifton Salloway?"

"I think you're afraid of just how powerful I could become, with or without him."

"I'm never going to call off the search for them, Roselle. I promise you I will find them, and when I do, I'll be back for you."

I rub my aching temples. "I'm going to call off the search for your soul, Agent Crow. I'm tired of looking for it. It's plain to me that you just don't have one."

He chuckles and walks to the doorway. "The physicians did an outstanding job on your face. You may be even lovelier now. I cannot wait for my turn to work on it." He leaves the room, and I have to fight the urge to vomit brought on by the sheer terror I feel at his parting words.

I make my way to the small closet on the other side of the room. Inside, I find Mags's ugly cloak. The hat that Reykin gave me is still shoved in the pocket. I tug it out and locate the thin, golden, star-shaped device in the brim. Taking the star to the bathroom, I set it down on the sink.

I hide the golden star inside the nest I create out of my hair, securing it in a bun with an elastic band I find in the cabinet. Then I evaluate my face for the first time. I tilt my head at different angles, eye my new thinner, straighter nose and smooth complexion. I look just slightly different than before—more sophisticated somehow. I'm not sure what they did to me, but I'm not going to object. I'm no longer in much pain. With the exception of a headache and some stiffness, I am as I ever was.

"Roselle!"

I peek around the door to see Emmitt standing next to Clara Diamond. He places his hand on his chest, dropping his chin and saying to Clara under his breath, "This place is horrendous. We have to get her out of here before any drone cameras get in. She will look horrible in this light."

"Emmitt?" I emerge from the bathroom.

"Roselle! My dear girl! It's so wonderful to see you!" He gives me air kisses on both cheeks. "Your nose is perfection! I always thought it was too big. Didn't I always say that, Clara?"

Clara nods. "He did say that a lot."

"Er . . . thanks," I murmur. "Why are you here?"

He draws his hands in front of him in loose fists. "No one has told you?"

"Told me what?"

"You are to be the guest of *honor* at the Sword Palace this weekend, in celebration of your triumphant return from behind enemy lines." He looks over at me with an expectant air.

"Oh," I reply. "That sounds . . . fun." I touch the bun of my hair, making sure none of the star points protrude. I don't know how I feel about returning home.

"It will be fun! And you'll have to bring along your delicious man, Clifton Salloway. He'll want to see you receive your medal. Maybe you

Secondborn

can wear it for him, you know, after the ceremony, when the two of you are—"

"What medal?"

"The medal for bravery that your mother will present to you for your actions in defense of the Fates."

"I don't want a medal."

Emmitt gazes at Clara. "She doesn't want a medal. Couldn't you just eat her alive? She's so adorable. Of course you want a medal, Roselle. Everyone wants a medal. I want a medal—and I should get one, too," he adds as an aside, elbowing my newly healed ribs, "for having to deal with your mother."

"But I wasn't a heroine. My airship malfunctioned."

"Don't worry about a thing. I'm planning your ensemble for you. Where are you staying? And please don't tell me that it's in some Tree Base," he says, wrinkling his nose, "because I really *cannot* go there and—"

Clifton breezes into the room with his coat slung over his arm, looking handsome and well groomed. "Why are you out of bed?" he asks, frowning at me in my flimsy smock.

"Did you get the invitation we sent out for Roselle's celebration dinner this weekend?" Emmitt asks. He practically breathes Clifton in.

"I did," Clifton replies. He gently takes my arm and leads me back to my bed. "I will have my assistant respond today. Roselle and I are honored to attend." He covers me with the blanket.

Emmitt almost preens with satisfaction. "I just need her address so that I can take care of all the arrangements."

"She's moving to a new apartment. I'll send you the address." Clifton crooks his finger at Emmitt, leading him into the hallway.

Clara comes closer to the bed. She glances over her shoulder at Emmitt and Clifton. From under her lavender-colored coat, she uncovers a white rose she's been holding. "This is for you, from a friend," she whispers, handing it to me. "You can get your messages to him through me. Emmitt doesn't know."

She backs away before I can ask her what she means and goes to join the two men in the hallway. I put the rose to my nose and inhale. Emmitt pops his head in from the hallway. "Aw, did Clara bring you a rose? That was thoughtful—consider half of it from me. I'm leaving to get started on your gown," he says. "I'll send you some mock-ups later." He grins and scurries away, taking Clara.

Clifton comes back alone. "Darling," he says, brushing his lips to my cheek, "you had me so worried. I thought for a few hours there that I might lose you." He seems tired. He sits beside me on the bed and takes my hand. "You had a cracked skull, Roselle. They had to go in through your nose and repair it. Why did you downplay how bad you were hurting when I found you?"

"I didn't want you to be mad at me," I reply.

"I'll only be mad at you if you ever keep something like this from me again," he says sincerely. "I don't know what I would've done if I'd lost you."

"It's a relief to know you didn't just think my nose was too big and you had to fix it," I tease. I'm not sure how to handle this Clifton. He's not acting aloof and entitled.

He laughs, an unreserved snicker. "I didn't tell them to make it smaller, if that's what you mean. How are you feeling? The physician tells me that your recovery is assured. They foresee no complications."

"I feel much better. Thank you for taking care of me."

My attention drifts to the window. On the side of the building across from the hospital, there's a moving image of me. It's a Salloway ad. In it, I'm dressed in a tight black leather outfit doing a choreographed sword maneuver in a faked combat scene. Simulated artillery explodes around me. I battle with the Dual-Blade X16 that Jakes designed. I frown.

Clifton flashes me his model's smile when I glance at him. He tips his head toward the ad. "The X16 is a bestseller, Roselle. Burton is hating life right now."

Clifton stays with me for the rest of the day, ordering us food and bossing the hospital staff around. He reads me some of the crazier things that the press has written about us. Some make me howl with laughter, like a story about his "undying love for his creative Muse, Roselle St. Sismode, the woman he tries so desperately to impress with state-of-the-art weaponry."

"How come you're not like them?" I ask.

"Like who? Like firstborns?"

"Yes. I mean, you're *super* arrogant, but you're also hardworking."

"I'm hardworking because my little brother died of a heart disorder when he was seven. I was nine. He didn't live to his Transition Day."

"I'm sorry."

"Don't be," he says softly. "It has made me who I am. My mother was not able to have another child to take Aston's place—they wouldn't approve her for a thirdborn. We suspect it was political. We lost our place in the aristocracy. We had to earn our own way. Being an Exo-ranked officer doesn't pay what you'd think it should. Fortunately, I come from a family that knows how to earn a living—we excel at it. It makes us undesirable to the current aristocracy, which receives large sums of money for no other reason than their names. They're quick to do favors for me, though, if there's currency to back it up. It's how I was able to buy my title back, reclaim my family home, and become part of the aristocracy once more. The Fates Republic is paying less and less these days. This war is sapping their resources."

"And building yours," I reply.

"Ours," he corrects me. "Don't forget that I set aside currency for you in a secret account. I don't just hand all of it over to your greedy aristocratic family. Your dinner this weekend at the Sword Palace will be celebrated with money you earned from me."

My mother, father, and older brother are entitled to most of my earnings as a secondborn. The rest is supposed to go to the Fates Republic to support people like Fabian Bowie and Grisholm. It's a completely corrupt system. I'm only entitled to a capsule in an air-barracks and three meals a day, and even that is subject to my commanding officer's whims.

"Let's not talk about money. It makes me grumpy," I reply.

"What would you like to talk about?" He runs his knuckles lightly over my arm. I shiver at the exquisite feel of it.

"Agent Crow was here when I woke up."

Clifton tries to look mean, but he's too gorgeous to look threatening. "I will murder my security personnel!" he says angrily. "They were supposed to be guarding this entire place! What did he say to you?"

I tell him about our conversation word for word.

"I have to take care of this tonight," Clifton grumbles, rising to his feet. "Don't worry about Agent Crow. He's not going to threaten you again." Reaching out, he brushes my cheek with his fingers. "Please get some rest. I want to be able to take you home soon. I'll see you tomorrow morning. We can have breakfast together."

"Okay." I nod.

When he leaves, I realize just how tired I really am. Snuggling into the blanket, I lift the white rose to my nose, sniffing it. One of the interior petals has a small black mark on it. I pluck it out, turn it over, and discover a message:

Hoping your head feels better.
—R.W.

Reykin Winterstrom. Clara has ties to the Gates of Dawn! Jumping out of bed, I hurry to the bathroom and flush the white rose petal. Returning to my bed, I search through the rose, but there are no other messages.

∽

A gentle breeze stirs my hair. I open my eyes to the darkness of my hospital room. The windows that look out into the hallway have been shuttered so that very little light comes through them. I don't remember doing that. Pushing up on my elbow, I notice the window on the other side of the room is open. The building across from me is mostly dark except for the light emanating from the explosions in the ad campaign. It paints my walls with orange, yellow, and red, dancing over everything, even me. A dark silhouette moves by the foot of my bed—an extremely well-built man stands there facing me. His outline is unmistakable, even dressed in an all-black jumpsuit with a black-knitted mask to hide his face.

"Hawthorne," I whisper. He moves quickly, going to the open window. "Hawthorne! Wait!" He looks back at me. Silent. "Don't go!" I plead. "I need you."

He turns away and leaps out the window. He's near the ground by the time I can get out of bed and make it to the window ledge. My hair tangles around me. Wisps of it slip from my bun as I lean outside, trying to get a better look at him. His gravity-resistant jumpsuit slows him down when he gets close to the sidewalk. Landing on his feet, he's gone from sight in a matter of moments. I don't know how long I stand there at the open window, but when I finally move, the sun is just coming up and shining between the buildings.

Chapter 22
Rose-Colored Crown

Clifton arrives midmorning and arranges for my release. Emmitt shows up carrying a highly stylized version of a Strato-ranked uniform that few real soldiers would be caught dead in. I hide the star-shaped device inside the calf of my boot. Clifton hands Emmitt an address. "Meet us here tomorrow afternoon. You can help Roselle get ready for her medal ceremony and accompany us to the Sword Palace."

Emmitt looks like he just tasted the most delicious morsel of his life. "I will be there by noon!" he squeals. "Everything will be ready! Trust me!"

We leave the hospital amid a circus of reporters, drone cameras, and—to my utter shock—fans. People are lined up outside to see me, shouting my name the moment I leave the relative safety of the lobby. Clifton's black bullet-shaped Recovener, the most ridiculously priced aircraft in production, is parked at ground level. His security team is ready, shoving the crush of people away from us.

Once we're inside the aircraft, he shifts into flight mode and veers off in the direction of the sea. "There." Clifton points as we near a gorgeous building that stands out from the others lining the beachfront. The shape of a silver-bladed broadsword rises from the sand, similar to the Heritage Building except that this sword stands on its hilt, pointed to the sky. The sword itself resembles an ancient blade, thick and heavy, with a steely sheen of metal and glass. A rose-colored crown rings the blade near the top. It's the physical representation of my moniker. We circle it a few times before Clifton lands the Recovener on the airship pad beside the crown-shaped penthouse.

"This," he says, "is your apartment." I stare at it a moment, speechless. "C'mon, I'll show you around." We walk hand in hand through a rooftop garden. "The plans for it were made a few years after you were born, but it wasn't constructed until nearly five years ago."

"Who else knows about it?"

"Up until now, not many people, but I gave this address to your mother's assistant yesterday. I'm sure Gabriel, Admiral Dresden, the Clarity of Virtues, and his son—the First Commander—know about it now as well. They can all track your moniker, anyway, so secrecy is not going to win the day."

"What will they do?" I ask.

"I have my theories. Othala has only herself to blame if she doesn't like it. She took no part in your Transition. Your life was left in the hands of secondborn commanders. She probably thought they'd find a way to kill you quickly so she could walk away with a clear conscience. Maybe she envisioned that you'd go out like her brother—killed as revenge against The Sword. Although I believe Bazzle was killed by your grandfather's order so that his firstborn, your mother, remained protected."

"There wasn't a Secondborn Bazzle Society?"

"No one shed a tear for him, poor creature. But the public didn't grow up watching Bazzle like they did you. Othala didn't anticipate that when she was masterminding her family's legacy. And you're not the kind of person to lie down and die. She probably never realized the impact Dune was having on your future."

"She said she gave me the tools to survive."

"You barely survived one day of active duty because of her. What she couldn't have foreseen was that you'd create a completely honorable military job for yourself, let alone make her and Clarity Bowie quite a bit of currency. Othala may want to get rid of you to protect Gabriel, but Clarity Bowie is just warming up to all your possibilities. You haven't gone unnoticed by the First Commander either."

"Grisholm?" I snort and turn away from the rose-colored windows. "He finds me repulsive."

"I wish that were the case, Roselle." Clifton taps his moniker, showing me a holographic image of Grisholm at a Secondborn Pre-Trial event. He looks perfectly at ease in his private box in the exhibition arena.

"Notice his sword, Roselle?"

I peer at the small hologram, which plays in a seven-second loop. "It's an X16. That means nothing. He probably likes the dual-blade design."

"You're the face of the design. They all buy it because you use it."

"He knows a lot more than you give him credit for, Clifton."

We walk together around the pool and up a short staircase to the veranda. The glass doors slide open to reveal an open floor plan with a 360-degree view. An elegant seating area with a bar looks over the skyline of Forge. Standing at the thick windows, I can just make out the Salloway Munitions headquarters and the hilt of the other sword—Gabriel and the Heritage Council's fortress. Putting me up here feels like a declaration of war, or at least a shot fired across his bow. Gabriel could see it as an implied threat.

We take the spiral staircase up to the next level. An extravagant master bedroom makes up the tip of the sword. The silver-tinted windows peak in a dagger point at the rooftop high above my head where a magnificent chandelier hangs, its crystals crafted in the shape of swords ringed by crowns.

"My room?" I ask, running my hand over the bright white blankets of an extremely large bed.

He nods. "Your room. You'll have a lot of security personnel around. They'll stay in the apartments below the penthouse, so you'll have privacy. I had clothing made up for you. You'll find the wardrobes and closets there." He points to an empty space.

"Where?" I ask. He laughs and touches the air of a holographic console near the door. Wardrobes rise from the floor, unmasking rows of clothes in every beautiful fabric imaginable.

"Oh," I say breathlessly when I near a wardrobe and find clothing that Othala would envy. I can't resist the impulse to run my hand over the luscious fabrics. "These are breathtaking."

"I'm tired of seeing you in rags, and you need clothing that reflects your station as a Salloway spokesperson."

"So this is all for me?"

"All for you, Roselle."

"Where will you stay?" I ask over my shoulder, trying to keep the note of suspicion from my voice.

"I'll be at my apartment at Salloway headquarters." He points in the direction of his office building. "It's imperative now that we maintain the utmost impression of propriety. We cannot give anyone any reason to call your conduct into question."

"Thank you, Clifton."

"You're welcome." He glances down at his moniker's timekeeper. "I'll let you settle in. I have an important meeting in an hour."

"You're leaving?" My smile falters.

He looks up at me. "I've rescheduled this particular client several times so that I could be at someone's bedside." Disappointment must show on my face because Clifton chuckles. "I'll return tomorrow to escort you to the Sword Palace."

"Promise?" I'm surprised by just how pouty I sound.

"I promise."

Clifton leaves and I play with the console. Glass walls rise out of the floor to hide the teacup-shaped tub from the bed. Another option frosts the glass wall of the bathroom. I can configure the walls in the bedroom into any floor plan I desire. A fireplace rises from the floor. A vent opens in an exterior window.

I reconfigure the room to my taste, then change into a tiny red bathing suit with sword-shaped metal buckles that rest on my hips. The weather is much warmer here today than it was earlier in the week in the Fate of Stars. I hang my clothing in the closet, hiding the star-shaped malware device that Reykin gave me in my boot that I stuff onto one of the shoe shelves. I spend the day by the pool.

By nightfall, I'm feeling restless. It seems unnatural now to be alone. I walk outside onto the terrace in my pajamas. Going to the railing, I gaze down at the ocean, inhaling the scent of the sea. It's so quiet here. Not since the Sword Palace have I known this kind of solitude. My stomach starts to hurt—my hands tremble. Impulsively, I climb up on the thin glass railing, teetering on its edge. The fall to the shore below would take some time. One misstep and I'll never have to worry about being alone again.

I walk the handrail like it's a tightrope. Adrenaline courses through my veins, making me feel alive again. My hands stop shaking. My eyebrows draw together. Something's wrong with me; I know that. This isn't normal. I shouldn't need to do this in order to breathe. Climbing down from the railing, I hug my arms around me.

Later, in bed, I stare up at the chandelier. The stars glow through the glass ceiling.

I awake sometime before dawn with a scream caught in my throat. A nightmarish version of the beating I took in Stars has left me panting. I touch my forehead and find it slick with sweat. I close my eyes, remembering the brutality of my dream. An angry mob was gathered around me, stalking, but the person who stumbled forward to hit me the hardest was Hawthorne.

Secondborn

Emmitt and Clara arrive to help me prepare for the medal ceremony this evening. Clara styles my hair, piling it high and decorating it with golden star pins. She applies a dark, smoky eye shadow to my eyelids and a light dusting of golden glitter to my cheeks. I wonder if she knows what I'm to do this evening. When she's finished, she excuses herself and leaves.

Emmitt helps me dress in a clingy night-sky-inspired gown. It has a daringly low neckline and a leg-hugging hem that flows into a small train. Black stiletto heels with a thick ankle strap complete the ensemble. Appraising myself in the mirror, I exude a risqué air of defiance.

"Where are they supposed to pin my medal?" I ask Emmitt.

"Not on this dress!" he screeches. "Just hold out your palm and let them hand it to you."

I know better than to argue with him. He gives me a small golden clutch.

"I think it's the most beautiful gown I've ever seen," I tell him.

"It could be better." He clucks and smooths the fabric again.

"No, it couldn't. It's perfect. You're a genius."

"Do you want to see the best part?" he asks coyly.

"It gets better?"

"You can unzip this seam on the side so that you can dance later at the event." He shows me the cleverly hidden zipper.

"That's brilliant, Emmitt." Impulsively, I find his hand and squeeze it. "I think I'm ready. Should we go now?"

He frowns at my hand on his. I quickly drop it. "Yes, it's time." He looks down his nose at me.

As we leave the room, I hesitate. "I forgot the lipstick. I'll get it and meet you downstairs." I rush back in alone and go to the closet. Locating the thin metal malware device in my boot, I hide it between the pad of my foot and the sole of my shoe before snatching up my lipstick on the way out the door.

265

Clifton meets me at the bottom of the stairs, attired in a black Exo dress uniform. A cape covers one shoulder, held in place by a braided rope attached to the other. On him, the look is roguish. He takes my hand and kisses the back of it. "There are no words for your kind of beauty, Roselle."

"It's a stunning gown," I admit. "Emmitt outdid himself. The only problem is there's no way I can wear my X16. The thigh scabbard doesn't work with this dress."

He smiles cunningly. "You're all the weapon we need."

Chapter 23
Secondborn Traitor

It's now, when I'm seated next to Clifton in his airship, that I begin to panic. I've gotten no further instructions from Reykin regarding the malware. Time has worked against me. My sweaty palms grip my star-beaded clutch. I stare out the side window at the dark sea as we lift off.

The closer we get to the Sword Palace, the bigger the fool I believe myself to be. *I haven't been home in over a year, and I'm going to get caught for espionage before I even make it through the front door.*

"What are you thinking about?" Clifton asks.

"The maginots. I miss them," I reply, trying to hide my true thoughts.

"You mean the ferocious wolfhounds that roam the Sword Palace grounds? Those maginots?" He's alarmed.

"Yes. They're my sweet babies," I reply with a soft smile.

"They're cyborgs that will rip your throat out," he teases me, but he also seems a little worried.

"Maybe *your* throat, but never mine." I grin.

We pull up to the security barricade by the iron fence. Iono guards with handheld wands scan our monikers. We're waved through, and Clifton pulls around the Warrior Fountain. Women in sparkling ball gowns float by, accompanied by a mix of uniformed and evening-wear-clad men and women. They make their way inside the Grand Foyer of the St. Sismode Palace.

When it's our turn to exit the Recovener, I wait for Clifton to come around to my side. I take his offered hand. We walk arm in arm into the glowing reception. Dozens of people are here. Some are standing on our family crest. The last time I saw the symbol, I had rifles pointed at me. It was a year ago, but I still feel the shame and fear vividly. I almost expect to see Mother on the balcony at the top of the staircase, hanging over the railing, screaming for her soldiers to shoot me.

Faking a smile, I allow myself to be drawn into conversation as we queue up in front of the security checkpoint. An older gentleman with a much younger companion takes an interest in me. Clifton introduces us. "Ah, yes," the man says, stroking his graying beard. "We watched the news of the Atoms rushing you into surgery, my dear. You took a severe beating, didn't you?" He doesn't sound sympathetic.

"The thing about beatings, Firstborn Houser," I reply conspiratorially, "is that if you have to take one, it's best to take a severe one. That way, you don't remember it."

He chortles. "I'll have to remember that, Roselle."

"Do," I reply with a forced smile.

Clifton presses his lips to the shell of my ear. "You are masterful at this, Roselle." His breath is warm against my skin.

"Roselle!" Gabriel's voice resonates in the domed room. Voices around us quiet as he cuts through the crowd. He's dressed in formal evening wear, with a midnight-blue cape styled exactly like Clifton's. When he reaches me, it's plain that something is not right about him. He has a feverish look. He throws his arms around me and lifts me off my feet in a tight hug. "I've been so worried about you. How are you feeling?"

He leans down and drops me to my feet. "I'm well, Gabriel. How are you?" I have to brace his forearms to keep him from swaying.

"Why are you in line with all of the common people?"

I try not to let my embarrassment show. "Because I'm common people," I reply, trying to calm him. "What are you doing down here with us?"

"You're not common people—you're my sister, Roselle!" His speech is slurred, his face is pale and drawn, and his lips have a bluish tint.

"I'm your sister," I agree. "And this is my friend, Firstborn Salloway." I gesture toward Clifton.

Gabriel sobers a little, his face darkening. "I know who he is," he leers. "What's he doing here?"

"Gabriel!" Hawthorne steps forward, placing his hand on Gabriel's shoulder and holding him back. I'm struck dumb, staring at the man I've never stopped loving. "Let them go. You're the heir to the fatedom, not her. Salloway will never be the Fated Sword, even if he has her." Hawthorne's words carry such scorn that I can taste the bitterness in my own mouth. I'm crushed by the weight of all the hours that I've loved him. I look away from Hawthorne and meet Clifton's eyes. He stares at me, seeing everything, but saying nothing. "I'm ready to go in," I tell him.

He leads me away from Hawthorne and my brother. I'm numb. I'm not even afraid when an Iono guard passes a wand over me and searches my clutch for weapons. Then we're through the checkpoint, walking a line of waiting ambassadors, shaking hands with familiar faces. "Welcome home." "Glad to see you back." I just say "Thank you" and move on.

The farther I move down the line, the more plastic this world seems. I feel like a real woman in a fake world. No one truly lives here. They just exist, surviving like parasites off other people they look down on and despise. I don't miss any of it, this oppressive regime that wants to cannibalize me. Something inside me burns. Something inside me rages.

Then I approach Mother. She's a vision in a white halter gown edged with golden accents. A golden laurel rings her chestnut hair.

Large bangles ring her delicate wrists. Her radiant smile immediately fades when she sees me next in line.

"Welcome home, Roselle," she says, air-kissing my cheeks.

Father is next to her. I blanch. Outwardly, he seems to be the same handsome man I remember.

Before we can address each other, Mother demands my attention. "Roselle!" She's aghast at my dismissal of her. "Aren't you going to introduce me to your . . ." Her chin points in Clifton's direction. "What shall I call him?"

"My apologies," I relent, hating this charade. "I believe you're already familiar with one another. May I present Firstborn Salloway. Clifton, this is The Sword, my mother, Othala St. Sismode."

Clifton bows his head in a formal nod of respect. "It's an honor to see you again."

"Firstborn Salloway, I hear that you're into gardening." Mother barely smiles.

"It has become quite a passion of mine," he replies warmly. "Especially roses. I have a weakness for them."

Mother cuts a dagger-like stare at me. "And what is he to you, Roselle?"

"He's my gardener." I step toward Father at her side. I look at his handsome face, thinking of my time in the hospital. It was a Salloway by my side, and before that, a Winterstrom. Not one St. Sismode or Abjorn came to see me.

Father looks at me as if I'm a stranger—and I am. "So, you didn't let them kill you, eh, Roselle? Good for you," he says with the same smug condescension and ruined humor that I remember.

"Thank you, Kennet." I reach up and straighten the collar of his unearned Exo uniform. "I'm sorry you let them kill you, though. I hate seeing the grass that has grown over you." My hand rests on his chest. I pat his heart. Then Clifton takes my elbow and we walk away in silence.

We're shown to chairs at one of the front tables by the podium. I set my handbag down as Clifton pulls out my chair for me.

"I'm not sure how you survived here, Roselle."

"Dune," I reply.

"Where is he now?"

"The Fate of Virtues with the Clarity."

"Sounds as if he can't avoid danger." He takes two flutes of bubbling beverages from the hovering tray as it passes by. Handing one to me, he clinks his glass to mine. "To danger."

"To danger," I reply.

Other guests are shown to our table, and we greet them cordially. Two are secondborn Sword soldiers from the Twilight Forest Base. They're both receiving medals for discovering spies with copycat monikers in tunnels dug into the Base almost a year ago. I feel sick.

Hawthorne sits almost directly behind me, beside a tall, attractive brunette with a soft floral tulle gown that reminds me of a beautiful flower. I straighten in my seat. Gabriel steps to the chair across from us, yanking it out for an elegant young woman in an exquisite, crimson silk dress. Marielle Cosova. She's a firstborn from a prominent Sword family. We've never been introduced. I'm secondborn. No one saw the point. "Why are we sitting with secondborns?" she asks disgustedly. She inches her chair away from the secondborn Twilights on her left.

Gabriel takes the seat beside her. "Because I want to see my sister," he replies, lounging back into his chair, his arm resting on the empty one beside him. Dark circles shadow beneath his eyes. An attendant tries to seat someone in that empty chair, but Gabriel growls. "Find somewhere else to sit."

Marielle slides a golden case from her clutch and opens it. Selecting a slender red cigar, she holds it between her fingertips, waiting. Gabriel doesn't move to light it for her. He's watching me. Clifton reaches across the table and ignites his lighter. Marielle places the tip to the flame, drawing on the cigar. Cherry-scented smoke wafts into the air as she leans back in her chair. She plays with a piece of her blond hair and studies him. "Clifton Salloway," she says. "It has been a long time."

"It's nice to see you again, Mari," he replies.

"How long has it been?"

"I was nine."

"I remember. Your brother died. What was his name, Astra?"

"Aston."

She ashes her cigar. "He was always so funny!" she flirts, but it feels callous and cold. Clifton takes my hand under the table. Marielle is oblivious, clearly accustomed to being the most desirable woman in the room. "My father wouldn't let me see you after that—when you lost your title."

"Your father was protecting you." Our food arrives. A plate is set in front of me.

"There's a lot more to miss now." She gives him a girl-of-summer smile. "You should never let your firstborn high go to waste, Clifton." Her eyes fall on me.

"You have no idea what gets me high, Marielle," he replies. He looks away from her to me.

"I'm interested in what gets you high, Salloway," Gabriel says. He pushes his food around on his plate. I wish he'd eat some of it. It might make him feel better.

Clifton lowers his eyes, cutting his steak. "Visionary highs, Gabriel. Creating something from nothing. Collaborating with brilliant minds who don't understand muted emotions or thoughts."

"Like visionary plans for rose gardens?" Gabriel asks with a hollow tone.

"Exactly like that. I'd like to plant one in a cemetery that I know. It'll cover up the bones of the dead. I was showing my plans to some investors in the Fate of Virtues. Their interest is absolute."

"You don't know her at all," Gabriel says with a sad smile on his face.

"And you do, Gabriel?" Clifton asks.

My brother toys with his food. "I know that if you look in her clutch you'll find half of a steak stashed inside it—treats for her sweet babies."

Mother steps to the podium. "It is my great pleasure to welcome you all here tonight. It's a night that is very special to me. We are here to honor the brave men and women who serve our Fate and all the Fates as their secondborn birthright."

Everything about this evening suddenly makes sense to me. Mother arranged for this—my medal ceremony—to motivate Gabriel into taking action against me. This is her way of pressing for my death warrant. Clifton knows it. He's issuing a threat of his own, letting Gabriel know that I'm not without allies. And Gabriel feels betrayed by me.

"For bravery behind enemy lines," Othala says, "I'm pleased to bestow the Medal of Valor to secondborn Roselle Sword."

I rise from my seat to a smattering of applause, picking up my clutch. As I near Gabriel, I lift my sharp knife. He doesn't move or show any emotion, merely stares at Clifton. He never flinches when I stab the knife into his steak, skewering it. I open my clutch and thrust the steak into it, a treat for the maginots later, though it makes my point now. Closing the clutch, I set the knife on the table and walk to the podium.

Mother lifts the medal, intending to pin it on Emmitt's dress. I hold out my hand instead. She places it in my palm. "Would you like to say a few words, Roselle?"

I nod and look out at the sea of firstborns before me. "I accept this on behalf of secondborn Swords everywhere, whose valor protects all of you every day." Instead of returning to my seat, I walk to the door at the back of the ballroom and slip outside to the stone veranda. Iono guards stand watch at all the entrances to this fortress, but they ignore me because I'm breaking out, not breaking in. I take the stone stairs down to the grounds at the back of the house. The lights overlooking the manicured lawns show off the glorious topiary maze and bronze statues of soldiers from other eras. I used to love to get lost among them.

My high-heeled shoes crunch on the gravel. I walk to the stone bridge over the koi pond and toss the medal into the water. The sound of the splash fades. I keep walking. The stone-tiled rooftops of the kennels come into view. The wolfhounds know me by my scent, and my sweet babies run to me and surround me, their iridescent yellow eyes following my every movement. They sniff the air and whine in anticipation of treats. I wait for the boldest among them to come to me. Opening my clutch, I take out Gabriel's steak and tear off pieces of it, tossing them to the pack.

My favorite maginot approaches me. "I missed you, Rabbit," I whisper. The giant wolfhound nudges me with his vicious-looking muzzle. "How's my good boy?" Standing on all four of his legs, Rabbit and I are at eye level. I scratch the thick fur of his neck. He licks my face. My fingers slide under his metal collar, and I feel for the lever there. The pin eases from the bolt, and Rabbit automatically sits and becomes still.

I nudge the bolt open. A port slips out of Rabbit's neck. From my shoe, I tug out the device that Reykin gave me. Inserted in Rabbit's port, the star-shaped metal spins like a glowing sun. Rabbit's muscles twitch as the cyborg accepts the device's program. The golden star slows and stops.

"Never outlive your usefulness, sweet baby," I whisper, "and never trust the pack." I hug him. In the morning, when Rabbit is called back inside the kennel, he'll be connected to the Sword Palace's main systems. His handlers will upload his security logs. They won't realize that when they do, Reykin's program will be among the data. The rootkit drivers in the malware will conceal it. "We're gonna burn it all down, Rabbit. You . . . and me."

Chapter 24
The Hand and the Heart

On the way back toward the ballroom to rejoin Clifton, I pause at the apex of the stone bridge. The koi pond beneath me reflects the stars of billions of other worlds. Bending the arms of the thin, star-shaped device in my hand, I break them off one by one and drop them into the water. Concentric circles ripple outward in the dark pool. Soft music floats to me from the orchestra inside. When all the pieces disappear, I exhale deeply, resting my forehead against the bridge's cool stone railing.

Footsteps make me straighten. A man stops at the edge of the bridge. I turn toward him. It's Hawthorne. His face is hidden in shadow, but I'd know him anywhere. He approaches me slowly, deliberately. I take a step back. I don't have a weapon. I step toward the other side of the bridge, and he moves to block my way.

"You can't be out here." My voice quivers, sounding weak. He takes a couple of more steps toward me. "The maginots will shred you."

"You're not afraid of those vicious cyborgs," he murmurs, "but you're afraid of me?"

"They've never hurt me."

He glances down, looking wounded. "You have to leave. Now. Just go—don't return to the ballroom." He takes my left hand in his. From the pocket of his uniform, he pulls out a small aerosol device and sprays the skin over my moniker. The holographic sword fades from view. "Don't go back to the Base," he growls. "Stay in the city. Clifton can't protect you at the Base like he can in Forge."

"What did you just do to my moniker?"

"I covered it with CR-40. It's a polymer. It'll block your signal for a few hours—enough time for you to get away from here."

"Why?" I ask.

"Gabriel is out of his mind right now. He's given a kill order for you. Assassins are being dispatched."

"I'm not against him. He knows that! This isn't him. He's not like this, Hawthorne!"

"He's like this now, Roselle. When I fail to kill you tonight, there will be others. Be vigilant—stay with your Salloway bodyguards at all times."

"How long have you been working for my brother?" After seeing Hawthorne with Gabriel the day I came back from the Fate of Stars, I didn't want to believe what I know in my heart to be true.

"Since the day we met. I was sent by him to look for you—to see if you survived the attack."

"So Gabriel saved me from Agent Crow, or was that you?"

Hawthorne scowls. "It's always been me, Roselle. Just me. Your family has always been fine with the idea of you dying. It's your living that concerns them." He looks over his shoulder, then turns back to me. Seeing that I'm not going to leave without some kind of explanation, he relents. "My brother was Gabriel's right hand on the Heritage Council. Did you know Flint?"

I shake my head. "After I turned eleven, I was kept away from Gabriel. Over the years, I'd sometimes see members of his council at the Palace, but I was never permitted to speak to them. I was beneath their notice."

Hawthorne nods, his expression grim. He's on the other side of the fence now—one of them—but he knows what it's like to be second-born. "Flint contacted me on Gabriel's behalf the day of the attack. You remember when I found you?"

I nod. "You thought I was in shock."

"They'd given us your last known position. It was Flint I was talking to in my headset when I located you. He hadn't spoken to me since I'd Transitioned, and all of a sudden, he wanted me to find you to see if you survived."

"Were they afraid I was dead?"

"They were only worried that you'd been taken by the Gates of Dawn," he replies. "They were afraid you'd slip out of their control. Once they found out you were alive, I was ordered to make sure you arrived at the Base for your Transition."

I don't think I want to know any more. My throat aches, but I have to ask. "So you thought you'd be finished with all of us as soon as you released me into Transition?"

"Yes, but it didn't go down that way, did it? Gabriel had you placed in my air-barracks. Since the morning I found you in the locker room, I was required to give Flint and Gabriel status updates. I never told them what you and I really talked about—I gave them false reports. When I told you I've loved you since I was ten, that was real. Everything we've shared together is real."

I don't know what to believe. "Why didn't you tell me?"

"I've agonized about telling you everything, but your *not* knowing made every lie I told them more credible. And you've been having nightmares since I met you. What would it do to you to know that my lies were keeping you alive? I would've kept on lying to you—lying to them—anything so they'd leave you alone. But Flint was murdered . . . and now I know the truth."

"What truth?"

"Gabriel is losing his mind. He's paranoid, especially since he found out about the Rose Garden Society—and before you ask, no, I didn't tell them. Othala found out and reported it to Gabriel. The danger to you is absolute now. Gabriel has sided with your mother. He wants you dead, Roselle."

The betrayal I feel is at war with my love for both Hawthorne and my brother. I understand everything Hawthorne's telling me. I might even be able to accept it, later, when the crushing turmoil and wretchedness abate. By earning Gabriel's trust, Hawthorne has kept me safe. I know Gabriel trusts him—it was in his eyes back in the Grand Foyer. And now Clifton has pushed Gabriel to the brink. "What are you to my brother, now that you're not his secondborn spy?"

Hawthorne winces at the term. "I took Flint's place as your brother's first lieutenant on the Heritage Council."

"You're Gabriel's right hand?" I pale. That's not a position awarded lightly. Killing me would prove Hawthorne's loyalty, but he's warning me instead.

"He's *made* me his right hand. But you, Roselle, will always be my heart." I can't deny the aching tenderness in his voice.

"Hawthorne, don't hurt Gabriel," I plead, grasping his forearm. "He's sick. Mother has made him ill."

"He has made himself ill, Roselle!" Hawthorne's jaw clenches. "The chemicals he ingests have rotted his mind. He's paranoid and delusional. One minute he believes you want him dead, and the next he's ranting that you're the only person who understands him and loves him. He's hardly ever rational, and your mother can no longer hide it. It comes down to your life or his. I have no choice. It's always been you. He has to die."

"Let me *talk* to him, Hawthorne," I implore. "He'll listen to me! I can make him—he's just afraid!" I try to push past Hawthorne, but he holds my arms.

"You can't talk to him, Roselle. He'll murder you if you get near him again. Your brother is beyond irrational. He's taking Rush."

My eyes search his face in the light of the glowing moon.

"It's a drug that turns your world inside out, makes you believe you're a god. It makes him insane. You have to go into hiding until after the Secondborn Trials."

"Why? What happens then?" I demand.

"Trust me. You have to go now!"

The desperation in Hawthorne's tone breaks through to my survival instincts. A part of me still trusts him, even though he's been lying to me since I met him. "I'll go," I whisper. Hawthorne wrenches me to him. My hand braces on his chest, the slab of virile muscle hard and unrelenting. His hand fists roughly in my hair. My blood roars in my ears and my knees weaken with fear and desire.

"You mean everything to me, Roselle," he whispers. He breathes heavily, fighting for restraint. His nose skims the surface of my neck. His mouth finds mine. He kisses me hard, demanding. "I've always loved you—I swear it," he says. "I never stopped. I'll never let them hurt you."

"I miss you so much, Hawth—" His kisses silence me.

His hands run over the thin fabric covering the sides of my breasts, my hips. I crave his skin against mine, the rigid bulk of his muscles. "We'll be together soon," he promises, "but you have to go now, before someone finds us."

His grip eases. I feel weak, but movement up ahead triggers my alertness. Iono guards are branching out, coming our way. Hawthorne sees them, too. He grabs me from behind and hauls me off the bridge and down the slope of the hill. We hide in the tunnel of darkness under the stone bridge, on a small lip at the water's edge. I hear them on the path above.

"Do you have a weapon?" His voice is hushed.

I shake my head. I'm shivering from fear and the damp night air. Hawthorne detaches the black cape from his Exo uniform and drapes it over my shoulders. With the aerosol can, he sprays his own moniker. It goes dark.

A harrowing shriek pierces the air.

"Where did the guards go?" My voice quivers.

He inches forward and peeks around the edge of the stone. "They went into the kennel."

I frown. "Which kennel? East or west?"

"West."

The pack of maginots I fed earlier answers the cry with a collection of howls. "We have to go! Now! They're programming the maginots for a hunt." I slip off my heels and unzip my dress on the side. I toss my shoes and my clutch into the water. Hawthorne's hand engulfs mine. Turning, we creep farther under the bridge, hugging the stone wall until we emerge on the other side of the tunnel. The pond here empties into a small river that winds into the woods. Another unnatural-sounding howl—something between the cry of a wolf and a thunderclap—echoes from the far side of the tunnel. We run.

In about a half mile, we come to a round stone structure within a wooded area near the perimeter wall of the Palace grounds. The river continues, but Hawthorne and I head for a tall, black iron gate with sloping steps in front. Gray stone pillars wrap around the structure, holding up the domed roof. It's only two stories high with four rooms inside. It's a meditation building, formerly used to make tributes to a god that has either faded away or died, as did the people who once used it. As a child, I'd come here to get away from the cameras. It was my secret place.

The doors of the building are always unlocked. Panting as I reach them, I push one heavy bronze slab open. It whines on its rusted hinges. The only light comes from tiny slivers that pierce the round dormer windows in the ceiling and the narrow stained glass windows on the main floor. The scent of incense is thick and old. We bar the doors and engage their thick metal bolts. I lean against the cold bronze, trying to catch my breath. Hawthorne takes his fusionblade from his scabbard and ignites it so we can see. Statues of warrior-gods line the walls. The marble floor is dingy with dirt and leaves, but it's in perfect condition otherwise.

Something heavy crashes against the doors, bowing them in and pushing me forward. Another blood-curdling yowl splits the air. "This way," I whisper. The stained glass beside us shatters. Colorful shards rain onto the floor. The monstrous muzzle of a maginot tries to push through the narrow window. Its jaws snap at me, dripping saliva, but it's unable to fit through. It isn't Rabbit; it must be a newer model because I don't recognize the silver markings by its eyes.

The gigantic maginot paces outside, throwing itself against the door again. The crash echoes in the domed building. Hawthorne fixates on the window. His jaw tightens. "Is there another way out of here?"

I lead him across the marble floor and behind a bronze statue of a beautiful male god who wears a crown of laurels and very little else. I reach for a notch in the wall. A piece of gray stone slides open to reveal a shallow staircase. Hawthorne's fusionblade lights the way as we take the passage down, the wall closing behind us.

"Where does this lead?" Hawthorne asks.

"I'm not exactly sure," I reply. "I've never been strong enough to pry open the door at the other end, but I know this hallway is long enough so that it must be beyond the Palace wall." We walk together down the corridor. I take the lead. "You need to stay on the west side of the tunnel up ahead. There's a security wall that you don't want to trip into."

We come to an animal graveyard. Piles of decimated rodent bones and molding fur litter the ground. I pick up a small pebble and toss it ahead on the left side of the tunnel. It explodes. Hawthorne picks up another and throws it to the right. It bounces on the ground. "C'mon." When we're on the other side, he asks, "Any more surprises ahead?"

"I don't think so, but like I said, I've never gotten through to the outside."

"How far does this go?" he asks.

"A mile or so."

"And you did this alone?"

"I do most things alone, Hawthorne."

"You don't need anyone, do you?"

"That's not true. I desperately need someone I can trust."

"I love you," he says softly, "and I'll earn back your trust again, even if it kills me."

"Don't let it kill you," I reply. "I don't think I'll make it if you're gone."

We walk on, coming to a spiraling ramp upward. It leads to a small rectangular room. I gesture to a heavy outline in the stone. The walls and the floor are embedded with small metal swords in a repeating diamond pattern.

Hawthorne passes me his fusionblade and pushes against the door. It doesn't budge. "There has to be a lever," he mutters. He pushes on a sword on the wall. It moves inward. Nothing happens. He lets go of it and it moves back out. He presses another one. It slides in and comes back out. He presses all of them he can reach. Nothing moves the door. He growls in frustration.

Cool air wafts through the crack in the doorway. Peeking through it, I feel mist on my face and hear the distinct sound of running water. I look up. I can't see very far, but I can tell that the walls curve inward above us. "This shape—an obelisk," I say. "We're west of the Palace, so that puts us in the park—Westerbane Heath. Is this . . . is this the Tyburn Fountain?"

"I think you're right."

"Tyburn was one of the earliest lessons Dune drilled into me."

"What do you mean?" he asks.

I hand Hawthorne his Exo cape and move into the center of the small room. "Which way do you think is west?"

He pulls out a pocket compass. *Typical soldier.* He points to the wall adjacent to the closed door. "That's west."

With Hawthorne's fusionblade still in my hand, I explain, "Tyburn is a demigod, known as the Warrior of the West Wind. To pay homage to the West Wind, you assume the warrior pose, facing the west." I extend my right hand out in front of me with my left arm behind, bending my right leg in front of me at a right angle, and my right foot to the west. My left leg extends behind me, my toes pointing south. I hold the pose for a moment. Then, extending the sword in my right hand, I point it straight up. Rising on the points of the toes of my right foot, I bring my left foot up behind me, holding it in the palm of my left hand until the pad of my foot touches the back of my head. I hold it for a few breaths, and then twist, jumping into the air and turning in circles over and over, like a whirling tornado. When I stop, I'm in the warrior pose once more, facing west.

Hawthorne follows the line of my right hand to a bronze sword on the wall. He presses it. It locks in place. Turning, he follows the line of my left arm, depressing the sword it points to. It locks into place. The door doesn't move.

"Try the ones by my feet." I wiggle my toes. He moves to the sword in front of my right foot on the floor. As he presses it, it locks. My left foot points to the last one. He touches it, and suddenly the whole building starts to rumble. A stone door drops from the ceiling, cutting off our way back to the Palace. The door on the north wall makes a horrible scraping sound and rolls open. Water cascades in front of it, and as soon as it opens all the way, it begins to close again. We scramble forward together, jumping through the wall of water, and land in a deep pool. My grip on Hawthorne's sword loosens and it extinguishes, but I manage to grab it before it sinks. I come up coughing and sputtering.

Hawthorne is beside me. He hugs me to him. "You're brilliant. Do you know that?"

I hold him, my breasts pressing against his chest. My lips move to his. I kiss him like I've longed to kiss him since his moniker turned golden. He stands and lifts me out of the water, my legs wrapping his waist as he wades through the fountain. Reaching the low wall, he sets me on it and sits next to me. I pass him back his sword and he puts it in his scabbard.

The fountain is lit from underneath. In the center, the stone obelisk points to the night sky. Wild-eyed bronze horse statues kick their hooves into the air. Ferocious sword-wielding soldiers and fierce demigod statues in horrific poses adorn the multilevel water feature that circles the obelisk. Tyburn is the largest, most virile statue, slashing with his vicious sword at Hyperion, the demigod of water. Water flows from the wound in Hyperion's side, an enactment of the tale of the West Wind giving water to the people.

The door we came through is on the north side of the monument. A statue points to it with a rose in its hand, a young naked woman—Tyburn's lover, Roselyn. She stares with a devil-may-care smirk. A thick crown of roses hangs low on her beautiful brow. Breathing hard, I whisper, "I think my secret hideout is a Tyburn temple."

"I think we should start worshipping him." Hawthorne sees me shiver violently. "We have to go," he urges.

We start jogging, looking for a way out of the park. It must be past midnight by now, and the park is empty. We stay on the grass and avoid the lighted paths.

"I don't know which way to go. I've never been in Westerbane Heath. I only know it from pictures," Hawthorne growls as he looks around, trying to decide in which direction we should go. "My family spent very little money educating me before turning me over to our Fate." He sounds ashamed of that. It must have been a rough few months trying to Transition from secondborn to firstborn. I can only imagine the ridicule he has faced not understanding their etiquette and rules. He must feel like a club-wielding barbarian among butterflies.

"Your training is better than their education," I tell him. "You know how to catch a fish, gut it, and cook it. You know how to pilot a fighter airship and rebuild its engine. You know how to defend yourself, and what it feels like to help a friend." City lights shine up ahead. We step up our pace.

"Exo training has helped Transition me," he continues. "It's soldiering, something that makes sense to me. It's geared toward special operations. I'm in a unique position, already having core secondborn training—a fact that appeals to Admiral Dresden."

"Admiral Dresden is an unscrupulous killer, Hawthorne. If he has taken an interest in you, it's nefarious at best."

"He has definitely taken an interest in me."

"He's my mother's right hand. Be extremely cautious where he's concerned."

We come to a wrought iron archway. Passing through it, we're on the sidewalk of a city street. Hawthorne hails a hovertaxi. We pile inside it, and the automated driver says, *"Please scan your moniker."* Frustration infuses Hawthorne's features. We're about to jump out when a shadow blots out the light from the streetlamp. A maginot broadsides the car with its thick head. The door crushes in, shattering glass all over us. The impact drives the hovertaxi from the curb into the middle of the street.

The automated driver garbles, *"Please scan your moniker."* The black beast with the silver markings circles the car. Its yellow eyes stalk me. Its open mouth drips with saliva. Hawthorne yanks me out the opposite side of the vehicle. Brandishing his fusionblade, he pulls me behind his back.

The maginot leaps onto the roof of the hovercar. Hawthorne slashes at it, but the cyborg deftly avoids the thrust. It poises on its haunches. Before it can pounce, a fast-moving hovercar slams into the disabled hovertaxi. Sparks and smoke blast from the wreckage. The maginot is thrown from the roof, and the hovertaxi explodes in a ball of fire.

The wolfish creature rolls. The fur on its left flank shears off, revealing its metal frame. A lopsided ear twitches as it gets to its feet, shaking its body, rebooting its systems.

A lumbering garbage vehicle trundles up a side street, driven by an elderly man. We rush to the passenger side of the hovertruck's cab. Yanking the door open, Hawthorne climbs inside. The fusionblade in his hand is enough incentive to convince the sanitation worker to vacate the cab. He jumps out. Hawthorne reaches down and hoists me up before sliding into the driver's seat.

"Do you know how to drive this thing?" I ask.

"No." He notches the gears, eliciting a horrible grinding sound. "You?"

"No!" I panic because he usually knows how to do everything. He shifts a lever and we lurch forward. The hovertruck lists into the vehicles parked on the side of the street. Sparks fly. Hawthorne corrects the levers and guides us back into the center of the channel. "This thing is like driving a humpback whale," he complains. "Can you see the maginot?"

I open my window. Cold air blows inside the cab. Sticking my head out, I search the area behind us. At first, the blackness is complete, but as my eyes adjust, the darkness takes the shape of a wolf, and it's gaining ground. "Give me your sword"—Hawthorne tosses me the fusionblade—"and just keep moving." Hoisting myself up, I sit on the edge of the open window. Holding the handrail on the side of the cab, I climb onto the roof. I brace my feet and ignite the fusionblade. It glows golden in the moonlight.

The yellow-eyed maginot is just a few paces back. It moves alongside us for a few strides, then leaps upward, almost making it to the roof. It falls back into the channel and continues without breaking stride.

I jump the small gap from the cab to the top of the garbage collector. Tapping my heel against the metal of the humpback, I hear a hollow ring. Wielding Hawthorne's sword, I slash through the metal roof, cutting as I run to the other end. I make a right-angle turn, carving a perpendicular line. Reaching the flank, I pause. The creature running below hurdles onto the top of a parked hovercar beside us and crashes over other vehicles that line the channel until it pulls abreast of us.

I make another right-angle turn and continue to slice through the rooftop. The metal glows orange, melting away. I run back toward the front, a spine-chilling howl shivering the air behind me.

Suddenly the whole vehicle shakes as the maginot lands on the roof near the tailgate. We sway, and my thighs burn with the strain of maintaining my balance, but Hawthorne keeps us in the channel. Hackles on the cyborg's crest stand straight up. The flews on the sides of its mouth rise, exposing its sharp fangs. Its massive forepaw steps toward me. Steely claws grip the surface of the humpback. I hold Hawthorne's sword in my sweaty hand, the burning blade angled toward my feet. I wait. One breath. Two.

The maginot lowers its head and rushes toward me. I plant the fusionblade into the roof and rake it across the hold, creating the final seam. The back of the rectangle falls first. The cyborg slides backward, its razor-sharp claws digging into the metal, trying to find purchase. Then the rest of the ceiling gives way. The beast falls, disappearing inside the belly of the whale.

An angry yowl comes from inside the humpback, and the rampaging maginot rams the side. The hovertruck careens. I sprawl onto my stomach, dropping Hawthorne's sword. It slides away. I reach for it, but another cataclysmic jolt to the flank of the hovertruck throws me toward the edge. I stop just short of falling over. The sword slides toward me. I stretch out and catch it.

Tearing away a piece of my hem, I hold the fabric against the fusion-blade. The cloth ignites. I drop it into the garbage hold. Smoke rises, and the reek of burning garbage is almost unbearable. A terrifying wail echoes from the hole. Turning, I leap back to the cab of the truck. Lying on the rooftop, I swing myself over the side and back in through the window.

"Stop!" I order, slumping against the seat.

Hawthorne reverses the engine. The chassis crashes to the ground and skids to a halt amid a shower of sparks. I'm about to speak when the cab pitches sideways again. Inside the refuse hopper, the maginot is ramming the walls of the hull. Through the side mirror, I see enormous dents radiate from the inside out. I pull a blue lever between Hawthorne and me labeled "Compaction." It triggers the hydraulic system. The garbage compactor whines, compressing. Smoke pours out of the hole in the rooftop. The framework rumbles and shakes, and a horrific howl cuts short, leaving only the sound of crunching metal. The blue handle shifts back to its resting position and the night grows quiet.

Sirens arise in the distance. "Can you run?" Hawthorne asks me. I nod. We get out on the shadowy side of the channel, ducking between the nearest buildings, and slip away into the night.

Chapter 25
A Rose Gardener

Hawthorne guides me to a stop beside a rather expensive-looking Fairweather. I try to catch my breath while he breaks into the luxury airship. Once inside, it doesn't take him long to manually start the engine.

We lift off the hoverpad and fly in the direction of the sea. Neither of us says a word about the maginot. The fact that we're both still alive is enough. Hawthorne finds my hand and threads our fingers together. About a mile from my apartment, I realize he's taking me home.

"How do you know where I live, Hawthorne? I only just moved in."

"I stalk you, Roselle." He sounds unapologetic.

"And yet all that time you never contacted me."

His lips form a grim line. "I couldn't. They'd have known, and they'd have killed you for it."

"It doesn't matter now. They plan to kill me anyway."

"And I plan to stop them."

We near my apartment, circling once. The terrace is alive with Salloway bodyguards. Instead of landing, Hawthorne flies to the channel a block from the building. He sets us down facing the sea, letting the engine idle. "I've been following you and Salloway. I've known about this place for a while now. It didn't take me a second, once I saw this building, to recognize your moniker. They can try to pass off its shape as that of a secondborn weapon, but I know the crown at the top is you. I know every curve of your body. Every contour. Every shape you take. This place was built for you."

"They have plans for me." I shiver and rub my arms. "Do you know about Hammon and Edgerton?"

"Agent Crow came to me, looking for them. I know you had something to do with their disappearance. I'm not sure how you pulled it all off—getting them out of Swords. But I know you paid for it. A beating like that means someone meant to kill you. What happened? Where are they?"

"I can't tell you," I reply, "for your own safety."

"You don't trust me." He sounds hurt, but not surprised.

"You're right," I agree, "but I also don't want you to be in danger because of me."

"I can accept that. Did the Star soldiers hurt you worse than the beating that I saw?" he asks through gritted teeth, his gray eyes bleak.

"I know what you're asking. They didn't rape me." *Reykin wouldn't let them,* I think to myself. I don't want him to see me cry, so I open my door, get out, and walk toward the beach. Hawthorne catches up and takes my hand. "I was afraid—I am afraid," I admit as we wander through the sand. "The kind of fear that makes me think if I had to do it again, I might not be able to. I might just let them die and that . . . that makes me feel"—my voice cracks—"angry and guilty. I'm afraid to go to sleep tonight. I'm afraid to dream that I'm in the middle of it all again, and there's no way out . . ."

His arms engulf me, tugging me to his chest. I breathe hard until I get my emotions under control. A tear escapes from the corner of one eye anyway. I growl and wipe it away with a trembling hand. "Hammon is pregnant," I murmur. "You're going to be an uncle."

Hawthorne swears softly. "I'm going to kill Edge! So thoughtless!"

"Believe me, he'd have welcomed it after the beating he took."

"Is he okay?" Hawthorne asks. "Is the baby okay—and Hammon?"

"Like I said, they're as okay as I can make them."

The tide is high. We don't have far to go until our toes sink into the wet sand and surf. It's the first time I've actually touched seawater. The sound of the waves is melodic.

"We have to scrub the CR-40 off your hand so you can go up to your apartment." Hawthorne takes a handful of wet sand and gently rubs it over my moniker. The glowing silver sword sputters to life, illuminating our faces with its shine. I reach down and take a handful of wet sand from the shoreline and rub it over Hawthorne's skin. His holographic sword shines golden next to mine. We rinse our hands together in the surf. "It was simpler when they were both silver," Hawthorne says.

"When you were mine," I add softly. *Was he ever mine?*

"I'm still yours." He bends and kisses me. It's excruciatingly tender, filled with promises that I'm afraid to let myself believe.

"I'll walk you up. I'll make sure you're safe—that none of Gabriel's men are waiting for you. Then I'll go."

I tug back on his hand as he starts to walk toward my apartment. He turns back and looks at me. "The other maginots watched you escape the Sword Palace with me. By morning, when their logs are uploaded into the Palace's main systems, my brother will know that you betrayed him."

"He probably already knows."

"Gabriel cannot publicly accuse you of treason. Ordering you to kill me is something he needs to keep quiet, but don't underestimate him or my mother. You must stay with me. I'll protect you."

"You can't be associated with me, Roselle. We have to give the appearance that we never had a relationship of any kind once I was Transitioned to firstborn."

"Why?"

"Because it's the only way to keep you safe in the future."

"Because you still intend to kill my brother?"

"I intend to do whatever's necessary to keep you alive."

"Hawthorne, to you this is strategy. To me, this is my brother's life. He no more asked to be firstborn than I asked to be secondborn. He's just as much a pawn in this as I am."

"Pawn he may be, but he has options that you do not. He has power where you have none."

When we reach my building, I scan my moniker. We enter together. A Salloway security unit is mobilizing in the well-designed lobby. Weapons are being distributed—the kind that aren't even available to the military yet. Clifton keeps the best weapons for himself.

The commotion grinds to a halt the moment Hawthorne and I appear. My bare feet make dark, sandy smudges on the white marble floor. I pretend I don't look like I've just been through a battle and casually ask, "Excuse me, but where might I catch a lift to the penthouse?"

The manic intensity of their stares is amusing, but I can't smile.

"Your lift is over there," a silver-monikered Sword says, pointing to the elevator in the center of the complex. It's made of glass and resembles the petals of a blooming rose.

"Thank you. Please, carry on," I murmur, taking Hawthorne's arm. The silence throbs. We enter the lift and the glass doors slide closed. Emerging from the hilt of the building, we step into the blade. A panoramic view opens: a seascape on one side and a cityscape on the other.

"Your cult has spared no expense," Hawthorne mutters.

When the doors open, we walk out into the magnificent foyer of the crown-shaped apartment. Grand chandeliers light the room. No fewer than ten Salloway security personnel are waiting for me. Clifton pays the government for the soldiers who protect him, and he secretly pays the soldiers as well, lowering the chance that one of them might be bought by someone else and turn on him.

Clifton's bodyguard approaches me. The fact that he is here is startling because he's usually the point man protecting Clifton in public. "Roselle," Crucius says, "are you hurt?"

"I'm just cold and wet. So is my friend. Do you think you can find him some dry clothes?" I'm not in the habit of asking for things from any of Clifton's security detail, but I'm going to have to get used to my new life.

"Anything you need," Crucius replies, surprising me again.

"And can you tell Clifton I'm here?"

"He knows. He's leaving headquarters now. You should know he's bringing someone with him."

"Who?"

"The Virtue."

"Clarity Bowie?" Suddenly, I wish I were still hidden inside Tyburn Fountain.

A team of uniformed soldiers patrols the rooftop. They're not Clifton's security, but the Iono soldiers who protect the Clarity of Virtues. A Verringer hovers near the rooftop, a halo-shaped crest of the Clarity of the Fate of Virtues on its side. I glance at Hawthorne. He's nervous.

The Verringer anchors to the railing alongside the building, blocking the view of the sea. A railed gangway ramp extends to the rooftop terrace, and Clifton emerges from the open doorway, followed by Fabian Bowie. They walk together toward the poolside entrance.

I only have a moment or two to panic before an Iono soldier opens the door. Clarity Bowie and Clifton walk up the stairs and into the apartment. I try not to fidget. Clarity Bowie has seen me looking worse, in my Census criminal attire. At least this time I'm in a dress, even if it's filthy.

"Roselle." Clifton says my name with a mixture of relief and concern. "Did they hurt you?"

"No one hurt me. I left the Sword Palace because Hawthorne told me what my family was planning for me this evening. He helped me get back here."

"Firstborn Trugrave," Clifton says with a curl of his lip, clearly not sure whether Hawthorne is truly friend or foe. "Thank you for returning our soldier to us. She means a great deal to my organization and to the war effort. I am in your debt."

Clarity Bowie strikes me as being even more powerful in person. He's dressed in a crisp uniform denoting his status as the leader of the Fates of the Republic, with a white cape styled much like an Exo uniform. "Clarity Bowie," I say with a deep nod, and then a smile. "I would offer you a seat, but I remember from my youth that you prefer to stand."

"I remember you as well. You beat my son's head in with a clock."

"He should've been quicker on his feet."

The roguish smile that passes over his lips fills me with relief. "Grisholm could use someone like you," he says, "someone who's willing to bash him in the head when he steps out of line. I think everyone else is afraid to stand up to him. He'll be the Clarity someday, and he'll need a strong Clarity of Swords."

"I'm sure that Gabriel will be able to assist him in that regard."

"Walk with me." Clarity Bowie extends his hand. I move forward and take it. He tucks my arm in his and we stroll toward the rooftop outside. We take the stairs down and wander past the pool surrounded by armed guards.

When we're out of earshot, he continues. "I look at you, Roselle, and I see your struggle tonight written in the cuts on your feet, the scratches on your face, the rends in your gown, the weariness in your smile. And yet, you still have a rigid command of everything and everyone around you. You handle a crisis as if it's an everyday occurrence."

"Forgive me, but in my world, crisis *is* an everyday occurrence."

"I intend to change that for you."

"How can you do that?" I ask.

"By offering you my protection. By taking you away from the Fate of Swords and allowing you a place in my household for a time."

"I have a position here. I am a weapons consultant for—"

"Yes, and Clifton is adamant about not giving you up. You'll still be allowed to work with him. He'll come and visit you in my household when he requires your consultation."

We approach the ramp leading into the Verringer. I glance over my shoulder at my penthouse. Neither Clifton nor Hawthorne has followed us, but they're both watching us through the glass. "I'm going with you tonight, aren't I?"

"Right now, as a matter of fact," he admits, ushering me onto the ramp.

"Can I say good-bye?"

"You can see them both soon. They'll be invited to the Opening Celebrations of the Secondborn Trials—to our private party, Roselle. You will be, after all, our celebrity guest of honor at the event." We enter the Verringer. The door behind us closes. Clarity Bowie offers me a seat by a window. "You can rest after your trying evening. We'll be in Virtues in no time. Your room is waiting for you, and someone there is very excited to greet you."

I gaze out the window at Clifton's and Hawthorne's grim visages. The Verringer purrs softly and rises into the air. "Who is waiting for me?" I ask absently.

"Your mentor. Dune."

I gape at him. Then I notice a shiny pin on his lapel. "Are you a gardener, Clarity Bowie?" I gesture to the pin.

"I've become very interested in the flower's beauty and incomparable essence."

"Roses come with sharp thorns," I reply.

"I'm counting on them."

Glossary

air-barracks. Kidney-shaped dormitory airships that dock on the military Trees in Bases like the Stone Forest. They transport troops and house them.

air-billiards. A game played on a multilevel billiards table with an airstick—a cross between pool and air hockey.

airstick. A cue stick that uses forced air to move a ball.

Anthroscope. An expensive sports-model airship.

Aspen Lake. The body of water located within the Stone Forest Base.

atom splitter. An invisible security force field that explodes the atoms of whatever crosses into its path.

Brixon. A port town in the Fate of Stars.

Bronze City. A port city in the Fate of Swords. It's located on the Vahallin Sea.

Burton Weapons Manufacturing. A Sword-Fated weapons manufacturing company owned by Sword-Fated Edmund Burton.

Census. A branch of the government comprised of agents whose mission is to hunt down and kill unauthorized thirdborns and their abettors. Their uniform is a white military dress shirt, black trousers, black boots, and a long, tailored leather coat. Their Bases are underground, beneath the Sword military Trees at Bases like the Stone Forest Base and the Twilight Forest Base.

chet. A nonaddictive substance that is used to relieve tension and induce relaxation. It looks like a white stamp.

Clarity. The title held by the leader of a Fate.

CO. An abbreviation for commanding officer.

cooler. A slang term for a detention center.

Copper Towne. A moderately sized city in the Fate of Swords. A Salloway Munitions warehouse is located here. It is also near the border to the Fate of Seas.

counter. A slang term for a Census agent.

CR-40. A topical polymer dispensed in an aerosol device that, when sprayed on the skin, temporarily blocks the signal of an implanted moniker. It can be scrubbed off the skin or it will wear off in a few hours, making it ineffective.

crella. A type of donut.

Culprit-44. A sidearm, also called a fusionmag. It's a fusion-powered gun-like weapon with a hydrogen-powered option.

death drone. An automated robot with a black metallic outer casing. It's shaped like a bat and used primarily on the battlefield to interrogate and execute captured enemy soldiers. The drone is summoned by a black-blinking "death-drone beacon" that emits a high-pitched sound, prompting a drone to respond to the location. Once the drone interrogates an enemy, it decides whether to kill the soldier or take it back to a containment airship for further interrogation.

death-drone beacon. A black, disc-shaped device the size of a thumbnail. It blinks with light and emits a high-pitched frequency that summons a death drone. The device is placed on a captured enemy soldier to target him or her for interrogation and/or death.

drone camera. A spherically shaped automated floating camera that has a multitude of lenses. Some are automated and can be programmed to follow a specific target, while others are operated remotely.

Dual-Blade X16. The Salloway Munitions brand name for the dual-sided sword—the fusionblade/hydroblade—designed by Star-Fated secondborn Jakes Trotter and Sword-Fated secondborn Roselle St. Sismode. It was sold to the company by Roselle St. Sismode.

evac (or evac'ed). To evacuate (or evacuated).

Exo. A rank in the firstborn Sword military. It is higher than all the secondborn ranks. Only the Admiral and Clarities are higher. Black uniforms. Clifton Salloway is an Exo.

Fairweather. An expensive, state-of-the-art airship.

Fated Sword. A title given to the spouse of The Sword (the Clarity of the Fate of Swords). Kennet Abjorn is considered the Fated Sword because he's the husband of Othala St. Sismode.

fatedom. The realm of a Fate, like a kingdom.

Fates of the Republic. Also know as the Fates Republic. The Fates of the Republic society is comprised of nine Fates or "fatedoms." The Fates highest to lowest in the caste system are Virtues, Swords, Stars, Atoms, Suns, Diamonds, Moons, Seas, and Stones. The leader of the Republic is the Clarity of Virtues.

First Lieutenant. A position on the Swords Heritage Council that is considered the "right hand" to the Firstborn Sword (the heir to The Sword).

Firstborn Commander. A title given to the firstborn son or daughter of The Virtue. Grisholm Wenn-Bowie is the Firstborn Commander.

Firstborn Sword. A title given to the firstborn son or daughter of The Sword. Gabriel is the Firstborn Sword.

Forest Base Tree. A tree-shaped military building used by Sword-Fated personnel.

Forge. The capital city of the Fate of Swords.

FSP (Fusion Snuff Pulse). A device that acts like an EMP (electromagnetic pulse), delivering a short pulse of energy that disrupts the fusing of atoms that create fusion energy. The device is a palm-size sphere with a silver metallic outer shell with a trigger button.

fusionblade. A fusion-energy-driven laser-like sword. The sword resembles a broadsword without the expected weight. Fusion cells reside in the hilt of the sword and create a stream of energy when engaged. The hilt is constructed of a metal alloy and usually personalized by a family crest or some other distinctive marking. The St. Sismode family is the originator of the fusionblade. They came to power because of their prowess with weapons centuries ago. They are the heirs to the fatedom of the Fate of Swords.

fusionmag. A gun-like weapon that fires energy in "bullets" hot enough to burn through skin.

glide mode. A mode of propulsion used by antiquated hovercars, such as the Vicolt. It uses magnetic attraction to propel a vehicle.

Golden Circle. The area just outside the walls of the Stone Forest Base where secondborns are processed on Transition Day.

gravitizer. The anti-gravity mechanism in a combat jumpsuit. It uses magnetic repulsion from the molten core of the planet to slow the descent of a soldier after he or she jumps from an airship. It disengages once the soldier is within feet of the ground, allowing him or her to land safely.

head case. A mentally unstable person.

heartwood. An escalator-like machine that carries occupants up or down levels through a vertical tube within a Forest Base Tree.

helium-suckers. A derogatory term meaning *morons*.

Heritage Council. A committee comprised of firstborn members of the Sword aristocracy. The leader of the council is the firstborn heir to The Sword. It's a junior council of sorts in which firstborn heirs hold positions of power until they assume their parents' roles as the leaders of the Sword aristocracy.

hover. An abbreviated term for hovercar.

hoverbin. A programmable drone that carries items from one place to another.

hovercar. A wheelless vehicle that hovers above the ground and is propelled by various means.

hoverstretcher. An automated, self-propelled stretcher that floats above the ground. It carries wounded people from one place to another.

hovertaxi. An automated hovercar for hire.

hovertruck. A large wheelless vehicle that hovers above the ground and is propelled by various means.

humpback. A hovering garbage truck that has a collection unit that resembles a whale belly.

hydroblade. A hydrogen-powered swordlike weapon.

Hyperion. A demigod known as the god of water.

Iono. A rank in the firstborn Sword military. Soldiers are tasked in the role of protecting heads of Fates, primarily Clarities from the nine Fates. Gray uniform. Dune is an Iono soldier.

Iron. A city in the Fate of Swords where the Stone Forest Base is located.

kill tallies. These black line tattoos extend from the corners of the eyes to the hairline of Census agents, denoting the number of thirdborn kills each agent has amassed. The marks can also be found notched on the necks of agents.

Killian Abbey. An abbey and collection of tombs where heads of the Fate of Swords are buried. Roselle's grandfather is buried there.

Lenity. A city in the Fate of Virtues. Home to the wealthiest country estates. It is considered the "sister city" of Purity.

mag. A holder for ammunition cartridges.

maginot. A canine-like cyborg that resembles a wolfhound. They patrol the grounds of the Sword Palace, acting as sentinels.

magnetizer. A feature on an Anthroscope airship.

medical drone. An automated robot with a silver metal outer casing. It's shaped like a cylinder. It uses a blue-lighted laser scanner to x-ray wounded soldiers in combat by hovering over the body of the fallen soldier. It has mechanical arms, which project from the underside of the robot. The mechanical arms can administer medication and perform triage. The drone is summoned by a red-blinking "medical-drone beacon" or "med-drone beacon" that emits a high-pitched sound, prompting a drone response. Once the drone performs triage on a soldier, it inflates a hoverstretcher containing a homing mechanism. It places the soldier on the hoverstretcher for transport to a rescue airship.

medical-drone beacon (or med-drone beacon). A red, disc-shaped device the size of a thumbnail. It blinks with light and emits a high-pitched frequency that summons a medical drone. The device is placed on wounded soldiers who need medical attention from a medical drone.

Meso. A secondborn Sword soldier rank in the military. It is two levels above a Tropo and one level below a Thermo. Royal blue uniforms. (Tropo, Strato, Meso, Thermo.)

moncalate. A tool used to surgically implant a moniker beneath the flesh.

moniker. Each person receives a symbol implant at birth that denotes class/caste. It is a brand that covers a holographic chip. The chip is loaded with the person's identification and other vital information, such as rank, family members, district, status, and so on. The holographic chips can be activated at checkpoints manned by security personnel. They are used to track people entering and leaving districts, to process secondborns, to denote firstborn status, and more.

ol' boy. A slang term for a firstborn.

ol' man. A slang term for a firstborn.

Old Towne. The historic district in the city of Forge in the Fate of Swords.

oosay. A motivational cry used by Swords.

Patrøn. A term of respect, like *sir*.

phloem. A pipeline or tube that transports items of cargo up or down levels via forced air within a Forest Base Tree.

Platinum Forest Base. A military Sword-Fated Base consisting of tree-like structures upon which air-barracks ships dock. It's located in the Fate of Stones.

Protium 445. A Twilight Forest Base air-barracks ship and unit of infantry soldiers. Their armor is embossed with a lavender-colored emblem.

Purity. The capital city of Virtues.

Recovener. An aircraft with both hovercar and airship capabilities. Bullet shaped in design, it is the most expensive small-craft airship in production.

reg. An abbreviation for regiment.

Rose Garden Society. A secret club dedicated to the preservation and welfare of Roselle St. Sismode. They have a vested interest in seeing her become The Sword (Clarity of the Fate of Swords). One of the most influential members is Clifton Salloway (firstborn Sword aristocracy), an arms dealer who owns Salloway Munitions Conglomerate. Members are called Rose Gardeners.

Rose Gardener. A member of the Rose Garden Society.

Roselyn. Tyburn's lover, known for wearing roses in her hair. Her statue is part of the Tyburn Fountain located in Westerbane Heath. She points to the secret door that leads to the hidden passage to Tyburn's Temple located inside the grounds of the Sword Palace.

Rush. A highly addictive drug that causes paranoia and delusions of grandeur.

Salloway Munitions Conglomerate. A Sword-Fated weapons manufacturer owned by Clifton Salloway. Headquarters is in the capital city of Forge in the Fate of Swords.

sapwood. A pipeline or tube that transports liquid (such as water, fuel, or waste) via suction up or down levels within a Forest Base Tree.

Sovenagh. A female composer who created the chamber music titled *The Rape of Reason*, her ninetieth symphony.

stinger. Sharp-nosed security drones that catalogue and ping monikers. They scan for unauthorized personnel and for soldiers who are in the wrong areas for their service-level access.

Stone Forest Base. A military Sword-Fated Base consisting of treelike structures upon which air-barracks ships dock. It's located in the city of Iron in the Fate of Swords, near the border of the Fate of Virtue and the Fate of Atoms.

Strato. A secondborn Sword soldier rank in the military. It is one level above a Tropo and one level below a Meso. Midnight-blue uniforms. It is Hawthorne's rank when he meets Roselle. (Tropo, Strato, Meso, Thermo.)

strike port. Located at the end of the hilt, this is the access point or source from which a fusionblade or hydroblade glows with golden energy.

summoner. Another name for a beacon.

Temperance. A small hamlet in the Fate of Virtue.

Thermo. A secondborn Sword soldier rank in the military. Highest rank. It is three levels above a Tropo. Sky-blue uniforms. (Tropo, Strato, Meso, Thermo.)

Tourmaline Mountains. A mountain range that surrounds the Twilight Forest Base.

Transition Day. A day in early autumn that happens annually, wherein eighteen-year-old secondborns are required to report to a processing Base set up by the Fates of the Republic to be indoctrinated into governmental service. Sword-Fated secondborns report to the nearest "Golden Circle" just outside of each Forest Base for processing. For a multitude of reasons, families bring their Sword-Fated secondborns to these Bases years too early, as young as ten years old. Parents often fear their secondborn will harm their firstborn to gain power and position in their society. Many parents don't want to grow attached to their secondborn, knowing they are to be given up later.

Tree Fort. The tower on a Forest Base that gives airships clearance to take off and land. Air traffic control at the military Bases.

Tree. A tree-shaped military building used by Sword-Fated personnel. Firstborn officers and high-ranking secondborn officers reside in apartments or air-barracks in glass Trees, while subordinate soldiers reside in apartments or air-barracks in concrete and steel Trees.

Tritium 101. Roselle's Sword regiment/air-barracks. Also known as T-101.

troopship. A large airship that transports soldiers to and from war zones or other military duties.

Tropo. A secondborn Sword soldier rank in the military. Lowest rank. Beige-and-brown uniforms. Roselle's rank on her Transition Day. (Tropo, Strato, Meso, Thermo.)

turner. A snitch; in particular, a secondborn who betrays the confidence of another secondborn or who reports another secondborn's infraction of a rule or law.

Twilight Forest Base. A military Sword-Fated Base consisting of treelike structures upon which air-barracks ships dock. It is located in the Fate of Swords near the border of the Fate of Stars and the Fate of Seas. It is surrounded by the Tourmaline Mountains.

Tyburn Fountain. A fountain in Westerbane Heath that depicts the West Wind demigod, Tyburn, defeating Hyperion, the demigod of water. The fountain contains a secret passage that leads to Tyburn's Temple on the grounds of the Sword Palace. The statue of Roselyn, part of the fountain, points the way to the hidden door.

Tyburn. A demigod known as the Warrior of the West Wind. He defeated Hyperion, the demigod of water, giving water to his people.

Tyburn's Temple. The domed stone building located on the grounds of the Sword Palace in the Fate of Swords.

underdeck. The sublevel between floors on an airship housing Stone-Fated workers. It has passageways used only by Stone-Fated workers.

Vahallin Sea. The sea that borders the Fate of Swords, the Fate of Stars, and the Fate of Seas.

vector spinner. A centrifuge device that simulates g-forces on pilots.

Verringer. A very expensive airship with the ability to dock on land, water, and air.

Vicolt. An antiquated hovercar made of chrome and glass that the aristocracy of the Sword Palace uses in ceremonial processions.

virtual access. 3-D visual access to an individual in real time via drone cameras that constantly document the individual's life.

visual screen. A television-like viewing apparatus that can be flat or holographic, as large as the side of a building or as small as a thumbnail.

Westerbane Heath. The public park on the west side of the Sword Palace in the capital city of Forge, Fate of Swords. The park contains the Tyburn Fountain, an ancient monument to the warrior god Tyburn.

Wingers. Advanced fighter aircraft.

Acknowledgments

Jason Kirk, that sunny day at Amazon in July 2015 sparked all of this. Thank you for your words of wisdom and inspiration. I'm eternally grateful.

Thank you to the best agent in the world, Tamar Rydzinski. Without your guidance, *Secondborn* would not have been possible.

To the staff of 47North and Amazon, it is a great honor to work with all of you. Thank you for making my dreams come true.

Tom, Max, and Jack, you are my heart. "I love thee best, oh, most best, believe it."

Mom, thank you for always reading my manuscripts before anyone else and giving me your strongly worded opinions. Honesty is love.

To the Four Horsemen of Facebook, no one gets me like you ladies do. Where would I be without you?

Amber McClelland, thank you for always being a shoulder to lean on (or cry on?) when deadlines loom nearer. You have the best take on life. I'm grateful for your friendship.

Dad, may you be at peace.

Thank you, God, for Your many blessings.

About the Author

Photo © 2016 Lauren Perry of Perrywinkle Photography

Amy A. Bartol is the award-winning and *USA Today* bestselling author of The Premonition Series, The Kricket Series, and a short story titled "The Divided." She lives in Michigan with her husband and two sons. For more on Amy and her work, visit her website, www.amyabartol.com.